The Cabernet Legacy

THE EVEREST EVULSION

BOOK TWO

I0627851

NICHOLAS HUNTLEY

"We... are the transmuters of the earth; our whole existence here, the flights and falls of our love, all strengthen us for this task (beside which there is really no other)."

– Rainer M. Rilke

Act 1, Prologue

The land that lies to the south of the great city goes too often underappreciated for all its natural beauty which it owes to the life-giving waters of the Kemano River. This river, at the center of the Walham Valley, sprang forth from the sharp coastal mountains few dare to tread, splitting through them and enlarging in size to become an immense body whose mouth pours out into the Hecate Strait. The fresh waters of this river were a murky green, but not contaminated by pollution, but populated with life within it and reflective of the life around it. As it would be typical year-round in this land, the dreary grey clouds of the sky that roll forth from the strait would pour their vapors downwards and like the spring river from the mountains, flow forth to sustain the flood plains of these surrounding parts and the crops they grow, who like the wild vegetation and animals, their existence depends upon. They are not alone in this need. From these southern lands, the rise of civilization sprang forth like a plant from its root, and like the plant, out of dependence of the fresh waters around it. These settlements of mutual peoples, most of whom were Christian missionaries, would thrive out of the compassionate love of one another as a cohesive society, and by their existence did they love one another; all those around them. The love that we have is a gift to be used responsibly, and this tale is a testament to a man whose compassionate life should remind us of that fact.

Everest Pepin Cabernet lay prone at a knoll that overlooked the bank of the Kemano River amid the remote parts of the region further east. From this mound, the dark sands and driftwood of the beach could be seen on one side, and at the other side close to a hundred yards on the other side, the tall evergreens that towered upwards towards the blue skies. There was a chill in the air, but not enough to see one's breath but still enough to make one shiver, especially as they lay carefully and quietly still in the tall grass. Everest, a young child in this time, was not alone, but accompanied on his left by an older male with similar blonde hair that could be seen at the side and backs of his tweed cap. Everest's hair was noticeably cut short at the sides as he wore a similar cap, his fair skin very pale from the cold, but spotless and pure with round cheeks and sky-blue eyes. He wore layers, at the top of which was a dark green tweed hunter's coat that matched his trousers. He also wore tall greenish-grey boots too. Beneath his coat, he wore a dark green turtleneck sweater and scarf. The man next to him, his father, Derby Cabernet, wore a similar outfit with a larger coat overtop, scarf around his neck, and collared shirt rather than a sweater. He had a bush of blonde hair around his chin, being unshaven for a few weeks, although around his head, the hair at the top of his head was clean-cut as though he had never left the British Army. The pair lay in the grassy knoll together, Derby with both hands around a pair of binoculars, and Everest with his hands around a scoped Lee-Enfield rifle.

From the early noon, into the late noon, the pair stay motionless in camouflage, awaiting their predator-prey to come out and approach the bait beforehand.

"Listen to me carefully, Everest," Derby quietly spoke in his East Anglian accent. "There she is, a she-bear, looking for a little snack, and unsuspecting to our presence. Do you see him in your sights, son?"

"Yes, father," Everest replied, placing his scope into sightline with a grizzly bear that appeared from the bushes. He spoke in a less eloquent accent than his father, a speaker of the vernacular English accent and dialect.

"Right then," Derby responded. "Just as we talked about then, she's approaching her meal, but the angle here is not perfect. You'll have to wait for a better sightline to her neck. Take in deep breaths, and trust in my voice – wait for the perfect shot."

"I will, father."

Everest brought his finger from the side of the rifle around onto its trigger. He brought the rifle closer to his body, his other hand firmer around the stalk.

"Breathe in, and out," Derby repeated. "Breathe in, and out."

Everest observed as the sow approached the bait placed on the riverbank near the driftwood. Her neck was obscured by the immensity of her body, especially her rear. For a split moment, as the grizzly bear poked at the bait, it turned its head around and faced directly towards where Everest and Derby were. He gently pressed down upon the trigger, but not fully enough to discharge a shot. The bear looked away and then proceeded to badger the bait with its claw. Everest continued to observe as it brought its teeth down to pick the bag up and then bring it around closer towards them, but still shy close to a hundred yards.

The pair lay silently as the bear attempted to tear the package open with its teeth, but it was wound too tight. The package fell onto the sands of the beach and the bear came around to pick it up by its teeth again, and then sit down on its bottom like a human person. It then took both of its arms and gave a tougher grip at the bait where its left side was exposed to them.

"You've got a perfect angle there, son. Take the shot," Derby quietly encouraged.

Everest looked forward at the bear as it sat there, attempting to get at its meal. He could hear the quavering of the sow as it struggled at the tightness of the rope but slowly began to get through the cloth.

"Everest, what are you waiting for? She's nearly ate her food," Derby warned. "Take the shot, son."

Everest breathed rapidly as he continued to aim down his sight, lining up the neck of the bear.

"Everest," Derby scolded in a quiet tone.

Everest took the shot. The gunshot echoed outwards from the rifle and caused the bear to drop the bait as blood poured outwards from the vein of her neck. She made a loud howl as she raised her head up in pain at the pierce of the bullet. In a panic, the bear came onto her paws and scrambled out and into the bush. Derby immediately stood up and put the binoculars away.

"On your feet," Derby commanded, "she on the move and won't be far to it."

Derby took the first steps forward, while Everest slowly stood up and with trembling hands began to step forward after his father who ran forward. Everest came up towards the beach where he saw the package of food lay waste with crows pecking at its remains. The blood of the bear stained the dark sand and what appeared to small chunks of flesh where the bear sat, were equally being poked at by the corvids. He poked through the shrubs and tall grass around the riverbank from where the bear ran, seeing the stains of blood around as well as the tracks of the sow.

"Everest, come quick!" Derby shouted.

Everest hurried through and came around to a small clearing where the bear fell to rest. He looked at the immense grizzly bear as she lay down on the sands beneath a tree. Her chin resting upon the ground, eyes still open, and torso raising up and down through slow labored breaths.

"She's still alive," Derby noted, looking over to his son. "Look at the size of her though."

Everest could hear through the breaths of the bear and speech of his father, cries that poured out from the female bear.

"She's in pain," Everest acknowledged.

"Yes, I bet she is, foul beast," Derby remarked, "but don't let what you see deceive you. There's been many more critters that this one has killed than you know, and more and more in the rest of the world than you can count. I've seen these kill and have at it at ducklings; their cruelty knows no bounds."

Derby examined the bear from afar and then looked back at his son. "Right then, lest we be cruel too. Put her to sleep, son. From this distance, you can't miss a clean shot at the head."

Everest stood frozen as he looked at the bear, continuing to cry out and breath laboriously.

"Everest!" Derby shouted. "Snap out of it, son. Kill the beast!"

Everest twitched and then looked over to his father who looked seriously at him, and then down towards the bear. He slowly began to take his rifle and point it towards the head of the bear. His eyes met the black eye of the grizzly. He brought his finger around to the trigger, but in reluctance pulled away and shook his head. His eyes tearful, he said, "No, I can't do it, father. I can't kill another animal."

Derby scoffed, took his revolver from his side, and effortlessly pointed the barrel downwards and towards the head of the bear. He took two shots. Everest closed his eyes through them both. When he opened them, he looked forward and saw that the eyes of the sow were now lifeless, and the labored breathing had come to an end. Blood poured out from the top of its head where his father had shot it. Derby took in a deep breath and then put his pistol away.

"You've let me down, son," Derby remarked. "Here I was thinking I could make a man out of you, the least that a father could do for his son out of love."

Derby took a large hunter's knife out from another pouch at the other side of his belt. He then stepped forward towards the carcass of the bear.

"Well, just stand there then and let me have at it," Derby said. "What use are you then if I can't even take you into the woods to killer a meager bear. All your complaining, and for what?"

Everest looked away as his father began to cut at the corpse of the bear. The camping trip cut-short after this moment; the hike from where they had camped back to the road where Derby had parked his jeep was a long and awkward one, as was the car ride from the woods back out to Skeena Plains.

Walham Valley, to the south of Greater Harlech, surrounded the Kemano River whose curves rolled through the land. At the west coast, at the river mouth, was the village of Helmcken, and closer inland at the very center of the region was the township of Lennox, the largest settlement even if it were small in these times and little more than a thousand people. From this township, the horizon to the east bore the daunting peaks of the coastal mountains, but to the north were the peaks of the skyscrapers from Harlech ahead whose heights knew no limit. To the south of Lennox was Kemano Plains, a large flatland with an abundance of farmland whose produce fed the urbanites to the north. Further inland, around the bends of the Kemano River, and from where Derby and Everest had to pass through to return home, was a smaller township than Lennox, Caritas. To the north of Lennox was Skeena Prairie, another flatland, although narrower in size. Even further northwards were forests while towards the east was the Lennox Regional Park, and to the southeast of this park was a smaller valley secluded between hills, Sanctus Lake, and the lakefront properties around this body.

By evening, Derby drove the jeep down the dirt road that came up to the gates of the Cabernet family mansion, Cabernet Court as it was known, a large historical estate from where the wealth of the Cabernet family began with its vineyards at all sides. The façade, frames, and walls, of the exterior of the mansion were all set in a grey stone in the same hue as the skies above them as the evening had become very cloudy. The mansion, built at the end of the last century, was built in Victorian style with tall, peaked rooftops at the left, right, and center. At the corner of the center partition were slender spires. In the midst of the mansion was a rectangular tower with the Red Ensign flag waving from one corner, and the Union Jack from another. The rooftop shingles were a reddish-brown, and every window with white curtains on the other side.

The jeep drove up to the front of the mansion where there was a gravel lot and parked right in front of it. A servant in a black suit met Derby at the front of the building and took his backpack from him as well as Everest's belongings.

"Welcome home, Mr. Cabernet," the servant greeted. "You're back early. How was the trip?"

"Not what I hoped for," Derby acknowledged, "no less with that one and his bleeding heart."

"Pity," the servant responded. "Mrs. Cabernet and young Ms. Cabernet have not yet returned from their voyage. Should I prepare something for you and young Mr. Cabernet?"

"Please do."

The servant brought their bags inside while Derby disappeared around the side of the grounds. He then came back and opened the side door for Everest who shot out like a cannon and ran inside.

The interior of Cabernet Court was nothing like the exterior, where the exterior consisted of stone, the inside was wood with only the floors draped in carpet. Everest went up the grand staircase and to his room in the right wing where he stayed put for the rest of the evening. He fell asleep atop of his bed without changing out of his clothes, opening his eyes to look around at his many possessions. The room was large, his bed king-sized with many pillows and the cover made of silk. To his left was a wardrobe and dresser, and to his right a bookshelf and desk. At the foot of his bed was an ottoman, and beneath the window across from his bed was a chest with many toys. At the left and right of his bed, along the same wall, were shelves with many more toys. The interior walls of Everest's bedroom were lined with wallpaper that featured childish caricatures at the top border and beneath a deep red with patterns of small suns.

Directly ahead of his eyes though, atop of a toy chest was a dark brown-haired fuzzy teddy bear.

Everest sat up from his bed and saw that the time was nearly midnight. His bedroom door was left ajar, but through the crack he could see a light and smell a small; the same smell of the campfire he was all too familiar with at this time. He made his approach into the hall and went down, coming around to the main atrium where he then went down the staircase to the ground floor and came around to the library. The Cabernet Court library was immense, as large as a school gymnasium in all its size. To the left of the library though were a set of doors that led into his father's study. A different smell now replaced the smell of the campfire, although that lingered not too far, and this smell was like that of the jeep; it was a very potent and hard smell, and it came from something soaked into the carpets and spilt on the floor. Everest was careful not to step in this liquid as he came around to his father's study where the light was on, but he was not present.

"Dad?" Everest called. "Dad, are you there? Are you okay?"

Everest looked around at the messiness of the study, books pulled out and piled around. Above the fireplace was a portrait of a man similar to Derby, but older and with slightly darker hair and a beard. A plaque beneath the portrait read, "Lycidas Cabernet." Everest came around to a table near the fireplace where there was a half-used cigar on a tray, a nearly empty bottle of scotch, and nearly empty glass with a half-melted ice cube. Suddenly, Everest looked out towards the entrance into the study as he heard a creak of the floorboard. He came around to hide behind a curtain near the French window out towards a veranda when he saw his father enter the room, carrying a jerry can and pouring that same liquid onto the carpet inside.

Derby, dressed in a lavish smoking jacket, tossed the jerry can to the side and then went over to the fireplace. He staggered as he walked, picked up the fire poker, and then began to poke at the fire as he rested his other arm on the mantle above. Derby took an ember and brought it down towards the floor, causing flame to shoot outwards wherever gasoline was poured. Everest rested his foot before him, causing the floorboard to creak, and causing his father to shoot his gaze out towards him.

"What are you doing here, Everest," Derby spoke in a slur. His eyes looked towards him and shined the reflection of the fire in them. "Nosy child, couldn't keep yourself in your room, could you?"

Derby threw the fire poker into the fire and then came towards his son.

"You see this, son? You see all this that burns? Meaningless, all of it, but you know not, of course. No, you were born into it, never had to struggle for it, and mind you, never did I have to struggle for it either. I shouldn't have been born into it either; I had to find my pain. For what does it all amount to? All this… opulence? Who does it serve, but to bind us to the past and make us soft?"

Derby stood before Everest. He grabbed him by his hand and took him away from the fire as it engulfed the entire room, and from this room the entire mansion. He led him towards the French window, which he unlocked, and they stepped out from.

"I'll show you, son. I'll show you; don't you worry," Derby expressed as he took him away. "Oh yes, we'll start anew, and maybe then I'll be able to make a man out of you."

Act 1, Scene 1

Everest opened his medium blue eyes and looked up at the plain white texture of the popcorn ceiling above him. He held his hands at the bottom of his ribcage, dressed in dark red silk pajamas, and tucked into the quilt cover of the king-sized bed in the bedroom he lay in. Everest Cabernet had light blonde hair at this time that was cut short at the sides and slightly longer at the front swept towards the sides. He also had a broad stature, a chiseled cheek bone facial structure, and no apparent facial hair although there was a bit of a shadow that had grown overnight. On his left, tucked in next to him and dressed in a lavender night gown was the love of his life who breathed lightly still in slumber. Everest took in a deep breath and then rubbed his eyes before he sat up, put on a pair of slippers at his bedside, and then stood up in the master bedroom to come around and enter the bathroom where he relieved himself. He then exited the washroom and came back around to the bed where he returned to it to lie down once more. The chirps of birds from outside could be heard through the glass pane of the windows around, a gentle breeze that came to the shrubbery and trees, but otherwise there was a peace and tranquility in the air. With another deep breath in, he lay on his side and began to close his eyes again, only to be woken up at the ringing of an alarm at his wife's bedside table. Everest opened his eyes and let out a groan as the alarm rang.

Within a few seconds, the alarm stopped, and Everest felt the movement of his wife as she sat up at her side of the bed and stood up to leave the room. At the sound of the door closing behind him, Everest pulled the covers over his shoulders and attempted to fall back asleep. From within the bedroom, a peace returned, only to be disturbed at the distant sound of a dog bark and the creak of the bedroom door met with the patter of paws on hardwood floor. Everest was then met with the loud bark of a dog from within his room, directed straight at him, causing him to squint and look ahead of him at the sight of the family Doberman.

"Baron, please," Everest complained.

The dog barked at him again, causing Everest to sit up and bring his feet back around.

"Alright, alright, boy," Everest said, walking forward as the excited dog continued to bark. "Come here now."

Everest led the dog out of the master bedroom and into the corridor outwards. He then guided him through the exit into the foyer.

"Sal, come and get your damn dog, he's keeping me awake!" Everest yelled.

"Coming dad!" Sal replied from afar.

Everest closed the door on the Doberman and then went back into the bedroom and closed the door firmly behind him. He then came back around, passing the curtains that covered up a bright sunlight that poured in to the room. Everest sat down at his bedside and picked up a glass of water on the end table to catch a drink. He then laid it down and got back into bed where he stayed and looked up at the ceiling again. Everest closed his eyes after a moment and listened to the chirping of the birds, the rustle of the wind, and now the barking of the family dog as it was let out onto the patio met with the speech of his youngest son to his bestest friend.

After a few more minutes in bed, Everest caved to the external forces and pulled the covers away from his body, dragged his foot over the edge of the bed, and sat up. He turned on the radio at his end table and changed the channel from soft rock to a news channel as the radio host said, "Good morning, Allabrese!"

Everest stood up from his bed and began to do some stretches. He then stepped forward and pulled apart the dark purple curtains at the three arched windows that faced the west. He gave a long look towards the Rocky Mountains and great plains behind Cabernet Manor. The skies were a clear blue and there was still a breeze that brushed the trees around the manor. Everest moved over to the windows that faced the north and looked down where a young adolescent male was playing with the family dog. Salmar Cabernet threw a tennis ball across the patio and into the gardens below, causing the dog to run after it. The patio between the south and north wing of the manor consisted of a swimming pool, patio dining table bedside, and numerous lounge chairs at the sides of the pool. Around the perimeter walls, there were numerous porcelain pots and plants, and on the walls were decorative pieces, porcelain butterflies, a stained-glass effigy of a sun, and around the corners were wind chimes that too sung in the wind. Everest looked at his son; Salmar appeared much like his father, tall, broad shoulders, and athletic stature, but with a lighter, thicker, and longer head of hair. He was dressed in a dark yellow collared shirt and beige pants. The Doberman came back from the garden with the tennis ball and Salmar knelt down to lovingly pet his companion. Everest stood admiring the scene with a smile before he went to the bathroom to get ready for the day.

After a few minutes, Everest came downstairs dressed in a short-sleeved collared shirt and grey dress pants. He wore a belt around his waist and at his feet were dark socks and his pair of slippers. He exited the south wing and came into the foyer where he looked down at the marble floor as light poured in through the east wall. The walls in the manor were painted a faint green, the crown mouldings and baseboards a chestnut wood. There were numerous framed photos on the walls around, very few if any artwork, and the paintings that were consisted of natural scenes. Everest stepped down to the main floor and then walked forward towards the north wing where he entered to a small seating area with a corridor that went further to another seating area with cabinets set up on the walls. Across from where he entered was another way into a colder room with stone tiled floor and arched windows that looked out from left, right, and center. There were many more plants in this room. Through this room, Derby entered into the kitchen. The kitchen was split between the cooking area and a small dining area where the windows were. On the left-hand side there were counters in a reverse U-shape with the stove in the middle and refrigerator on the left. Behind the right-hand portion of counters was a small glass table where six seats were set up in total, two at the head, and two at each longer side. Behind one head of the table was a door that entered into a pantry storeroom and also provided access to the basement. A second door was beside the stove and went into the ball room. Salmar sat in front of the windows that looked down to the driveway that went into the garage, eyes pointed towards a small television set propped up beside the stove on the counter. Everest came around to the kitchen refrigerator to join his wife who was at the stove making breakfast.

Vienna Edelweiss Cabernet turned and smiled at her husband. She was a petit lady, nearly a foot shorter than her husband (who was five-foot eleven inches). She had small hands and fair skin nearly as white as snow with rosy cheeks. She had small button nose and deep blue eyes. Her hair was very blonde, like wheat in the sun, or fine sands on the seashore. Her hair was also thick like her son's, although cut short and up to her neck. She wore an apron over her yellow blouse and golden polka dot skirt. She returned her attention to the stove and danced around the kitchen merrily. Vienna turned to Everest as he poured himself some coffee and gave him a kiss on the cheek.

"Good morning, my sweet one," Vienna greeted in her southern German accent. "How was your sleep?"

"Fine," Everest responded in his local accent, smiling at his wife, "restful. How about you? You seemed quite at peace."

"Ah, at peace it was, but restful is how I would describe it," Vienna remarked, passing him a plate of eggs on toast. On the side were some cut up fruit. "For Salmar, my sweet one. Yours is soon."

Everest took the plate and brought it over to Salmar to place before him.

"How's it going, sport?" Everest greeted with a warm-hearted laugh. He put a hand on his shoulder and placed his coffee down at the head of the table. He then looked over to the television as it played the national news. "What's going on in the world today?"

Everest looked as he saw police vehicles that looked to belong to the Harlech Police Department in front of a rundown apartment. The caption read, 'One killed, another in custody in drug raid in Harlech.'

"I'll tell you what, the more I see what's going on in the cities, the more I'm glad to be out here."

"Aw, come on, it's not all that bad, dad," Salmar responded in a local accent like his father. "I really would like to see the city one day. It's not fair that Charles and Allodia been there more than I have."

"There's nothing out there of interest," Everest dismissed. "You listen to the news so much, I'm not sure how you couldn't find reluctance to be where they're at. Charles... your brother being who he is, would place himself anywhere there is danger. Your sister on the other hand... well, somehow, she's doing alright over there. I suppose she isn't exactly in the city as much as she is in campus at the university. If I know her, she wouldn't step out of that place."

"What if I decide I want to go to school at the University of Harlech? University of Toronto?"

"We'll support you, but there's no need to be chasing for adventure where there is only... futility and vainglory," Everest expressed. "Leave it all to Charlemagne – he takes right after your granddad in that regard, chasing highs and risking their neck for nought."

"Now then," Vienna interjected, putting Everest's plate down before him, "leave Charlemagne alone. He's doing what his heart wants most, and that is important in our decision-making. If I did not choose what my heart wanted me to do, well, I would not be here now, would I?"

"And where exactly is here?" Salmar questioned.

"At the side of your father and you, where I am needed most now," Vienna answered.

"And what about when I decide (if I decide) to go to college?"

"Then it will still be here with your father," Vienna said. "The heart knows; if I cannot love my kindred, then what use am I?"

"You will always be one to provide many gifts to the Earth, my dear," Everest remarked, taking his wife's hand and kissing it. "You are an example to all of us."

Vienna gave a warm smile as she blushed. She returned to the kitchen to serve herself, and then returned to eat with her family. After breakfast, Salmar went off on his own to go to school, driving his own year-old 1988 Armstrong Hoosier pickup truck. Vienna set off to wash the dishes, while Everest set off to walk back to the foyer and make his stroll towards the south wing. He entered a short corridor and opened a door on the other side that led into the library, although in these times it was split up between being a library and a recreation room. On the right-side there were bookshelves that held numerous old books collected in the last forty years, while on the left were sofa chairs and a large television set at the center. A grand piano was at the corner at the far-side, while on the immediate left was a jukebox. Next to the piano was a small bar. On the second-floor veranda was a billiards table. Everest passed through this room to the right and entered through a door that went into his study. The study that belonged to the head of the household was dark, blinds closed, bookcases hiding the panel walls. There were very little decorations in this room. Immediately across from the entranceway was a table with a fax machine. At the bottom tray of the fax machine were several dozens of papers piled up. Even as Everest entered, the machine wurred and printed out the latest document to be sent through. Everest approached the machine and picked up the latest sets of papers. Next to the fax machine were piles of transmissions sent through. To the left of this table were two more tables with even more piles of papers set up around. Everest took the latest bunch and made his way across the study towards the desk on the other side. He passed a fireplace where before it was a simple rug. He came around to the large wooden desk which before it were two brown armchairs, and sat himself down in a leather brown office chair. Everest's eyes skimmed the headline and details of each piece of paper, turning through each detailed and intricate report with all its data and key performance indicators, and other nuances, at less than a minute per sheet. When he was finished, Everest placed the papers aside and looked at the answering machine as a light flashed. Everest pressed the button, and it began to go through voicemail as the tape rewound.

"Mr. Cabernet…" a voice on the recorder said. Everest immediately pressed the fast forward button to skip the message. "Mr. Cabernet," the next voice said, speaking deeper than the last. He skipped through this message to come to another, "Mr. Cabernet…" He skipped once more to another person who said, "Everest, I need…" Everest hit stop and sat back in his chair. On his right was a monitor sat atop of a computer; a Bertrand-Schmidt machine. The screen was turned on and displayed a log-in screen. Rather than look at a computer screen all day, Everest stood up and left his study.

Everest returned to the foyer atrium where he met his wife as she came around to go upstairs.

"Hello, my little darling," Everest greeted, taking her by the arm and swinging her around. "What do you have planned for the day? I'm all yours if you need me."

Vienna gave a light laugh as she looked at her husband and replied, "Thank you, my sweet one, but I am all booked. The league and I have to tend to our garden now that the sun is out, and then we are going to go out and have some tea."

"Ah, what a shame then for me," Everest remarked, bringing his finger to the top of her nose to boop, "but you enjoy yourself, my pretty."

"If my big man is not busy, I'm sure the parish could use a helping hand…"

"Yes," Everest remarked, lowering his smile, "but come to think of it, I do have some errands I've put off which need to get done…"

Vienna looked at her husband and returned a smile. She replied, "You see, you do not need me to fill your day." She kissed him on the cheek. "I'm going to get ready and be out in a bit. You go and get started on those errands you have to do… hopefully, by the time I return, the house should be painted…"

"Yes… not quite those sorts of errands," Everest expressed with a chuckle.

Vienna winked at him and then parted to climb up the stairs to return to the master bedroom. Everest lowered the smile on his face as he looked around. His face turned to Baron who was sat nearby looking at him.

"What are you looking at?" Everest questioned.

Baron barked at him. Everest sighed.

"Well, I suppose it's just you and me then, again," Everest said, walking over to the dog. He knelt down and began to stroke his head. "The misses is out in the community again, and here we are with the palace all to ourselves."

After Vienna had left, Everest came out to the patio with a towel at his side and collared shirt unbuttoned to expose his chest and abdomen. He had also changed from his trousers to a pair of shorts and wore a pair of sunglasses. He lay the towel down at one of the wooden lounge chairs and sat back in the chair, looking up towards the sky as the sun beat down. He applied sunscreen lotion and then tipped his head back while Baron went out into the garden on his own. Everest stayed put in the chair for the better part of the morning into the noon, getting out only to drench himself in the pool where he again lay back and floated on its waters, eyes silently looking up towards the skies while he lay motionless on the water.

Act 1, Scene 2

Later in the evening, Everest sat by the poolside at the head of the patio table with Salmar to his left, facing the pool. Both Everest and Salmar each had two playing cards in their hands, while before them were three cards unturned. Between them were some sums of cash in bills and coins, some put forth into the pot. In Everest's hand, he had queen of clubs and six of clubs that he retrieved from the deck. Salmar himself had two cards in his hand. Between Everest and Salmar, each of them had a crystal glass on a coaster, where Salmar's was dark, bubbled and fizzed, Everest's did not and had a soft transparent brown color to it. Each of their drinks had ice cubes. Beside Everest's drink was an ash tray where there was a cigar that he would pick up to take in.

"Alright son, on you," Everest stated, putting forth a dollar coin. He held a smug look on his face after he blew smoke away from his son's face.

Salmar put forth two dollars in coins while Everest looked at his cards.

"I'll call," Everest remarked, putting an extra dollar in for an even four in the pot.

Salmar looked at his cards with a degree of uncertainty in his face. "I'll check," he said.

"Right," Everest responded, putting his cards down on the table and flipping the three between them. The cards were a queen of hearts, a king of clubs, and a king of diamonds. A slight twitch came at Everest's eyebrow. He paused for a moment as he took his cards back into his hand and then said, "I'll check."

"Me too," Salmar responded.

Everest reached over to place a fourth card in the series before them. The card was a jack of spades.

"I'll bet," Everest remarked, putting forth two more dollars.

"Call," Salmar replied, meeting his bet. There were now eight dollars in the pot.

Everest reached forward to flip another card. The card was a five of hearts.

"I'll bet," Everest remarked, putting another two dollars forth.

"I'll call," Salmar responded, meeting his bet again.

"Right, let's see what you got, son," Everest said, laying down his cards.

Salmar overturned his cards to reveal a nine and four of clubs to Everest's queen of spades and six of clubs.

"Aha, two pairs, king and queens win out," Everest remarked with a smile. "Come to me." He took in the pot and added it to his cache. "What were you thinking with cards like those?"

"I was hoping for a straight…"

"You haven't even got one pair there," Everest remarked, putting the cards together to shuffle them and then pass over to Salmar to deal. "Your go."

Salmar laid three cards face down between them, and then gave one to his father, one to himself, and then another to his father and then a last one to himself. Salmar flipped his cards and saw that he had a ten of diamonds and three of hearts. This time, Salmar put down one dollar to start while Everest had two.

"I'm not any good at this," Salmar complained, putting forth another dollar to call.

"Don't be dismal," Everest responded, tapping his fingers on the table to signal a check. "Neither was I when I started to play, and even now I'm by no means a professional. It's just fun and games."

"I don't see what the thrill is here," Salmar questioned, flipping the cards in front of them to reveal a three of clubs, five of diamonds, and seven of diamonds.

"You will," Everest encouraged, "just you wait." He tapped his fingers again.

Salmar paused for a moment and then decided to put forth six dollars.

"Oh, what do you have there?" Everest questioned, looking at his cards and then down to those between them. "I'll raise." He put forward twelve dollars."

Salmar didn't respond and instead met his father's raise to include another six dollars. There was now twenty-eight dollars in the pool. He then flipped the card between them to reveal a ten of spades.

Everest's eye looked at the ten and then back down to his ten. "Check," he said.

Salmar went ahead to raise five more dollars forward. This time Everest didn't respond as he called his bet and included another five dollars: thirty-eight dollars in total.

"You must have a mighty good hand, son, to now be really gambling your cash like that."

Salmar didn't reply and placed the last card between them: a queen of spades.

"I'm going to call your bluff there," Everest expressed, putting forward what cash he had left, close to forty-nine dollars. "All in."

Salmar groaned and placed his cards face down. "Fold."

"Now come on there," Everest replied with a wider smile. "What'd you have there, really."

"It doesn't matter, just take the money," Salmar remarked, hiding his cards in the deck. "I don't want to play anymore."

"Don't be such a sore loser," Everest chuckled, taking in the pool. He took back his forty-nine, and then began to put together the rest of the pot. Everest looked over to what Salmar had left, which was only thirteen dollars left. "You're not going to get anywhere if you don't lick yourself after a bad fight and learn from it. Your mother taught me that, you know."

"I don't like poker," Salmar responded. "I don't understand it, or the appeal for it. How can anybody find a game like that to be fun?"

Everest sighed and replied, "Perhaps I thought you'd enjoy it the way I do. I couldn't get you into racing either." He finished counting the money in hand and then began to set down money before him. He counted fourteen dollars and then passed it over to Salmar. "Here, for what you lost in that last round."

Salmar continued to look displeased. Everest returned thirteen more dollars.

"For what you started with," Everest remarked, looking at his money again. He sighed and then passed on twenty dollars. "And here's for what you deserve."

"I didn't do anything," Salmar remarked.

"You gave me a good time," Everest replied, "sitting here with my boy. What more could a father want? Come on, treat yourself too," he said, pulling over a wooden box and opening it. "Take one if you'd like."

Salmar looked into the box and picked up a Cuban cigar. He then also picked up a lighter.

"I'll tell you what, Sal," Everest expressed, sitting back, "we don't know how good we have it, living here in Allabrese, in this home, with this weather."

"You sound like Allodia," Salmar replied, flicking at the lighter to try and light his cigar. "She's always saying how fortunate we are, and how unfortunate other people are."

"Well, not like your sister says it then. I just... on days like these, I can't help but feel a little gratitude for what we got. Life is just good – not that I feel unworthy of it."

Salmar continued to struggle to light his cigar. Everest set his down and helped him.

"Put it in your mouth and breath in while you light it. There you go... easy breaths, don't inhale any of that smoke. You don't want that in your lungs."

Nonetheless, Salmar coughed out at his first breathes.

"Isn't mom going to kill me if she sees me smoking this? She's warned me about cigarettes."

"She's warned you about cigarettes, but this is a cigar. It isn't anything like those death sticks they keep talking about on the TV. No, a cigar is meant to be enjoyed and last longer. You aren't supposed to inhale the smoke into your lungs either, but to let it simmer and fester around you. Like a fine glass of scotch, don't speed through it but stop, enjoy it, and take your time."

Everest and Salmar sat back in their seats as they each enjoyed the aroma of the cigars that burned in their hands and came up and around their bodies like incense to a temple. Everest blew smoke away from his son's face and then looked over to him.

"If you don't want to play poker with me anymore, then tell me about your day," Everest asked. "How was it?"

"It was alright," Salmar responded with a light cough.

"I remember when I was your age, in my last month of high school," Everest acknowledged. "I couldn't wait to get out that place... Harrow Preparatory, what a nightmare of a place. Allodia and you ought to be thankful we never sent you to a boarding school. If it were up to your grandfather... well..."

"Isn't that the school Charles went to?"

"By choice, I might add," Everest remarked, shaking his head. "An all-boy's boarding school straight from hell."

"Harrow is an all-boys school? I thought you and mom met in high school."

"We did," Everest admitted, "but your mother was at a nearby all-girls school. There are all sorts of boarding schools near the university. I believe the one your mother went to was called Our Lady of Roses Academy, or something to that regard. Anyways, this school was less than a few blocks away, across the street from the dorm rooms, and often times we would see these girls pass by... I considered your mother to be the most beautiful of them all."

"Hang on, how old were you when you met mom?"

"I was fourteen years old when I first saw her with my eyes, but I didn't come to speak to her until I was fifteen. What an astounding feeling it was to know that this girl who I ogled at for the past year had feelings for me as well. I was even more in luck of course when she felt as madly in love with me as I did with her. I remember before your brother was born, your grandfather met your mother for the first time and without knowing that we were in love, he immediately threatened me to stay away from her. I don't know if I ever mentioned this about your late grandfather, but oh he hated Germans with a passion; remnant from his war-experiences to some degree, I believe, and your mother of course isn't German, she's Austrian, but your grandfather thought them all to be the same. He could wrongly sense the German within her by her accent and such of course."

"Wait a minute," Salmar interrupted, "when was Charles born? 1961? If Charles was born in 1961, and you in 1945, doesn't that mean that you were..."

"Fifteen years old, because Charles was born a few days before my sixteenth birthday, and was it the worst birthday of my life. My grandfather found out about your mother being pregnant when her family contacted him a few months before she was due. Her family found out of course by the school because she couldn't hide her pregnancy from them for too long. Your brother, a fact in which he prefers to not be reminded of, was born out of wedlock because I in the least was too young to marry, and neither of our parents consented to allow us to marry. Strangely though, my father supported your mother in these times, when there was tremendous shame upon her from her family. They were aristocrats and looked down upon such a thing, but my father... I guess he took her in around the time your brother was due to be born, and he was born out in England where we lived at the time. Your grandfather was right there with your mother in the hospital."

"Where were you?"

"I was… not there, unfortunately. I mean, I was in England at the time, but I just… missed the moment in which your brother was brought into the world. Your mother stayed with us at our home, in a guest room of course because my father suspected me of being a miscreant, but I didn't want to approach. I felt ashamed… too ashamed. I went back to Harlech in September to continue school, while your mother stayed with my parents in England, by her own choice, because she had no home to return to in Austria. Her parents had disavowed her outright, so your mother stayed with your grandparents with no choice of where to turn to, and from what your mother told me about the experience, she was treated well, even by my father. Heck, she made good friends with my sister, your aunt. Your mother and I didn't talk for a while until she finally approached me when I was back home for Christmas break, but I remember she tried to get me to hold Charles in my arms, but I couldn't bring myself to do it. I felt fearful… as if I would drop him, and too…. I kept my distance from them both for the first year, but then when I returned to high school for my last, I was relieved to know that my parents would pay for her to attend her final year at Our Lady of Roses while they cared for Charles on their own. Your mother and I made up too, and we found ourselves back in love with each other so much so as soon as I turned eighteen, we made our vows and got married. My father surprisingly approved of the marriage (as if he had shame that Charles was born out of wedlock), so we were set to wed at a nearby church. Of course, it wasn't enough that we were to get married that we had to do so in a Catholic Church, and let me say, it was a pain in the ass doing so. No less because my father and the priest father forced me through the confessional to feel repentant because I had extramarital relations when I had no such remorse. I was ashamed, but not guilt-ridden… but to the say the least, that and the weeks of preparation up to the wedding were the hardest I thought I would have to go through, but nonetheless in June 1964 we finally married, and then since your grandparents seemed to love Charles so much and were willing to continue to take care of him, we went on our honeymoon, and… that was that."

Salmar looked back at his father as she finished his story. "Wow," he replied.

"The moral of the lesson in this story, son, is that if you have any interest in any girl at school right now, learn from my mistake," Everest stated. "Kids these days seem to have it way better off with contraceptives than I did in mine, even though it was taking off…"

"Oh dad, that's gross…" Salmar rebuked. "Come on…"

"I mean it," Everest replied, "attitudes in my times were just changing, but now in yours those attitudes have set in, and you kids seem to do and want to do whatever you want, just as long as you do it in a safe manner, and don't make the mistake I did…"

"Mistake," Salmar repeated, looking at his father.

Everest realized, looked back at his son, and said, "That's not what I meant now. I love Charles very much, even if, unfortunately, he seems to be the spitting image of your grandfather, but he's my son and I love him. I just wish… I hadn't brought him into the world like I had done."

"Don't you worry," Salmar acknowledged with an embarrassed laugh. "I won't be doing anything like that."

"Weren't you interested in that one girl though?"

"Me? Nah, I mean, I like her and all, but I don't know."

"What was her name again?"

"Gloria," Salmar remarked, "Gloria Pasini."

"Oh, Italian?"

"Yeah, she lives on that side of town."

"Well, come on, I don't think that side of town is a bad one."

"I'm not saying it is either, but it's just… they're awfully quiet and keep to themselves."

"What's she look like?"

"She's… well, she's got tanned skin and brown hair. She's a little shorter than me, a few inches taller than mom. She's got hazel eyes."

"Well son, let me just disclose to you, I have no prejudices towards Italians. I know some folk in this town do for some reason, but that's between them. We're just strangers on the other side of the river sometimes… at least I am. Your mother seems to get right along with the Anglo-folk, especially those in the parish."

"Yeah…"

"I'll tell you what though, why don't you invite this Gloria girl over for dinner some time, or invite her out. They've got a fine restaurant in town you could take her to."

"Maybe… what if it works out though and then I decide to go to school, say in Harlech for example. What then? And what if I really like her but suddenly, I feel conflicted about where to go?"

"Well son, just lead by my example on that one," Everest remarked, standing up as he picked up his glass to leave, "see how I do. I'm sure it'll all work out in the end."

Act 1, Scene 3

Everest stood up in his pew as the tune of the organ rang through and the parishioners, his wife included, sang the closing hymn of praise. He held the hymn book for his wife who sang beautifully in tune with the choir, *'How deep the Father's love for us, How vast beyond all measure, That He should give His only Son, To make a wretch His treasure.'* Salmar stood on his right, not particularly in full attention but leaning over with hands on the top of the pew in front of him, eager to leave. Vienna wore a white blouse and skirt with a belt around her waist. Salmar wore a white dress shirt and golden sweater. Everest wore a navy-blue suit, golden-yellow tie, and white dress shirt. They stood among the back rows of the center right-side of St. Allan's parish. Everest stood straight as his eyes looked at the lyrics, but no music came from his mouth while the faithful sung and the parish priest, deacon, and altar servers gathered in front of the altar.

St. Allan's parish was a small Catholic church in St. Allan's Plains in Allabrese, built in the latter half of the twentieth century. The church had two main rows on the center left and center right that consisted of longer pews, with space on the far left and far right with smaller pews besides the stained-glass windows. There were about twelve pews up to the altar and a wide sanctuary that was raised up from the rest of the church. On the left and right from the sanctuary in the transepts there were small shrines, one to the Virgin Mary and another to St. Allan, with candles set before and kneelers. Behind these shrines were large arched stained-glass windows. Behind the sanctuary there was an even larger stained-glass window. All these windows had no particular design or depiction and were instead in a random assortment of colors. From a balcony above the back of the church and accessible via stairs sung the choir. The interior design of the church was plain, not quite modern, but without a particular historical aesthetic. The half-paneled walls were painted an off-white, and the floor wooden panes up to the sanctuary where there was carpet. Overall, within the parish there was a decent amount of people, although it was not entirely full.

At the sight of the parish priest, deacon, and altar servers exiting the church to enter the atrium, Everest closed the hymn book and set it down. Vienna seemingly did not need the hymn book to continue to sing, but understood her husband's desire to leave and so she picked up her coat from beside her and folded it over her arm. Salmar took the initiative too to begin to shuffle out from the pew as others, although not the majority of parishioners, began to exit out to the aisles. Salmar quickly bent his knee, although he did not fully reach down for a genuflect, he quickly raised himself up before doing so and turned around to leave. Next, Everest came out of the pew and rather than bend the knee, sort of nodded his head down as though to bow, while Vienna came out and in the least gave a full bow towards the sanctuary. Within less than a minute, the singing stopped but the tune of the organ continued, and the rest of the parishioners motioned to exit the church.

Everest watched as he saw parishioners douse their hands in small brass cups of water at the doors and then motion their hands to their forehead, chest, and shoulders before they exited. Vienna dipped her hand, but Everest and Salmar continued through to come into the atrium where parishioners began to gather. The parish priest, dressed in a white chasuble, and deacon in a white dalmatic, stood at either side of the main entrance through where they shook hands with the faithful as they made their way out. Rather than immediately leave, Everest and his family moved towards the right where there was a small gathering hall. The atrium was not particularly large in the parish, but the floor did consist of smooth terracotta brick tiles. Towards the left was the sanctuary where bookshelves, wardrobes, and the altar servers could be seen within as they removed their vestments overtop their regular Sunday clothes. The gathering hall on the left consisted of a few tables, an alternative exit on the left to go out to the entrance patio, and a small kitchenette to the right. The smell of coffee wafted through the air from the gathering hall, so Everest gravitated towards it to grab a drink while Vienna became lost as she smiled, greeted, and shook hands with the couples of friends and others. Salmar stayed with his father, although there were some males around his age, he chose to rather stay together and join him in the meeting room where they each took a small cup of coffee and went to stand in the corner. Everest watched around him with skeptical eyes as many people met up with each other, each with smiles on their faces, and also too each dressed in formal clothes appropriate for Sunday worship.

Suddenly, a hand came down on Everest's shoulder from beside.

"Well, how are you doing there, Ev," a man greeted in a coarse voice. Everest turned and looked at the man. He was an older male in his early to mid fifties, slightly unshaven or with a short grey beard and grey hair. He was on the slimmer side, wore glasses, and was dressed in a blue blazer and dark navy-blue trousers.

"Hi Clarence," Everest greeted with tad of bitterness.

"I didn't see you last week," Clarence remarked. "Do you sometimes go to the eleven o'clock? That'd be explain why sometimes I see you, while sometimes I don't."

"Maybe," Everest lied.

"Right on," Clarence replied, "anyways, I wanted to express my condolences. It's a shame what happened with the tourney and all. I really thought you had it – to lose everything you had…"

"You win some, you lose some," Everest responded. "It's the way that life goes, you know."

"How true, how true," Clarence replied. "So what are you up to now? What do you usually get up to during the off-season?"

"Not much I can do," Everest answered. "I've just been around, doing a bit of work around the house right now, and in a couple weeks Salmar will be graduating from high school."

"Oh, that's right isn't it," Clarence said, looking towards Salmar, "congratulations, young man."

"Thank you," Salmar replied.

"Any plans for September?"

"No," Everest answered for him, "he's yet to decide, so he'll be taking a year off."

"Very nice," Clarence responded, "suppose you'll put him to work over at the office."

"Yeah," Everest sort of sarcastically replied, looking at his son, "I may take him over to the branch office in town. We'll see... there's really not much work to be done, and I think Sal has his own interests."

"Fair enough."

"There he is," a younger male, around the same age as Everest, spoke, "Mr. Cabernet."

Everest looked over as a man dressed in a grey suit and pinstripe collared shirt stepped forward. He had dark brown hair and cold fair skin.

"Can I help you?" Everest questioned.

"No, but perhaps you can help give us all some hope to understand how your company's operations led to the deaths of hundreds of people and destroyed a small village in Tanzania."

"What are you talking about?" Everest questioned with doubt. "My company has done no such thing. Don't you think I would have heard about it?"

"Apparently not," the man criticized, "and it was not too recent either for you to feign ignorance, or do you really not know what the corporation with your heredity name gets up to?"

Everest clenched a fist in his hand and looked over to his son to gauge his reaction. He then looked back over to the man.

"Now hold on," Clarence instead spoke, "pardon my own ignorance, but what are you talking about?"

"Last Thursday, the collapse of two dams at a Cabernet Industries mine in the northern region of Tanzania caused the deaths of hundreds, the destruction of an entire village, and displaced all the survivors. The initial report suspects foul play to some extent that led to these deaths in what in other words could be described as an avoidable disaster. Their blood is on your hands, Mr. Cabernet."

Everest looked at him with suspicion still but had no response. He looked over to Clarence as he looked at him, and then back over to the man.

"Cabernet Industries is a large international organization. I don't know what exactly you are referring to…"

"How can you not know, it's your damn company!" the man spoke a little louder. "Hundreds are dead! It's your company!"

Everest looked in his periphery as he noticed others turn their gaze towards them.

"Keep your voice down," Everest complained. "I'm sorry, but I don't know what you're talking about, but I'm going to have to ask that you leave us be." He stepped forward and took Salmar by his arm. "Come on, son."

Both of them walked away and moved to exit from the church hall.

"Walk away," the man taunted, "it doesn't change the facts!"

"Who was that creep?" Salmar questioned.

"I have no idea… I hardly know anyone here."

Everest approached Vienna near the main entrance where she stood in front of a young couple with their two children. The mother had long reddish-blonde hair and fair skin, while the father had light brown hair and a beard. She wore a pink summer dress while he wore a dark suit. They had two children with them, one with each parent, a young girl around four-years old with dark red hair and a two-year old male with light brown hair in his father's arms.

"Oh, how adorable," Vienna expressed. "How mighty young Everett has grown to be…" she said, adoring the young boy.

"Hello," Everest greeted the couple, "Vienna, dear, I think it's time we head out."

"Yes, very well," Vienna responded, looking back to the couple, "well, it was so nice to see you again. Take care."

The young couple walked off and Vienna turned to her husband with a smile.

"What's wrong my dear?" Vienna questioned in her accent.

"It's time for us to go," Everest expressed. "Come on now."

"But it's Sunday," Vienna replied, bringing a hand to her husband's cheek. She then caught a look in his eye, and without further words, she understood. "Yes then, perhaps it is time." She lowered her smile and took his hand. She then raised her smile again as they walked out. However, before they left, they caught the attention of the parish priest outside where the sun shined forth. "Goodbye, Father," Vienna departed. "Wonderful sermon."

"Thank you, Vienna, have a blessed Sunday you three," Fr. Wilfred smiled and waved.

Everest and his family passed him as they walked towards the right and into the parking lot. They entered into an SUV, a navy blue 1986 Asano TTV. He turned the engine key and began to back out while Vienna and Salmar were still putting on their seatbelt. He then drove out of the parking lot and proceeded out.

Vienna stayed quiet as they drove back through St. Allan's Plains and crossed the bridge. The sun beat down hard and shined across the Nattau River as they crossed over to the west bank. The car drove around and came down towards Cliffside Way where Cabernet Manor rested upon. Everest drove the vehicle into the driveway, looking up to the large home.

Cabernet Manor was constructed in Edwardian architecture-style. The exterior walls consisted of grey stone and there were many shrubs around the front of the building. The windows were panelled and consisted of white frames. The stairs that came up to the front entrance were white too, and led up to the three columns. The entrance inside was wide and at either side of it were tall rectangular windows that looked inside. Around the property there just a few shrubs, but no fences or gates in these times. Everest drove up the driveway and then down towards an annex that stuck out from the side of the manor. The garage doors opened, and Everest drove the car inside, making a U-turn and parking right next to the corridor that went towards the elevator. Vienna continued to stay quiet as the car shut down and Salmar got out.

"Well, thank you two for joining me today," Vienna expressed. "I know it is a bother for you, but it makes me glad for us to be there together, as a family."

"At least part of," Salmar expressed, stepping out of the car. "I don't think we've ever truly been there as all five of us (nor would it really ever be possible)."

"Now then," Vienna scolded, "you never know. One of these days, it would do me good. What about when one of you gets married? Do you mean to tell me, or believe your brother or sister won't be there like we would be?"

Salmar didn't respond as he closed the door and walked off. Everest looked to his wife.

"Don't you look at me like that either," Vienna expressed, "you are not off the hook as they say."

"What did I do?" Everest questioned as his wife exited the car and slammed the door. He shook his head and replied, "Everybody seems out to get me today."

Everest got out and went up behind his wife towards the elevator up to the kitchen. They each went up and came around to the atrium, from there Salmar went upstairs to his bedroom while Salmar walked off to the library and Vienna went upstairs to the master bedroom. Everest got out every document and fax notice he could gather from across his study, and sitting down at a table, he began to go through them.

After a while, Vienna came around with a tray that had his breakfast and sat it down at one of the tables as she looked around the mess about.

"Such a busy man," Vienna expressed, "too busy to clean up after himself."

"Not now, Vi," Everest pleaded.

"A grouchy man too," Vienna remarked. "What is the problem, my big mountain? Why did you rush us out when it is not even the racing season anymore?"

Everest sighed as he sat back, releasing the papers in front of him from his grip and bringing his hands to his temples with tension. He then released and looked up to the ceiling.

"I messed up, my beautiful city," Everest expressed. "I may have let something slip by me, and I'm beating myself up for it."

"What did you let slip up?"

Everest explained to him the encounter he had with a stranger at the parish, and the allegations that Cabernet Industries was responsible for an industrial disaster in East Africa.

"Ah," Vienna remarked as Everest described the man to her, "Mr. McKay. He is the editor of the Allabrese Advocate newspaper. He was likely attempting to provoke you for a response, assuming you knew about what happened."

"The thing is that I didn't know about what happened, and now I looked like an ignorant fool in front of him for him to write about. I'm going to have to go and talk to him about it, but before I do that, I need to find out what the heck even happened... Why wasn't I made aware of something like this?"

"Yes, good question," Vienna agreed, "you are the man of the company, so why have you not heard from the people you pay to work for you? Cabernet Industries is your company, and they are your people."

"Well, the ownership of the company is not that simple," Everest replied. "It's not entirely my company anymore."

"What do you mean?"

"Do you remember the last time I had to go to Harlech? When they urgently needed me to make some decisions?"

"Yes."

"Well, a part of those decisions in that entire mess involved making Cabernet Corporation not privately-owned, but opening it up to public ownership. As far as I am aware, I am still a majority shareholder, but about forty-percent of the company belongs to other people, the shareholders."

"I don't understand, but it is still your family name," Vienna responded.

"Yes, to my begrudgment, because I wanted them to change it to something else, but they liked the idea of legacy," Everest expressed. "They didn't want to rename Cabernet Corporation to something unfamiliar at a time when they looked to sell shares, so they opted for a different rebrand. They changed the end of the name from corporation to industries, and that was that."

"And are you not the leader of the company anymore?"

"I am, technically," Everest confirmed. "I'm the Chairman, and I... I make decisions and such, but look at me. I'm not a businessman. When all that business was going on five years ago with Medici Bank and such, they all told me there was a very real risk of going to prison. I had no idea how or why the company got implicated in all that, and yet still they told me I was at risk. I was fearful, I thought for sure I would be on the chopping block when they had famous people like Quigley Burton and Raymond Halloway going to prison. Even some politicians were swept up, like that American politician, the secretary of defense, Clark Clayton. I had no idea if the weight of it all would come down on me for what the company was up to. The company had been mine for just about fifteen years at the time, but I had never made any decision, ever. I left the decision-making to the executives, like my father did, and I still do. I try to stay involved now and then, but for the most part I trust their judgement, especially since nowadays since that mess they're a lot more capable and experienced people."

"And who are these people you trust so much that they did not share with you about this travesty?"

"The board of directors, or board of investors really; they're the new executive council that run the company, and they've been doing so since the scandal. A majority of them each hold a sizeable share or represent someone who holds a sizeable share of the company, and there's about six of them in total, more than half of whom are foreign investors and two local investors. There's three seats that were given to the most senior executives at the company who survived the scandal and weren't implicated, but I don't hear from them too often, if ever. How many is that? Nine, not including myself? I'm supposed to be a tiebreaker when it comes to decisions, but not every time do I vote only to break a tie."

"Well then, it sounds like since you are still the majority owner, and you are still the chairman, you are still the man whose family name is also the company name. In my opinion, these directors, or investors, or what have you, should be answering directly to you."

"I've been through all these papers, and I can't recall seeing anything about anything in Africa," Everest expressed. "Either I threw out the paper, which I don't tend to do, or they didn't tell me."

"Well, then if you ask me, it is time that you have these men answer directly to you and give you an answer for this situation," Vienna encouraged. "As it should be that these men ought to answer directly to you, whether the company is entirely yours, a majority yours, or even if it were just a small percentage yours. You are a part of that board of investors."

"Yes, I agree," Everest quietly replied, looking around. "I will have to go into town later today, to the supermarket, and pick up a copy of the national news to see if there's anymore information."

"Good."

"I'll then go into the office tomorrow and insist to meet with the executive council," Everest expressed, "and when I do, I'm going to make sure that all this mess is dealt with promptly and atoned for. Those poor people…"

"Well, now that the racing season is finished, I believe this mission could be good for you too; a project to keep your mind at ease since that loss at the races," Vienna expressed. "I hope that you can do more than just ensure that the sins of the company are atoned for though, but to avoid whatever leads to these scandals and insist that something like this never happens again in the Cabernet name."

"Oh, I will."

Act 1, Scene 4

The following day, Everest woke up in his usual routine, but as he dressed himself, he put on one of this suits, a black one, and tied his tie as though it was Sunday again. He came downstairs to the kitchen and smiled as he met with Vienna in the kitchen, and Salmar at the kitchen table. Baron was sat in a bed next to the pantry door. Salmar looked at his father as he went to kiss his mother on the cheek.

"There is my other handsome man," Vienna expressed, accepting the kiss. She returned to the stove and resumed to cook pancakes for the boys.

"Where are you going?" Salmar questioned, slightly confused.

"I'm going to the branch office downtown," Everest replied. "I have some business to take care of."

"About that stuff going in Africa, right?"

"Yes, that would be right," Everest expressed. "You see, son, Cabernet Corporation (sorry, Industries), as a whole has become the subject of some terrible news, and I plan to see what all the commotion is about and why I wasn't apprised of it appropriately."

"I can't remember the last time you went to the branch office, other than for their summer barbecues or Christmas parties."

"Even if you haven't seen me come around the office, I do go on occasion when you are at school (at least once every two months). Where I haven't been in years is the corporate offices at Cabernet Tower. However, I'm sure I can raise enough questions and make enough requests that the situation shouldn't be so dire that I would need to travel to Harlech."

"I would hope you wouldn't go to Harlech without me. How about we do it in the summer. Please, dad?"

"No," Everest denied, "what would possess you anyhow to want to travel to Harlech when the world's an oyster with many more sites to see? Your grandfather used to take me and your aunt around the world from when we were a young age. Even then, there is so much more to see in the world that I still haven't seen and would be much more pleasing to the eye than Harlech. This year, I thought it would be nice if we travelled somewhere easterly, less caught up with the rest of civilization."

"Like Tanzania?"

"Why not?" Everest questioned. "I won't have anyone at this table think that a country like Tanzania is less worth a visit than Harlech. Dammit, we stare at that TV box every morning for news, and had that disaster been in Europe or the United States, we would have certainly heard hell raised for it, but because it was in Tanzania, an under-developed country, the lives lost appear to be worth less or the intrigue of lesser value than a likewise disaster?"

"Nobody is saying anything to that degree, dad."

"Yes, all life has value," Vienna agreed, "now eat. You will need a full stomach if you are to confront those executives of yours."

Vienna sat down their breakfast, and they ate in silence before the parted ways. Salmar went off on his way to school, while Everest went to his study to prepare papers for his meeting. He put together some papers in a briefcase, closed it, and then left his study as the clock came close to nine. Everest sat down in his Asano TTV, opened the garage gate, and then drove out and to the left to make his way across the river.

From across the river, where St. Allan's plains was, there was plenty of farmland spread across the river bank all the way southwards towards the marshes. Travelling eastward, up a steep hill onto a plateau, one entered into Allabrese proper, where in these days there were fewer suburban homes and more farms, or forest. As one travelled closer to the downtown core, the number of homes was spread out a block or two away. Cabernet Industries branch office was located on the south side of the main park looking towards the Curtia Dawson Memorial Library. On each of the other faces of the park was the civic centre, a government building, and a line-up of shops and such. Cabernet Industries branch office was above a line-up of shops, the main entrance through a small lobby on the ground floor.

Everest parked his car behind the building and then walked through an arcade through the ground floor to reach the sidewalk that looked towards the park. He walked a short distance to reach the glass doors into the main lobby. The main lobby for the branch office consisted of a coffee table flanked by two sofas at either side in front of a glass window. Next to it was a small reception desk with the corporate logo behind, and at the very end was an elevator, if not a stairwell door next to it. On the left, on the long wall opposite from everything else were some large historical pictures of Cabernet Industries, particularly in the oil and lumber industries that was specific to the prairies and this office. Everest walked towards the reception desk to meet with the receptionist, a young lady who looked to him with a smile.

"Welcome to Cabernet Industries, how can I help you?" the receptionist greeted.

Everest gave a hearted laugh and replied, "I have a meeting this morning with the branch vice-president, Conrad Adlington."

"Certainly," the young woman replied, opening a large agenda book on her right. "Could I get your name?"

"Yes, that's Everest Cabernet."

The young receptionist wrote the first letters of the name before she stopped and looked at Everest. "Oh…" she replied, looking at him and then picking up the phone. "One moment, please."

The receptionist dialed a four-digit number and then waited. "Hi Augusta, it's me. I have a Mr. Cabernet here to see Mr. Adlington. Is he here? Yup… Yup… I'll send him up." The receptionist stood up and looked over to Everest. "Mr. Adlington is expecting you upstairs. Let me get the elevator for you."

"Thank you."

Everest walked over towards the elevator while the receptionist called for the car. The doors then opened, and the receptionist stepped in with a key in hand, turned a switch, and then stepped out. She held the door open and allowed Everest to step through.

"Ms. Glover will meet you on the third floor," the receptionist remarked. "A pleasure to meet you, Mr. Cabernet."

"Thank you," Everest replied, stepping inside. The doors closed and the elevators made the short trip upwards to the third floor. The doors then opened and revealed the quiet atmosphere of the branch office.

"Hello, Mr. Cabernet," Augusta Glover, a middle-aged woman with golden blonde hair cut short in a dark red dress greeted. Mr. Adlington was expecting you in his office."

"Thank you, Augusta" Everest said again. "I haven't been here since... oh, around February? Seems like you go through receptionists downstairs so quickly..."

"It's a high-turnover position, I'm afraid, but don't worry, all of us upstairs are still the same," Mrs. Glover responded as they passed individual offices to reach end of the corridor. "Here we are."

Everest looked at the door in front of him. The door bore the name plate 'Everest P. Cabernet' on the front of it, and title below 'Chairman'. He pivoted to the office on the side which had the name plate, 'Conrad H.J. Adlington, M.B.A' with the title below, 'Executive Vice-President'.

Mrs. Glover opened the door as an older male came around to shake Everest's hand. He appeared to be in his seventies and had very short hair light grey hair that was combed back and held in place. He had wrinkled fair skin that was tight around his forehead and temples, flabbier around the cheeks. He had a tall nose and blue eyes that evoked a strict, but dignified and respectable look on his face. He wore a grey suit with a golden-yellow tie and white shirt that was fine pressed and clean. He was a tall man, at least three inches more than Everest who stood at an inch less than six feet. He had an average body-type.

"Ah, Mr. Cabernet," Conrad greeted in a mundane tone. "A pleasure to see you again."

"Hello, Mr. Adlington," Everest remarked, shaking his hand. "It's been a while, at least since I've been here. I saw you just yesterday, didn't I."

"Yes, that would be so."

"Can I get you anything?" Mrs. Glover asked.

"A drink, Mr. Cabernet?" Conrad offered.

"Perhaps just some water," Everest expressed. "There's something I want to discuss before we go to the boardroom."

"Certainly."

Everest looked around at Mr. Adlington's office. His office was unlike those in the rest of the office because the desk faced perpendicular to the window with its view towards the park. The curtains were stretched open, and behind his chair there were three filing cabinets with a vase of flowers on the left and a large crucifix on the wall behind. The desk was covered in newspapers and other documents, and in front of it were two chairs backed up against half-bookcases with many books inside and memorabilia and pictures atop. Among these pictures was one of Mr. Adlington with Everest's father, Derby Cabernet, and a family friend and former executive with the company, Horace Turner. The picture was taken in front of the building, where Derby appeared to be in his late forties with his grey hair and moustache. Everest looked at the photo and then back over to Conrad who came around to his desk.

"Please, take a seat, Mr. Cabernet," Conrad insisted.

"Thank you, Mr. Adlington."

Everest went to sit down, and Conrad respectively sat down after him.

"What did you want to speak on?"

"You've been with Cabernet Industries for a long time," Everest stated. "You're on the executive council. I'll be honest with you, the subject of today's meeting in the next hour is to do with information that I was not made aware of and was questioned about – to do with an industrial accident that happened with Cabernet Extraction in Tanzania."

"Ah, yes," Conrad remarked, "we, or at least the board, had a short meeting on it on Friday, in Harlech. You were to be invited, but nobody could get through to your landline, but ultimately decisions were made, and an investigation is on the way."

"I could find very little information on the matter. The least that I could find was in *The National Focus*. What do I need to know before I press the rest of the councilmembers on it?"

"Well," Conrad responded, pausing for a moment, "the situation transpired in the early morning hours of Thursday, April 28th, when two of the tailing damns above a local village collapsed. The upper dam broke first, and then the other, and when that did it released a combination of mud, sand, and water towards the village, destroying everything in its path and only stop at the adjoining river below."

"How awful," Everest expressed. "What was the cause?"

"We don't know quite yet, but we've sent a team to investigate the situation and report back on what went wrong to avoid a future occurrence, especially to determine whether it was a mechanical failure, an act of God, or human error."

"Act of God?"

"I don't mean so literally. It's a technical term to mean something out of our hands, or unanticipated in which no human is responsible for. An example of which would be a natural disaster, or strike of lightning."

"And there's a possibility that the cause was human error?"

"It will need to be ruled out, but to be honest with you, it is quite possible," Conrad remarked, pausing for a moment. "I don't mean to be dismissive with you, Mr. Cabernet, as this tragedy is a heart-felt one, but these accidents do happen more frequently than you may think. Not too long ago, an oil refinery that the company owns in the south region of Mexico ignited and took the lives of several dozen. An oil rig that the company owns found itself completely washed away on the coast of Canada some years ago too. We are not the only corporation that suffers from such ill-fates, but it is a consequence of industrial work at a large-scale. What I mean to do in addressing these unfortunate issues is for you to consider the frequency of events, and not take such a harsh approach on the matter."

"People died, Mr. Adlington."

"Yes, it is unfortunate, sir, so please, what is your intent then in this meeting?"

"I want to know why I wasn't informed. A telephone call I could have missed, but there was no recorded message on the answering machine about it, and I didn't find any fax notification about it from the council either. I was pressed about the issue after church on Sunday by a reporter from the local newspaper, and I had no idea how to address questions to do with something in my own company. Can you imagine my embarrassment towards that?"

"So… your concern is not the loss of life then?"

Everest flinched at the question. He moved in his seat before he answered and said, "Well, of course I care about the loss of life. It is a tragedy, not that we could undo the losses, and as much as we could attempt to atone for the actions, we've done serious harm with the local communities."

"Yes."

"I want to hear what Mr. Roness and the rest of the council have to say with what action Cabernet Industries is taking though. I thought for sure that if something like this tragedy had occurred, then corrective actions must be taken and put in place. I wouldn't know what sort of correction actions those would be, but I'm confident in our present leadership to action them."

"The actions that would include would be an in-depth investigation to determine what the cause had been, and if the cause had been human error, to learn more from them so as to ensure that such errors could not be done again by reviewing policy and procedure; if the fault was mechanical in anyway, to ensure those failures do not occur again the way they did either through replacement of machinery or routine maintenance, and then if the fault had been constructive or structural, to review the schematics with the architects and hold those accountable for the oversight in structural failure. I can only speculate on what sort of corrective action would be needed without a clear insight into what had gone wrong, but so far only the investigation has been launched."

"And in these other incidents that occurred, what have been the outcome in those investigations? The disappearing oil rig, and the oil refinery fire? Has there been increases in safety measures for our oil rigs, or improved fire safety at our refineries?"

Conrad took in a deep breath and replied, "Unfortunately, the least I can attest to is for our industry here in the prairie region and rest assured lessons have been learned from the mistakes of others to safeguard our workers and the company here, but I'm afraid I cannot speak to the rest of the company. You would have to ask Mr. Roness about those incidents."

"You must have an approximate idea."

"I would rather not provide speculation to you, Mr. Cabernet, out of respect for you."

Everest nodded, looked at his watch, and then stood up. "Well, how about we go to this meeting then." He picked up his briefcase and then proceeded to walk from one side of the third floor to the other where at the very end was the executive board room.

The board room was smaller than the one kept downstairs for corporate meetings, had less seats, but had a view westward towards the Rocky Mountains. Everest came around to a chair near the head of the table where there was a telephone set, while Conrad came to the telephone set and began to dial in. He then placed the telephone down while Everest sat down. He sat down across from Everest, leaned back, and placed his hands together before him. Meanwhile, as the telephone rang, Everest opened his briefcase and began to sift through papers.

"Hello, Mr. Adlington," a woman spoke on the other end. "Can you hear me?"

"Yes, I can hear you, darling."

"Alright, perfect. I have with me here at Cabernet Tower, Mr. Roness, Mr. Clifford, Mr. Leroy, Mr. Paterson, Mr. Wan-Cheung, Mr. Holmes, Mr. Locke, and Mr. Bennett."

"Thank you, my dear. Gentleman, I am here at the Prairie Region branch office in Allabrese, Alberta, with Mr. Everest Cabernet."

"Howdy there," a man spoke on the other end, "Dallas Dwight Roness, but you can just call me, Dwight Roness, Mr. Cabernet. It's always a pleasure to get to speak to the man whose roots started this glorious company, doing the work that we get to do. To what do we owe the pleasure on this fine Monday morning to speak with you, sir?"

"Hello, Mr. Roness, and hello everyone else," Everest sheepishly greeted. "I've called this meeting to address a serious concern that I had with the operations of the company."

"Right then, did you have something specific in mind, Mr. Cabernet?" Roness questioned.

"Yes, I did," Everest answered, "it has to do with the dam collapse in Tanzania last week."

"Ah, yes. What of it?"

"I wanted to know why I was not apprised of it; not even a memorandum, or a small notice. I was harassed by a news reporter as of recent about the incident, and I couldn't provide any information about the event whatsoever and instead seemed plain stupid to the news."

"Yes, yes, yes," Roness responded. "I see the issue here, that sounds like quite the unfortunate situation. Those reports, let me tell you, they cannot play nicely. Well, Mr. Cabernet, I am sorry that you had to go through that moment. Let me express to you just how sorry I am. However, I do believe that this information to do with the event was disseminated to you, if not in an operational notice, then in the daily operational reports that you receive via fax everyday."

"I receive many notices and reports, Mr. Roness," Everest responded. "Some from different branches, and some from different conglomerates."

"No, no, no," Roness denied, "you want the daily executive report that Julie sends out every morning. It should have been right there at the top of the page…"

"Is that so…" Everest remarked, shuffling through his papers.

"Yes, and as well as being in that report, I do believe that we held a meeting about the event between ourselves and corporate communications before we went to the media about the situation. We also held another meeting with the executive for Cabernet Extraction. Both meetings of which I'm sure you were invited to, but as is the case often times, we don't ever receive a response from you. Even so, if we had known that such incidents were of particular concern to you, we could very well assured that the communication was made outward to you in case something like this incident were to happen again."

Everest raised his head up at that last word. He then slowly began to continue to search for the report.

"Let me tell you though, Mr. Cabernet," Roness continued to speak, "we've made a response to the press on the issue, and we've sent a team out towards that part of the world to take a deeper look into what the cause of this incident had been. An incident like this one is a rare occurrence you know."

Everest looked over to Conrad and then over to the telephone.

"It's not every day we have dams or mines collapsing, or have to deal with the travesty of a hundred or so lives lost. I speak out of years of experience in international business, close to thirty years of it, and there has been worst catastrophes, but often times that's the way it goes in the world. In the early days of the oil rush at the end of the gold rush, accidents in those times were much more common, but we've gotten smarter, work harder, and now despite the high-velocity of such operations, we are extracting much more oil, much more minerals, and keeping our people and other people safe in doing so. Cabernet Industries has one of the safest guidelines for workers; we care about our people...

"And how has our response been to this situation? How are we aiming to ensure that those affected in his tragedy are compensated for their loss? I assume that workers, and perhaps worker families were included in the casualties?"

"We had a rough estimate to the losses, but yes workers and employees were taken in those losses, but I wouldn't worry about those numbers. What's important right now is that we are getting to the bottom of this situation, and I assure you that we do not take events like these lightly, no less when the media are breathing down our necks about it. Believe me."

Everest found the report titled 'Executive Summary' at the top for April 28th, 1989. He looked down the list of events that transpired where at the very bottom of the page there was a notation: 'April 27th, 1989 – Dar es Salaam, Tanzania – Incident at Site C' Beneath the notation was a description: "All operations have halted at Site C pending a safety inspection as a result of an unknown failure that has led to the destruction of both tail damns. Revenue losses and timeline of repair are to be determined; an assessment is underway for continued operation, if possible, as soon as possible, and statements provided to corporate communications.' Everest re-read the report once more before he looked back over to the telephone as Roness continued to babel.

"… What matters is that Cabernet Industries, and the reputation of Cabernet Industries, is secured and assured, because we don't let a small hiccup like this get in our way."

"Mr. Roness, what about safety measures? I am certain that safety measures will be looked into, and whether consideration of a dam failure was made, or if backstops were placed in consideration."

"Absolutely, Mr. Cabernet. You can be assured that we will be reviewing where we went wrong in this situation, and how that, being the largest failure in this entire situation, could have occurred to have resulted in the deaths of people. I hope though that you would consider too that while safety is our number one priority, especially a safe work environment, we can't account for acts of God and the sort, and sometimes, accidents happen and while we can always certainly do all that we can to make it certain that these situations don't happen again, often times, they don't happen again because it is a once in a lifetime occurrence rather than some overhaul in operating procedures. I'll always be honest with you, Mr. Cabernet, and tell you how it is – it is a common corporate, even political reaction, to always want something done to every situation, but sometimes there are just situations you can't account for, and I know that's not a favorable answer, nor am I saying it is the answer to this particular situation, but rest assured I am not just providing assurance to you that we will make revisions for the sake of slapping a bandage on our reputation and negative occurrence. No, we will do so because we care and hold this situation, like any safety incident, in high regards. Does that answer your question? Let me know if I need to explain that a bit more thoroughly to you."

"No, Mr. Roness, it is plainly apparent to me," Everest responded with a sigh.

"Excellent," Roness responded, "is there anything else I can do for you? Any other questions, or inquiries you had?"

"No, I... I think that'll be all for now," Everest expressed, looking aside.

"Alright then, thank you then Mr. Cabernet for making the time to talk to us. We always appreciate getting to hear your voice, and we hope that we'll get to see you in person sometime soon."

"Yes..." Everest muttered under his breath, "I'll tell you what," he said in a louder tone, "why wait? I believe it's been quite enough time – I think now is a better time than any to come to Harlech. I would like to see closer details to our response to this particular situation, and also to play a part and make a statement to the media. I think it would be important to show that Cabernet Industries truly is invested in and concerned for what has happened at Site C."

No immediate response came from the telephone as both Mr. Adlington and Everest looked at the phone.

"Sure," Roness finally responded. "Sure, that sounds like a fantastic idea. I couldn't ask for a better idea than that, but I also don't want to impose on your, Mr. Cabernet. If you have the time, let's do it."

"I have the time, Mr. Roness. I'll have to make some arrangements of course, but expect me in Harlech sometime by the end of the week. I think it's a ripe time to say some hellos and see how it's going at the corporate headquarters."

"Certainly, how about I leave that for Mr. Adlington to arrange, and if you need any assistance, my assistant will liaise with your assistant, Mr. Adlington," Roness expressed. "We'll want to be assured we get an itinerary and such so that we can ensure that Mr. Cabernet is given a proper welcome."

"Very well," Conrad responded.

"Excellent," Roness said, "well, if that'll be so, then we look forward to seeing you in-person, Mr. Cabernet, for your visit over here. If there's nothing else to discuss, I believe now would be a good time to divulge and adjourn this meeting."

"Thank you, Mr. Roness," Conrad remarked, hanging up.

Mr. Adlington stood up and looked over to Everest.

"Is everything alright, Mr. Cabernet?" Conrad questioned, looking at him.

Everest looked to the side, over to him, and then over to his briefcase as he tidied his papers. He then stood up and looked to him, shaking his head and raising his hand up.

"Everything is not alright," Everest expressed. "Our company had an accident, and everything will not be alright until we see this accident through with a proper response. Can I trust on you to help with my travel arrangements to Harlech? I assume the penthouse is still available and is not in use?"

"I will have to check with Mr. Roness' assistant, and don't you worry, I will ensure your travel arrangements are set. I will of course join you on your voyage to Harlech."

"Thank you, Mr. Adlington. Do you have anything else for me?"

"No, Mr. Cabernet," Conrad responded, prompting Everest to step aside. "I hope that you can make the desirable impact on your visit, for all peoples."

Everest nodded and then left the room. He left Mr. Adlington behind who took a seat back as Everest left, while Everest with heavy breaths through his nostrils, returned downstairs via the elevator with a twinge of anger in his eyes.

Act 2, Prologue

"Open your eyes," a soft English-accented voice said.

Everest opened his eyes as small soft hands were removed from his eyes. He looked ahead of himself and saw a large cascade before him, seen from up high but ever taller than one could see with mists that sprayed upwards. Everest was sat atop of a grey elephant, which itself loomed over and made its way through a calm stream in the midst of a humid rainforest jungle. Young Everest, who appeared ten-years old at the time, was sat atop of the saddle of an elephant with his mother behind him. Ophelia Cabernet at this time had short light brown hair and fair skin. She wore a white blouse tucked into cargo pants with a jungle hat over head and boots at her feet. She also had a small backpack behind her. Everest was dressed in an open collared shirt and white undershirt. He also wore cargo pants and boots. Behind them was another elephant from which Britannia Cabernet, who appeared to be seven-years old, was sat with her father, Derby Cabernet, behind. Britannia Cabernet had light brown hair like her mother, except hers was longer and tied in a ponytail. She wore a pink blouse, cargo pants, and boots. Her father was dressed in a khaki collared shirt and cargo pants. He also wore boots and had a safari hat. In these times, Derby was clean-shaven, although older as much as he was wiser, being in his early thirties. His blue eyes were focused in front of him as the family journeyed out from within the jungle and came through the shores of a lake from which the wide waterfall poured itself into.

The elephant that Everest rode raised up its trunk, and he looked at it as it slithered around. Ahead of them were two local Indian males who took lead and guided them through the jungle. An elephant let out a cry, causing some birds to flutter and disperse into the skies. The sun poured forth through the tall trees and their vines, while the waters below were as green as the jungle itself.

"Isn't it a wonderful sight?" Ophelia questioned in her west Londoner accent. "My, it brings me to my childhood when my father would bring us to the Raj for holidays."

"I wouldn't suppose those holidays were filled with these sorts of adventures though, were they, my love," Derby remarked aloud from besides. "We should almost be at the village, from there we will have to stop momentarily before we proceed on a hike to reach the temple."

"Sorry if I sound like a broken record, Derby darling, but how safe is it for the children in the village?"

"Plenty safe, most of times village folk are the most kind and blessed souls a man can hope to meet on an adventure as such."

The elephants continued down and began to curve right away from the lake and back on a river stream for another mile. The river was wide, but they travelled on the shores. The elephants waded through the waters without difficulty. After close to half an hour, Everest began to see a village on the coast of the river. The tour guides ahead could be heard speaking in their local language, which none of them understood. Along the coast of the river, a wooden dock stuck out where there were some boats on one side. The elephants continued upwards to this dock where they slowed down and made a stop as the tour guides led theirs to kneel and allowed them to climb down.

Once the tour guides were down, the elephant stood up and one of the guides led it away with a lead so that Everest and Ophelia's elephant could make room so they could climb down. Everest was assisted down the side of the elephant first, and then afterwards Ophelia made her way down to join him. Afterwards, Derby assisted Britannia down, and then took his rucksack and began to make headway into the village.

Derby stopped at the end of the docks where his tour guides began to discuss with him, but Everest rather than listen, began to look around the village and its many buildings. He saw many structures unlike any those he had ever seen before, even in India since his arrival. These structures were small, primitive, and made of bamboo and/or wood. The rooftops consisted of nothing more but foliage or straw. There were many children in the village who looked at them with piercing white eyes that contrasted to their very brown skin, much noticeable as most of them were barely clothed, wearing nothing more than locally made garments to cover their private parts. Everyone here had very dark black hair and the boys had thick eyebrows, while the girls' were a bit finer although their hair was long. The boys had shaggy, thick hair. Everest stopped looking around as he went over to his father and mother. His sister was behind them and looked over at Everest.

"Why are they looking at us?" Britannia questioned with concern. She spoke with an accent similar to Everest's having been raised in the same home. "It's weird."

"Wouldn't you stare, if strangers like us suddenly appeared on such tall animals?" Everest suggested. "I'm sure they're only curious at us."

"Make them stop."

"What am I supposed to do about it?" Everest questioned, annoyed.

"Children, enough," Derby warned. "Come now."

Derby and the party walked forth into the village where the tour guides led them further in. Everest and Britannia stayed close to their mother at the back, whereas Ophelia looked around with wonder at the local village. As they ventured deeper into the small village, Everest began to hear a peculiar noise that he had never heard before. The noise sounded as though someone was yelling, as though in danger, but it was melodic as if they were singing. The sound echoed forth too. The adults with Britannia attached to her father's leg, began to greet some adults in the village centre, but rather than join them, Everest began to wander in search of that noise.

Everest went into the village as he looked around, the villagers too looked at him. The adult males wore rags and dirty clothing, while the adult females wore very long colorful clothes, and there were many women and very few men. Finally, Everest began to close in on the noise as he came around to a larger building on the outskirts of the village that had a foundation constructed out of light grey cinder blocks. He went around the perimeter of this building as the noise dissipated until the building adjacent to this one, he found a shrine. The shrine consisted of a tent built similarly to the houses around, but with no walls. The base of the shrine in the least consisted of stone with steps up to an idol. At either side of the steps were anthropomorphic statues of creatures similar to those of apes, but with noses like elephants. They were crouched with their knees raised up to their chests, and their heads were tipped down. Beside these statues were pots that contained green plants in bloom. Within the shrine itself was a mural on the backwall with a depiction of all sorts of caricatures with blue skin and white tattoos. The mural was very colorful, with a palette of pink, yellow, green, red, and blue. In the midst of the shrine where the idol was, there was an arched shelter within the shelter made of painted wood. The arch had a wavy blue groove that came out of the mouth of green, red-horned dragons at each pillar. At the center of the arch was another dragon-link face, although this image also appeared as though one side was mirrored at the other side. The monster-like creature had a flat nose like a snout, horns that protruded from underneath at the top of its lip like tusks, and it spat out a blue flame shaped like a bell or anchor. The eyes of the creature were orange, and it had upon its head a crown-like hat. This creature watched over the idol within, which was much more anthropomorphic although it did have four arms and hands. The idol had blue skin and wore a yellow robe. The palms of its hand were pink. The icon was sat upon a plain grey rectangular box. It had one left leg flat on the stone base, while the right was raised and touched on the side of its left knee. Each foot had sandals, and the toenails were painted white. Around the torso there was a yellow belt, and around the chest there was a yellow amulet. The shoulders were draped in a turquoise capette. Around all four wrists were circular yellow bands. The bottom most arms had both hands palms facing forward, fingers straight, but the left-hand fingers pointed up, and the right hand fingers pointed down. The upper arms had both hands palms facing forward, but only the thumb, middle and index finger pointed up, and the ring and pinky bent. The idol had yellow earrings similar to the necklace, and wore a domed pointed crown on its head. It had ears and nose like a cow, and on its forehead there was a white sigil. The eyes were human-like. On each of the palms were red sigils too. Everest went towards the idol, looking at the life-like eyes of the idol that stared forward in its pose, but then he heard a voice cry out from behind him.

Everest jumped and looked as he a saw an older male, nearly toothless and what teeth he did have were deeply yellow, in the basement of the building with a cinder brick foundation. He had dark eyes and very long hair. He spoke incoherently to Everest as he tugged at the bars of the window. He extended his arm outwards towards Everest as though to lure him towards him, but Everest did not go forward. Suddenly, the throat singing could be heard again, echoing outwards from the prison cell beneath the building. Everest looked away from the prisoner on the left, and looked towards another older male on the right. This man appeared defeated, his arms were outstretched and lay lifelessly on the dirt path, and his head rested on the cinder brick and he appeared with tired eyes. This man had white hair and a thick bushy beard. His skin was a tad lighter shade than the rest of the locals, and he muttered to himself as the prisoner from within continued to sing. Everest looked back towards the prisoner who was attempting to get his attention, to which the other prisoner noticed and then looked over to Everest.

"He wants you to set him free," the other prisoner spoke in clean English. "He thinks that you are a messenger, sent from Allah to set us free. Do not be tricked by him. He has been locked up in here for many years, although he has not known freedom since the day he was born."

"What is Allah?"

"Allah is the god of the Muslim people, which he is one of, although that is not solely why he is in prison. He has been a very bad man, so have we all…"

"Is the man singing – is that because he is a Muslim too?" Everest questioned.

"No, he is a Sikh, and the singing that comes from the throat a custom of his people, to keep spirits raised."

"He's sick?"

"No, a Sikh, his people come from the northwest, and he found himself here and was thrown in prison because his people are not viewed any better than the Muslims."

Everest got a closer look at the man inside who was cross-legged and sat in the far back of the prison. He wore a garment above his head, similar to the crown of the idol, but made of cloth. He had skin similar to the man before him, not as dark as the others.

"I think you all look very similar. Are you not all Indians?"

"We are," the older male answered, "but what we do, what we believe in, is different."

"What do you believe in?" Everest questioned.

"I am a Buddhist," the older male stated. "I follow and teach the wisdom of the Buddha, the awakened and greatest among us."

"I don't know who that is either."

"The Buddha was a great teacher, very wise and mystical. He taught how to avoid and relieve oneself from suffering, from misery and pain, because all these things are illusions. Are you familiar with these terms? Have you ever known sorrow? Have you ever cried?"

"I have," Everest answered. "How does a person avoid to those feelings?"

"The path to enlightenment begins first by accepting these four truths: we all suffer, because we all have selfish desires, and if we continue to desire then we will continue to suffer, and so the only way in which we can avoid and relieve oneself from our sufferings is to cease all desires, and when that is done, you will be enlightened."

"What if I want my desires?"

"Want is the ultimate expression of desire, even need can be an expression of desire. You must cease first to not want or need, because the human spirit neither wants nor needs."

"I don't understand... is the desire to not want to desire, or to suffer, a desire? Do you not have wants or wishes? Don't you want to be set free?"

"I have been in this prison for many years, but what difference do we have? The way I see it, you are in the prison, and I am free, because if I were where you were, there would be more suffering than where I currently am. Here I am at my freest, away from the desires of the world. I have nothing, and can lose nothing, and because I can lose nothing, I can feel no sorrow for loss. I am empty, poured out to the world around me, and all I have left is what I can offer to the world, and when I have had my last breath, to dust I shall return to the earth that made me. I am content with where I am, even if it were here or there, the possibility to suffer is more out there than here."

"Isn't there a single want in your heart? To be happy?"

"I am happy," the guru replied. "I was once a prince, with endless riches, but riches could not buy the wants of the heart because the wants of the heart are flawed and cause others and oneself to suffer. I stopped listening to those wants, and I stopped to act on those wants to be as I am now, and there has been enlightenment when those wants were let go. You must let go of your own wants and desires, and cast them away."

Everest looked back at the guru. The man from within began to throat sing again.

"There you are!" Derby expressed, grabbing Everest by the arm. "What are you doing over here? Talking to prisoners? Allowing yourself to be blind-sided and manipulated? Come on now!"

Derby grabbed Everest and began to pull him away. Everest struggled at first as he continued to look over to the guru. The guru raised up his arm with what strength he had and reached out towards Everest.

"Let go of your desire, the wants of the heart, and you will achieve Nirvana," the guru remarked. "The loss of all your sufferings."

"Don't listen to him," Derby rebuked. "How long have you been over there? Listening to pagan nonsense? I swear, Everest, you're about as easily manipulated as you are dumb."

"They didn't do anything, pa," Everest expressed as he was let go. Derby confronted him. Everest raised his arms in a cross as though to protect himself. "Please, I'm sorry."

"Pull yourself together," Derby barked, "and pay attention. What do I always say when we're in foreign lands? Show some respect and keep in line. I don't want to have to go out looking for you again, do you hear me? Now come on."

Derby took Everest's arm and tugged him behind.

"What do you desire, pa? Why do you suffer and make me suffer?" Everest questioned.

Derby stopped and let go of Everest. He turned around and looked at his son who was tearful. He scowled at him and replied, "I desire that my son shows himself a bit more dignity around these locals and quits his whining – that's what I desire." He took out a canteen from his belt as well as a handkerchief.

"Now wash up that face of yours and dry yourself too. It'll be a whole lot less embarrassing to know that my ten-year old son isn't teary-eyed."

Everest received water into his hands, and briefly washed his eyes and then took the handkerchief to dry them. When they were finished, Derby had calmed down a bit and took Everest by the hand to guide him back to his others. Although Everest had washed the tears from his face, his face still expressed sorrow.

Act 2, Scene 1

Everest sat in the seat of a small lounge where beside him was another plush seat, and across from him two more. Behind this seating area there was a couch outstretched to the rear wall, and before that couch were two armchairs with a pillar that contained a cabinet at the bottom and a nook at the top where there was a television box nestled inside. At Everest's feet was a fuzzy blue carpet, the walls white and smooth. On the opposite side from the seat, he was at there was a small kitchenette. At the rear wall there was a door with a latch door handle that went into a storage hull, and at the other end was another door that went into a space before the cockpit where the exit and bathroom were located. Across either side of lengthier walls on the left were shelves, directly above of which was a briefcase and suitcase that belonged to Everest. Beneath this shelf, on both sides, left and right, were small cubical thick-glassed windows. Everest sat in his seat directly next to a window, across from him was a copy of *The National Focus* newspaper.

Rather than a view of Harlech, the view that Everest caught sight of was the region to the south, the Walham Valley. The Kenman River stared out at him from above, slithering inland from the sea with its murky waters. Helmken on the coast, and Lennox midland, almost united with each other with a bit of farmland between them on the north and south sides. Lennox had grown from a township to a city of its own with apartment blocks and construction sites that promised towers of their own. From this city that centered both the highway and river, the river followed to connect with Caritas at the base of tall hills covered in pine trees and forests between. His eyes fell upon the forests around that vicinity, and then down towards Skeena Prairie where properties took up immense acres of land, more land than one could ever hope to find in the densely populated city to the north. The Kenman River then continued onwards inland.

As the plane made its approach and descent, it began to turn as it went too far from the island city and flew over the Hecate Strait. The view shifted to the tall mountains over New Harlech, Penultimate Bridge uniting it with King Island beneath it and the downtown core; Jarsdel Island with the city centre and Cliffe Island with Harlech Old. In a stark contrast to the Kenman River, the Harlech River at the south of Cliffe Island appeared visible too, its waters blue but no doubt polluted, and its width at least four times the width of the Kenman River. The Harlech River curved inland around New Harlech, Rosalynn Regional Park at the peninsula end. The river carved into the land like the Kenman, buts its curves and turns less sharp although it did narrow out. The private jet descended towards Harlech International Airport on the eastern side of Cliffe Island.

Once the jet arrived, Everest, dressed in a dark grey suit, stepped down the steps to arrive at a black Dolores-Ganß luxury sedan. A chauffer dressed in a black suit with a black tie opened the car door for him. Conrad Adlington exited the limousine, himself dressed in a pinstripe black suit that was tailor-fit and custom to his stature. He extended his hand to Everest, and they shook on the tarmac.

"Welcome to Harlech, Mr. Cabernet," Conrad greeted. "The board is waiting for you at Cabernet Tower. Please, allow the driver to take your luggage and take a seat."

"Thank you, Mr. Adlington," Everest responded, surrendering his luggage to the chauffer. The chauffer took his bags and placed them in the trunk of the car while Everest got inside the vehicle and Adlington sat across from him.

The sedan departed from the airport tarmac and exited out onto the streets of Leicester where they made their way towards the highway. Everest looked out towards the city and then over to Adlington as he was reading a copy of *The Financial Focus*. He asked, "How long have you been with Cabernet Industries?"

"I've been with the company since 1946, Mr. Cabernet," Conrad answered, folding the newspaper and placing it beside him. He sat with his ankle resting on his opposite knee. I began as a general manager, made my movement upwards to operations manager where I stayed until 1973 with the decline. My entire branch was laid off that year and I was assimilated into the corporate staff where I worked as a director until 1985 at which point, as part of the many changes that happened that year, I was put in charge of the Prairie Region branch office."

"I'm glad that we were able to retain you, but why didn't you quit in 1973 and find somewhere else to work? With your experience, you could have stayed where you were if not moved up."

"1973 was the start of a recession, Mr. Cabernet. It was impossible to find another job in that same position, and in leaving I would have lost seniority and the connections I had made within the corporation. My wife encouraged me to hold through and stay put; to endure. She had confidence that I would be rewarded for my patience."

"Have you?"

"I would say so," Conrad answered.

"My wife stayed home because of my eighteen-year-old son. When you travel to Harlech, does your wife stay home?"

"She used to."

"Oh, is she with you now?"

"No, she passed away two years ago."

"Oh... I'm sorry to hear that," Everest responded. "How about children?"

"I have eight children, all adults now."

"Wow, that's quite the number of children. I can hardly keep up with three. How did you manage so many?"

"With much love, much patience for each of them," Conrad answered, "and the skills a man gathers when he shepherds his workers like a good shepherd, to care for them and be like a servant."

"That's very good of you."

The car continued to drive from Cliffe Island northbound to King Island. The skies on this particular day were clear and blue. The sun pierced gently and there was a mild breeze that made it neither warm nor cold. Once at King Island, the sedan made the first exit and came out onto Bailey Drive. They turned right and went north, turning left then onto Campbell Street. The car continued westbound, passing Stephens Street, Bennett Street, Barnard Street, and Bourassa Street as they went into Central Harlech.

Everest looked out his window at the many different people, young and old, of different races and sizes, hair styles and getup, elegant and fancy, to the simplest, most common, to dirtiest of clothes. He looked up at the tall buildings around him that stretched upwards. The car passed down Farrant Street, Cahan Street, Price Street, and Hound Street. At Dowager Street, Everest looked out with familiar eyes at his surroundings, seeing Dominion Square directly ahead of the Bank of Harlech.

At the corner of Campbell Street and Earle Street, the base of Cabernet Tower could be seen. Cabernet Tower was an exceptionally tall skyscraper that occupied the entire block. The base of the structure had four square shop windows on the left and right from the main entrances at the center on Campbell Street. The main entrance came in three rotating doors that were two meters tall, the same height as the shop windows. Above these windows and doors were taller windows the same length, but twice as tall in height with a stone panel through the centre with a decorative herald similar to the Cabernet crest except with no animals. From these windows, there was a similar height gap, and then double rectangular panel windows up for the entire length until the twentieth or so floor. This length up to the twentieth or so floor was the base of the structure, and it was in a rectangular U-shape with a gap above the main entrances from the tallest windows. At the front of these gaps was an arch in the structure in which the Cabernet Industries logo was depicted like a seal. At two and half meters, the façade of the structure consisted of smooth, polished, greyish-tanned stone, and then above that it consisted of tanned bricks. From the base, the building continued upwards, smaller in square-size than the base, but still a significant size nonetheless that reached upwards, dwindling in size until the ninetieth floor were just below the penthouse in lit letters the words, 'Cabernet Industries' came out, and then at the rooftop was a large C initial. At the corner of Campbell and Earle Street, the car turned left onto the one-way road and drove northbound.

Eight more square windows lined the ground floor up to a side entrance into the building, and then ahead the building stuck out to form an arcade over the sidewalk with more shops and windows ahead. The sedan merged to the curb where a lane led into a gap in the arcade that came into the underground parking lot. The car stopped before it as they pulled over and came off the busy road. The chauffer then got out to open the car door for them, while a young man in a suit stepped forward from the side entrance to assist. Mr. Adlington stood up to exit, and then he held the door for Everest to step out. The chauffer came around to get Everest's bags from the trunk of the car and then placed them down. The young male in a black suit came forward to take the bags onto a luggage cart.

"Have these taken up to the ninety-eighth floor," Conrad directed, turning to Everest. "Mr. Cabernet, right before you set in at the penthouse, the board of directors wishes to greet and meet you."

"Certainly," Everest casually replied.

Rather than enter through the side entrance, where the attendant disappeared through, Conrad brought Everest down to the street corner and around to the main entrance. Once at the main entrance, Conrad allowed Everest through first. Everest pushed the rotating door in front of him as he could see through the glass, the presence of many people who were looking towards him.

Everest entered the main atrium of Cabernet Tower in its brown marble walls and floors, and gold-colored rails, frames, and beams, where there were at least more than a hundred persons in business clothes that awaited his arrival and now begun to clap for him. The main atrium at Cabernet Tower was two-stories tall with an open space in the middle. The shops that could be seen around the ground floor could be entered through the main atrium. At the very center of the atrium was a gold-colored metal circle in the midst of the floor with a cursive C. Around this C were curved planters with shrubs and benches in front of it. Everest looked around him as he saw people, men and women, on the ground floor and second floor above, looking down at him with smiles on their face, clapping for him; all these people of whom he did not know, not even their first name. Everest looked at all these people, people who worked for a company that he was a majority shareholder of, and which years ago were of his own entire ownership. They all clapped for him, and as they did, his smile began to slowly lower but not entirely disappear. He simply stood in a combination of awe and discomfort. Everest entered forth past these people as Conrad guided him towards the elevators where the luggage cart disappeared into an elevator car.

In front of the elevators were a few people that Everest squinted as though in mild recognition. Among these people was a young man in a blue pinstripe suit with fair skin and medium-length brown hair. He continued to clap as he stepped forward, and then he extended his hand out.

"Mr. Cabernet, Lucius Clifford, President of Cabernet Industries, very pleased to meet you again," the male greeted. "How was your trip?"

"Very comfortable," Everest answered, "there was so much space, it felt almost lonely."

The people in their surrounding continued to clap, while the executives on Clifford's left began to stop which within a few minutes stopped the rest of the people who began to chatter amongst themselves.

"Mr. Cabernet, allow me to introduce to you members of our board of directors," Clifford remarked, turning around. "Here we have Mr. Marie-Pierre Leroy, who I am sure you are familiar with. He has been our appointed president with our branch in France."

"Welcome, Mr. Cabernet," Mr. Leroy greeted.

"Next to him we have Mr. Brian Paterson, president of our British branch."

"Greetings, Mr. Cabernet," Mr. Paterson said, shaking his hand.

"Here we have Mr. Xu Wan-Cheung, president of our Chinese branch." Everest shook hands with Mr. Wan-Cheung, and then moved on to the next man. "This is Mr. Theodore Holmes, executive vice-president for our human resources department."

"Nice to see you again, Mr. Cabernet," Mr. Holmes spoke in a deep voice.

"This is Mr. Andreas Locke, vice president of our operations department.

"Nice to meet you," Everest greeted, shaking his hand.

"Lastly, John Bennett, executive vice president for the Pacific branch here."

"Hello, Mr. Cabernet," Mr. Bennett greeted. John Bennett had dark hair and fair skin. He was clean-shaven and wore a black suit. He also had dark eyes that pierced back at Everest.

"Nice to meet you," Everest simply replied, shaking hands and then letting go. He looked around and then back at Lucius.

"Where's Mr. Roness? I would have thought he would have been here for this… welcome party."

"Sorry, Mr. Cabernet. He wanted me to let you know with regret that he would be unable to join us now because of an important meeting with stakeholders. However, in the meantime, we could go up to your office on the top floor."

"My office?" Everest questioned. "Certainly."

Lucius led the way forward to the elevator. The rest of the board of directors followed, but only Conrad, Lucius, and two females stayed with them. Everest looked at either female as they wore colorful blouses and skirts. They were both young and beautiful. The elevator door opened and all six of them entered in, while the others waited for the next one. Lucius punched in a code and selected the eighty-eighth floor. The elevator doors opened, and they stepped out into a corridor. Everest looked around, as though nostalgically at a sight he had long thought to have forgotten. The corridor and space around them was drastically quieter than the atrium in the least. The interior space consisted of fluffy brown carpets and plain yellowish walls with incandescent cone lamps spread out around. At the top and bottom of the walls were wooden moldings and baseboards. Lucius led the group down the corridor and then around a corner where they passed a set of double doors into the conference room to come to another set of double doors into the chairman's office.

"Here is your office, Mr. Cabernet," Lucius remarked. "Kept in its original state from when you were last here, rest assured."

Everest looked around the large gymnasium-like room with its large open space in the center. The floor consisted of polished dark brown wooden floorboards, the walls of a similar darker wood in panels. The ceiling had gold-colored lamps that hung down on chains. At the far-side there were tall windows, at least two stories tall, from where light poured in through. There were two layers of curtains, a dark red opaque outer layer, and a white translucent inner layer. These curtains were pulled open, and the view through them looked out to the mountains of the northern mainland. In front of the windows directly across from where they entered there was a large globe and a table beside it from where there were more boxes. On the right there was an unlit fireplace with a tall life-like portrait above it. Everest looked at the portrait and saw that it was of his father, when he was still young too as his hair had its color and his face was clean-shaven without its moustache. He was dressed in a grey three-piece suit with a hand at his side and standing confidently as his blue eyes looked ahead. Although, to Everest, they looked as though in his immense stature, they looked directly down at him. There were a set of doors at either side of the fireplace that led elsewhere. On the left, on the opposite side from the fireplace, there was a large desk that was mostly empty apart from a few boxes piled around. Behind the desk was a tall leather chair. Besides the desk were two more sets of doors that went elsewhere into the building. As they went further into the room, Everest turned around to face the wall besides the door they passed through where he saw various frames, one of which was of the upper half of Cabernet Tower, another of which was of Cabernet Court in its former glory, and the last of which was Cabernet Manor in Allabrese. These were not paintings, but architectural sketches set in frames. There was nothing more to the office than these items. Everest looked around once more and then to Lucius and Conrad.

"What's a man to do with this much working space?" Everest expressed.

"I'm not sure," Lucius replied, "but the office is yours to do with as you please."

"Where is Mr. Roness' office?" Everest asked. "I can't remember the layout of this building."

"On the opposite side of this floor, there are three corporate executive offices: mine on the east side, Mr. Roness' on the west, and a vacant office that belonged to the chief financial officer in the center. The role of CFO though has been vacant for some time."

"Why's that?" Everest questioned.

"At our current efficiency, we've been able to run the company smoothly without such role. The board of directors has determined it to not be needed, or necessary."

Everest nodded and then said, "How about a tour of the rest of this floor?"

"Absolutely," Lucius replied, "please follow me."

Lucius led the group out of the chairman office, down the corridor and through a set of doors on the right that came into a large conference room. In the midst of the conference room was a long table with many chairs. The windows on the opposite-end of the room looked outwards to the west, over the rooftops of the rest of the downtown core. From the conference room, Lucius led the group back into the corridor, and then over into a large space in the center of the building from where there were cubicles and desks around. Everest took notice of the smaller offices at the back that were labeled with city names, 'Paris,' 'London,' 'Taipei,' but also 'New York,' 'Tokyo', and 'Bonn.' The office space was mostly quiet, aside from the occasional ringing of a telephone. The office workers in this space talked quietly, even when on the phone. Lucius led the group around and towards the middle office that belonged to the CFO.

Everest walked inside and saw a smaller office, half the height of his own, a third of its length, but with a window that looked out southwards towards Dominion Square and then over the downtown core outwards to the rest of the city. On the left there were beautiful paintings of natural landscapes set up in three, while on the right there were empty bookcases. Before the window there were empty shelves. The desk in front of these shelves, and tall leather chair, were smaller than the one in the chairman office, but still large pieces of furniture. Everest walked right up to the window and looked out at the view, seeing it go as far south as towards the mountains near Caritas in the Walham Valley.

"I would have preferred my office to look out to the south than the north," Everest remarked. "At least the view from the penthouse gets me there."

"I thought I heard you all in here," Roness remarked, opening the door behind them.

Everest turned around and saw Mr. Roness enter the room. He was an older man than Lucius, dressed in a grey pinstripe suit with a blue tie. He had fair skin and blue eyes. He was balding at the top of his head with short flat grey hair, buzzcut at the sides, and he had flabby ears. He was around the same height as Everest and held a proud smile on his face as he walked on.

"Nice to see you again, Mr. Cabernet," Roness expressed in a Texan suburban accent, offering his hand to shake. "It's been how many years? Five or six?"

"Three years," Everest remarked, "and it's nice to see you again too."

"How has the tour been?" Roness questioned, looking around. "Educational? This place sure doesn't change much, I'll tell you what. Not much time, or concern for interior decorating, around here. I've seen places that have taken concern in their aesthetics, but in my opinion it's nothing short of a waste of time and money."

"I could agree to that."

"Well, isn't this nice then," Roness said. "Have you been able to see much since you got in? How was your flight?"

"Not much," Everest responded. "I just arrived, and the flight was short but comfortable."

"Good," Roness remarked, stopping to sit down atop of the desk. "Well, I'm one to jump right into business... I suspect you wouldn't want to stay in Harlech for too long."

"I don't mind. I'm here for important business, and I want to take all the time that I can to sort this out," Everest expressed. "I've set aside Cabernet Industries for enough time as I have."

"How long do you intend to be in Harlech for, Mr. Cabernet? You intend to do a lot of sightseeing while you're here on vacation?"

"I'm not here on vacation, Mr. Roness. I'm here to work."

"Right," Roness simply replied, brushing off that remark, "well how about you get settled in. If you'll be in Harlech for a while, let's set up a meeting time for later. I'm sure you have many questions, and much to discuss with us."

"Right now I would like to know what progress has been made into the investigation for the incident in Tanzania."

"It's a work in-progress. You can't rush these things, you know. We'd rather our boys get all the information they can and then get back to us rather than get back to us now with only a bit of information."

"I see…"

"We won't keep you waiting too long though," Roness expressed. "I know you are here for one issue, and that one issue being that particular incident, but like I said over the phone, we've got a handle into it, so don't you worry, Mr. Cabernet. As far as any sort of controversy in the news is concerned, it's in the past and old news isn't likely to be brought up anymore. As far as any reparations are concerned, Cabernet Industries is in the region and doing its best to assure that those affected are attended to and consoled."

"Good."

"As far as you are here to work, Mr. Cabernet, we'll get this situation sorted out quickly and then you can be on your way home to that lovely home of yours out in the prairies."

"I appreciate it, but like I said, I want to ensure that everything is seen through appropriately, so that something like this tragic event doesn't happen again."

"An investigation like this one could take quite a while in its entire length, and while we do want to get operations up and going again…"

"I don't think it would be wise if we did continue to operate at Site C until we know for certain what the cause of the accident was."

"Yes, of course, but while that investigation is ongoing, Cabernet Industries does have logistics on the way to repair the infrastructure. We have to be efficient to stay on top, right?"

Everest didn't respond. He instead looked at Mr. Roness and then back out to the view.

"How long do you really intend to stay in Harlech, Mr. Cabernet?"

Everest turned his neck to look back at him.

"As long as it takes, Mr. Roness."

Act 2, Scene 2

After Everest had met with Roness and Lucius, he travelled up on his own to the ninety-eighth floor. The elevator exited out into a small corridor on approach to the main entrance doors of the private residence at the top of Cabernet Tower. At the end of the corridor were a set of large, wide smooth wooden doors with panel grooves. The walls in this corridor consisted of wooden panels similar to those in the chairman office. The floors though were not of carpet, but wooden floorboards. Everest made his approach to the door and retrieved the keys from his pocket, identifying the key for the penthouse and then inserting it through the lock. He opened the door and then stepped inside. The walls in the penthouse were different to those in the exterior corridor. They consisted of panels on the bottom half and green wallpaper with a golden cursive ribbon motif. The main entrance led into a small foyer with three double-set doors left, right and forward. Everest found his luggage directly on the right, which he left for a brief moment as he pushed through the doors ahead of him to enter into the parlor. The penthouse was furnished, although the furniture was covered with white clothes. In the midst of the parlor was a brass chandelier. The northside of the penthouse continued to the dining room on the left, which then continued onto the kitchen. Everest looked forward out to the view of New Harlech from the parlour, frowning as he did so before he turned around back to retrieve his luggage. He entered into a stairwell corridor where there was another double door on the right going to the library. He began to take his things upstairs along the U-shaped wooden staircase ahead of him that came up to the second floor. Everest opened another set of double doors that came into a long corridor. Both left and right, with gaps of space between each respective door, there were at least half a dozen total bedrooms. Everest made his way to the closest bedroom on the left and took his belongings inside. The bedroom he came into was large, set up like a hotel room with a king-sized bed on the left, end tables at either side, a dresser at the opposite-end with a television box, and an armchair in the corner near the window covered with translucent white curtains. On the right was a door that led into a windowless bathroom, while on the immediate left was a walk-in closet. After Everest had left his belongings and refreshed himself, he travelled back downstairs to look around the rest of the penthouse.

From the foyer corridor, Everest travelled directly across from the stairwell corridor to enter a cross-shaped corridor with three more double-set doors. The doors on the right led into the dining room. Everest walked into the doors on the left and came into a dining room. He stepped forward to the glass window at the very end, walking right up next to a grand piano in the corner, and looking outwards to the south of the city. From this view, Everest could see as far as the Walham Valley and the mountains beyond along the southern coast of the province. From this height, Everest could even see beyond the Hecate Strait and Queen Charlotte Island ahead. However, he paid particular attention to the valley region, the countryside, with nostalgia in his eyes. From the ballroom, Everest entered into a room at the side with a patio in the southwest corner of the building. This room gave a greater view of the horizon outwards to the Pacific Ocean.

Everest walked back to the cross-corridor and opened the final set of double doors to enter into a study, but this room only looked out towards the ocean. He looked at the bookcases on the left and right, the large desk in front of him (although smaller than the one in the chairman office), and then he left to come to the elevator to leave.

• •

"Perhaps there is no better place to start our tour than the main atrium," Lucius expressed, walking around the central courtyard of the atrium. "I'll spare the details of this building's history as I'm sure you are familiar with them."

"To be quite honest," Everest expressed, "I can hardly remember much of it."

Everest walked with Lucius, Conrad, Marie-Pierre, Brian, Xu, and John Bennett.

"Let me give you a refresher then," Lucius remarked. "I've been told that Cabernet Tower was built in 1921 at the time that similar structures were being built across North America, particularly Chicago and New York. Your great-grandfather at the time, Lycidas Cabernet, built this behemoth to be the central hub of Cabernet Industries, which it still is to this date. Beneath Cabernet Industries too we have many sublevels, including the underground parking garage, as part of the firm foundation that the corporate towers is built on, and likewise those departments too have become so pivotal to Cabernet Industries operations. The main department that is kept downstairs is Research & Development, or R&D, where scientists and engineers create state-of-the-art technology for test, preview, and development. Now, Cabernet Tower remains the central hub of the worldwide empire, but across the world there are many branches," he expressed, approaching a globe in the center of the courtyard. "Cabernet Industries does business in nearly forty-two different countries, including all G7 countries, where branch offices maintain the day-to-day operations and workforce management. In Canada, we have a similar case with regional branch offices here in Cabernet Tower overseeing the Pacific Region, out in Allabrese overseeing the Prairie Region, in Toronto overseeing the Eastern Region, and in Halifax for the Maritime Region. Although these branches maintain those such necessities, they also provide touchdown spaces for local operations for our many conglomerates in nearly every industry known to compete in today's economy: shipping, shipbuilding, metallurgy, chemicals, construction, mining, millwork, manufacturing, fisheries, oil extraction and refinery, and agriculture. We have also taken foothold in some up-and-coming industries, such as aerospace, electronics, and pharmaceuticals. By these sectors combined, Cabernet Industries has never been better or healthier, and the work that we've put forth as a board has assured a high stock price."

"Uh, excuse me," Everest interrupted, "but you'll have to explain – what is the benefit of a high stock price? Is it a measure of the company's health?"

"Absolutely," Lucius confirmed, "that's a simple way to put it. You see, a stock is a share in the ownership of the company. As the majority shareholder, you own the largest amount of stocks, greater than all other stockholders combined, and these stocks are to some extent the measure of the company's worth. It all comes down to supply and demand, where the supply of stock is limited, therefore the demand for a stock will be gauged by the price of the stock. A pricier stock means there is a greater demand because the stocks are worth more, whereas a cheaper stock means there is a lesser demand because the stocks are not as desirable. You, Mr. Cabernet, would have a vested interest that we keep that stock price high with our success because that means that your shares, a form of monetary asset, are worth more and therefore that means more money in your pocket."

Everest did not inquire further. Lucius moved on as he pressed a button to call an elevator.

"From Cabernet Tower, each conglomerate has its central office staff and key management figures who then liaise with our branches across the world to assist in their respective operations. For example, Mr. Adlington, who runs the Prairie branch, will often liaison with Timothy Gallagher from Cabernet Lumber, or Chad Boeser from Cabernet Extraction, and likewise members of either Gallagher or Boeser's team will venture to the Prairie branch, or sometimes work directly from Allabrese if space is available, to manage the field staff in that part of Canada."

The elevator door opened, and half of the tour party entered inside, including Lucius, Conrad, Everest, and John.

"Now, contrary to what you may believe, but Cabernet Industries does not hold the entire building on its own. Like the ground and second floor, Cabernet Industries rents these areas out to tenants (in their case, shops), and so too is the third floor up to the twenty-second floor also rented out, and also the forty-fifth up to the eighty-seventh. The income from their rent is a sizeable portion of what keeps the lights on around here, and they too also pay for the building management, which we contract out to SBPG. All these floors which belong to tenants are accessible to the public, but in order to get anywhere elsewhere, you'll need a keycard or to at least know the override code."

Lucius swiped his card and rode up to the twenty-third floor. They exited out into a similar corridor as that on the eighty-eighth floor, except it was a short corridor with a sign that pointed to the left for, 'Cabernet Industries'. Lucius led them to a double door that came into a large, carpeted foyer with armchairs in two groups, left and right, and a reception desk directly ahead of them.

"Welcome to Cabernet Industries," Lucius boasted. "On this floor, we have the bulk of our corporate head office staff, including our human resources department, our Marketing department, and our Business Initiatives department. For many people, a visit to Cabernet Tower to see Cabernet Industries will be in this room, waiting to speak with either one of our hiring advisors for a job interview, or to go to one of our many meeting rooms on this floor."

Lucius proceeded to guide Everest through a set of double doors on the left, which he had to gain access to by swiping a card. He then led the party around a corridor where there were sub corridors that came out to spaces with cubicles."

"It's quite a lot," Everest expressed as they came around.

"Yes, it is," John Bennett replied. He spoke in an English, south London accent. "At Paladin Group, we have a fraction of the number of staff for the entire nation. The company takes up a single floor in Lincoln."

"Paladin Group?"

"A security business," Bennett answered. "I was with them before I joined up with Cabernet Industries. You see, their owner holds a small share of your company, Mr. Cabernet. He appointed me to be on the board of directors on his behalf."

"I see... but insofar as your job here, Mr. Bennett, you are qualified, aren't you? Sorry if that sounded rude."

"Not at all, Mr. Cabernet, and I am quite qualified, otherwise I wouldn't be in both the role of director and executive vice president. I've been with Paladin Group since its very beginning fifteen years ago, and with my help it's become one of the largest security companies in all of the company. Paladin Group even holds the contract to provide building security here."

"It does? That's interesting..."

"Now, of course, Paladin Group is a smaller business with one goal: to provide security services, and we have expanded in both security system services as well as risk consultant and private investigation. Those recent expansions have resulted in additional office spaces on other floors in the same building, but the idea is the same."

Everest continued to walk as they came around to the main lobby, and then exited out to visit the specific conglomerate offices. In fairness to the extent of size, office floors from the forty-fifth floor to the eightieth and upwards were smaller than the base set of floors, so each conglomerate took up at least two floors for themselves. Each conglomerate had its own office from the twenty-fourth to the forty-fifth floor, totalling twenty-one different conglomerates. In order these were Cabernet Food, Cabernet Fisheries, Cabernet Lumber, Cabernet Extraction, Cabernet Construction, Cabernet Steel, Cabernet Chemicals, Cabernet Pharmaceuticals, Cabernet Electronics, Cabernet Aerospace, Cabernet Shipping, Cabernet Ships, Cabernet Oil, Cabernet Power, Cabernet Textiles, Cabernet Mills, Cabernet Manufacturing, Cabernet Water, Cabernet Retail, Cabernet Wines, and finally Cabernet Arms.

"Arms?" Everest questioned as they arrived at that floor. "As in, armaments?"

"Yes," Lucius confirmed, "Cabernet Industries has been in the weapons business since the start of the century, profiteering heavily from the Great War and Second World War in the supply of arms to the government. Didn't you know that?"

"No, I didn't. I didn't realize Cabernet Industries sold weapons… who are we selling weapons to?"

"The same governments that we've always sold weapons to, and their friends of course. Now, Cabernet Industries does not focus on firearms, but on artillery and ammunition more than anything; that's the business that your great-grandfather brought Cabernet Industries through."

"What little I do know about Cabernet Industries, is that we didn't start out as arms dealers, but as vineyard owners."

"Yes, and Cabernet Wines stands strong with vineyards across the world now."

Everest stood unimpressed as he looked at the plaque of names and offices on the forty-fifth floor where Cabernet Arms was located.

"How about we go into the sublevel now? I want to see what's below," Everest requested.

"Of course, Mr. Cabernet, whatever you wish."

Lucius led the group back into the elevator and they travelled down to the sublevel floor. The elevator doors opened and they walked into a concrete corridor. The air was cold in the tunnel.

On the right was a reinforced glass door with a sign above that said, 'Parking Level 1,' while on the left was a double set metal door with a card access reader. A sign on the door said, 'Staff Only.' Lucius led the group through the tunnel and down a short corridor that broke off to the right with a sign that said, 'Loading Bay.'

"Cabernet Industries has up to ten stories of subterranean levels, this floor is half executive staff parking on the north end and the loading bay to the south."

Lucius took the group around the corner to a set of double doors that looked out to a large space. A ramp that diverged from the causeway to the underground parking lot led into this area where there were three spots for trucks to unload, and also barges for garbage to be thrown out and collected. Lucius took the group backwards to the elevator where they went down another floor, which led to a similar lobby with metal double doors into a tunnel and a reinforced glass door to a section of parking.

"On the second floor, we have data bank storage and also the hub of our new-fledged Information & Technology department."

Lucius showed the group a series of rooms that had machines with wheels that turned large data cylinder reels. They came around to a laboratory where there were a few technicians at work, operating Bertrand-Schmidt computers. They then travelled downwards again to another sublevel where facilities maintenance, security, and plant services were situated. Lucius showed the group the generator room from within the control room.

"Cabernet Industries has its own steam-powered generator that provides electricity to the entire building. In the event of an emergency, there are also backup generators ready to power necessary lights and elevators."

From the third floor, the group travelled down past the fourth and fifth floor where on the latter half, Lucius explained there were storage rooms. At the sixth floor, the elevator doors opened and they stepped out not onto a concrete floor, but carpeted floor in a wide corridor that came up to a set of double doors. There were four chandeliers spaced out in this room, with armchairs and coffee tables on the left, and cabinets that hosted various prizes R&D had won over the years, as well as picture memorabilia. Around the double set doors at the end were windows that looked inwards to a large open space where there was a reception desk at the other end and Cabernet Industries logo behind.

"Here, we have Research & Development," Lucius introduced, guiding them to the right where they entered a corridor. "Everything that has ever been known to be created, patented, and created in the Cabernet name has come through these halls."

Everest looked as he saw a similar room with cubicles on the other side of the corridor. At the end, they turned right and passed a large conference room on the right, and individual offices on the left. Around that corner, the east side mirrored the west side, and so they travelled deeper underground to the rest of the levels that mirrored the layout of the upper floors, but rather than offices within, these contained laboratories. Everest looked and saw scientists at work, on computers, and in discussion with each other.

"And that's Research & Development for you, Mr. Cabernet," Lucius declared as they reached the end of the corridor.

"I'm a bit confused," Everest expressed, "but what sort of innovations does this department do exactly? So far I've seen that they consist of the most space out of all the other departments, but I have yet see any example of their innovation."

"Well, there are lots of examples; any invention that Cabernet Industries has developed came from these labs."

"What invention though?"

"There are numerous ones," Lucius expressed, "irrigation systems that we use in Cabernet Food, the vessels that we build in Cabernet Shipbuilding."

"And I suppose the entirety of this department is dedicated towards providing that innovation outwards to the rest of the company. How come though it does not simply rest upon each individual department?"

"If I would have to hazard a guess, I would say for sake of efficiency," Lucius replied.

"You underestimate what R&D does, Mr. Cabernet," Brian Paterson interrupted. "This lab built state-of-the-art artillery and cannon modifications for weapons that were sent to the Allies in the Second World War, and many other wars after that including the Korean and Vietnam War."

"I can also say," Marie-Pierre remarked, "that innovations in rocket technology has been of immense value; these have included self-propelled and guided missiles that are the future of warfare, and many breakthroughs in rocket munitions and other explosives."

Everest looked at these men with a bit of a glare and then looked back at Lucius.

"Well, at any rate, that concludes our tour for this afternoon," Lucius remarked. "Do you have anymore questions, Mr. Cabernet?"

"No," Everest denied. "I don't."

• •

Everest retired to the chairman office where he began to rummage through the boxes which had stacks of paper within. He pulled out documents that were dated 1984 and 1985, reviewing them with care. He pulled out a chair and thoroughly read the reports. These papers contained data reports, or key performance indicators, which were highlighted data pieces from various sectors and branches within Cabernet Industries that showed the success of that sector or branch.

After a moment of reviewing these reports, Everest stood up and left the office. He walked down the corridor all the way to the end where he pressed up his ear to the door to hear that it was silent and then knocked heavy knocks on the door.

"Come in," Roness remarked from the other side, so Everest entered. "Ah, Mr. Cabernet. How can I help you?" Mr. Roness looked up from his desk and put a cigarette out in its ash tray. He wore reading glasses and put his hands together. "How was your tour today?"

"The tour was very informative," Everest answered. "I have a question, Mr. Roness."

"I may have answers."

"A request actually," Everest said. "I would like to have these KPI reports pulled for my review for the current fiscal year, March to present, and the last year, April 1988 to last March."

"For Tanzania? We don't really have a specific report for that part of Africa, although our branch office is in their capital. The KPI reports consider all of Africa: Tanzania, Cameroon, Namibia…"

"I don't want just the report for Africa; I want all reports and a comprehensive report on corporate operations, branches, and our conglomerates. I would like to know every detail of what this company is up to across the world."

Roness looked at Everest suspiciously. He then gave a chuckle, stood up, and then came around to put a hand on Everest's shoulder. "Mr. Cabernet, consider it done. I'll have my administrative coordinator Kathleen have those to you as soon as possible," he said, beginning to guide him out of the office. "Is there anything else you need?"

"Not at this time."

"Do you play golf, Mr. Cabernet? A lot of us fellas here are big golf players. Every Saturday, if weather permits, we're at the range."

"No, I've never played."

"Well, if you're going to be around here, Mr. Cabernet, then you ought to learn how. How about you join us? I don't imagine you'll have much to do over the weekend…"

"I was looking forward to meeting with my daughter, but she's gone out of the country on a trip."

"Then it's settled then," Roness expressed. "You'll be with us. We play at the Foxwood Country Club in New Harlech. A man of your stature should have no problems being received in; we'll sort that out later. We'll also get you a proper set of golf clubs."

"Thank you."

The pair made it to the door where Roness stopped and put two hands on each of Everest's shoulders.

"Now if there is anything else you need, Mr. Cabernet, you let me know and we will get it for you. If I'm unavailable, then please reach out to Kathleen. Her desk is first through this door. Why don't you get some rest now, Mr. Cabernet? I'll let Kathleen know what you need for tomorrow morning."

"Thank you, Mr. Roness."

"No, thank you, Mr. Cabernet." He patted Everest on the shoulders and then saw him. He put a hand in his pocket as Everest walked down the corridor. Halfway down the corridor, Everest turned around and saw that Roness had closed the door behind him.

Everest let out a deep breath and then returned to the chairman office where he picked up some notes he had drawn out on a legal pad, and then decided to leave to return to the penthouse and retire for the night.

Act 2, Scene 3

The following Saturday, Everest readied himself to head out to Foxwood Vale in New Harlech for a day of golf with Roness and other executives. He dressed himself in a light blue polo and beige trousers, and then came around to the foyer of the penthouse where a small gift box was kept on a square table in the corner. He picked it up, opened the top of the gift box, and picked up a set of car keys. A note on the gift box read, 'Welcome to Harlech, Mr. Cabernet!' Everest took the car key and also a key set in his pocket. He attached the two and then left the penthouse, closing the door behind him, and then going to the elevator to call a car and ride down to parking level one. The executive parking lot, reserved for directors, vice presidents, and executive vice presidents and above, was nearly entirely empty on this Saturday morning, providing a view of the full size of the underground parking lot as being half a city block. Near the exit from the elevator lobby was a crimson Spyros EX, a luxurious SUV and make variant from the Asano Group company. Before Everest got into the car, he came around to the rear of the vehicle and opened the trunk to see that the car was loaded with a brand-new golf bag. He took in a deep breath, inhaling into his nostrils the new car smell that came with the vehicle, and then closing the rear door and coming around to the driver's seat. Everest readied himself by adjusting the mirrors and car seat, and then he started the car engine and shifted gears to set out.

Everest drove the Spyros EX up a ramp that came up to a T-intersection just before the exit. A sign pointed forward for the loading bay zone, and to the left for the exit. Everest drove out from the parking lot and came onto a left-hand lane on Earle Street (which itself was a one-way street). He drove forward with the bit of traffic that accompanied him, passing Maurelle Street and then over the highway that cut through the downtown area. The highway through downtown was entrenched through

Central Harlech. Everest passed Federal Street and then signalled to turn left onto West Stuart Street. He passed Durham Street, Seyward, and Moloney Street, and then driving even forward the road began to curve as it reached its end and merged with the highway. Everest drove onwards as the highway rose up from the earth and began to raise upwards to connect with Penultimate Bridge and take him to New Harlech.

The traffic through Penultimate Bridge and onto the highway was mild; the vehicles he passed varied: Ford, Asano, Armstrong, Moore, Hiawatha, and Honda. However, few compared with Everest's Spyros. He drove uphill once on the mainland, coming around a bend at the top and then driving eastbound at the near base of the northern mountains. The view outwards towards the islands was obscured by tall pine trees. Everest passed the exit for Mount Harlech, and then continued onwards towards the exit for Foxwood Vale. From the exit ramp, Everest stopped and then turned left onto Legionnaire Ways. He then drove upwards until he arrived at Foxwood Road, going right and eastbound again. The traffic through Foxwood Vale was mild too, although the sight of vehicles like the Spyros was more common in these parts: BMW, Doloros-Ganß, Thiessen, Bentley, and Rolls-Royce.

Foxwood Vale was a small mountainside village above Westford. For a few blocks on both directions from the intersection with Legionnaires Way, small shops lined the way, a majority of these shops of which were small businesses rather than retail chains. These buildings were also ground level with no apartments above. Around the street corner were some multi-level buildings, including a long-term care home across the street from a synagogue, and an apartment complex on the other side. Everest passed three blocks worth of shops and began to see residential homes. These homes were grand estates, large homes on proportionate land, but none as large as Cabernet Manor and its disproportionate acres of land. The average size of a home was half the size of Cabernet Manor. Foxwood Country Club was on the left by these suburb homes and it was a large facility, like a hotel, three-stories in height with a white exterior and plane glass windows.

Everest parked the Spyros EX in the parking lot, retrieved his golf bag from the back of the car, and then walked around to the main entrance where there was a sliding door into the main lobby of the private recreation centre. Everest approached the reception desk where a man in the black suit looked to him.

"Can I help you, sir?"

"Yes, I'm set to meet with some colleagues. They told me to check-in at reception for guidance. I've never been here before."

"Certainly, can I get your name?"

"Everest Cabernet."

"Ah, yes. Mr. Cabernet, our newest member. We received your membership request earlier yesterday evening... Welcome to Foxwood Country Club, Mr. Cabernet. I have a note here from Dwight Roness that you will join them at the golf range. Allow me to give you a brief tour. At some point we will need you to complete the rest of your paperwork."

"I don't recall ever putting in an application to join this place," Everest remarked.

The attendant ignored his remark and then instead continued, "Foxwood Country Club is one of the most prestigious country clubs in all of Greater Harlech on forty-seven acres of land. Our amenities include a weights gym, ice rink, tennis courts, golf range, an Olympic-sized swimming pool, sauna and spa, private locker rooms, bar and lounge, and a premium restaurant. What sort of recreational pass-times do you enjoy, Mr. Cabernet?"

"Me? Oh, I'm more of a lounge by the poolside type of person when it comes to free time," Everest remarked. "Back home where I'm from in the countryside of Allabrese, Alberta, I enjoy the horse races and great outdoors. I like to camp, fish, and especially hike."

"You'll be pleased to know then that hiking is an up-and-coming trend enjoyed in these parts, especially by folks in New Harlech. The mountains and coastal mile provide many trails that lead to very scenic views."

"Well, I look forward to visiting them then," Everest replied. "I'm not much of an indoor person, although I do enjoy card games, either Texas Hold 'Em or Blackjack."

"Hm, we don't have any of that here," the attendant responded, "but Jarsdel Island has many casinos that could be worth your attention. Do you need to visit the change rooms before I take you to your friends, Mr. Cabernet?"

"No, I'm dressed as I need to be."

"Very well, Mr. Roness and his company are awaiting in the lounge still."

The attendant took Everest upstairs and on their way to the upstairs lounge, they passed by a few classes that were being held, an aerobics class, the weightlifting gym, and then they came around to the restaurant where besides it there was a social lounge with a view outward towards the rest of the property. Behind the main building there was a wide balcony with lounge chairs, armchairs, and small tables for members to gather beside the deck. Beneath the balcony was another deck with a large pool too. Beyond that deck was another drop, where there were four tennis courts side-by-side each other, and beyond them were three badminton courts, and besides these two squash courts. Beside the courts there was also an additional parking lot that stretched out from around the side. Beyond this section was an outstretch of perfectly green pasture amongst the hills that surrounded tall pine trees. Everest could see people on the golf course, and golf carts too. The attendant brought Everest around to a table where Roness was sat, dressed in collared shirt with a sweater vest and cap.

"Ah, Mr. Cabernet," Roness greeted, hands at his hips until he extended one out to shake hands. "Glad you could join us. We were just on our way down. You know Lucius, Brian, Xu, and Marie-Pierre. Also with us are some old friends, Jeffrey Youlden with Blackmore Industries, David Brooks with Fletch Corporation, and Chris Cullen with Kiefer Industries."

"How'd you do, Mr. Cabernet?" Youlden greeted.

"Nice to have someone of the Cabernet prestige join us," Cullen greeted, shaking hands. "Always a pleasure to meet a new face."

Youlden was an older male, around the same age as Roness, with fair skin short grey hair, and glasses. He was of average stature. Brooks was likewise an older male with grey hair and glasses, but slimmer and shorter. Cullen was a larger stature around the waist, athletic build otherwise with a receding hairline and jovial round face. He spoke in a deeper voice than the others and appeared a lot friendlier.

From the deck above, Everest was guided down a set of stairs and then another set of stairs to reach the gravel trail that led towards the golf course.

"Dwight told us that you'd come and join us," Cullen remarked. "You ever play golf before?"

"Never," Everest replied, "I don't anticipate I'll be very good at it. I was never an athletic child."

"Oh, you don't have to be athletic to succeed at golf, just look at Brooks. He's easily the best player among us and you don't see an inch of athleticism in him."

"Very nice of you to say so," Brooks sarcastically responded.

"Do you know at least the basics of golf?" Cullen asked.

"To hit the ball in with the least amount of strokes? I know enough to say that, and to understand the different uses of these clubs."

"Well, there's not much to it than that. Otherwise, it just comes down to experience, knowing how much power to put into a stroke, and where to go to get that good score."

The group came around to the golf course where they broke off into groups of three. Roness took hold of Everest and kept him among his party, separating himself from Cullen and the others to have him join Lucius and him.

"What a marvelous day on the course," Roness remarked as he sat front with Lucius. "Are you excited Everest?"

"I'm eager to see what sort of excitement is supposed to be in store here. No offense, but I don't particularly think of golf as much of an exciting sport."

"Oh, no offense taken, Mr. Cabernet," Roness replied. "You see, golf isn't thrill-rush adventure, but a game of turn-based strategy and decision-making against your competitors. It is a much more elegant sport in which the fruits of labor provide reward when you hit the mark. You won't find the same satisfaction in any sport-ball or other physically intensive sport where the brawns and blood result in success."

Everest stepped out of the golf cart as they came around to the first of nine holes. He stayed back and watched as Roness came around to the tee and before him was close to four-hundred yards of curved land with sand ditches at the sides, and trees off-course. He looked ahead of him, but Everest could not see where he was supposed to be aiming for. The others came around to join Everest in watching Roness take the first shot off. Roness took the heaviest club known as a driver which had a very thick clubhead. He raised a thumb up as though to aim, and then positioned himself at the tee where his golf ball was placed. He then swung his arms up with the driver and then brought them down to hit the golf ball forward, shooting it off in an arch and sending it flying across the nearly four-hundred yards to the other side of the initial hole where Everest realized there was a small fluorescent triangle shaped flag where the hole was. The others clapped as Roness nearly put the golf ball in the hole, while Roness scorned at himself. Everest simply looked about with confusion, and then Lucius stepped forward for his turn.

The rest of the executives teed off in a similar manner, most of which were able to deliver the golf ball forward to a close enough range of the hole while none was able to get a hole-in-one. Afterwards, Everest stepped up to the tee for his turn, placing his golf ball down, and then taking his driver into his hand.

"Go ahead, Mr. Cabernet," Roness remarked, nodding.

Everest looked ahead at the distance in front of him, all four-hundred yards, or close to four-hundred meters worth. He took in a deep breath and positioned himself, brought the driver upwards in a swing and then brought it down, connecting with the golf ball and sending it forth. The ball shot forwards into the course in an arched motion, going to the other side where the hole was and landing straight into a sand ditch next to the hole.

"Oh, bad luck, Mr. Cabernet," Roness expressed. "Straight into a bunker. Let's go then."

Everest joined the others as they came around to the golf carts and rather than walk the four-hundred meters, they each drove to come to their golf balls. Everest came to his golf ball and looked into the pit of sand.

"Ah, there it is," Everest expressed, stepping forward into the pit and then reaching over for it. "I'll just move it."

"Ah, not so fast," Roness warned. "We're playing by official rules, and official rules state that bunkers are a hazard zone. You'll have to play it as it lies, or take a penalty drop."

Everest looked up to where he stood and then down to where his ball was. As the others took their turns, Everest came around to his to take his ball out from the sand pit but as he swung with the driver again, he caught a heap of sand to create a cloud and did little more than move the ball over a few inches for it to roll back into place where it was. The others took their turn, and then Everest again, this time changing his golf club from the driver to a putter, carefully attempted to hit the ball out from the pit. This time he caught some air, but the ball hit the side of the bunker and then fell back over. Again, the others took their turn, and this time Everest took his second-smallest club, the wedge, and with a bit of patience at the third stroke while everyone else had finished with par, birdies, or at most a bogey, Everest was still attempting to get his out from the ditch. Everest looked up as the ball rolled forward and then slid back into place in the ditch at the eighth stroke from the pit, causing him to growl as he grit his teeth.

"Alright, Mr. Cabernet, that's as many as you'll be able to play on this hole," Lucius expressed. "We're moving on to the next. Just leave your ball there and let's get going."

Everest didn't respond as the others began to move out, and rather than leave the ball behind, he continued to swear under his breath as he tried to get the ball out. At last, he sighed and simply hit the wedge into the sand. He didn't say anything to the others as he rejoined them, and then they carried on.

"So, what brings you to Harlech, Mr. Cabernet?" Youlden asked. "A courtesy visit to come out to these parts?"

"Yes, something like that," Everest expressed. He had calmed down since the first hole. "I've been chairman of Cabernet Industries for more than fifteen years and haven't shown much interest into the company, but I thought that should change."

"Would we be expecting to see you more often then?"

"Perhaps," Everest expressed, "I don't think so though. I have some work to finish here in Harlech with Mr. Roness and Mr. Clifford, but then I think I'll return home. I'm trying to show a bit more interest for the company's activities and what it's been up to, and if I can, lend a helping hand."

"Cabernet Industries is an illustrious corporation with a global impact," Youlden replied. "Never has the corporation had a better time, no less since that scandal that held it up for deletion."

Everest didn't respond as Youlden walked off. He caught up to him and asked, "What sort of global impact does Cabernet

Industries make, in you opinion? I know what the corporation does, what it produces, and what it provides to the world economy, but I want to know what specific difference the company makes in the lives of people."

"Easily," Youlden expressed, "it helps drive the global economy, especially nowadays when the promise of this Cold War seems to be at its end. Communism has shown itself to be a dead subject, a worthless ideology of little return, while what we know as 'capitalism' will be triumphant and take the next century, the next millennium, by storm as the age of capitalism. Blackmore Industries and Cabernet Industries have a strong partnership through Mr. Roness and Mr. Clifford, and never has the time been better to be side-by-side than now when we are set to win the Cold War and pounce upon the receding economies of the communist nations."

"But what difference does that make to individual lives, Mr. Youlden?"

Youlden shrugged and replied, "To be honest, I couldn't tell you. All I know is that it makes your company successful, and it makes Blackmore Industries successful, which secures our jobs, our investments, and overall, our affluence and riches. You are a rich man, Mr. Cabernet, but in the next decade you will be an even richer man than you could ever imagine." He gave off a laugh and then passed Everest who looked plainly.

"Don't listen to that madman," Brookes responded. "He and I used to work with each other, and that's all he cared about: money."

"What do you care about?" Everest questioned.

"I care about the game that is played, Mr. Cabernet," Brookes expressed. "Like the swing of a golf ball, even business has its need for precision. Golf is a game of perseverance and resilience; it's about attention to detail, not paying attention to the moves of your opponents, but what you can do to succeed.

Whether you win or lose, others may lose more than you while others may win more than you; that's business, Mr. Cabernet."

"So, what do you desire then in your work efforts?"

"To make sure that I'm winning, of course, and not losing. You want to cut your losses and be at the top to win at golf. You can't afford to take losses."

Brookes shot off his ball and nearly got it straight into the hole in the next course. Cullen moved up and Everest watched him while the others prepared to move out.

"I'll teach you the secret, Mr. Cabernet," Cullen expressed. "The secret to golf is that there is no secret. You'll want to be patient, but not obsessive like the others. For me, golf is about the reflection, being outdoors, and putting your mind at ease of the problems at the office. Aside from today, I like to come to the range after the busiest days of work to just let off some steam."

"You take your work seriously, I imagine," Everest expressed. "What motivates you in your job?"

"I'll be honest with you, its business, Mr. Cabernet. Ashley Kiefer and I are good friends, and in my role as president, I'm there to make sure his company succeeds in its business ventures."

"Is that what you wanted to do when you grew up? To help serve another man in his business ventures and capital gains?"

"I'm a people person, Mr. Cabernet. I like to talk to people if you couldn't tell, and to meet people, and what drew me into business was the negotiations, the arrangements; I scratch your back if you scratch mine, the win-win scenarios. We do this, if you do that, and we both gain from that arrangement. Those sorts of bargains and barters. The business that we do puts jobs in the market when we succeed in the expansion and success of the company, and after the recession in the last decade has always been appreciative component of our work, no less in an ever-expanding city where jobs are needed so that people can have an income so that they can live their lives. To sustain a growing population like our own we need jobs of all kinds, and I've been happy to be a part of that component, and so should you with Cabernet Industries. I suppose you could say I'm a people-first kind of guy, and I like to look out for my people most of all. That's what it's all about for me, to be that kind of person in society, and play that role."

"I suppose then for you, when you aren't able to make those arrangements, or when there is any sort of loss in the corporate fortune, you suffer then too?"

"I certainly feel the hardships whenever there's a lay-off," Cullen answered.

"And what if the actions of our companies have a dramatic effect on the lives of others? A disastrous effect, for example – like in an explosion at a factory that puts not only our people, but locals at risk."

"Such situations are obviously a hardship for anyone, but I would feel them too. The problem though is that it's easy to go about assigning blame when something like that happens without realizing that tragedies are a part of human nature, and whether it is the explosion at the private-company's mill, or the explosion at the government-owned mill, it's going to happen and more times than others, it's a part of life, something that just happens, than it was an avoidable accident."

"What if it was avoidable?"

"You learn from your mistakes, hold those responsible accountable, and try to move on. You can spend all the time you want lamenting the losses, and as normal humans we should certainly grieve the dead as far as our hearts are concerned, but only as much before it turns into a political charade. I say that because whether it was a tragedy at the hands of our company, or the hands of another company, or no company, a loss is a loss and deserves to be mourned, but not to hang our heads upon, if you catch my pitch."

"I'm right there with you…" Everest responded.

Everest continued to play the rest of the holes with the others, moving up for his next turn, and hitting a swing. He did a bit better for a rookie but continued to perform worse than the others who played golf for however many years. The entire effort with nine players took the entire morning and went into the noon, at which point the group retired to have lunch at the restaurant. Everest continued to ponder on his own while others discussed business, economics, and politics.

"Mr. Cabernet," Marie-Pierre expressed, putting a hand on his shoulder and sitting down with him. "You are a man of few words… why don't you speak?"

"Not much to express, I'm afraid," Everest responded. "How are you, Mr. Leroy?"

"Please, call me Pierre."

"Where do you come from, Pierre," Everest asked. "I seem to recall some sort of corporation from metropolitan France."

"Yes, I was with La Bastion for thirty years," Leroy said. "Before, I was in French government as a representative. I was too young to fight in the war, around fourteen when it ended."

"I was just born," Everest responded. "My mother gave birth to me late February, just before the war ended. My father fought in the war, and he was young when he did. He joined when he was eighteen and came out of it twenty-three years old. My aunt used to tell me that the war changed him, he went in a youngster and came out a man. No less did he have to succeed as a business leader when he returned since his father, my grandfather died a year before I was born." He took in a deep breath and then replied, "My father of course died young too, and I know he's not a popular man who's practically been denounced by the rest of the world, but I do believe all that and more came from the war that changed him, and never particularly did him any good."

"The world has not completely renounced your father, Mr. Cabernet," Leroy expressed. "Even with his change of character in later years, for his service, as a Frenchman, I and those alike honor him for his part in our country's liberation."

Everest nodded but then replied, "I just… wish he could have had a fuller life than he did."

"Regardless, he would have been proud of what you've done for Cabernet Industries, and in you."

"I… I don't think he would have. His desires in me were never the same desires I had for myself."

Act 2, Scene 4

Everest spent his first month in Harlech in much solitude. He very seldom came downstairs to the chairman office and would spend his days in the room next to the ballroom in the penthouse. Everest transformed this room into his personal study, although smaller than the actual study, the view outwards to the south and the patio where Everest would often lounge in the evenings gave him a place to smoke a cigar and drink some scotch as he thought to himself and wrote in a notebook. He had dozens of folder boxes brought up to the penthouse and slowly went through each of them, analyzing them one by one with detail and patience. He received no visitors otherwise, and came downstairs only to attend meetings with the other executives, especially those that concerned the developments in Tanzania, but he would sit in them and not comment at all. Only seldom would he ask a question, often for clarification on a particular subject or for something to be explained to him. Afterwards, Everest would speak with some of the directors before he returned upstairs to continue what he called work. Otherwise, Everest would also leave the penthouse to wander the halls of Cabernet Industries offices, speaking to everyday blue-collar office workers to gain their perspective on the company, the work they do, and what they appreciate or have criticize about the company. For the most part, the opinion of others was positive and none dared to provide the chairman a negative review of the corporation until Everest presented himself to someone who did not recognize him nor knew who he was.

"I've been with Cabernet Industries for fifteen years," the worker expressed from the staff lounge. "I've never received any sort of recognition for any of my hard work. As far as I'm concerned, I come in and do what's expected from me, and then I go home. I don't give this company even an extra second of my time, and when I'm home I don't think about the company."

Everest looked attentively at this worker as he expressed his frustrations. The worker was a middle-aged male with glasses and dressed in a collared shirt and dress pants. He held a cup of coffee in his hand as he vented to Everest and some other co-workers.

"I don't get paid for overtime, nor would I stay overtime even if I was asked. I do what work that I can, and if I can't get all of it done, then I leave it to the next day and don't think another minute about it. I'm paid for a set amount of time, and nothing more. The only time I ever hear from my supervisor is not to tell me that I'm doing a good job, but it's a criticism or request to do something else. I know some hard workers who have only ever heard from their boss for worse. This company has no praise for me, so why should I have praise for the company? All I have is gratitude that at least I have my earnings, although little they may be."

"Amen to that," another worker responded.

Everest stayed silent for a moment and then expressed, "What would you want different then?"

"I don't want anything different," the frustrated worker replied. "There's nothing more this company could do for me now than to give me a raise, and maybe some more vacation time. To think that we get two weeks; three weeks if you've been here for more than five years and then an extra week for every five years after that."

Everest didn't respond, although he did look at the worker with some doubt in their desire. He finished drinking his coffee and then left the staff lounge to return to the corridors. He walked back to the elevator and entered alone to return to the penthouse.

The elevator doors opened, and Everest saw the administrative support coordinator approaching him, Kathleen Summers. She was a young female in her mid twenties with lengthy blonde hair and fair skin.

"Oh, Mr. Cabernet," Kathleen greeted. "Just who I wanted to see. I tried to phone you, but there was no answer. I assumed you were either on the patio again, or went out for a walk."

"You were not far with your guesses," Everest replied. "How can I help you?"

"An update on the Tanzania situation is available. Mr. Roness wanted me to deliver it to you right away. He said you may want to read up before your meeting later this afternoon."

Everest took the folder into his hand. A sticky note on top said, 'Everest'.

"Thank you, Ms. Summers."

"You can call me, Kay," Kathleen replied. "Remember that," she said with a smile. She then left. Everest watched her leave and then returned to look at the report. He flipped through the first pages, and then stepped forward to enter into the penthouse so he could read the rest.

Everest sat down at the desk in his study which looked over to the patio. He began to go through the report slowly, flipping through the pages. He then reached the final page where he stopped, read it, and then paused for a moment. He looked to the side, took in a deep breath, and then took off his reading glasses to place them on the desk and stand up to walk over to the window that looked outwards. He then returned to his desk, picked up his notebook and tore some pages inside. Everest threw these pages into a bin at the side of the desk and then sat down to quickly jot down some notes. He wrote for close to two hours before three o'clock in the afternoon at which point he left to go downstairs. Everest sat down at the head of the executive board room table, dressed in a suit, and looked to his peers.

"Good afternoon, everyone, and happy Friday," Roness greeted as he entered five minutes past. He held a folder in his side and came around to sit at the opposite head of the table. Ms. Summer sat around the corner from Roness with a typewriter, ready to take the minutes. "I hope I didn't miss anything."

"We haven't started yet," Lucius said, sitting across from Ms. Summer.

"Good, as I'm sure everyone in this room is aware, our investigators in Tanzania have provided us with their final report on the incident that occurred in April. At this time, measures have been made that have put the mine back into operation, and we still have a long way to go before regular operations can resume, but I thought it was worth taking the time to approve the final report so that we could move forward with those steps. Sorry, Mr. Cabernet, I know that you wanted to use this meeting time to speak."

"No apology needed," Everest spoke from the other side of the table, sitting comfortably in the chair, "I would have prioritized this report too."

"In case anybody in this room has not yet read the full report, the final conclusion that was made has stated that geological and meteorological conditions was the cause of the collapse," Roness expressed. At the request of Mr. Cabernet, geologists were sent to the site to inspect the damages, and they determined there to have been damages to the sediment around the bank and reservoir that played into a buildup of pressure that caused the upper dam to collapse, followed by an overflow that caused the lower dam to collapse too. Additionally, weather reports and confirmation from a meteorologist we also contracted confirms there has been an above-normal level of rainfall in the region which has had devastating effects in the neighboring areas that have caused floods. I believe that this conclusion is both logical and satisfactory to the aims of this board of directors to put this business to rest."

A few of the others agreed, but Everest did not.

"Mr. Cabernet?" Roness questioned. "Any comment?"

"Yes, I wanted to point out an eyewitness account that was included in the report. The eyewitness account from an engineer who worked on site and survived the wreckage expressed personally that there were limitations in place to the extent of maintenance that could be performed on the dam. He also further noted there had been numerous requests for logistics to aid in the upkeep, particularly in pipes. This engineer, among a team of nearly a dozen, most of whom survived, believes that because the dam was poorly maintained and safety measures limited, that this caused the dam to collapse."

"And yet the conclusion makes no mention to there being a structure failure, Mr. Cabernet. The cause of the dam collapse was because of above-average rainfall and a lack of consideration in the sediment. The scientists you had us contract have signed-off on that conclusion. I can understand that this particular worker would have a guilty conscience for what transpired, but independent engineers that we also contracted have validated that the standards and architectural plans for the dams were in now way flawed in their creation, and for what they were expected to handle were enough."

"Enough is not good enough," Everest argued. "Although not included in this report, those same engineers also warned that any lack of appropriate drainage from the reservoir to be dangerous as they could lead to a buildup of pressure that could damage the dam structure. I move to contract engineers to inspect the wreckage and report back before any final report is approved for submission."

"Mr. Cabernet..." Roness contested.

"Additionally, I want a deeper investigation into what sort of safety measures were incorporated within the African branch, what material was used, structural plans, and how that would have compared if this dam was built in the first-world."

"Mr. Cabernet..." Roness expressed with less patience.

"Lastly, I would like to have the maintenance records pulled and for the rest of the maintenance crew who have survived to provide testimony on the state of the dams prior to the incident."

"Mr. Cabernet," Roness called out.

"Yes, Mr. Roness?"

Roness didn't immediately say anything as the two looked at each other. He took in a deep breath, looked at the other members, and then replied, "We'll search for the best scientists we can find to send to Tanzania to do as you ask."

"No need," Everest responded. "I've been doing some research, and I already know which ones should be sent. I will have Ms. Summers make the travel arrangements – they will be reporting to me with their findings." Roness didn't respond. Everest looked to the others and asked, "Are there any objections?"

No response came. Roness stayed quiet for a while longer and replied, "Why would there be, Mr. Cabernet? This board of directors endorses your recommendations, and we look forward to seeing them through. Are there any other additions to this meeting related to the incident that occurred in Tanzania?"

No response came through.

"Very well," Roness replied, sitting back, "we can carry on with the actual topic of this meeting. Mr. Cabernet... what did you wish to discuss."

"Thank you," Everest responded, leaning forward and looking into his notebook. "I wanted to gather everyone here to express some key observations that I've made in the course of the month that I've been here in the corporate offices. I know that my original aims had been to rectify and see through this investigation with the situation in Tanzania, but as I've waited for those conclusions to be made, I've preoccupied myself in looking over financial and operation reports for all our branches and conglomerates to gauge the overall health of the company. Additionally, I've taken some time to better familiarized myself with the company, the people who work for us, who represent Cabernet Industries, and of course our leaders. To not waste your time any further, I've drafted fourteen points for what I wish to see changed within Cabernet Industries."

Everest proceed to pass around carbon copies of points that had been typed up on a computer and printed out.

"These points are made out of an overarching vision I have for the company that focuses on the people that we intend to reach out to in our business ventures, and the people who support us with their daily contributions to the corporation. First point, I wish to see Cabernet Industries hire the right sort of people. Too often during my tours did I notice that there just wasn't the right person in the right job. It did not seem that our hiring standards were kept up to speed, and so I'm going to ask for an overhaul in our human resources hiring department to see that through. Secondly, we must train our people more than adequately. Most new hires are not adequately trained in their job which results in misunderstanding to what is expected from them, so we need to ensure that they are trained thoroughly. Thirdly, we must ensure that our new hires are in the right place, and that our current hires are in the right place in the company. A lot of wasted talent lies at our feet, and I hope to see these people move to where they are most comfortable to thrive. Fourth, we must support our people in their goals and aspirations. This point comes down to benefits, financial compensations, and also moral support from their leaders. A lot of workers feel as though they are in a dead-end job, and that attitude must change for them to believe that there is no stop in their achievements. Fifth, we must recognize our workers in their work, especially when they work well. Here I am going to ask for Mr. Holmes to target a vision I have for our human resources department that focuses on people and culture. We must create a positive work environment that has no tolerance for nepotism and supports people who have been with the company for a long time with recognizing their work. I'd like to discuss this point in deeper detail with Mr. Holmes at a later date. Sixth, we must ensure that we never give up on our people and always be there to coach them through a tough time. Disciplinary action and reprimanding should be a word of the past – the tolerance for failure should be expanded upon, and patience made with our workers to see them succeed. Everybody makes mistakes. Seventh, I would like to see the right people promoted into positions based on knowledge and experience rather than connections. A standardized approach to promotions should be made with each role that allows for competition and for us to gauge a pool of candidates rather than to know someone we would like to see in such role.

"For the corporation as a whole, here are the changes I would like to see: eighth, the aims of the corporation must be made in the interest of both the employer and employees, and neither made to compromise one or the other. Ninth, the expansion and involvement of the corporation on foreign soil must be done respectfully to the local communities, and any developments to the interest of those local communities. Tenth, Cabernet Industries will form an occupational health & safety department distinct from the present desk within human resources that mandates and overhauls a universal safety approach at every branch and for all conglomerates. Eleventh, Cabernet Industries will adopt a public presentation and advertisement campaign that seeks to label and present itself as a people-first corporation. Twelfth, Cabernet Industries will in no way, shape, or form sell or do business with countries that are considered hostile to Canada or the North Atlantic Treaty Organization members, and their allies. Thirteen, Cabernet Industries will in no way, shape, or form, conduct the business practice known as outsourcing that would put jobs at branches at risk. Fourteenth, and last, on the subject of annual reports and reviews, I did notice some inconsistent approaches in reporting structure, what reports were filed and for what, and so: Cabernet Industries will reform and adopt an organized and consistent reporting structure, and an organized and consistent incident notification structure to ensure that there are no gaps in communication or misunderstanding between departments, branches, and conglomerates.

"These fourteen points are not recommendations, but actions I would like to see done throughout Cabernet Industries moving forward to correct some of the gaps that I've seen in the conduct of business around here. Any questions?"

The board of directors was silent. Roness looked at the sheet of paper in front of him and placed it down. He took off his glasses and looked back at Everest.

"Mr. Cabernet," Roness spoke in a strict tone, "you can very well be assured that we will honor and respect these important considerations you have made and presented for us."

Everest was taken back at his response. Roness stood up and produced a smile on his face. He then put a hand in his pocket and began to walk around the table.

"I can't speak for the rest of the board, but I for one endorse these action items wholeheartedly. Mr. Cabernet, it's been a pleasure to have you in our offices this past month, to sit in on meetings, and learn the works of the corporation that came from your family name… it's even more of a pleasure to have a fresh take on the interest of the companies which we have not been able to produce within the thoughts and minds of this select group of individuals. I for one take these points like a breath of fresh air as to what was missing from our wonderful corporation, and you have my guarantee that they will actioned off as soon as possible. I look forward to seeing them through," Roness expressed, coming around to Everest. He offered his hand. "Mr. Cabernet, it's been an honor to have you become involved in the affairs of Cabernet Industries, and I look forward to what else we can do to work together to see this company flourish even more."

Everest look at Roness' hand, and with a brief moment of hesitation, he then stood up and took his hand. "Thank you very much, Mr. Roness. I'm glad to finally be a part of the board."

Act 3, Prologue

Everest sat atop of a windowsill as he looked out to the street below. He wore a pair of dark blue socks, dark blue shorts, and a white collared shirt. He also wore a dark blue blazer with a striped light and dark blue tie. At his breast pocket was a sown white crest with the words, 'Harrow Preparatory School.' Everest appeared a little older than when he was in India, being little more than fourteen-years old. His blonde hair was cut short at the sides and had lost a bit of its color to appear nearly light brown. He held a sunken look on his face too as he gazed out of his dormitory window on the third floor and down the street beside it. His skin was pale, his eye sockets dark, and eyes bloodshot. His dormitory bedroom was small and consisted of a bunkbed with two desks and dressers. There was also a closet near the exit. The room was empty, mattresses stripped bare, drawers open and vacant, and a suitcase and backpack ready in front of the dormitory door. Beneath the window there were cars and taxis parked, and students in raincoats loading their suitcases into these cars, some with the assistance of other adults who held umbrellas in one hand. A heavy downpour came down onto the students, parents, and faculty members, and the skies were a deep grey so that it was almost nighttime despite it being noon. Slowly, one by one, students vacated the dormitories and cars came and passed. Within a few hours, one car came every twenty minutes for another student as the last were set free for the summer. Still, Everest sat at the windowsill with his right leg stretched out and left knee bent.

Across the street from dormitories was another building, in a similar Neo Gothic architectural design with tall windows. Everest could hear a choir singing from within the walls of this tall annex, although he could not see through the windows. The singing was cut off with the sound of classical music, met with cheers and applause. Everest stayed where he was, looking towards the building across the street. The annex was joined with a two-story building that wrapped around the street corner at the end. Our Lady of Roses took up the entire opposite block across from the all-male boarding school, both of which were located at the far corner of the university. A signpost at the end of the street corner on the right named the street between them Irving Street and the perpendicular one Coyle Street. To the left was another four-point intersection, and at the end of it residential homes at either side up to a cul-de-sac at the end. The perpendicular street one that side was named Suchet Street.

Everest continued to stay seated atop of the windowsill as he overheard the celebrations take fold from the other side of the street. Within another hour, no cars came to pass, and it was quiet. The commencement ceremony at the all-girls school came to a close, and still no car came to pick up Everest from the dormitory. He let out a long sigh and brought his feet into the room so that he could stand up. However, before Everest stood, he began to hear some commotion on the streets and turned his neck outwards to see what was going on. He stood up and turned around, leaning his body into the window to look down the street on the right. He could hear some incoherent arguing combined with laughter. The fire exit doors from the annex ahead were opened by two older females, and two other females were attempting to push out another girl who resisted their attempts to banish her.

"Hey!" Everest shouted out. "Stop that!"

The girls took notice, and so with a final push, they cast this girl out into the rain and then quickly closed the door behind them. The girl fell over onto the sidewalk on her side, quickly pushed herself off the ground, and then rushed towards the fire exit doors but they were one-way metal doors that were now closed shut with no handle to even attempt to force open. In the least, the girl stood underneath a nook in the building so she was out of the rain. She banged hard against the metal door, crying out for someone to let her in. The girls that had bullied her out had long left, but Everest wasted not a single moment longer to rush to his shoes, go downstairs, and exit out to cross the street.

Everest came around to the fire exit nook where the girl held her arms crossed. Her uniform was different than Everest's. She wore stockings rather than socks, and black ballerina flat shoes instead of dress shoes. She wore a kilt skirt that came down beneath the knees rather than shorts, and a blouse rather than a collared shirt. Although Everest had seen the other girls wear burgundy sweaters, this girl wore neither a jacket nor a sweater. She only had her white blouse on her back with the letters sown in at the breast pocket, 'OLR.' Her blouse was also short-sleeved, and so her forearms bare. She huddled underneath the shelter and looked at Everest through her light blue eyes as he met her. This girl had short light blonde hair that came down to her shoulders. Her hair was neatly combed, smooth and clean, and here eyebrows fine. Her skin was fair like Everest's, and her nose tall but small. She was young, slim, the same age as Everest and as she was met with him, she gave off an embarrassed look on her face.

"Hey, are you okay?" Everest asked.

The girl did not answer. She instead looked down. Everest was taken back by her lack of response, but he looked her face, saw the stains on the side of her blouse and on her stockings from when she had fallen, and also the scrape at her elbow.

"Do you need any help? Anybody I should call?" Everest questioned.

The girl continued to not answer. He looked at her once more and then both sides of the street. Nobody was around except the two of them. Everest took in a deep breath and began to take his blazer jacket off. He then stepped forward into the shelter and offered it to the girl.

"Here, take this," Everest remarked. "You're practically naked out here. I can see you're shivering. Please, take it."

The girl looked over as the boy held the jacket in his hand for her. She did not grab it, although she did uncross her arms as though hesitant to take it. Everest though took the initiative in the moment and unbound his jacket with both hands, slipped her hand through one arm and then brough the coat around where she became more compliant to slip the other through. The jacket was too large for her, but as she took both flaps and brought the fabrics closer to the body, there was an intense relief that came upon her and a shift in her face from discomfort to gratitude.

"My name is Everest," the boy said. "Like the tallest mountain in the world."

The girl looked on at Everest now with timidity but also desire to speak that could not be kept back as she spoke in her German-accent, "My name is Wien... Vienna... like the city."

"The most beautiful city in the world," Everest corrected, causing her to blush. "My family has been there many times. It's really beautiful."

Vienna brought the fabrics of the blazer jacket even closer to her.

"Thank you for your coat," Vienna expressed, "it's very warm."

"Why did those girls throw you out into the rain like that for?"

"Oh, those girls? Don't you worry about them, they're just not very nice. It's no problem..."

"It seems like a problem," Everest replied. "Nobody should have to treat anyone like that – that's just not okay."

"It's nothing really."

"You may think it's nothing, but where I'm from, it's not a problem. I deal with this all the time at home."

"And where are you from? Vienna?"

"No, Salzburg," Vienna answered, "in Austria."

Everest didn't respond.

"Where are you from?" Vienna asked.

"I'm… well, I was born in Reading, in the United Kingdom. My father was born here though, in Harlech, but my mother was born in Britain. We live here, or we used to until we moved east to the prairies."

"You don't speak with an English accent," Vienna remarked.

"You speak with a German accent."

"It's Austrian; we in Austria don't consider ourselves to be German, at least not anymore."

"You mean since after the war," Everest remarked. "My father talks about the war a lot. He never fought in Austria, but he did fight in Germany. Did your dad fight in the war too?"

"Yes."

"I bet he talks about the war a lot with you too."

"Not particularly," Vienna responded.

"Oh, how come?"

"My father died in the war, before it ended, which happened shortly before I was born."

"Oh… I'm sorry to hear that."

"It's no problem," Vienna remarked, "it was so long ago, and I don't remember it. I've grown up my entire life without my father, but his parents, my grandparents, have been good to me, my brothers and sisters, and my mother. They sent me here after all, so that if war ever comes to Europe again, at least I will be far and free."

"What about your siblings?"

"They're all older than me. They live their own lives," Vienna responded. "I'm the youngest of eight."

"Wow, that's a lot of brothers and sisters," Everest expressed. "I have one sibling, a sister, and she's a nuisance as she is. I can't imagine what it must be like to have eight siblings."

"Oh, it's nothing," Vienna dismissed. "I can't imagine what it must be like to have such a small family."

"Yeah…" Everest responded, smiling as she smiled.

Vienna lowered her smile as she blushed, and Everest too lowered his smile. They each fell silent for a moment.

"Can I walk you back inside?" Everest offered. "I don't imagine you want to be here all day."

"Yes, I would very much like that," Vienna responded. "There's an entrance down the street, but this rain... it's summertime and yet it still pours."

"Yeah, and it's not that warm either," Everest expressed, "but that's Harlech for you. Never seems to stop raining around here, even in the summer."

"Yes," Vienna agreed, stepping forward.

"You won't want to be in the rain for too long. You ready for a little run?"

"I can't run in these shoes," Vienna objected.

"You'll have no choice unless you want to walk in the rain and get all wet."

Vienna brough the blazer up to cover her head. She then looked at Everest and said, "Now I'm ready."

Everest took the first step out into the rain, which followed with Vienna taking a timid step behind him. She lurched as she felt the rain come down on her.

"Come on, we can get through it faster if we go together," Everest encouraged, laughing as he became drenched.

Everest took her hand and began to guide her through. She let go of the right side of the blazer but continued to hold it up by the left. They both hurried down the sidewalk together, coming around to some steps that went up to another shelter at a side entrance.

"You see, that wasn't so bad," Everest expressed, laughing.

Vienna gave a warm smile at Everest as they stood in front of each other. Everest was close to half a foot taller than Vienna.

"Thank you," Vienna expressed. "You're a very kind boy, Everest. Thank you for giving me your jacket and for walking me to the door."

"It was nothing," Everest replied. "It was nice to meet you, Vienna."

The pair looked at each other as they stood a foot from each other. They became silent again until Vienna asked, "I suppose you want your jacket back…"

"Yeah…"

"Everest," a deeper voice spoke in an English accent.

Both looked to their left at the man that stood next to a black car that had just recently parked across the street in front of the dormitories.

"Dad," Everest replied, looking over to Derby who wore a raincoat overtop his suit.

"I'll see you sometime later, Everest," Vienna expressed in her German accent, leaving.

"Wait…" Everest said, but Vienna left without a trace. She entered the building and left him with his father.

Derby Cabernet appeared not much different than how he appeared in India. He wore a formal hat over his head that tied in with his three-piece steel bluish-grey suit. The coat he wore was dark grey and went down to just above his knees. He also carried a black umbrella that he used.

"What are you doing, Everest?" Derby spoke in a strict tone. "Look at you… you're amess, standing out in the bloody rain without even a cloak on."

"I'm sorry, dad," Everest replied, stepping down to the sidewalk as Derby came around to him. "I was… I was just…"

Derby gave Everest the umbrella and then looked across from him through the doors where Vienna disappeared to.

"Who was that girl, Everest?" Derby questioned. "The one you were speaking to?"

"Her? Oh, I don't know…"

"Don't lie to me, Everest," Derby expressed in a sterner tone. "Who was she?"

"She's just a student at the school," Everest replied. "I was just talking to her."

"Her accent... she sounded German..."

"She's Austrian."

"Same thing," Derby replied, looking across the all-girl school grounds with suspicion before he looked back at his son. "I don't want you to talk to that girl, Everest. You don't want to get involved with a German lass."

"Why's that?"

"Why? Because of the manner by which I speak, you alone should be in agreement to what I've said," Derby strictly spoke. "Do you not have trust in the words of your father?"

"No," Everest responded. "I mean, no I do not trust you. I'm sorry...."

Derby looked down at Everest with disdain. He huffed at him and then began to walk back across the other side of the street.

"Come along, now," Derby expressed. "It's time for us to leave. Your mother and sister are waiting for us at the penthouse. Go along and get your things. I'll be here waiting..."

"Yes, dad."

Derby came around to the sidewalk near the car while Everest was made to walk down the sidewalk with the umbrella to return into his dormitory. As Everest returned to his room, and was about to close the window, he looked over to the all-girls school and took in a deep breath. He then let it out and closed the window, picked up his belongings, and then returned downstairs. Derby came around to the trunk and helped him load his suitcase, and then the pair got into the front of the car together where Derby started the engine and drove off.

Everest gave one last look into the rear-view mirror as they drove away from the boarding school. He then took in another deep breath and sat back, with a content look on his face, no doubt as he thought of and remembered his encounter with Vienna at the time.

Act 3, Scene 1

"Welcome to Cabernet Tower, my dearie," Everest expressed, guiding Vienna by the hand through the sliding door at the main entrance of the tower and into the atrium.

"It's so different to how I remember," Vienna responded in her Austrian accent. "They've made some changes… look at all these shops. It's been how many years… ten? Fifteen?"

Vienna held her right hand at her luggage behind her, while Everest was linked with her left arm. Salmar appeared behind them with his own suitcase in one hand, and a leash that held Baron in the other. He looked around the main atrium with astonishment.

"It's larger than I thought it would be," Salmar expressed. "I've never been here before in my lifetime."

"If you think that the sight from the ground level is something to behold, then wait until I take you to the top, son," Everest responded. "The view is to die for up there."

"Oh, they have a *Groß Heilker* here," Vienna expressed. "I've not seen one since we were in *Wien* a long time ago…! Look at those shoes!"

Vienna attempted to stir off the path as she saw a high-end Austrian boutique store. Everest held on to her and stopped her.

"You'll have plenty of time to come down and explore soon enough, dearie," Everest expressed. "Besides, what do you need new shoes for? You already have plenty…"

"Please, my mountain, just a peek."

"Later, not now," Everest responded. "You've just arrived at Harlech, let's get your bags and you settled into the apartment."

The family made their way through the atrium and towards the elevators. Everest helped them bring their suitcases into the elevator car, and then they rose up to the penthouse level.

"Is that all that prevents a stranger from coming up to the penthouse floor?" Salmar questioned. "Just four-digits of an easily guessable number."

"It's a backup code that only a few people know," Everest dismissed. "I have cards for you both upstairs so that you don't have to use that code in front of others.

The elevator doors opened at the penthouse level, and the three of them got off and then approached the penthouse door. Everest took his keys from his pocket and began to find the one that was used to unlock the penthouse. However, as he was about to unlock the penthouse, Everest heard a noise from the other side of a door shut close. His brow furrowed and he began to unlock the front door. The front door opened at his hand, and he stepped inside, jumping at the sudden appearance of a young woman who raised her arms up with glee as she saw her family.

"Surprise!" Allodia expressed.

Allodia Cabernet had lengthy and thick wavy golden blonde hair with bangs that covered her forehead. She had fair skin like her mother, but a deeper blue shade in her eyes like her father. She wore a light blue pair of jeans, a thick black belt around her waist, and a pink silk long-sleeved shirt. She appeared youthful, very youthful at nearly at the start of her twenties.

"Allodia," Everest greeted with a smile, embracing his daughter. "My little dear. When did you get back? I thought you were away on that trip to Europe."

"I just got back this morning," Allodia responded. "I didn't realize the entire gang was here. I wasn't expecting a family reunion."

"Not entirely a family reunion. Charles isn't here," Salmar responded.

"I meant the whole family, except Charles."

"To be quite honest, I'm surprised we haven't heard from Charlemagne in some time," Vienna expressed. "I hope he's alright. It isn't like him to not in the least write for more than a month."

"Wherever Charles is, I'm sure it is somewhere peculiar, dangerous, and preoccupying his time."

"I heard he was in the UK," Salmar remarked. "Something to do with a research project with his friends."

"Charlie has friends?" Allodia questioned.

"Now, be nice," Vienna scolded. "Just because Charlemagne is not with us, does not mean we do not hold him in our heart. He's a busy man, looking to make a name for himself."

"Oh, he's certainly succeeded in being able to make a name for himself..." Everest remarked. "If he keeps up, it'll be the same name his grandfather made for himself."

"Everest, please," Vienna pleaded, "do not speak of our son that way. Charlemagne will rise higher than either of us could hope. I know it in my heart that he will do good, and we have to be patient that he cannot be with us for that reason."

Everest and the others did not respond. Vienna took in a deep breath and then took her luggage.

"I'm going to get settled," Vienna expressed. "Which bedroom is ours?"

"First door on the left," Everest replied, watching her off and then turning to Allodia. "Wait a minute. How did you get inside?"

"I have my own key," Allodia replied, showing her key set. "How else?"

"I understood the penthouse to have been abandoned," Everest replied. "You don't mean to tell me you've been coming in here?"

"Not really," Allodia responded, petting Baron. "Charlie was supposed to be living here, so I had the key as a backup for him in case he lost his while travelling. I didn't even know it was abandoned."

"Hm…" Everest replied, "that's right. I completely forgot he was supposed to be living here. When I arrived, it seemed like this place was kept in stasis. I couldn't imagine where he's living nowadays then."

"I couldn't imagine he's living anywhere. He doesn't exactly have any sort of job," Salmar responded. "I heard that sometimes he earns some royalties from patents."

"I heard from him that he lives off grants he receives for research projects and such."

"Well, it's his life. I'm sure he knows how to live it, otherwise he'd be here," Everest expressed. "Sal, why don't you go get settled in a bedroom? I imagine you've already gotten settled in," he said, looking at Allodia.

"That's right," Allodia expressed as Salmar began to move. "I'm at the end of the hall, Sal, so stay out!" Salmar left with his luggage. She then looked at her father and asked, "So, what brings you to Harlech? I would have thought this city to be last place I would ever find you."

Everest explained to her what caused him to come to Harlech, his concern in the lack of communication for the news from Tanzania, his oversight on that investigation, and then his observations that led to the fourteen-points.

"The investigation is just about complete, but now I'm bogged down in seeing these fourteen-points realized and it's taken some time. I didn't anticipate spending my summer in Harlech but seems like I'll have to stay for a while."

"I think it's great that you're taking the reins on the company and exerting a humane vision for its future. I don't really follow what goes on with the company (despite being a shareholder), but I heard about what happened in Tanzania because a friend brought it up. It's just awful, all of it…"

"Yes, and I'm getting to the bottom of it, don't you worry."

"Good," Allodia replied.

"And how are your veterinarian studies at the university going for you?"

"Just finished my second-year last month. Two more years to go in my undergrad, and then I got to apply for vet school. I think I have long way to go still…"

"You'll do just alright," Everest expressed. "My little girl is far more intelligent than her old man. You'll be a great veterinarian."

"Yeah…"

Vienna returned, dressed in a different outfit. She wore a long white blouse with a black belt around her waist.

"I am ready," Vienna announced.

"For what, dearie?" Everest questioned, looking at her as she turned around to show off her outfit. "Where are you going so soon?"

"To the shops downstairs," Vienna expressed. "I did not get a chance to see the ones in the airport, so now is my chance. Allodia, my darling, will you join me?"

"I would rather not look at items that I don't have any money for," Allodia replied. "I can barely afford food and rent as it is with my part-time job."

"Did you not just return from Europe?"

"Oh, and that…"

"Fear not, my dear," Vienna expressed, "*mutter* will buy you clothes."

Everest cleared his throat and remarked, "With our joint bank account." The girls then glared at him, so he said, "I better come along just to ensure there's some proper supervision. I don't suppose Salmar will want to join. I'll let him know we'll be leaving for a while." He then went upstairs and came around to the first bedroom on the right. He knocked on the door, eliciting the bark of Baron followed by Salmar opening the door.

"Sal, we're going out," Everest remarked. "Do you need anything?"

"Where are you going?"

"Just down to the shops below, and possibly to Cascadia Mall too. I don't suppose your mother and sister will be content with just those shops below. Come on, why don't you join us. I'll be with you, and you did want to get a taste of Harlech, well here you are – a bastion of consumerism awaits you."

"Sure, alright. Can I bring Baron?"

"I haven't seen any signs that have forbidden dogs, so why not?"

Everest, Salmar, and Baron came downstairs to rejoin the girls, and then the five of them went down the elevator to the main floor where they proceeded to get lost in the shops on the main and second floor of Cabernet Tower. Aside from *Groß Heilker*, there were other foreign brand shops, particularly German/Austrian ones such as *Hanneke, Maack*, and *Kothe*. There were also Italian brands: *Zenteno, Santini*, and *Passarella*; English brands: *Orcutt, Lowery*, and *Mullins*; and also other European brands: *Gustafson, Guillory, Declerc, Nowacki*, and *De Koomen*. Cabernet Industries hosted all these exclusive name brands on the main and second floor. Vienna and Allodia became lost in the assortment of high-end products before them, trying on just about every pair of shoe they put their hands on, every coat, and every dress. Even Salmar became enticed by the luxurious male brands that showed off their products on muscular mannequins, sporting the latest polo, shorts, or collared shirt that stood out from regular brands. He gravitated towards the men's watches, colognes, and suits especially. Everest and Baron were renegaded to sit down and watch from the sofa couch in each store or outside in the main atrium while the others grasped every item that took their interest. He watched as Vienna encouraged Allodia and Salmar to put on clothes, try on different styles, and to put together something that they liked. When they were finished, they would go to the checkout desk and Vienna would pay for the items. Everest made an uncomfortable noise with Baron as he saw from afar, far enough so that the totals could not be seen ring up on the cashier box screens, but not far enough to hear the costs amount to over four-digits per purchase. The family came around to the atrium with their bags of items, Vienna passing bags to both Everest and Salmar so they could make a trip up to the penthouse before they carried on to Cascadia Mall nearby.

Everest stayed quiet as he helped out, but what they did not see was the tension in his jaw as he grinded his teeth and bit his tongue. They returned downstairs and came out onto the streets of downtown Harlech with the early summer heat pressing down through the skyscrapers, and a steady stream of motor vehicle and foot traffic moving either side of them. The family went eastbound towards Earle Street, crossed it, and passed the other side of Dominion Square where Chamberlain department store had display cases of luxurious dresses and suits. The Royal Harlech museum stood from the other side with banners for their feature exhibition: the Industrial Revolution. At the street corner with Hardwicke and Campbell Street, the opposite corner from Dominion Square was the plaza entrance into Cascadia Centre. In contrast to Cabernet Tower, Cascadia Mall had a variety of brands, especially mainstream ones that could be found in just about every mall in North America. Some brands of which included clothing brands such as Gates, Lucinda, and Wally's. There were also electronic and bookstores: Radioshack, HMV, A&B, and B. Dalton. The mall consisted of two floors, a main floor and a sublevel floor. The sublevel floor stretched backwards from the city block around Hardwicke and Campbell, to the city block around Hardwicke and Maurelle Street. From the sublevel, one could also cross underneath Hardwicke to the sublevel of Chamberlain and board the subway at Hardwicke Station. On the opposite side from Chamberlain, on Dowager and Campbell there was a Sears that was accessible via the sublevel. Above the mall there were two towers, one of which was an Equinox Hotel and the other, Cascadia Tower, an office building.

Eventually, towards late afternoon, the family came around to the food court where there were a variety of food brands: Sander's Chicken, Royal Burger, Dairy Duke, Mr. Kroc's, New Jersey Fries, Nara, Taco Space, Boy Slop, and Orient Express.

"Smells so good in here," Salmar expressed.

"We have plenty of food upstairs," Everest replied.

"But Everest, my dear," Vienna complained, "how could you expect me to cook when I'm so tired? How about we just get something to eat? With so many food options, there's something for everyone."

"You want to eat here?" Everest questioned. "No, if you want to eat out, then I know a better spot. Come on."

Everest took them away from the food court. They returned to the penthouse to drop off more bags, and then afterwards they crossed the street to the Windsor Hotel where Everest took them up to the fourth floor Palm House restaurant. The restaurant was quiet and there were few people, most of whom wore suits. They sat down at a table with a view outward towards Dominion Square.

"I came here once for lunch with some of the board," Everest expressed. "Very nice."

Vienna opened the menu and began to look through. "It's so expensive… sixty-dollars for a steak? I could buy enough food for a week with that same money, no less a one-time meal."

"You don't understand," Everest expressed, "it's not just any beef. It's prime rib, the tastiest and most desirable piece of steak from a cow."

"Meat – gross," Allodia complained. "Do they have any fish?"

"They have a three-salmon entrée," Everest expressed. "Three types of salmon with risotto on the side."

"You sound like you've been here often, dad," Salmar chipped in, "if you know the menu that well."

"Well, we do come here for lunch a lot of the time. I never mind the prices either; I never pay my meal. Someone else usually gets the bill."

"Oh? How generous of them?"

"Yeah, I suppose so," Everest remarked. "It's become a running gag even that we order whatever we want since someone else is going to get the bill, and they often joke at times that it'll be me. I've offered to pay, but they haven't let me yet."

Everest looked through the menu. He got for himself and Vienna a glass of Italian wine, and he and Salmar both ordered a plate of nine ounce prime rib steak to be cooked medium-rare. Allodia went ahead with her father's recommendation, and Vienna got the seafood salad.

"So, how are you liking Harlech so far?" Everest asked the group. "Allodia, you've been here longer than your mother and brother, we'll start with you."

"It's... big," Allodia replied. "I couldn't imagine living here all my life. I like the university though. It's nice and small and secluded."

"Vienna, you've been here before – is it as enchanting as you remember?"

"It's certainly has a lot more stores than I remember. When we were last here together, it was brief. The memories I have of Harlech are from my youth, and I almost never left the university or that island except on school trips. We never came to the downtown either. There's certainly a lot more people in Harlech than in Allabrese."

"And you sport? Is everything you ever imagined?"

"It's great," Salmar concluded. "I love it."

Everest nodded and then sipped his wine again.

"What about you dad? You've been here for what? Two months now? How do you like Harlech?"

Everest shrugged. He thought for a moment and then answered, "I'll tell you what – the conveniences to get whatever you want, so quickly, have grown on me. The penthouse is nice and quiet most times of the day, there's never anything you cannot do, but the only thing that I've missed in that time has been the pool… and you guys of course. I have to go all the way to the country club in Westford to find a nice pool, and even then it's not exactly private. You'll like the country club. I'll take you over there some time."

"How has work been?" Salmar asked.

"You know, I always despised the thought of being involved in Cabernet Industries, but in the time I have been, the board of directors has been very considerate and nice to me. They've been listening to my requests and my advice, and I really feel like I'm making a difference in the company and getting to push it away from what it used to be, from what my dad left it as (mind you he never really got involved either), and into something good. I'm happy about that."

"Well, I think we can toast then," Vienna remarked. "To continued success for Cabernet Industries and the Cabernet name." They then clinked their glasses and drank to that cause.

Act 3, Scene 2

Everest woke up the next morning, eyes looking up to the ceiling above him and light pouring in through the blinds of the window. Vienna was next to him, on her side with a hand towards Everest. She wore a pink nightgown that she had bought the day before. Her arms were slim and skin was smooth. Her fingernails were perfectly polished and not too long. Everest sat up and placed his rugged hand over hers and then came out from his side of the bed, stood up, and went to the washroom. He showered and got dressed in one of his suits, and then he went downstairs to make some coffee and then go to his study for an hour as he reviewed faxes that had come in overnight from around the world. Once Everest had finished his morning briefing, he went back upstairs to brush his teeth and then went downstairs to the elevator, going down to the executive floor and stepping out to come around to the executive board room.

"Gentlemen," Roness expressed, "after a long wait, the final results have been made available to us regarding the incident that occurred in Tanzania little more than two months ago. Mr. Cabernet, please."

"Thank you, Mr. Roness," Everest responded, putting on his glasses. "A final report on the cause of the damages to the dam in Tanzania has been produced, and similar in conclusion to what was previously provided to this board, our contracted engineers and scientists have reviewed the wreckage area and determined there to have been a fault in the architectural design of the dam. The dam was not designed in consideration to the collapse of soil that should come through excess of water and buildup of pressure, nor was the dam design with enough consideration to the ability to ensure that water was allowed enough flow. Additionally, maintenance of existing pipes was completed at a below minimal level, which also resulted in the failure to take notice of pipes at the upper dam to be sending off enough water to clear out the reservoir. In fact, in the unprofessional opinion of some leadership at Site C, the excess of water in the reservoir, or above average levels of water, was seen positively despite the damage it was doing to the sediment around the surrounding banks and pressure it was creating against the dam. In conclusion, the fault of the disaster that occurred at Site C is owed to flawed design and poor maintenance not within corporate regulation. A review of the blueprints and comparison to the wreckage made available to engineers determined there to have been shortcuts made in the cost of materials that averages to below what was provided in the overall budget. In cooperation with Tanzania police, an investigation has been launched to embezzlement of those funds, while in the meantime our report is ready to be shared with the police too to charge leadership at that site with manslaughter for their part in the collapse of this dam."

"Thank you, Mr. Cabernet," Roness responded. "Obviously, what has occurred at Site C is a tragedy, but this report has shown us it to have been a culpable and avoidable disaster. Rest assured, these men will face justice in due time, which should put the survived victims of this tragedy to ease for their losses. Have all members had a chance to read the report that Mr. Cabernet shared on Friday? If so, are there any objections to the report?"

No questions, comments, or concerns came through.

"Can I get a show of hands to approve the final report?" Roness questioned.

The vote was unanimous.

"Can I get a show of hands to approve the dissemination of the report to Tanzania police and request to press charges for this tragedy?"

"Have we consulted with our legal team before doing so?" Bennett questioned. "We don't want something like this report to spring back upon us."

"Not to worry, Mr. Bennett," Roness responded. "We've worked in cooperation with the Tanzanian government who see no lust for blood in us. They've cooperated with us likewise. This report will be made available to their government office, not to the press, so there is no fear for reprisal against Cabernet Industries."

Bennett nodded.

"A show of hands," Roness requested.

The vote was unanimous.

"Excellent," Roness remarked. "The report will be sent off at once. At this time, our new occupational health and safety department, or as it was called by Mr. Cabernet, 'People Safety,' is in the works of reviewing the recommendations that were made, and which were approved last week. Mr. Cabernet, is there any update on that department?"

"No update at this time, although the final report will be shared with that department and recommendations will take into account this tragedy so that it can be learned from to not happen again."

"Thank you, Mr. Cabernet. As for the culpable under our employment, Mr. Holmes, we will need to be in contact with Mr. Juma at the branch office in order to ensure that these employees are terminated before they go into police custody. Please ensure that your department, 'People and Culture,' are able to see that task through."

"Yes, Mr. Roness," Holmes responded, taking note.

"Well, I think that this meeting has been a positive start to our Monday, and the new month," Roness expressed. "Any additions to the agenda before we break off?"

No response came through.

"Good," Roness replied, standing up. "In that case, I wish the best to all of you have a good rest of your day."

Everest stood up and organized his papers into his briefcase. Mr. Bennett then approached him from the side.

"Mr. Cabernet, can I expect to see you at the mill later today," Bennett remarked. "I hope you haven't forgotten about this tour you've strongly requested."

"Yes, with you and Mr. Holmes. I haven't forgotten. I'll see you then," Everest expressed. "Err, what street was the facility on again?"

"Coventry Street," Bennett stated. "You'll want to take Stuart Street to ger there."

Once the morning meeting was concluded, Everest returned to the penthouse and joined his family for breakfast. He then retired to his study where he drank another cup of coffee and then left at a quarter to one o'clock in the afternoon. He went downstairs to the underground parking lot where the Spyros EX was parked, got inside, and drove off onto Earle Street where he went northbound and across the highway into Whitney Harbor. Whitney Harbor was not much different than Central Harlech, except it was closer to the water. There were still numerous skyscrapers and shops, but with less of the chaos around the highway and Campbell Street. There were also a lot of restaurants on the ground floor of these skyscrapers. Everest stopped at Stuart Street and turned right onto it. He then proceeded down to reach Hardwicke, Dowager, up to Hound Street when he observed the atmosphere to shift. The structures at his side were different than those he was departing from, turning from high rises to brick-laced buildings no greater than four stories tall. Stuart Street also narrowed and rather than asphalt, became brick-laced as of the Hound Street intersection. Everest also took note that various structures on the ground floor had barred, reinforced windows. He passed Hound Street, Cahan Street, and Bourassa Street as he noticed the people that roamed the street walked with a slow shuffle, some of them were under-layered or over-layered in dirty clothing, messy hair, and a lot of them sitting at steps and street corners. As Everest stopped at the next streetlight, and among those who passed the crossroad was a man with a shopping cart and another man with a limp due to a prosthetic leg. Everest looked on as the men continued to travel, eliciting the car behind him to honk at him. He returned to focus and drove forward, but rather than continue the rest of the direction as the neighborhood ahead seemed quieter and more industrious, he decided to merge left to signal left on Bailey Drive as he reached the industrial district.

At the light, Everest came onto Bailey Drive and made a loop around Keswick as he turned left onto Kent Street. He passed down the street where there were more impoverished people roaming the sidewalks, some of whom did not care to even jaywalk across the street. Everest observed a police presence by vehicles and patrol officers walking the streets in this particular area, and the native population did little to acknowledge or notice them, and likewise the police walked around these people. He pulled over to the sidewalk at a park that took up an entire double street block and turned off the car engine. He continued to look about with curious eyes. The surrounding area was quieter than Stuart Street. Everest came out of the car, dressed in his suit, and closed the door behind him and locked the car before he began to walk about.

Keswick, despite being a neighborhood of impoverished individuals, or slum in other words, still had shops and apartment blocks above them with essential businesses that included markets, pawn shops, laundromats, and liquor stores. Everest passed an alleyway where he saw two vagrants in a physical dispute. He then continued past and came around to a street corner where suddenly he was met with a sight of an older male sat atop of some steps in front of a café. The male was not dressed entirely in rags like the others. He wore a canvas coat and cargo pants with tall military style boots. He had a greyish beard that was not too long, fair skin, and medium length thick grey hair. He had a lone look upon his face, blue eyes staring ahead of him, his hands together, elbows at the knees. He was very tall. He looked as though he was waiting for something, or someone, although a cardboard sign in front of him read, 'Please help – hungry.' Everest looked at him, and then over to the café. He stayed put where he was, looking at both of them for a moment too long. He was frozen, although not in fear.

Everest let out a deep breath and turned around. He walked away from the man and returned around the street corner from where he came to run into a two police officers. He attempted to pass them, but they sidestepped as he approached to block his path.

"Excuse me, sir, but are you lost?" the police officer asked.

"No, I'm not lost. I'm just parked at the park," Everest responded.

"What's someone like you, dressed in a *Hanneke* suit, doing around here then?" the other police officer stated. "You're not from around here, are you? Keswick is a bad neighborhood; you may want to move along and be on your way before any of the locals give you trouble."

"Yes, of course," Everest replied. "That's just what I'm about to do."

Everest passed them, proceeded down the street and back around to his car when he noticed a line-up of people at a venue across the street from the park. The venue had a sign above it that said, 'With Open Arms'. The building was about two-stories tall, constructed of white stucco and had barred windows. The door into the building was narrow. At the top peak of the rooftop of this building was a Christian cross. Among the people around the building, there were some who held bowls in their hands as they sat on the curb or beneath a tree nearby, eating from those disposable bowls with plastic spoons. Everest's attention broke as he saw a vagrant approach him down the street. He nervously continued to walk down, crossing onto the street and keeping his distance by the cars between them. He got into the car, ignited the engine, and then pulled out from the street. He went forward on Kent Street and turned onto Cahan Street where the vagrant across from the café was. Everest passed the curb he was sat on, but the man was gone; he continued back to Stuart Street then and continued forward into the Industrial District to resume his way to the tour.

Act 3, Scene 3

"It was strange," Everest remarked, recounting what happened in Keswick. "I... I felt like I made the wrong choice."

Everest drove across the Penultimate Bridge as he finished telling his wife what happened last Monday. The pair of them sat in the Spyros EX as it went northbound. They were dressed in formal casual clothes; Everest in a collared shirt with his sleeves rolled up and wearing beige trousers, and Vienna in a collared blouse, red leather belt, and floral skirt. Everest paused for a moment. Vienna patiently listened and did not interrupt. Everest merged right onto an exit lane, onto a curved lane that came around, and then continued onwards onto a coastal road that went away from New Harlech and even further northbound.

"I felt like I should have offered that man some money, or a meal," Everest explained. "Maybe not money. When I first got here, the golden rule they told me was to not give beggars money because there's a rising drug problem in Harlech. I should have asked that man if he wanted something to eat and bought him something from the café. I feel ashamed that... that in my spirit, I was powerless to get out of my comfort zone. I felt like a bit of a coward because I didn't. The craziest part is when I drove past the street, he was gone, and I lost my chance in that moment. I... regret the choice that I made."

"And now is your opportunity to never make it again," Vienna reasoned. "When I was a little girl, I was told that you should never presume with the vagabond because they may be an angel in disguise to test your charity."

Everest didn't immediately respond as he continued to drive. "I don't think I had an encounter with an angel, dearie."

"Do not dismiss so easily," Vienna remarked. "A good friend of mine once shared with me that when she was in the city that she too had an encounter much like yours; the presentation of a homeless man in help and in need, and herself in a position to assist. She did so, but then when she returned no more than five minutes later, the person she had helped was gone just like that, with no possibility that he could have fled so quickly. No... if I was ever in a similar place as you or her, I would not think twice because I would know that whether this person be an angel or not, I have an obligation in my heart to help, even if I may be limited in my charity."

Everest did not respond. The conversation ended there, and he continued to drive down the northern route. The northbound route had two-lanes on either side and these lanes were close to the cliff edge that was more than twenty meters above the water. For some stretches of the travel, there were off-shoot roads to houses and homes in the outskirts of Harlech. Soon afterwards too, a sign listed the next destinations: 'Penultimate Shores – 15km; Ralagah – 64km; Radloff – 121km; Vollmer – 145km' However, Everest did not travel as far as Ralagah as they instead came into the suburbs of Penultimate Shores where houses were on the coast, cliffs, and mountainside.

The couple parked in front of a driveway at the end of a short cul-de-sac, which was attached to a longer road that came off the freeway. The house was secluded by tall hedges and had an iron gate that was pulled out for the occasion. The sun beamed down hard from over the eastern skies. Eventually, they arrived at their destination, a mansion on the pacific coast, rectangular in size and structure with flat rooftops and plain stucco walls. The driveway looped around in front of the main entrance with a concrete beam upholding a shelter in front of the main entrance. The couple came around to the front entrance of the mansion they parked at, and Everest raised a fist to knock at the front door.

The door opened and the couple were met with a woman with fair skin on the other side. She had dark wavy brown hair and blue eyes. She appeared to be in her early fifties. She wore a floral dress like Vienna, except the blouse she wore was sleeveless and not collared. She looked at the couple with a pleased look on her face, although it faintly showed expression.

"Ah, welcome," the woman expressed. She spoke in a sort of breathy tone, "it's so good to finally meet both of you of Cabernet fame. I am Magdala Roness, but I prefer Maude."

"Hello Maude," Everest greeted. "Nice to meet you."

"Vienna Cabernet," Vienna introduced, gently shaking hands. "A pleasure to meet you too." The couple walked into the foyer of the mansion. Maude closed the door behind them. "My, such a nice home you have."

"Thank you, I do take quite a bit of pride in the decoration," Maude remarked.

"Where's Mr., err... where is Dwight?" Everest asked.

"He should be downstairs in the den," Maude answered, guiding them through the foyer. "This way."

Everest looked around the foyer, it was nothing like the one that Cabernet Manor had. The entire mansion had a very distinct modern architecture structure with plain painted walls. Some pillars on their right were made of sheer concrete. A staircase on the left with glass railings led upwards to the second floor. Ahead of them were some steps that came up to platform where there were statues positioned in the centre, and further ahead in this long corridor foyer was a living room. Windows on the left looked out to the sea. On the right there was another staircase from the living room that led upwards to the second floor too. Overall, the foyer corridor was about two-stories tall and was very spacious. Everest looked around as Maude led them into the living room where a chandelier hung from the ceiling overtop some cubicle lounge chairs and sofas. Behind a wide plain white pillar with a television set in front of it the corridor extended further to reveal the dining room with windows on either side that looked out to the sea. The windows also looked out to the wide patio on either side. Overall, the mansion was very spacious and the rooms presented themselves as sizeable.

On the right, the dining room led into a very long kitchen that existed parallel to the foyer corridor. Everest looked closely from the dining room as the mansion consisted even further and deeper beyond the kitchen outward, but his concern was not in the rest of the mansion but in going down a set of stairs next to the one that went upstairs into the depths.

"My husband is just down these steps and then around the corner on the right," Maude explained. "If you won't mind, I would like to show Vienna the rest of the house and gussy up with her."

"No problem at all," Everest remarked, waving to them. He then proceeded down the stairs and came around to another wide corridor with a tunnel on the left and right that went deeper in. He followed Maude's directions and went right along a curved and narrow tunnel. Some cabinets in this tunnel held various different bottles of wine. He came around to the end of the corridor and up to a door left ajar. He knocked and then pushed the door in to enter into a large room with wide windows that looked out to the sea. On the left and right of this room were cabinets that contained various sea memorabilia, books, and trophies. In the midst of the room, hanging from the ceiling, was a chandelier crafted from the steering wheel of a ship. Just a bit beyond from this chandelier was a wide desk. Behind this desk were the windows, one portion of which was open and led out to a dock which was L-shaped. Everest saw no boat moored on the dockside, but saw Dwight Roness sat behind the desk with his feet up and listening to the voice of Frank Sinatra singing classical pop tunes. "Hello there, Mr. Roness," Everest greeted, waving to him from the doorway. "Quite a place you have here."

"Ah, Mr. Cabernet!" Roness remarked, lowering his feet and standing up. He wore a captain's cap, and a faint blue polo tucked into beige pants. He came around to lift the disc from the jukebox in his study and then smiled to Everest. "How are you,

Mr. Cabernet? Ready to catch some waves on the high seas there? Where's your wife?"

"With your wife," Everest answered, looking around again as he stepped inside. He then looked out towards the dock. "I don't see your boat."

"Oh, Mamie is nice and safe in the garage, don't you worry. Risky business keeping a boat moored out all day and night," Roness expressed, "no less all year long. Come along, Mr. Cabernet – you know what, I'm going to call you Everest from now on, if you don't mind. I think we've gotten to know each other long enough now."

"No problem with me, Mr. Roness – sorry, Dwight," Everest responded.

"Right on," Roness replied, gesturing him to follow. He led Everest through a door on the left from the desk between some cabinets. They came through another curved corridor, this one shorter than the last that came around to a large garage-like room, though with a ditch in the midst from where a large yacht was parked. "You see her, isn't she beautiful?"

"She's quite a large ship," Everest remarked.

"Yes, nothing like those superyachts you hear about, although who needs a boat as large as your home?" Roness questioned. "No, she's just the right size for a recreational boat."

The Mamie measured approximately ten meters from bow to stern. She was equipped with a sail and motor, and a small cockpit in the midst with seats around. She also had a fair-sized deck in the back with lounge chairs and fishing equipment laid out.

"I'll have her brought out in a jiffy," Roness expressed, climbing aboard. "You see that control panel over there, Everest? I'm going to need you to do me a favor and raise the gate and lower the tracks to set me down."

"Sure," Everest replied, coming around to the panel. He paused for a moment and then took hold of a lever. The gates began to rise at the end of the drydock. Once they were raised, he began to lower the boat down the ramp and into the water. "How's that?" he shouted.

"Perfect!" Roness shouted back. "I'll bring her around – wait for me at the docks!"

Everest watched Roness bring the boat out before he came around to the study again. He gave another closer look at the memorabilia in the cabinet. He found some war memorabilia, medals and pictures of Mr. Roness when he was younger with dark brown hair, dressed in a U.S. Army officer uniform. Another picture showed him in his combat uniform with some friends in the midst of a jungle. Beside these objects was a tattered American flag with a plate that said, 'Recovered from Pearl Harbor after the Japanese Attack on December 7th, 1941.' Some other pictures in the cabinet showed Mr. Roness with some famous figures, one of which included a picture of him with the illustrious business magnate, Mortimer Schildman. There was also a picture of Mr. Roness with U.S. president Lyndon B. Johnson and some members of his cabinet, men in suits, including the son of John Blackmore, Daniel Blackmore. He looked at these items and then noticed that Roness was sailing the boat around to the docks. He stepped out onto the dock and then stood by. Everest watched Roness bring the yacht around, prompting Everest to go further to assist him in mooring it to the docks.

"There we go," Roness expressed, climbing down. "Now where are those fine ladies of ours?"

After a few minutes, Maude and Vienna arrived to join them aboard the yacht with a cooler that carried drinks and snacks. Maude lounged on one of the seats near the steering wheel prompting Vienna and Everest to sit down on the other side while Dwight took the wheel. He took the boat out into the Hecate Strait until they were a fair distance from the shores and the sight of Harlech could be seen from afar too. Everest could even look farther down the coast and see Grafton Bridge and Walham Valley beyond. There was a mighty breeze in the air, the sight of seagulls above them, circling around like vultures, but after a few more minutes they were along calm waters, sailing according to the wind, so Everest released the steering wheel and came around to sit out in the sun. Maude and Vienna sat together as they were now deep in conversation, so Everest went and joined Dwight on the stern deck.

"You ever fish, Everest?" Dwight asked, fetching some poles. "Surely you must have."

"I have actually," Everest answered. "If there was one complaint I had about where I lived at the moment, in Allabrese, it would be that there just doesn't seem to be that great of fish in that river there except once per year you'll catch a good stream of salmon."

"Well, fortunately when you live in these parts, there's an assortment of fish to be caught," Roness remarked, passing him a fishing pole and then sitting back in his lounge chair as he let out a sight of relief. "Yes, this is quite nice, isn't it, Everest. Say, what a name is that, Everest – like the mountain, right?"

"That's right," Everest responded, "just like the mountain. My father, Derby Cabernet, was an adventurer as you know, and since I was born while they were apart because of the war, and there was limited contact between them, she named me after Mount Everest because my father always wanted to climb that mountain."

"Did he ever get to climb Mount Ev?"

"No," Everest answered, "he didn't. He was beaten in 1953 to be the first person to summit that mountain, and when that passed him, he lost interest ever since. I remember I was around eight-years old when that happened – my father was desolate at the news. He held that goal with such high aspirations, and he never met it… but of course, he had his other accomplishments over the course of his life. To be honest, I sometimes think that the reason why my father never got to succeed in his lifetime wish was because he was too busy raising my sister and me. I was born shortly before the war ended, and she was born three years later. All those years, the two of them stayed put in raising up first near Lennox in the Walham Valley, then for a bit in East Anglia at the summer home we used to have, and lastly in Allabrese. By the time I was ten-years old my father began to travel again, with us too, and he did that for a couple of years until he had to stop again."

"Why's that?"

"Well, it was a personal choice of his really," Everest plainly expressed. "It didn't take long for him to decide to retire and move back to England, but then he grew bored and began to travel again for the last stretch of his life."

Roness listened as they grew quiet together. He held two fingers at his cheek and then moved them to say, "You know, over the course of my time as CEO for Cabernet Industries, and then before for Blackmore Industries, there's been few men I've heard more about in the megacorporation business than Derby Cabernet. Even with all those cold words that are said about him post-mortem, as a military man myself, there's a lot to respect in a man who braved the war from start to finish, and then the tales of him afterwards that have put him in the likes of many great British explorers. It's a shame he never got to climb that mountain though," he said. "You were quite the lucky fella though to have such a father. My own old man fought in the war, out in the pacific against the Japanese, and then I fought myself in Vietnam for a while. It's not easy out there, let me tell you that much. I hold a lot of respect for your father, and I take it with great servitude that I am in the position I am for his – for your family's company."

"Thank you, Mr. R- Dwight."

"I only regret that I never got to work with him, or to know him in flesh before his accident," Roness expressed. "We have a lot of work to do between us though, to honor his memory, that's why it's important that Cabernet Industries is held up its standards and not let to deflate."

Everest didn't respond. He looked out to the sea and then back around to Roness.

"I still have a hard time believing, or even seeing sometimes what sort of effect we have on this world that does a good value to human lives," Everest expressed. "What charitable contribution are we making to the rest of the world?"

"Charitable contributions? Mr. Cabernet, Cabernet Industries is not a charity. It's a multi-billion-dollar international corporation with subsidiaries in just about every economic sector in the world. If you want to know what contribution it makes to the lives of everyday people, then consider this: if Cabernet Industries did not exist, then roughly one-and-a-half million people would not have the steady stream of income that they have now in various parts of the world – they would be unemployed. Those same people would not have many of the economic activities that add to the global economy in their local regions, such as mining, lumber, agriculture, or in other parts manufacturing and refinery; all of which results in an end goal of a product on the global market for purchase from a consumer. The effects from then on are like a ripple effect," Roness expressed, casting his rod. "The contributions from one sector, aids in the contribution of another sector; the global economy is like a network of corporations, delivering products and goods into the market which adds wealth into the pockets of everyday people. It's called trickle-down economics, Mr. Cabernet. Even then, you also have to consider the quality-of-life improvements that Cabernet Industries makes in the poorer parts of the world, how we've added infrastructure to these places where governments dare not to touch. All this activity was made possible by Cabernet Industries, and you ask now about charitable contributions to the world when Cabernet Industries has given the world so much already?"

"I fail to see how guided missiles and ammunitions add to the positive contributions to the world," Everest argued. "How do our weaponry ever do anything but disrupt the peace of the world?"

"If it were not our weapons, it would be weapons of some of the other large-scale producers like Smith & Wesson or Lockheed Martin. We've fought hard to stay competitive in this growing market; aerospace weapons are all the rage now, a Strategic Defense Initiative, lasers and satellites from the sky are what's hot right now – the defense of the first world is a priority."

"The defense of the first world? The Cold War is at its end – the first world has won that, so who do we have left to fight? Even then, I don't see our weapons being sent to Afghanistan, or to aid in the Central Americas. I see our weapons shipped to Africa, to Lebanon, to Iraq and Israel."

"All nations allied to the United States," Roness pointed out. "Look, you may not see it, but Cabernet Industries plays an important role in the global order," he remarked. "Believe it or not, but that win that you foresee and which I hope in the Cold War was played out with participation from Cabernet Industries. What more of a greater contribution in the scope of human history than that win, and the wins of the Second and First World War?"

Everest did not respond.

"You almost question whether there is any net positive good that Cabernet Industries does for the world," Roness said, "You're not seeing the bigger picture even when you look far and wide." He paused again for a moment and then reeled in his line. "Cabernet Industries poses no ethical challenge to the world. What happened in Tanzania was one-off, and not the company's fault. Rarely are problems such as those the fault of the company or organization. You just have to see it… Cabernet

Industries does not exist to give and provide, even from our abundance, but to participate in society as a corporate entity. There is no room for charitable contributions in business because it is illogical to the business processes as there is nothing to add or receive in such transaction."

"Fine," Everest finally responded, "you say Cabernet Industries is not a charity, and that's fine because it it's just as you say. Whether C.I. has a positive contribution, I struggle to see as you argue, but maybe I do have yet to see it even though I've searched for these past months and not yet seen it. I just want to believe that the work that we are doing is making a difference…"

"You want proof, evidence? Just tell me how you wish to measure such proof, and I'll give it to you."

Everest did not respond. Roness looked at him, gave a chuckle, and then went back to fishing.

"Exactly, you can't measure happiness, and you can't measure goodness," Roness expressed. "You want proof that isn't tangible – you'll always keep searching unless you trust and believe in the work we do. You'll always bog yourself down with doubt and at worst case come to despair unless you let go and just trust in us. Believe me, we are leading Cabernet Industries to the future."

Act 3, Scene 4

Everest sat on the patio of the penthouse later in the evening, smoking a cigar as he looked out towards the view ahead. The skies were orange and clouds presented like strokes of a paintbrush. The door opened and Everest looked over to see Vienna approach and sit down next to him. She swatted her hand at the smoke and moved the ash tray closer to Everest who put his cigar down as he looked at her. Vienna sat on the side of the chair and looked forward towards the horizon with him.

"Is everything alright with you?" Vienna questioned. "You've been quiet since we returned from the Roness home."

"Vi, can I get your honest opinion about something?" Everest asked. "I've been in Harlech for two months, trying to get this company off its feet to start to do some damn good in this world, and for as much as I push and provide guidance in a vision for Cabernet Industries, the others seem to lag behind and I just fail to see any good that I'm doing here. Today I asked Roness if he thought Cabernet Industries was making a charitable contribution to the world, and he basically laughed in my face about it. He said that C.I. is not a charity and I shouldn't think of it as such because it has nothing to gain from charity, but I… I don't want this company to take and exploit others. I understand that people need to earn their paycheques and such, but why do we have to embezzle so much wealth from others? Why can't this company do more social good for the world?"

"Hm," Vienna responded, "yes, I hear your frustration." She then sighed and placed a hand on Everest's hand as it rested on the lounge rail. "Perhaps you are both not wrong, but your perspectives are just different. Perhaps, you both speak two different languages. Mr. Roness as I understand is a businessman, and with all due respect to you, my mountain, you are not a businessman. You are a kind, loving human being. A company needs to be a company in order to succeed; how would you suppose it would flourish if it did not continue to grow? Do you not think that Cabernet Industries makes a difference in the lives of others?"

"If it weren't Cabernet Industries, it would just be some other company doing the same crap we do. I want Cabernet Industries to stand out and be different. What frustrates me the most too is the fact that this company develops and produces weapons that get shipped abroad to foreign countries to be used in their wars, in the death and destruction of other people's lives and livelihoods."

"Why not tear that down if it bothers you so?"

"I could never do it," Everest admitted. "Cabernet Arms and joint ventures in the arms industries cover a significant portion of our revenue. It would have a significant toll on us if we were to shut it down. Believe me, I already looked into it. Not to mention the backlash from the board of directors... Although, I have been thinking about another part that does bleed into that sector and which hasn't really contributed as much as it should to the company – the research and development department of Cabernet Industries is an absolute blackhole when it comes to money it receives, and it's just about impossible to measure its success because patents and such make so little revenue compared to what they receive and the net positive they have on the rest of the company. What I want to do is just shut down that entire part of the company for good."

Vienna took in a deep breath and then stood up. She went to the railing and looked out. "I do not envy what you have to deal with, even as I wish it were not a burden on you."

"You know, when I was in Keswick, I saw a soup kitchen not too far from where I parked. I suppose it was a part of a Christian mission of some sort. That soup kitchen probably does a lot more good in this city than Cabernet Industries does. If I take the R&D department apart, I should funnel all that money to a charity like that one to feed the earth," Everest expressed. "Hell, if it weren't for the fact that many charities are so unbelievably corrupt, I would funnel money into other ones too."

"Hm, and why not start your own charity then?" Vienna proposed. "If Cabernet Industries has the leadership and you have the vision, then you can build your own soup kitchens and shelters for the vulnerable people of this city."

"In other words, why not make Cabernet Industries into a charity – the board would never agree. 'There's no money to be made in that business,' they say."

"Not Cabernet Industries as a whole, but a department or separate company?" Vienna explained further. "Why not take what is given to the researchers and give it to the poor?"

"How would I have the board of directors agree to that? I would need to sell it to them, and if there's no profit to be made in something like that then what's the use?"

Vienna thought for a moment and then spun around. She came over to Everest and sat down next to him. "The selling point will be much more modern than those gentlemen could hope to believe – Allodia is involved in so many charitable contributions, and that's the *mode* with children her age these days. It is to be hip to be charitable and peaceful, so the selling point for these men to understand is for the public eye. You want to remake the image of Cabernet Industries, don't you?"

"Not particularly. I don't care for the image. I care for the people."

"Yes, you do, but as a businessman, a businessman must care about what others say about their company. They must care to know that other people, especially young people, and people like us too who grew up through the protests of the sixties, care about the earth, other human people, and in ecology and such. You must tell the board of directors that it is for the sake of marketing interest, propaganda, even if in your heart you know it is more than that."

Everest thought for a moment and then responded, "The problem though would be to find leadership. I can provide guidance, but I'm so caught up in so much already to see it through. Where do I find someone I can trust to take on that endeavor and who has the time?" Everest paused as he looked aside, and then he looked over to Vienna. "You – you should be in charge of the charity. You and I think the same without even talking sometimes; at times I can hear your own thoughts. You would be perfect for the role."

"I could not," Vienna refused, "I know nothing about business and management. Everest, I have never worked an honest day of my life outside of the home."

"Exactly, outside of the home, but you've worked in the home, managing me, the kids, and even putting in leadership with your women's league at the church and all those activities you get up to. You'd be a perfect fit – with your permission, my love, I want to nominate you to that role. I'm going to go down to the board tomorrow, announce my intentions to close R&D, and announce the creation of a new endeavor – Cabernet Charity."

••

"Cabernet Charity?" Roness questioned as he leaned forward in his desk. "Why would we want to sponsor, or create a charity?"

"I thought you might ask that," Everest responded as he sat on the other side, "and in consideration, I thought about what is the latest fad with adolescents and young adults, even some adults that lived through the civil rights era – it is popular to be charitable with one another, to give to the poor; these old Christian ideals of giving from your own pocket your last copper penny. My own daughter returned not too long ago from a trip in which she went cross-country with some friends to raise money for the poor for the sake of the environment. A lot of people are into those prospects, so why not us? Why not renew the image of Cabernet Industries from a rigid, mechanical gears and cogs type organization to one that gives back to the Earth?"

Roness did not respond as he looked to Locke on his right. "Is this true? Would a charity be suitable for our public image?"

Locke paused for a moment as he hesitated and then answered, "In honesty, Mr. Roness, charitable contributions from a corporation has made a resurgence since the Great Depression. In those times, large firms such as Kellogg and Ford established charitable foundations to collect funds in the support of charitable projects. These became popular again in the late sixties, early seventies, and now they're projected to be on the rise again. However, what would be more favorable in the interest of the company is not a charitable organization, but a foundation."

"What the hell's the difference?" Roness questioned.

"A charitable organization raises funds and gives those funds back to those in need, usually in the form of some sort of service. A foundation is a charitable trust that funds others for charitable purposes through grants. A foundation would be easier to manage as it would purely involve raising money and giving to other charitable groups or people, whereas a charitable organization would require us to raise funds, organize charitable missions, and executive those plans – a lot more laborious."

"As much as it could be laborious," Everest interjected, "I would prefer to trust our funds into our own hands to manage how they are given to those in need. What if they were to come into the hands of a corrupt organization, and their corruption exposed? We wouldn't want to risk our publicity in such a scandal."

"No, we wouldn't," Roness agreed, hand around his chin, "but still, these processes are costly and we're talking about an entirely new department for the purposes of these projects. We would need to start small in the least, and also allocate funds in the first place. Any decisions that were to be made would need to be done in your consideration, Mr. Locke, to get an idea of ensuring that we get as much bang as we can for our buck, and also insight into market research into what is popular among the masses."

"Yes, as for funds, that brings me to my second proposal," Everest remarked, "I've reviewed the numbers for this quarter, and Research and Development continues to be a drain in our expenditures. I wish to shut down this department in its entirety, and individual projects put under the administration of their respective subsidiary company. The subsidiaries that require a degree of innovation can have research teams grafted into their being, but an entire department for the sake of research and such is a waste of money, and on the subject of marketing, plays no use in it."

"So, you've finally decided to go to war with that department then," Roness expressed, looking plainly at him. "So be it. I think the board could agree to understand that a large department like that on its own is pricey, and what cannot be placed anywhere we could also sell to fund this ambitious new project of yours, although I am still not yet sold on the idea of a… a Cabernet Foundation."

"Charity," Everest corrected, "and you will see. Cabernet Charity will reshape our image."

"If provided the right guidance, it could very well," Locke agreed, "it is a dual approach. On one hand, among consumers there is a bias towards corporations that contribute and support the current social movements, and corporations and investment agencies are catching up to these ideas; ideas of civil and women rights, nuclear non-proliferation, anti-apartheidism, and world hunger. These social movements have proven popular among young people and the media."

"Who would we dare put into such a role to take leadership?" Roness questioned. "There's nobody I could think of in their right mind."

"I have an idea," Everest remarked. "I would like to nominate my wife, Vienna Cabernet, to that role. She and I are of one mind on the objectives of the charity, so she would be perfect."

"With all due respect, Mr. Cabernet," Roness responded, "it would not be a wise choice to do so. For a start, your own policy on nepotism would make that choice a clear violation. I don't disagree with you that she would be a right fit, but it would just not be passable to the public, or the rest of the board. The most we can offer her is an advisor position. We'll need to find someone else, but I suppose we'll have time. We'll need to engage with Mr. Holmes on the closure of R&D, transfer those who we'd like to keep to the respective sub and layoff the rest. A layoff of this calibre, we may need to provide close to two months notice to such a workforce. If all goes smoothly, you may have your foundation by end of Q3. In the meantime, we'll need to work on our PR for its launch, and also address this liquidation of R&D appropriately."

"Layoffs?" Everest questioned.

"If we're to liquidate Research and Development, some staff will be transferred to a conglomerate their expertise may serve, while others will need to be laid off. I will have to discuss with their chief executive officer, but it should be close to two-hundred employees so that should equate to twelve-weeks notice. If less than a hundred, than only eight weeks. As for some of their equipment, assets, property, I'm sure we can find a home for them or sell them off."

"For the sake of public relations, we could frame it as a restructuring within the organization and provide our announcement first before we announce Cabernet Foundation," Locke expressed. "It could soften the blow."

"Yes, that would be nice," Roness agreed. "Many of these workers are skilled, and I'm sure they'll find employment elsewhere. There is a high demand for skilled workers at this time. Just not what Cabernet Industries needs right now. We aren't a tech company after all." Roness looked back to Everest as he stood up. "Is there anything else you would like to address, Mr. Cabernet?"

"No," Everest plainly stated, "that was all."

"Good," Roness replied, offering his hand, "I think we've come to a mutual agreement here. Yes, I think the idea of a Cabernet Foundation will be good, and the liquidation of R&D to be worth the sacrifice. Let's present our idea to the board of directors and get started then."

Act 4, Prologue

A taxicab pulled up in front of Cabernet Manor sometime in the early night. The sun had just set over the Rocky Mountains and light could still be seen around the peaks like an aura. The front light of the manor was turned on, and lights from within could also be seen on. A door opened from the cab and Everest stepped out from the car, wearing a raincoat, a flannel underneath tucked into denim jeans, and boots. He had lengthier hair than when he was an adolescent; of course, he was not an adolescent anymore. He appeared older, a young adult by comparison, although still very much young. He was a fair five feet and eleven inches tall and slim. He opened the trunk of the cab and began to take out one suitcase followed by another. The opposite door from where Everest came out was opened, and a young female stepped out. She was dressed similarly to Everest, although wearing a denim coat and beige trousers. She helped Everest take out the rest of the suitcases and then the two of them made their approach up the steps of Cabernet Manor where Everest placed his luggage down and took out some keys. He opened the door and then they stepped inside together.

The foyer of Cabernet Manor was constructed similarly to how it was in the present age: marble floors and half-panelled walls. The décor was a slight difference to the present, and there were a few lamps turned on around that provided light on this particular evening.

"Alright, we got to be quick," Everest stated. "The plane won't wait for us for more than an hour. We're just here to pick up some winter clothes."

"Oh, but Everest," Vienna expressed, "you promised."

"Do what you have to, but be quick," Everest replied. "We can't waste any time. Go and get some clothes and then come back."

"You know what clothes I need," Vienna insisted. "I am going to go find him."

Everest did not respond as Vienna walked to the left, while he went upstairs and came through to the door on the right. He entered into a corridor foyer with a door ahead of him that went into what was his bedroom. He began to rummage through the dressers and closet to take out some clothes. He laid them out on the bed and began to pick through them. However, as he turned around, he realized he had left the suitcases downstairs. He growled and came out of the room, but rather than go downstairs, he stopped and then went down the corridor. He passed an empty bedroom on his left which had been his sister's bedroom, emptied and plain, passed another room which was transformed into a den, and then past another room to finally reach the end at the last. At the end of the corridor was another bedroom, this one with a balcony and connection to the bathroom between this room and the den. This room was similar to the one that belonged to his sister, but with a bit more personal items, such as photos of Vienna and Everest together, some black and white photos of Vienna as a child, and a photo of a young infant in her arms from a hospital bed. He began to rummage through the closet as he pulled items that belonged to Vienna and placed them on the bed. He opened some drawers in a dresser and found not her clothes, but child clothing. When Everest was finished, he then went down and around to the main foyer again. Everest did not waste another moment to begin to pull the suitcases, one in each hand, towards the staircase but they were particularly heavy together.

"Ugh," Everest groaned, pausing for a moment to catch his breath. He sat down on the steps to take a break and then stood up again. "Vienna, honey, come on! Let's go!"

No response came forth. He paused to listen for a call back, but no voice could be heard except for some muffle of someone speaking as though through a microphone. There was also a cheerful tune playing. He stepped down to the bottom of the staircase, came around to the living room on the right from the main foyer, and saw the room to be dark with nothing more than the light from the television set illuminating the room. It was also found to be amess in the midst of the carpet where numerous construction-based toys were scattered around on the floor. Some loose pieces laid out on the floor around the central carpet in the living room, while other pieces took part of constructs and creations. At the base of a coffee table in front of a sofa that looked towards the television set was a young toddler, at least three-years of age, dressed in overalls with a green long-sleeved shirt underneath. This toddler had smooth medium length light blonde hair and fair skin. He also had light blue eyes that pierced back at Everest as he saw him. The light from the television shined towards him. No response came forth from either Everest or the toddler as they looked at each other, which for Everest was met with sharp breaths as though frozen in fear.

Everest swallowed his fear and remarked, "Charlemagne – boy have you aged up since I last saw you." He continued to grind his teeth as he looked down at the boy. He looked down at the toys again and said, "I see dad has been taking care of you. He never got me this many toys to play with, that's for sure…" Everest looked back at Charlemagne as he simply stared back at him. He sighed and said, "You probably don't even know who I am, do you…"

Charlemagne didn't respond as he looked at Everest with almost a bit of awe.

"What do you want kid? Say something, I can't read your mind," Everest expressed. "Do you need something? Where's your mother?"

Suddenly, Everest heard footsteps on approach from the left as Vienna came around. She stopped at the doorway and dropped her face as she saw Charlemagne on the floor. Charlemagne's blue eyes shot towards her. "*Mutter! Mutter!*" Charlemagne cried out, leaning forward to stand up and rush to her.

"Hello, my little boy!" Vienna gleefully replied, squatting down to embrace him. She then lifted him up. "How is my little Charles? Oh, how long it has been since I last have seen you, and how much I missed you too…"

"Vienna…" Everest interjected, but to no avail. She continued to spin around with Charlemagne in his arms. Charlemagne buried his face into Vienna's chest as he held his mother tightly.

Vienna walked over to the sofa, around the bits and pieces on the floor, and sat down. She placed Charlemagne on her lap and brought a finger to his cheek.

"How beautiful is my little Charles," Vienna expressed. "How precious and handsome is this little boy."

Everest simply stood from the other side of the room as he looked at both of them. Charlemagne began to moan, and his face turn to pout as though he was about to cry.

"Oh, what is it, my dear?" Vienna questioned.

Charlemagne had made fists to his eyes and extended one arm over towards the coffee table where there was an empty bottle.

"Is my little prince thirsty?" Vienna asked. "*Möchtest du etwas zu trinken?* Yes?"

Charlemagne nodded as he brought both fists to his eyes again.

"He's a little thirsty," Vienna said to Everest with a smile. Everest held a plain, unimpressed look on his face. "My dear, could you please fetch him something to drink from the kitchen? See if there is any juice, if not some water."

Everest did not grumble, but simply obeyed his wife's will and picked up the bottle. He walked into the dinette, which in these days had a small round table inside with iron-frame chairs. He came around to the kitchen, which was just as it was in the present but without the table on the other side. He opened the refrigerator and found a pitcher with some juice, poured it into the bottle, and then closed the cap. He then walked back to the living room with the bottle.

"You see, Charles, your father has brought you something to drink," Vienna said, shifting herself in the sofa to give Everest some room. "Come, my dear, sit down."

Everest walked over and sat down, doing so with an uncomfortable look on his face. Charlemagne saw the bottle in his hand and reached over for it.

"Here you go," Everest simply said, passing him the bottle.

"You say, thank you, father," Vienna responded for him. "Can you say, thank you? *Danke?*"

Charlemagne instead looked over to Everest with anxiety. He turned his face and proceeded to drink the juice without acknowledging him. Everest grunted and stood up.

"Alright, well, we don't have much time," Everest remarked, looking down at them. "You've seen Charles, he's grown up a bit since last time we saw him, time to go again."

"Now please, Everest," Vienna replied. "We still have much time to wait."

Suddenly again, the pair turned their faces at the creak of a floorboard and appearance of another person from the doorframe. Derby Cabernet loomed from the other side of the room, a hand in his pocket as he was dressed in a dark suit with a tie. He had a moustache at this time, but his hair was still blonde and at medium length, although starting to turn grey.

"Mr. Cabernet," Vienna greeted with a smile on her face. "It's such a blessing to see you again. We found Charlemagne..."

"So you have," Derby responded in a crude tone. "I had no idea you would be coming in this evening. I also have the faintest idea of where you two have been."

"We've been across Europe," Vienna responded. "Everest, you told me that you told your father where we went before we did, didn't you?"

Everest didn't respond as he brought a hand to his neck.

"Where is Mrs. Cabernet?" Vienna instead asked. "I could not find anyone…"

"We were on the patio," Derby replied in a cold tone. "Ophelia is in the garden. Why don't you join her for a while… I need to talk to my son."

"Yes, of course," Vienna remarked, standing up with Charlemagne in her arms.

Derby stepped out of the dark living room and into the foyer, allowing Vienna to pass through while Everest came around. Derby placed a hand on Everest's shoulder as Vienna went ahead and then they were left alone.

"Come, my son," Derby coldly expressed, walking him across to the library. They came around to the study and Derby closed the door behind him.

Everest walked forward, turned around, and crossed his arms. "If you're going to yell at me, may as well get on with it."

Derby instead looked back at him with a plain face, a little bit of disappointment in his eyes, but no anger. He turned left and came around to his desk where he stopped and looked over to Everest.

"Where have you been?" Derby simply asked. "Did you not think to let either me or your mother know before you and your woman slipped out? It's been how many months since we had last seen each other? Since the last summer at least… for what?"

"We were on our honeymoon," Everest answered, "We went to Europe, and stayed to see all of it, at least the western parts. Look, I knew you or mum would never approve, so why would I bother to waste any time in seeking that approval?"

"And Charlemagne," Derby said, "yet again, you have left him in our care without even asking for our permission, or support in the matter, but presuming in our kindness that we would of course take care of our grandchild."

"You've basically adopted him for yourself since the day he was born," Everest remarked. "You and mum have both made that pretty much clear, so why look for permission when he's already yours?"

"But he's not ours, he's your son," Derby replied. "He's been yours and Vienna's since the day he was born, and what we've done in the least of our abilities is to support the two of you in the raising of that child with expectations that someday when you were ready you could take the reins in raising that child for yourselves. I had thought that now you two were married, it would be that time."

Everest did not respond.

"Of course, I misjudged to believe that given a few years, you could reach where Vienna has been all this time. Since the day Charlemagne has been born, Vienna has been very much a woman, a natural mother to the son, while you... you've yet to reach that manhood that is necessary and which I so hoped would come to you to raise that boy."

"All you ever want to do is insult me," Everest replied.

Derby ignored his remark and instead asked, "When, may I ask, when do you plan to take responsibility for your own creation of this earth and choose to raise Charlemagne as his father?"

"When? I..." Everest paused for a moment and then said. "I don't see why I should. You seem to take more enjoyment in being his father than I would. You may as well have him..."

"He's not mine!" Derby cried out. "He's your son, the fruit of your loins, not mine."

"And I'm supposedly the fruit of yours," Everest replied, "and yet you seem to treat Charlemagne better than you ever did to me. I know you don't yell at him; you don't berate him, you don't have these incessant expectations from him, and most of all I know that you don't hit him. And I don't know, father," he said, eyes tearing, "I don't know if that's because you love him more than you loved me, because he meets those asinine expectations of yours or what."

"Everest…" Derby complained.

"So keep him, father, for all I care. He's yours to keep, even if I were to somehow change my mind. He's better off with you than he would be with me."

"Everest," Derby strictly stated, "don't be a fool." He took in deep breath and sighed. He then walked over to his son and raised his hands. Everest twitched at him, causing Derby to get annoyed and place his hands on his shoulder either way. "Listen to me, please." Derby looked at his son, eyes engaged with his. "I want you to know that I'm sorry. I'm sorry for the expectations that you believe I placed on you, and most of all for the way that I treated you as a child and adolescent. I was wrong. I was wrong to treat you in such a way that no man should ever treat a child. I hear the pain of your heart, a pain of which I myself have inflicted on you most of all, but no more. I'm not here to cause you anymore pain… I was in the wrong in those days, surely I was. I was a drunken fool, shellshocked beyond belief over what I had to go through in the war, in what I had to give up for the sake of the country and empire. I was sick. Very surely, I was a sick man. I wish… I wish I could have loved you as I have loved Charlemagne, with greater patience and kindness than I loved you, but I cannot change the past. I can only assure the mistakes of the past are not made in the future, and a part of that responsibility and wisdom is to beg you to not make the same mistake, or similar mistakes. Please, I implore you, for the sake of Charlemagne, he is approaching the age of reason, and now is the time to be with him more than ever. If you postpone this responsibility to be his father, he will come to resent you, and as a father and a son, myself resented and having resented, I want nothing of the sort. Please, son, stay here and care for your son."

Everest looked at Derby with disdain. He took Derby's hand and slid it off his shoulder, and then he stepped back. He then said, "If you have so much remorse in the way you raised me, then take Charlemagne as your second chance. I – Vienna and I – will not be staying." He then took a step to the side to leave.

"Leave then," Derby said, "but know that when you shall return to this place, it will be empty. If you've chosen to abandon Charlemagne, then I will take it that you are assured of your choice, and I will have to take measures to ensure he is given the best upbringing I could hope to offer."

"Where are you and mum going?" Everest questioned, turning his head to the side as he paused. "Where?"

"To the English countryside at our summer home," Derby answered. "When Charlemagne is ready to enter into school, he'll be going to the same grammar school I went to as a child. A very fine school, and there we will raise him in a fine institution, in a very moral upbringing. This house is yours, for you when you come home, and for you when you choose to stop running away from your responsibility, of being a man."

Everest did not respond as he left the study. He slammed the door shut behind him.

"Stupid, idiot, old fool," Everest muttered under his breath. "He thinks because he's found religion, he can call himself a changed man. He's the same, stubborn and foolish, and to think that I want to take up that burden of a child."

Everest came around to the main foyer, looked out to see that the taxicab was still parked, and then turned around to yell out, "Vienna! Vienna, let's go! It's time to go!" He then picked up the suitcases, took them upstairs, and quickly put together some coats and sweaters from each of their wardrobes, smothered them into their suitcases together, and then take them out. By the time Everest was back in the foyer, Vienna had returned with a puzzled look on her face.

"What is it, my mountain?" Vienna questioned. "What is wrong?"

"Nothing is wrong," Everest replied in a bitter tone, "but my father has given us clairvoyance, so don't you worry about him. He'll be taking care of Charlemagne as long as we need, while we get to travel the world."

Act 4, Scene 1

Everest sat in his lounge chair on the patio in front of his study in the penthouse. The sun beamed down hard upon him, and he wore boardshorts and an open Hawaiian shirt as he laid back with sunglasses on his eyes. The sun passed directly above him, and he stared at it through his glasses. He held his hands behind his head, arms flexed as he did so, and he took in a deep breath and let out a peaceful sigh. He closed his eyes again as he took slow breathes, in and out. He listened to the honks, skids, and overall metropolitan commotion that came ninety stories below. He took in another deep breath and let it out. His body became still as he held this pose and his chest slowly rose, up and down, as he breathed.

"Everest, my dear mountain," Vienna suddenly expressed through the door to the study, "come quick. There is a surprise waiting for you at the front door."

Everest released his arms as he looked over to his wife. She quickly disappeared. He sat up and raised his sunglasses up to his forehead. Everest had recently gotten a haircut that exposed his receding hairline a bit more closely than it did before. He brought his feet around and stood up, putting on his sandals nearby, and then he came around and into his study. Everest held silence as he walked from the study, through the ballroom, and around to the main entrance where Salmar, Allodia, and Vienna surrounded a tall person in front of the main entrance. Everest released his breathe out as he muttered, "Oh no…"

"Hello there, father," Charlemagne greeted from the doorway. He spoke in an East Anglian accent like Derby, although his tone was less deep. "It's been a long time, hasn't it?"

"Charles," Everest greeted in a plain tone, "it has been a while, hasn't it… I didn't anticipate I would be seeing you anytime soon."

"Oh, didn't you now?" Charlemagne questioned, taking his hand to shake. Everest reeled him in for a hug, holding him tightly. "Oof…" he expressed.

Everest let him go and said, "Sorry there, son. Boy, you sure are looking thin and pale. You aren't eating much, are you, or getting enough sunlight for that matter. Nice moustache, just like your grandfather's."

Charlemagne was six feet tall, taller than his father by an inch and Salmar by a few inches, and then his sister and mother by half a foot. He was thin though, as Everest described, boney and lanky with very fair skin, whiter than his mother's and almost sickly. He had a moustache like Derby's at the top of his lips, blonde haired, like his own which was cut short. He wore a mustard yellow short-sleeved collared shirt with a white undershirt underneath. He also wore brown trousers, and his shirts were tucked into his trousers too although they were a bit short for him as they came up to his ankles to reveal his white socks and slacks.

"You on the other hand look well-fed and sunkissed," Charlemagne responded, looking back at him. "I see that a life of luxury continues to sustain you."

"Luxury? Well, I wouldn't go so far to call it such," Everest brushed off. "We've lived the same humble lifestyle that your grandfather passed on to us is all."

"I see…" Charlemagne replied.

"Where've you been, Charlie?" Allodia questioned. "Sal said you were in Britain?"

"Yes, for a while," Charlemagne answered, "been travelling between there and France. In the midst of a project that was supported through Research and Development, but I've heard that's been put out of existence, so that work was put on hold until a beneficiary could be found."

"Oh…" Everest responded.

"Yes," Charlemagne insisted, "anyways, at least you've all been able to add some life to this apartment while I've been away. I hope none of you have touched any of my stuff…"

"I haven't touched any of your stuff, Charles," Salmar replied. "I've left it just as it is after I saw you were using that room."

"Good," Charlemagne said, looking back to his father, "well, it's so lovely to see you all again, but I really should settle in. I've only arrived from Heathrow an hour or so ago, and I am tired."

"Yes, here," Vienna replied, looking to Salmar, "let's help your brother with his things."

"Jeez, how many bags you got with you, Charles?" Everest noted, seeing close to four suitcases as he helped pick one up. "You got that much clothing?"

"No, some of these have important documents, tools and items," Charlemagne responded. "Please do be fragile with them as they are expensive."

"Right…" Everest replied, looking over to Allodia, "Allodia dear, could you get the door for us."

Allodia went around and opened the door to the staircase corridor. Charlemagne walked through first, followed by Vienna, Salmar, and then Everest who looked at Allodia with the same look on their faces. Each of them helped Charlemagne bring his luggage upstairs, and when he was finished, they went downstairs to the parlor where Vienna brought a kettle with some tea. Charlemagne sat in the large armchair like a throne by the coffee table, whereas Salmar and Allodia were on the sofa, and then Everest in the smaller armchair across from Charlemagne. Allodia went on and on with questions to her brother, followed by questions from Salmar while Everest simply sat back and cracked jokes in between.

"Tea is here…" Vienna expressed, bringing down a tray onto the coffee table and then sitting between Everest and Charlemagne, immediately between Allodia and Salmar.

"The revolution of the computer will change the world," Charlemagne expressed as he continued to share in his story. "The advances in computation will advance our abilities to have these devices better the lives of future generations. There are some people who believe that a computer cannot advance anymore than it has without increasing in size; that the processing power of a computer could not be matched even more than it has. At this point we have supercomputers that take up entire rooms, and it was our wish that we could dwindle that size to fit on a desk. If the processing power increases and operating system were to become more user friendly as it has become, we could have these systems incorporated into the difficult areas of human lives – to do menial tasks that would ordinarily require tedious and difficult calculations from a human person. For this reason, the computer is called such because it replaces the menial job of one who computes."

"Would that not put those who do these menial tasks out of the job?" Everest questioned. "I've seen the television sketches, of fears that one day robots, artificial beings with computers for brains, could replace even humans."

"Bah, that's a load of baloney," Charlemagne responded. "Even if we were to hypothetically create such an advanced computer, the computations of a computer could never replace the human mind. A computer will always rely on input and data from a human person; it cannot create on its own or rationalize like the human mind. In a similar way, at the hubris of the transhumanists, one cannot upload the human conscientiousness and mind to circuits, no matter how sophisticated that circuitry may be. For as much as I would like to believe in such a future, it is far too illogical even for me."

Nobody responded and the room grew quiet for a moment. Everest took his tea served by Vienna into his hands.

"Now, augmentations of the human body, increased longevity of our human lives through gene therapy and rejuvenation – that's where my money is at," Charlemagne encouraged. "It is the hope that a person born now could live beyond a hundred years old, and further – the goal is human immortality, and it is there that I can agree and have hope in some of the transhumanist arguments."

"Well now, all that sounds like science fiction," Everest disregarded. "You can't replace the human heart and the human mind with cogs and gears."

"We're not talking about cogs and gears," Charlemagne dismissed. "We're talking rejuvenation and empowering the body to transcend from its predestined end from our births, and doing so through advanced medicine; alas, a subject I wish I could endeavor on if I found the right medical researchers to endeavor with. Perhaps I will use my now free time to do such."

` "I wouldn't know where you'd begin to find those sorts of people," Everest replied.

"There's many of them in the universities; they're a breeding place for this sort of free-thought and creative output," Charlemagne stated. "A place of champions really in the academic and intuitive progress."

"I wish I could say something," Allodia expressed, "but sometimes I don't think even my professors know what they're teaching… I used to think science was so settled, but there's so much we don't know and they don't seem to know with certainty why certain parts of our body do what they do."

"There is still much work to be done," Charlemagne encouraged, "and so if you ever wish to abandon this aspiration of yours to be a pet doctor, then medical research could be to your benefit to expand that level of understanding. The same goes for you, Sal," he said, turning to him. "Did you ever decide on where you would go to university?"

"I… I haven't decided yet," Salmar replied, "but since I was in Harlech, I thought I would take a chance to explore my options."

"You haven't decided?" Charlemagne responded, annoyed at that answer. "My God, what have you been doing all this time while in school? Is there not a single thing that you could wish to put your mind into?"

"Not really," Salmar said. "I was just enjoying my senior year. We had a really good football season, and prom was great too."

"Hmph," Charlemagne simply responded.

"Did you finally ask out Gloria Pasini to be your prom date?" Allodia questioned.

Both Everest and Vienna looked over to Salmar who began to blush. He leaned over slightly as he avoided to look back at them.

"Why the embarrassed look, Sal," Everest said. "Never be ashamed of a girl in your life."

"We had Ms. Pasini at our home as a matter of fact," Vienna confirmed. "Sal brought her to the house after picking her up and going to the prom together. They took lovely photos together."

"Must be a shame that you're all the way here and she's all the way over there…" Allodia remarked.

"Yeah…" Salmar said.

"At any rate," Charlemagne replied, taking hold of the conversation, "you ought to think quickly, Sal, in what you want to do and where you would like to go to be your alma mater."

"I've been talking to dad a lot about what he does for the company, and what all that is like," Salmar expressed. "I think I want to do something like that, managing people, making decisions, and leading the company."

"Business?" Charlemagne questioned. "Hm…"

"I hope I'm not influencing you," Everest remarked. "I also hope I'm not giving the impression that I'm enjoying what I'm doing right now in being in Harlech. The management of this company is difficult, especially since sometimes getting other people to do something can be like guiding a really stubborn ass through a gate. I've raised horses that are better at following directions than these folk in the company, believe me – managing people is… very difficult and stressful."

Charlemagne scoffed and replied, "Now, how hard could it be? Is Mr. Roness and his compatriots giving you that much of a hard time?"

"It's not Mr. Roness, or Mr. Clifford, although a few of the directors on the board can be hard to work with, but it's the people who report to them. We've been trying to implement my fourteen-points for the past two months, and corporate leadership has been having such a hard time following through. I don't know what it is about other human beings that make following directions so difficult; it's nearly impossible to find loyalty. Every day I hear about such and such incident that occurs in which it could have easily been avoided if they followed corporate policy. These people who work for the company are supposed to be educated too, and yet they really either present themselves as wholly ignorant or willfully stubborn."

"People will always be as such," Charlemagne remarked, "but provide them the proper guidance to be led, and they will do as you do. What they need is appropriate leadership."

Everest did not respond to Charlemagne's comment. The family grew quiet for a moment until Charlemagne cleared his throat.

"So, what's happened with R&D?" Charlemagne said. "I was on the phone with Dr. Cockell in London, and he tells me that he was provided notice that in eight weeks time, R&D would cease to exist. His position as Chief Research Officer would be terminated, and many of his colleagues were either also being terminated or transferred to other subsidiary companies, some offered jobs in industries they have no such expertise in. In other words, shutting down R&D has become such a ludicrous undertaking, my question is whose bright idea it was to shut it down?"

Everest did not respond. Nobody answered him.

"And now rather than continuing to assist in the funding of scientific research, I also hear that in its stead there will a new subsidiary moving forward devoted to charitable projects rather than scientific projects, a charitable foundation," Charlemagne expressed. "I find it hard to believe that a man as callous as Mr. Roness could be responsible for that undertaking, although I could believe it was his idea to liquidate R&D."

"As a matter of fact, Charles, Mr. Roness does not make the decisions in the company," Everest told. "I do. I wanted R&D shut down, and I had a very good reason for it: it is a monetary blackhole. Cabernet Industries pumps millions of dollars into that department, millions more than any other department – it has the budget of a large subsidiary, but it does not produce any goods or services. Why in God's good, green earth would it be a wise idea to keep a department like that?"

"It's not about the money," Charlemagne refuted.

"Oh, so was it about the publicity, or the marketing?"

"No, not really," Charlemagne argued, "although we did have a network of connections across the scientific community, and a strong rapport with universities – it was about our contributions to scientific and technological innovation – innovations of which were shared in respective subsidiaries where they fit, if not patents shared on the larger market. What you've done, father, is killed the brains of the company. From now on, Cabernet Industries will never innovate, or be on the cutting-edge of innovation in the global market. What you've done is perhaps the most idiotic thing I have ever heard a company do."

"You shut your mouth," Everest immediately shot back. "You are way out of your depth, and you have no idea of what you're talking about."

"How would it have been possible for Cabernet Electronics to compete in the computer industry, or Cabernet Energy to develop fuel-efficient generators?"

"Yes, and the irrigation systems of Cabernet Food, and ships used in shipbuilding," Everest mocked. "I've heard it all – I've also heard about the missiles, the bullets, the firearms, all being sent to tyrants overseas to fight in wars that cause the deaths of thousands of combatants and civilians alike. Don't proselytize me. You have no idea of what this company does."

"I would hazard a guess that I know more about it than you do," Charlemagne jibed, arms crossed. "It isn't rocket science."

"You know - you're nothing more than a privileged, rich kid who thinks he knows more than he does and thinks that the world revolves around him!"

"You're a classical representation of what's wrong with your generation – hippies in suits, living through the sixties on songs of free love and peace, and now recklessly wielding power and having havoc at the lives of others while willfully ignorant of the consequences."

"What does that even mean?" Everest complained.

"Oh, you know exactly what it means!" Charlemagne shouted, standing up. "You'll just have to wait for it to process in your feeble mind!"

Everest did not respond. Charlemagne walked off and slammed the door shut behind him. He shook his head as he sat in shock. The others were in silence until Vienna began to silently clean up the table.

"You win," Allodia expressed to Salmar, "that was less time than I thought it would be."

"Enough you two," Everest pleaded, "please. Let me believe that there can still be peace in this house, even if your older brother is home."

Act 4, Scene 2

Everest sat at the head of the executive conference room with his head pointed up to the ceiling. He closed his eyes for a moment, took in a deep breath, and then lowered them to continue to listen to the executives speak.

"We've examined a few charitable foundations for several large companies like Cabernet Industries, and we've found so far that this sort of hierarchical structure should work best," Mr. Clifford remarked, presenting a diagram to those seated with them. "The structure is small, like a foundation should be with very few employees. This group would be responsible for the organization of charitable events and fundraisers meant to raise funds for particular projects."

Everest looked at the diagram before him. He then looked back over to Mr. Clifford at his far-right. Clifford was seated with Vienna on his right and Ms. Summers on his left. On the other side of the table, Mr. Holmes, Mr. Bennett, and Mr. Locke were sat. They all sat close together.

"The positions needed to fill would be as such: President and CEO, Vice-President, Operations Director, Public Relations Director, Financial Manager, Communications Manager, and Events Manager. Between Finances, Communications, and Events, those three departments would then need their own coordinators and staff. We would also need to hire an executive assistant for administrative affairs."

Mr. Holmes made a note on a legal pad and then said, "We'll begin to hunt for these roles as soon as possible, perhaps see if any promotions can be made from within."

"No need to search for a President and CEO," Clifford remarked. "We've already found a candidate, highly recommended from Mr. Roness: Yolanda Walters. She's been the senior consultant for a philanthropy organization in Eastern Canada for almost ten years."

"Perfect," Holmes remarked, writing down her name, "I'll reach out to Mr. Roness for us to interview her."

"I would like to be in that interview too, if you'd please," Everest noted.

"Very well," Holmes agreed.

"Now, as for workspace, our options are limited," Clifford remarked. "I discussed with Mr. Bennett, and we can't just clear an entire floor of tenants to make room for a new subsidiary just like that. These tenants have leases that are signed for more than a few years."

"R&D had several sublevel floors," Everest said. "Their sixth sublevel floor if I remember correctly was spacious, had plenty of office and workspace. They even had an office there for their CRO we could use for the President and CEO."

"An office in the sublevel is not the most suitable place for a charitable organization," Locke noted. "We want this office space to stand out and be welcoming for photoshoots and meetings."

"Well, we better make some use of that space," Everest replied, "there's five sublevels there that will otherwise go unused."

"We could transfer one of the other subs down to that floor," Clifford suggested. "It would be best if a larger sub took it, and then we used their space for Cabernet Foundation."

"Any subsidiary in mind?" Bennett asked.

"We can review later," Clifford replied, "but otherwise once all the assets are either sold or moved into storage, those lower levels will have to be condemned until we can find use for them."

"Now let's talk operations," Everest said. "We've settled on a name, Cabernet Foundation, and we've squabbled between differences of charitable organizations versus foundations, but at its heart I want C.F. to be in part an organization that provides funds to important projects that it can support, namely clean-water projects, food and clothing banks, homeless shelters, etcetera. C.F. should extend a hand into every branch and work with branch leadership to see what needs to be done in the community to help, for the sake of marketing," he said, looking over to Locke, "with our Cabernet image in that region."

"I understand your intention, Mr. Cabernet," Clifford responded, "but I find it unrealistic and it unsustainable for the Cabernet Foundation to extend itself so wide."

"If we keep an ear out to every branch, at least one executive vice-president could come to the table with something they would like to help out with in their community."

"However, that intention comes with the presumption that every executive VP would want to help out with their regions," Clifford replied. "Furthermore, what charities that help the poor are we talking about, because in a charitable organization, it is the charitable organization that does those such tasks you described. In a foundation, we provide the capital to be seen as a sponsors of these already in place organizations – in that sense, we gain credit. Do you expect us to open homeless shelters, food and clothing banks, and hospitals in every part of the world? We can't do that. We... we're not the Catholic Church."

Everest frowned at his remark. He grew quiet for a moment. Vienna then replied, "If the Catholic Church, which earns no revenue and yet sustains thousands of clergymen and religious orders around the world is able to also act in all these charitable missions, then why can't we?"

"We're not a religion, Ms. Cabernet," Clifford simply rebuked.

Everest continued to frown. The conversation at the table grew quiet as people flipped pages to move on.

"If we're to endeavor then to support charitable organizations, provide grants and funds," Everest said, "then I want this foundation to support local and grassroot charitable operations – none of the major league charitable organizations –

the bigger the organization, the more likely it is to be corrupt, my father would say…"

The others at the table looked up to him as he finished his sentence. The table grew quiet again.

"Very well, we'll take a note of that demand," Clifford replied. "Moving on…"

Everest seldom spoke for the rest of the meeting. By the time it concluded, he continued to sit back in his chair, looking out towards the window. The other executives proceeded to leave the room, while Vienna readied her purse and then placed a hand on Everest's shoulder. Everest placed a hand on hers. Vienna wore a pink blazer and skirt to the boardroom meeting. He kissed her hand and then looked back up to her face.

"I'll be back in the penthouse in just a bit," Everest expressed. "I'll catch you soon."

"Take it easy, *meine Leibe*," Vienna responded. She then left the room.

Everest was left alone in the board room where he sat back in silence, eyes closed, before he leaned forward and began to go through the documents that were presented to him in the last meeting. Everest made notes in a legal pad as he went through the documents, stopping to pause for a moment and then look to the side. The skies were bright and clear. He took in a deep breath and then reached over to his side to pick up his briefcase. He pulled out some files and began to review them. These were termination notices. Each notice had a letter that was signed in his name, expressing appreciation for their service and giving a brief amble for why their job was being terminated with notice. At the end of these papers was a total list of employees that were served notice, numbering less than one hundred.

"Ms. Summers, could you please bring me the most recent files on the liquidation of R&D," Everest expressed, talking into an intercom on his right.

"Certainly," Summers responded, "give me five minutes."

Everest shut off the intercom and then sat back. He put his hands together at his abdomen and then leaned back in the chair. He closed his eyes again, began to take deep breaths, and then stayed perfectly still as he waited. The breaths came in through his nose, and out his mouth, in through his nose, and out his mouth. He was at peace. He was still. He breathed carefully.

"Mr. Cabernet," Ms. Summers spoke from the side entrance.

Everest jumped. He sat up in his chair and then looked over to Kathleen Summers as she entered into the room. She wore a pinstripe white dress with a black belt around her waist. Her dirty blonde hair was wavier than usual. Everest looked at her. She was slim around the waist, arms too. She looked back at him, and Everest gave a warm smile to her.

"You startled me," Everest remarked with a lighthearted laugh, "I didn't realize I had drifted off. I was just trying to clear my head and I suppose I fell asleep."

"I hope I didn't ruin any sweet dreams," Summers replied, walking over with a stack of papers. "Here are those files you requested."

Ms. Summers stood right next to Everest as he looked down at the files. She placed an arm over the top of the chair as she began to go through them.

"Mr. Roness has been very busy recently seeing through the liquidation of R&D," Summers expressed. "I have all the minutes for his meetings tied with agendas, lists of assets (it's a lot), and current efforts to sell those assets if not where those assets will be transferred to. I also have a list of employee transfer letters, termination letters, and a summary of projects in progress and which ones will be cancelled and others relocated."

"Thank you, Ms. Summer," Everest replied. "I appreciate it."

"It's a lot of reading, so I'll let you get back to it," Ms. Summer responded.

"With this much reading, I may just fall back asleep," Everest joked. "I was having such a pleasant dream as a matter of fact."

"Oh really, what about?"

Everest paused for a moment as he looked down and then back over to her, "You know, it's interesting, I was mountain climbing, not merely rock climbing, but crampons and ice picks, scaling upwards to the peak of a snowy mountain who knows where."

"Mount Everest?"

"Maybe," Everest replied, "I couldn't tell you for sure, but this mountain… it was tall, and the pathway upwards was narrow, and the descent if I were to make a slip and fall… lethal."

"Sounds exciting," Summers pointed out in a dull tone.

"You know what, it wasn't," Everest said, "not in the slightest. I did not feel excitement, I felt stress and anxiety, and despite the view from how high I was: a cosmic view, a serene very light, nearly white background with the sight of planets in the distance, it did little to empower me. I instead felt the weight of the universe on my shoulders, and also a great loneliness. I would look up and the top of the mountain could not even be seen, and yet I continued to climb."

"Hm, interesting," Summer responded.

"Yes, very interesting," Everest replied, "but anyways, thank you for fetching these files for me. I'll let you get back to work."

"Forgive me if it's not my place, but you feel an immense pressure in implementing and seeing Cabernet Foundation launch, aren't you?" Summers pointed out.

Everest did not immediately respond. He looked over to her and gave a kind smile. "I just want Cabernet Foundation to do what it should do: to help other people and not benefit the suits up here."

"And to make Cabernet Industries look like it cares about poor people," Summers said. "You know, the marketing angle."

"There has to be some benefit to Cabernet Industries for this pitch to have worked with the board of directors," Everest responded. "I just don't know how though I'm supposed to see this subsidiary come to life. We're on a set budget, and I want a majority of that money to go to projects rather than salaries. Perhaps they're right. Perhaps my vision for Cabernet Foundation has been too large, and it should instead strictly focus on supporting existing charities than being its own charity."

"Before I was with Cabernet Industries, I used to work for a hospital foundation," Summers stated. "I was the receptionist and at times would assist the administrative assistant in that role. A lot of the events they hosted were attended by doctors, politicians, and hospital administrators and businessmen. They raised thousands of dollars, and sometimes they would receive large donations for their larger projects to fund new equipment or wards. I used to think it was strange that a hospital needed to have its own charity, but then I learned that the government only provide a set amount to individual hospitals to run that anything else to expand quality of care relied on the foundation."

"I did not know that either," Everest replied. "Do you still have contacts with these people you worked with?"

"Yeah, I believe my former boss is still in her current position," Summers said. "Why?"

"Just want to add healthcare improvements to the list of endeavors I wish for C.F. to participate in. So far, I have a list of what I want to see the foundation strictly support, but I want to add healthcare improvements to that list. It'll be important that we make contacts with some of these organizations across Harlech and at other parts of the world, so if you're still in contact with someone there it would certainly help break the ice."

"Ah yes, I see," Summers responded. "I'll have to see if I still have a business card lying around somewhere. Anyways, I'll let you get back to your work."

"Thank you, Ms. Summers... sorry, Kay."

"It's alright, Mr. Cabernet," Summers replied.

"Everest."

"Right," Summers replied, giving an awkward smile before she left. She stopped as she was about to leave and said, "I hope you know the difference you will make in the world in having a charitable organization as a part of the company. It really makes me feel different about the work I do around here, almost like I felt before I came here."

"Thank you, Ms. Kay," Everest responded.

Ms. Summers finally left, and Everest let out a sigh and leaned back in his chair. He looked towards the stack of papers that she had provided him, and then began to slowly go through them one-by-one, skimming headlines and random paragraphs without much intrigue. He skipped entire bunches of paper until finally he decided to just put these copies into his briefcase and then leave the boardroom. He came around to the elevator lobby and called an elevator to go upstairs.

"Ah, there you are, father," Charlemagne greeted as he came out from around the corner of the corridor that led to the chairman office. "I've been looking for you." Charlemagne was dressed in a black suit with a black tie.

Everest sighed and replied, "What do you want, Charles? What are you doing here?"

"I've been keeping myself informed," Charlemagne answered. "I am a shareholder after all – it would only be right to keep myself as informed as possible for a company I am invested in. I have to say, you've quite outdone yourself these past few months."

"I'm not looking for your criticism or praise," Everest said in a bored tone. "Save it for someone who cares."

"I wouldn't waste my breath on deaf ears," Charlemagne replied, "but I will make another plea that you reconsider your actions against the R&D department. You talk about taking a step towards charitable ambitions, but you willfully ignore the

180

detrimental harm that shutting down the R&D department will have. You fail to see the larger scheme of things, the bigger picture, and what more good R&D could do than a charitable office that gives money away in a marketing scheme."

"I'm not going to change my mind, Charles."

"Oh, but father please," Charlemagne pleaded. "Where is your compassion? You've willingly allowed this corporation to lay-off a hundred employees."

"Less than a hundred," Everest corrected, tensing his hands around the handle of his briefcase, "and I'm sure these folk will be fine. They'll be receiving severance packages when at this much notice they shouldn't have, and those being terminated are all skilled workers who will find jobs elsewhere."

"You are so certain of yourself, so? These people have committed their lives to service this company, and you ignore them. You're a hypocrite."

"Goodbye, Charles," Everest remarked as he looked up to see the elevator arriving. "I'm going back to the penthouse. Please do not follow me."

"Hmph," Charlemagne simply responded.

Everest stepped into the elevator and swiped his card to go upstairs. The elevator doors then closed, and he looked back at an annoyed Charlemagne, arms crossed, looking back at him from the other. Once the doors closed, Everest let out a much needed sigh.

Act 4, Scene 3

"Here we are," Everest expressed as the car came to a halt, "after months of waiting for the season to restart, it's time we finally get a chance to catch a game."

Everest sat with Salmar in the cab of a taxi that pulled up at the front steps of Polaris Arena. Salmar was dressed in a hockey jersey, while Everest wore a leather coat, dark grey trousers and a collared fleece shirt tucked in. The hockey jersey that Salmar wore was black with thick double red stripes around the upper arms and a single thick red stripe around the base. At the sides of his arms were in white numbers '22' and on the front portion of the jersey was the simple depiction of an evil greyish-black wolf-like dog with pointed ears and red eyes. The dog had sharp teeth and fur around its lower lip like a goatee. At its forehead was a third red eye. At either side from its nose, it had red whiskers that came out like smoke. To contrast the black fabric of the jersey with the logo, a white outline surrounded the beast. Salmar moved out of the cab first while Everest leaned forward to pay the cab driver in cash. He then moved out and saw the surname of the jersey that he wore, 'Fesette.' Everest stood up from the cab and closed the door behind him, turned around, and saw the many more fans gathered around the Matilpi Street entrance of Polaris Arena.

The pair made their way towards the main entrance to present their tickets, and on their approach they each saw the large red banners that advertised tonight's game. Each banner had the same logo on Salmar's jersey, but with the words above that read, 'Polaris Arena' and below, 'October 2nd, 1989 – 07:00PM' followed by 'Harlech Hellhounds vs. Seattle Totems.' The pair made their way to the ticket booth where they presented their tickets and then walked inside and made their way to their seats.

"Do you want anything to eat?" Everest questioned, eyeing the various food stands. "Gosh, I guess we should have saved some room…"

"Yeah, I guess so," Salmar responded, looking about as they went along. "I'm honestly good though."

Everest eyed some fans with tall glasses of frothy beer and face paint. They exhibited hype as they bantered with each other. He looked over to one particular stand that served beer.

"Wow, look at that," Everest said, seeing the various different sized and designed cups that one could buy beer from. "Say, I wouldn't mind if I spent this game having just one beer with my boy. You're eighteen anyways."

"Legal drinking age in B.C. is nineteen," Salmar corrected, "it's a crime to sell or give alcohol to a minor."

"Bah, what government can tell me it's a crime in one place but not another to give alcohol to my own grown son?" Everest expressed, looking at the stand. "Go and find our seats, sport. Your old man is going to get you a beer."

Salmar did not argue with his father. He instead let his dad walk into the line-up of people. After a moment, Salmar left and went as his father directed him. Everest stood in line as it slowly progressed with each person ordering and receiving their order of beer. As he waited, Everest saw the various types of fans that were stood around: regular people, to regular people with fan-attire to full blown fanatics. The vast majority of people in the hall that wore fan-wear were Harlech Hellhound fans, while one or two persons could be seen donning the green hockey jersey of the Seattle Totems with its white-black indigenous art design of an eagle totem. Everest did not have to wait too long to move up to the front of the line and approach the cashier.

"Two beers, please," Everest requested, putting his hand in his jacket to fetch his wallet. "Tall glasses, twenty-four ounces. How much is that?"

"Two talls?"

"That'll come as thirty-dollars," the sales attendant said, punching in to the cashier box.

"Thirty-dollars? For two beers? You've got to be kidding?!"

"I'm not, sir. Did you want the two beers?"

Everest nodded and placed forth two twenty dollar bills from his wallet. He was returned a five dollar bill and some bits of change as it was little over thirty-dollars. He placed the coins into his pocket and put the five dollar bill into his wallet with the other numerous bills he carried. He then stepped to the side to wait for the two beers, at which point they came after a few minutes wait and then he took them both into his hand and carefully carried them outwards. Everest walked around to the other side of the stadium corridor, and then up a flight of stairs to come out to the large arena.

Polaris Arena interior was large and consisted of thousands of seats that looked down towards a small hockey ice rink. The seats were cushioned and had many rows. Everest went down the steps to come around to the mid-section where his seat was with Salmar. He passed Salmar the beer and then came down into his own seat.

"Well, isn't this nice," Everest expressed. "I've never been in this place before. When did they open?"

"I don't know."

"I remember I went to a hockey game once, when I was young. It was with some friends from boarding school. We got permission to go to a hockey game because my friend, Ethan, his dad got them tickets but he was too busy to go with him so he made a deal with his son to get all his friends tickets, which I was included in. Anyways, we went but it wasn't here… it was down south, closer to the boarding school in a smaller arena than this one. Also, the hockey team in those days wasn't the Hellhounds, but the Harlech Harbourmen… a lot less catchy I suppose."

Everest continued to look around at the many seats. He also noticed the VIP seats above all the rest, individual boxes where people could sit down with plenty of room to themselves. These seats were also isolated from the rest of the crowd. Above these seats there were larger boxes with windows that looked down below, one of which Everest could see was where the sports announcers could be seen.

"Well, I'm glad we were able to make it here," Everest expressed, continuing to look around, "I needed a night out of the apartment... boy, your brother. You're frankly lucky you didn't have to grow up with him all that much."

"Why's that?"

"Why's that? Sal, you know your brother and what he's like. He's a nightmare, just... a really difficult man to work with, oh and he's so full of himself," Everest said. "I've really never met anyone like him, and I just don't know where he gets it from sometimes because his dad – sorry, my dad, was never like that for it to have been him."

Salmar gave an awkward chuckle and replied, "I never knew grandpa to say."

"Yeah, I know you didn't, Sal. You didn't get to know either of your grandparents. Although come to think of it, he does sort of remind me of my mom's dad. He had a sort of cockiness to him, although we never really got to see much of him except once or twice. He didn't like the family either."

"Who was that man again?"

"He was your maternal grandfather, Sal."

"But what was his name?" Salmar asked. "Charles told me about him once. He was an admiral?"

"Louis Mountbatten," Everest responded. "From what little I know about him is that he's related to the Queen, which I suppose means we're related to her in some way too."

"Yeah, that's what Charles was telling me. He was saying that we were British royalty and how he thought we should all be knighted and attempt to restore ties with that side of the family."

"Typical," Everest remarked, shaking his head. "I've never talked to anyone from that side of the family since the last time I saw granddad, and then he died and your grandma died – not together, of course. She sort of… withered away to say the least after my dad died, which was very sad to hear about although I never got to see it. She lived with her folks which I suppose was a mistake seeing how they neglected her. I don't carry a lot of regrets, Sal, but letting that side of the family take care of my mom… that's up there in my list."

"You have regrets, dad? I thought you didn't have regrets."

"We all have regrets, Sal," Everest stated. "Even if we don't admit it – there's always something that bothers us or that we wish to have gone different. We all have those desires that bother us and make us suffer. I don't believe it's possible to let go without repressing, like the Buddhists seem to think."

"What's the top of your list then?"

"Oh, well, Sal," Everest remarked, "it's got to be never getting a college education, or having an idea what I genuinely wanted to do with my life professionally. I wasn't a dumb kid in school. Neither your mom or I were, although we made dumb decisions. Heck, we were in love, so madly in love that we didn't care about the world around us. She almost didn't finish high school, and we certainly didn't want to waste our time in school anymore either when we were both so passionate about travelling around the world."

"Yeah, Charles told me about this too," Salmar replied. "How before Allodia was born, you guys visited practically every country in the world… when you lied to your dad that you were both were going to university."

Everest cleared his throat and responded, "We didn't lie about anything… we just gave the wrong expectations. I don't regret the travels we did, and we didn't get to visit every country in the world. We spent a lot of time in Europe, especially West Germany and Austria. We got involved in the anti-war demonstrations, especially when the Berlin Wall was constructed. We also did a lot of travelling in the United States, and most of that time was on the road, visiting place to place, sleeping in nothing but a van and such. We also went to Australia, New Zealand, and the islands around those parts. Nothing too fancy... and don't think it was all me, your mother advocated to see the entire world. She wanted to meet someone of every race, of every nation and be able to say hello in their language. She has a very kind heart, your mother, that's why I fell in love with her."

"How many countries do you guys suppose you visited?"

Everest thought for a moment.

"Supposing there's around two-hundred or something," Salmar added.

"Probably, thirty-five or so... how much is that? Less than twenty percent?" Everest stated. "Yeah, it'd be nice to finish that dream of ours, but you know, just like your grandpa, I don't think I'll get to finish my lifetime aspiration the same way he didn't get to finish his..." he said. "Wherever we end up when we die, he's probably looking down upon me a little glad that I stopped travelling the world too. I've got too many responsibilities, a lot of trust – people who trust me, and... I guess comforts that I have, to want to even go back to that lifestyle."

"What about mom?"

Everest shrugged and replied, "She's probably the same. She'd say we're too old for that lifestyle..."

The pair began to quiet down as the pre-game show began and the lights in the arena dimmed. The pre-game show did not last very long and before long the announcer moved on to officiate the singing of the national anthems. The crowds stood up as they removed their hats and headdresses, and Everest awkwardly stood up and looked around as he saw others place a palm on their chest at the singing of the Canadian national anthem, *Oh Canada*. Afterwards came the Star-Spangled Banner, and then the face-off at center ice.

Everest observed the hockey players on the ice, a majority of whom were older males in their late twenties to early thirties. This age range was where the bell curve peaked, and then at either end were those in their late thirties plus and early twenties below. The player whose jersey Salmar wore, 'Fesette' was in his early twenties. In addition to the black jersey, the home uniform for the Harlech Hellhounds consisted of black pants and black shin guards with thick red stripes around them. The opposing team, the Seattle Totems, wore in their away uniform a white jersey with green around the shoulders and gloves. There were also yellow-green stripes around the upper arms and lower half of the jersey. The pants and shin-guards were both green, and there was a yellow stripe around the shin guards.

The game proceeded from period to period, the Harlech Hellhounds in good hustle to the opposing team, scoring twice in the first period. In the second period, the Seattle Totems scored but were shy in making it even, but in the third period they brought it around not just once, but three times to make the score five-two.

When the game was over, Everest and Salmar left the venue and began to walk down Matilpi Street together. They came around to the base of Cabernet Tower and had to sneak into the loading bay zone to get back into the building. They then came around to the elevator lobby in the basement where they waited for a minute. Salmar held a wide smile on his face and looked over to his father.

"Hey dad," Salmar stated.

"Yeah, son?"

"Thanks for taking me out tonight," Salmar remarked. "I didn't anticipate we'd actually get to see a hockey game together."

"Why not? I told you I would get us tickets to the first game of the season," Everest responded. "Am I not a man of my word?"

"You are," Salmar agreed, putting his arm around his dad's shoulder. Everest put an arm around his son's shoulder too, and the two came together for an embrace. Everest pat his son's back and then the elevator arrived, and the two of them went upstairs to the penthouse.

Everest quietly opened the penthouse door, and the two snuck inside and came around to the second floor where they stopped.

"Thanks again, dad," Salmar remarked. "I'll see you tomorrow. Love you."

"I love you too, son," Everest replied, seeing him off. "Rest easy."

Everest watched Salmar walked down and enter into his bedroom. He shut the door behind him, and then Salmar came to his shared bedroom with Vienna, opened the door, and walked inside. Vienna was sat up in bed with a book in her hand and glasses. She looked over to Everest as he entered inside.

"I thought you said the game would finish around ten o'clock? It's nearly midnight," Vienna expressed with slight concern. "Is everything okay?"

"Oh, yes, quite alright," Everest replied, chuckling. "We had a good time, the game went on a little longer than I thought, and then we walked home since the rain stopped. By the time we got here, we realized we'd have a hard time getting into the building after-hours, but we managed through the loading bay with my key card."

"Good riddance," Vienna answered, "I may have sent the dog searching for you two."

"No matter, we're okay," Everest said, removing his coat and preparing to go to bed. "Sal had a good time, and so did I."

"Good."

Everest finished removing his clothes and putting on his pajamas. He brushed his teeth and then came out to sit down at the side of the bed.

"You've been so busy with the launch of Cabernet Foundation," Vienna said, "I'm glad you were able to find a night to enjoy yourself."

"Ugh, don't remind me," Everest replied. "We've got that fundraiser next week... it's slowly dawning upon me."

"You'll do fine."

"You know, Sal and I were chatting at the rink before the game started about how I wish I actually went to college, but instead we went around travelling about... He made a good point about how we never really got to see the world as much as we thought we were."

"I seem to remember that was because you didn't want to get out of your comfort zone," Vienna remarked. "I wanted to see every nation at the time."

"I did too," Everest responded. "I did too, but it made think... do you think there'll ever be a time where we could see that through? To actually meet every people and learn to say hello in every language?"

Vienna did not immediately respond. She looked at Everest and gave a warm smile. "The ambition has passed me, my mountain. There are more important things to fess about, but who knows... God only knows, perhaps sometime, we will get to see much of the world again..."

"Yeah, that'd be nice..."

Act 4, Scene 4

"Welcome, welcome, one and all, to the Cabernet Foundation fundraiser launch party!" a male spoke from the front of a stage. "My name is Howard Graham…"

"… and I'm Leanne McClaren," a female spoke next to him.

"And we are your hosts on behalf of the entire Cabernet Foundation for tonight's event."

Everest looked down from the side of the stage at some cue cards he had readied.

"Now, before we officially begin tonight's fundraiser," Leanne said, "we would just like to remind everyone for what cause we are here to seeking to raise money for. The Harlech Health Care Society, representing our largest hospital, Harlech General, the University of Harlech Teaching Hospital, and the Lincoln Centre, is seeking to support the Harlech General Foundation and raise funds for the construction of a new psychiatric facility on the same grounds."

"That's right," Howard affirmed, "tonight's goal is to help raise just one-million dollars, but we're not just going to stop there as the total capital cost of this new facility is projected to be at forty-million dollars, and the provincial government has already pledged to cover thirty-million, so we want to go above and beyond to help meet the hospital's goals for advanced care in mental health and substance abuse."

"Now, before we officiate the start of tonight's fun-filled night, we would like to introduce Mr. Everest Cabernet to the stage to give a few words."

Leanne extended a hand towards where Everest was stood. He then stepped forward and made his way onto the stage, waving over to the audience of a few hundred people who were in attendance. He accepted the microphone from Leanne, and then she and Howard stepped back so that he could speak. The audience applauded to Everest, and he continued to wave until the crowd settled down. He wore a black tuxedo with a bow tie. He had also cut his hair again, which showed his increasingly receding hairline.

"Thank you, you two," Everest accepted, "and thank you everyone who bought tickets to come to tonight's lovely event that has been two months in the making. We are excited to have you all here not just for the cause of the evening, but also because today marks the official launch of our charitable foundation, Cabernet Foundation."

The audience applauded.

"Should a corporation be involved in the social and economic stewardship of the local citizens it does business from? My son recently bored me with the technical details of what it means to be a corporate entity, that in the eyes of the law, they are persons just like you and me despite being mere entities on paper. If a corporation is to be considered a person in the eyes of the law, then I suppose it should act like a decent person too, and with the amount of wealth and affluence that Cabernet Industries is lucky to generate, I believe it is long deserving that this corporation, of whom I am the fifth generation descended from Sennett Cabernet, begins to give back to the people, all of you, to whom we owe our success to. I think that we should give you all a big round of applause."

The audience applauded. Everest joined in as he clapped with one hand.

"Just as a reminder, Cabernet Industries intends to match the donations received tonight. Our partners here at Elysium Casino have also pitched in to cover the costs of tonight's events, so half of all profit tonight will be going to our charitable cause. If we make our one-million dollar goal, which let's be honest, should be a piece of cake, then let's aim even further to five million dollars, and we can get this new psychiatric facility built in no time to serve the good people of Harlech, and all those who suffer from psychiatric illness and substance abuse, the care they need in no time."

The audience then applauded again. Everest returned the microphone to Leanne and then walked off stage. He threw the cue cards in a bin and then made his way around to rejoin the others as they gravitated into the casino. He met with Vienna and Allodia as they left the ballroom to enter into a corridor on the second floor of the hotel. The corridor had a tall window from the ground floor that looked outwards to the highway. Vienna was dressed in a glittering white dress with one sleeves, while Allodia wore a silk white one that was sleeveless.

"Where's your brother?" Everest questioned Allodia as they regrouped. "I thought I saw him with you."

"Charles is… around, somewhere," Allodia replied. "He said he was going to have a look around. I don't think he was going to stay very long."

"Hm…"

"Come on, dear," Vienna remarked, taking his arm. "Let's join the party."

The couple began to walk towards the main entrance into the casino at the end of the corridor where security let them in. Even the security in the venue were dressed in formal wear. They had ear-pieces that went into their suits, nearly unnoticeable that they had both radios and handcuffs around their belts. They were also all very tall and intimidating persons. They entered into the casino floor without issue, stopping for a moment before they continued onwards to look around.

"I've never been in a casino before," Vienna acknowledged. "I wouldn't even know what to do, I've never gambled, nor do I want to."

"You made your gamble with me when you married me," Everest corrected to her dismay. "If you go downstairs, I think there's supposed to be live entertainment. You girls could go and enjoy yourselves there if none of these games are to your interest."

"What are you going to do?" Vienna questioned. "You stay away from those slot and other bright machines. They are the snares of the devil."

"I'm not going to go to the machines, I'm going to go play cards," Everest said. "Don't worry about me. You and Allodia go find something you'll both enjoy."

Elysium Casino had an immense casino floor, rows upon rows of slot machines on one end of the oval casino floor, met with tables upon tables of tabletop games. Around the center of the casino floor was a triangle opening to the ground floor below with stairs at either side and a cascade fountain down to a circular bar where there were round tables and stools scattered about. Some additional slot machines could be seen beneath the main floor where it was darker and easier for one to lose themselves.

Everest led Vienna and Allodia to the top of the stairs that went down, and then saw them off as they went to go enjoy the live entertainment. Meanwhile, Everest proceeded leftwards to the tabletop games where there was roulette, poker, and blackjack games.

"Oh look, it's the man with the charitable heart," a voice called out. "Mr. Cabernet, come over here!"

Everest turned and saw Roness wave over to him as he stood at a table where a game of poker was about to be played.

"Mr. Cabernet, have you played poker before? Specifically, the Texas special," Roness asked. "Either way, come and sit down."

"I have played poker before," Everest replied. "Not professionally though. I'm just an amateur. Although it seems like you have enough players."

At the table there were seven people seated, including Roness, but not including the dealer at the head of the table.

"Not at all. We can make room," Roness responded. "LeClair, why don't you leave us?"

A man nodded and stood up. He left the group, and Everest came over to sit down. Roness then sat down as well.

"The game is Texas Hold'em," the dealer announced. "The buy-in is two-hundred dollars, per player."

Everest took out some cash from his wallet and then placed it down at the table. The dealer gave out chips to the players totalling two thousand credits, and then afterwards he began to shuffle the cards.

"Why not some introductions before we get started," Roness expressed. "My name is Dwight Roness, CEO of Cabernet Industries."

"Dr. Mark Lundstrom," the second person greeted. "Medical Doctor."

"Jack Kong."

"Alexander MacTavish," the fourth person greeted in a Scottish accent, "and as long as we're sharing our job titles, mine is mayor for the City of Harlech."

"A pleasure to finally get to meet you, Mr. Mayor," Roness replied, looking to the next person.

"Sean Irwin, Vice President at Penultimate Hospital."

"Everest Cabernet."

"Welman Parr."

"Gentlemen, please ante up," the dealer asked. Since Welman Parr was on the left-hand of the dealer, both he and Everest were required to put chips in as part of the blind: Welman with a small blind at twenty and Everest with a large blind at forty.

The dealer proceeded to hand out cards to each person on the table, one and then another. Everest looked at his cards: he was given a queen of clubs and eight of hearts. As Everest looked at his cards, the person on his left made their move; Sean Irwin decided to call and put forty in. Alexander MacTavish also called, while Jack Kong folded and Dr. Lundstrom raised the bet by twenty. Roness called his raise and put in sixty. Welman called and put in forty more for a total of sixty, and then the table went around again, and everybody called and put twenty more until it came to Dr. Lundstrom. By the time it came back around to the doctor, he checked and the game proceeded. The dealer put down three cards before him: a nine of hearts, a five of hearts, and a ten of spades.

"So, does this table like to make light chat while they play poker, or are you all a dry crowd? I can at least make conversation with Everest and the dear mayor, I think," Roness expressed as they went around the table. Nobody raised or folded; they all checked. "Anyone?"

"I think most of us would like to concentrate on the game ahead," MacTavish replied.

The dealer put down the fourth card to add to the other three. The card was an eight of diamonds. There was a minor twitch in Everest's eyebrow.

"Well, if that's the case then I'll be ordering a margarita," Roness said. "Waiter!"

The game came back around to Welman to decide what to do. He folded. Irwin then raised, putting down another twenty. MacTavish folded, but Lundstrom and Roness called, and it came back around to Everest. He looked at his cards again, called the bet, and then it came back to Irwin. Irwin raised it by another twenty.

"If I had to hazard a guess, it would be that someone has some good cards," Roness said, looking at Irwin. He did not illicit a reaction. Lundstrom called, while Roness folded. "Well, Mr. Cabernet?"

Everest raised by twenty to call Irwin's raise and another twenty to send it around the table again. Lundstrom and Irwin both called. Everest then checked.

"Jack of spades," the dealer announced, placing the fifth card in the community pool.

Everybody who remained checked proceeded. The pool was now at five hundred and forty. By the time it came back around to Everest, the players who remained showed their cards, starting with him.

"Straight," Everest announced.

Irwin and Lundstrom placed their cards before themselves. They had an ace of diamonds and seven, and a ten of clubs and jack of clubs, respectively.

"Very good, sir," the dealer remarked to Everest. He set aside a few chips from the pot, and then pushed the rest over to Everest. The players proceeded to give their cards over to the dealer.

"Well done, Mr. Cabernet. You said you were an amateur at this game?" Roness questioned.

"Nothing more," Everest responded, counting the chips. The dealer had taken around sixty chips worth as part of a house rake.

The game proceeded to continue in this fashion, except the persons required to put in blinds rotated clockwise with every play. Roness collected a few martini glasses at his side, and Everest slowly drank a scotch with ice. As the game went on, players bought themselves drinks and most of the same players went steady until Welman Parr lost all his money and had to buy-in. Shortly afterwards, Dr. Lundstrom cashed out and left with less money than he entered in. A man approached to take the doctor's place, putting a hand on MacTavish's shoulder.

"Do you mind if I join?" the man questioned, speaking in a North English accent.

"Certainly," MacTavish responded, "we know it won't stop you though."

The man laughed and went to sit down in Lundstrom's seat.

"Who's your friend, Alex?" Roness questioned.

"We're doing introductions," MacTavish encouraged the man. "Why don't you let our friends here know who you are and what you do in this great city."

"Of course," the man replied, "my name is Victor Buckley, and I am the current Executive Vice President of Paladin Group."

"Hm," Roness responded, "interesting. Nice to meet you, Mr. Buckley, I don't think we've met before. I've met some of your colleagues though. My name is Dwight Roness with Cabernet Industries."

"Which of my colleagues have you met?"

"Your boss, Mr. Dunn, and I work with another colleague of yours who worked for Paladin Group for a while, Mr. John Bennett."

"Oh right, John is over at Cabernet Industries," Buckley remarked. "I forgot he was there."

MacTavish laughed. Roness gave a sly smile.

"Would Mr. Montgomery be here by chance? I've yet to meet him in person," Roness questioned. "I've heard a lot about him, both the positives and the negatives."

"Ah, but don't believe the negatives," Buckley assured him. "He's been the victim of vicious rumors for more than twenty years. Unfortunately though, he is out of town at the moment. Are you from Harlech, Mr. Roness?"

"Not really," Roness replied. "I'm South by blood, Texas born and raised, but spent most of my time out on the East Coast."

"Trust us when we say then that Mr. Montgomery is an upright character, a sort of philanthropist to this city in the service he provides."

"Through Paladin Group?" Roness questioned. "I didn't realize Paladin Group also endeavored to establish its own foundation," he joked.

"Not in that sense," Buckley said, "but in the overall good that we do for this city, like all corporations."

Everest frowned as he overheard the conversation. He then eyed the *turn*, the placement of the fourth card on the table by the dealer, and it was an ace of spades, and in his hand, he held an ace of hearts and king of diamonds. On the table there was a king of spades too.

"I'm going to raise," Buckley remarked.

"I'll fold," MacTavish announced. "I'm also going to cash out after this round. I have to get going."

"I just sat down, Alex," Buckley whined.

"I'll call," Roness said, putting his money forward (the stakes had gone up at this time, blinds bets were triple what they were initially).

"I'll also call," Everest remarked.

"Brave men, are we?" Buckley heartedly laughed. "How far will you go though?" he asked, raising even further.

"I think you're bluffing," Roness expressed, calling his raise, "and even if you weren't, I have better cards than you."

Everest looked over at both of them and then silently called the raise.

"All in," Buckley remarked.

Roness frowned at that demonstration. Everest could see him gritting his teeth through the tension in his jaw.

"Damn you, I'll fold," Roness beckoned. "Your move, Everest."

Everest looked at his cards again and then at the cards in the community: king of spades, two of hearts, five of spades, and ace of spades.

"I'll call and match," Everest said (not going all in since he held more than Buckley).

The dealer placed the *river*, or fifth card, and it was an ace of clubs. Since Buckley could not bet anymore, they revealed their cards instead.

"Flush," Buckley announced, showing a queen of spades and jack of spades."

"Straight," Everest remarked, putting down his cards.

"Rotten luck," Buckley chipped. "I won't buy-in. I've had bad luck all night. Good game, gentlemen. Enjoy yourselves."

"Yes, good game," MacTavish agreed. "I'm out for the night. A pleasure to meet you gentlemen. Let's stay in touch."

The two men left, and the seats were left empty as another round continued with five.

"What a strange man," Roness balked. "The pair of them. I can't stand those men from Paladin Group, Bennett included. He can be a real problem on the board, essentially a crony for that Oswald Montgomery."

"Doesn't Paladin Group provide security services for the building?"

"Unfortunately," Roness simply said, "they are cheap and decent at least. That mayor too, he's another character... him and his political party. Very tough to deal with, and controlling. For example, I heard they've been opposing government plans to regionalize healthcare, to amalgamate the hospitals under a single corporate entity to centralize healthcare – that sort of rebellious spirit I can support, but then it comes around in stubbornness towards us. Those times they can be too... arrogant and unsupportive of our plans for the city, and lacking in the American spirit to let the people build. I don't know whether to love them or hate them at times.

"The health authorities are the future of healthcare in this province and will revolutionize the nation," Irwin rebuked. "The Harlech Health Authority is inevitable. As an American, you can take plenty of envy in our progressive and modern way of healthcare services."

"As an American, I have to say I don't agree with what you're saying," Roness replied. "Your disregard for what the invisible hand of the free market can provide, and what will lead to vast corruption in a larger organization and a dwindling in the standard of care. Eventually then who knows... maybe this communistic government of yours will just start to euthanize the lot of you, all at the taxpayer's immense expense. How's that for compassionate care?"

No further comment was made, and another round began. Everest received his cards.

"I'll fold," Everest said.

"This man," Roness expressed, "he's fifty-fifty each round to either stay or fold. Where's your sense of adventure, man?"

"Oh, I'm plenty riled up," Everest assured him, sipping his scotch, "Poker and games alike are my sense of wilderment."

"Really?" Roness questioned. "I had no idea you even knew adventure. Perhaps there is a fun bone in you after all." He then laughed.

Everest glanced to his right and saw Charlemagne, dressed in a tuxedo, wandering around. He quietly groaned as he made his approach to their table as a new round began.

"Hello, father," Charlemagne greeted. "Hello, Mr. Roness."

"Well, well, if it isn't the crown prince himself," Roness expressed. "How're you doing, Charles?"

"Fine," Charlemagne responded. "Just fine."

"I didn't realize you two had met before," Everest remarked.

"Of course we have," Roness replied. "From the many times this rugrat has barged into my office. If he weren't your son, I would have gotten a restraining order by now."

"Hm..." Charlemagne groaned, looking down at his father, "I should have known I would find you here of all places, indulging yourself."

"Yes, well, it is a charity event, and what good is a charity event if you can't have fun playing your favorite card game?" Everest replied. "Why don't you loosen up and sit down."

"I would rather not," Charlemagne expressed, looking down with disdain at the card table. "I find the frivolous spending of money on a game of chance to be most unwise."

"Suit yourself, son," Everest replied, looking at his cards. Charlemagne stood behind him. He had a jack of clubs and ten of clubs.

"There is a lot of people here, wealthy people," Charlemagne expressed, looking about. "I hope your charity event is doing what you hoped it would do, father."

"People like fun, and like a company who knows how to have fun," Everest remarked. "All this money is going to do a tremendous amount of good for the people of Harlech."

"All in," Roness said.

"You really believe that there is some sort of redistribution of wealth going on about here?" Charles questioned as his father put his chips in too. "The rich giving to the poor? Why not cut the middleman and just given the entire budget for R&D to charity than endeavor on this charade?"

Everest growled as he attempted to concentrate before him. The cards played were a queen of clubs and ace of clubs, as well as a ten of diamonds and six of spades. The next card played was revealed as a jack of hearts.

"Dammit," Everest swore under his breath.

"Alright, show 'em cards," Roness remarked, revealing his as a jack of diamonds and jack of kings. "Straight."

Everest tensed his jaw and dropped his cards down. He had just two pairs.

"Oh, nice try, Mr. Cabernet, but this round is mine," Roness said, taking in the pot. "Thank you."

Everest sighed, stood up, and fixed his coat. "I think I've had enough," he said. "Give the rest of my winnings to the cause of this event. I'm going to get a drink." He then left.

Charlemagne stayed behind while Everest went downstairs to the bar. He sat down atop of a stool and then received a scotch on the rocks. Charlemagne came around soon afterwards to sit down next to him.

"What do you want, Charles?" Everest sighed. "Why can't you leave me be?"

"You're a fool," Charlemagne expressed. "The odds that card would have been a king of clubs, or even just a king, were incredibly low. Your senseless addiction to take risks cost you the equestrian centre, and it cost you that game."

"I really wish you'd just learn to shut up," Everest responded in a rude tone. "I'm sick of hearing you talk. There's nothing of value that comes out from your mouth."

"Hmph," Charlemagne replied, "well then old man, how's this? Your efforts here tonight have fattened the wallets of the casino owners, a Greek man who bought this place on sale from the Chinese mafia after terrorists had shot it up years ago. You've allowed the rich men and women of this city to enjoy themselves in their sinful delights, and all this event will have built is a psychiatric building that would have otherwise been built at taxpayer's expense. Bravo."

"Ugh…"

"And to add to that, you continually allow yourself to be blindsided and manipulated by that cartel, the board of directors, who have no interest in the good of Cabernet Industries, but only seek to carve it out with your presence being a blessing to do so."

"You're cynical, Charles."

"I'm expressing the truth, father," Charlemagne replied. "Since I've returned to Harlech, I've been sure to keep myself busy, especially as a concerned shareholder in a company that bares our ancestral name. I've been sure to look in depth at what your actions have done for the good of the company – frivolous spending in the restructuring of the human resources and occupational health and safety department is one thing, but did you know that the property of Site C was sold?"

"What?"

"Site C was sold to a British geological company," Charlemagne said," which was the result of downsizing measures at the Africa Branch to settle all the losses incurred as a result of a very prolonged and expensive incident investigation, financial compensation from the heart of a very generous chairman, and loss of profits in the delay of work at that site. The results of which too have resulted in the layoff of hundreds of workers; men now without jobs, some of them already victim of that senseless tragedy earlier this year."

"So, the geological company that's taken over will just rehire them."

"Possibly, but not for many months and likely at a lesser pay."

Everest sighed and replied, "You're trying to demoralize me, Charles."

"I'm only giving you the truth in your efforts," Charlemagne responded. "Site C is not the only asset to be sold to foreign buyers. I looked at all the assets on the market from R&D, and there certainly was a lot of them, most of which were bought by four companies in particular: Blackmore, La Bastion, and Harriot-Windsor, and Ursicon. Coincidentally, the four companies that Roness and Lucius, Leroy, Paterson, and Wan-Cheung all used to work for, and certainly have colleagues that continue to work for. No doubt the willingness of those men to carve out the innovative brain of Cabernet Industries can be explained then… and their willingness to install a useful charitable foundation in its place. By all means though, take all the credit you want, father, and believe that you've made a difference, because a difference you have made – you've allowed that cartel to fool you to destroying this company from inside. They don't care if Cabernet Industries loses, no less if they can flock to the investors they represent afterwards. They will tear our family's company to bits, and you'll be their scapegoat."

"Charles, that's enough," Everest rebuked, downing the rest of his drink. "I've had enough of you and your conspiracy theories for a lifetime. Go and tell it to someone who cares, because I'm not buying into anything you have to sell me. Get the hell away from me…"

Everest walked away from Charlemagne, wandering into the aisles of slot machines in the lower levels where he stopped to sit down on a stool. He stared around him at the people staring at the machines before them. He then turned around, eyes slightly squinting at the bright machine and then looking back at those others that looked at it, almost without blinking as they put coins in and then pulled the levers. He looked for another second, and then visibly disturbed, left. Everest walked away and towards the showroom, reuniting with his wife and daughter for the rest of the night.

Act 5, Prologue

"Ladies and gentlemen," Everest spoke from a podium, "I would like to express my upmost thanks that you should join me on this day at the inauguration of a very special memorial. With permission from the French government, my wife and I decided to exhume the remains of my late father, Derby Cabernet, from his gravesite in northern France to be flown over and laid to rest in this graveyard in particular where his dearest wife, my mother, was buried."

Everest paused for a moment as he looked at the paper in front of him, and then to the crowd. There were close to twenty to thirty people, all of whom wore coats and had umbrellas above their heads. Everest was young, in his mid-twenties, skin fair and hair medium length and blonde. Behind him and on the sidelines was Vienna, dressed in a black dress with a veil, and next to her was a small cart with a nearly two-year old infant inside.

"When my father died little more than two years ago, we ensured that we stood together with my widowed mother. We attended the funeral and all the events and occasions that took place in that week afterwards, for us to show our support in her trying times. My mother, Ophelia Cabernet, was an elegant woman who rightly matched my father in his sense for adventure, but also held the social values of her aristocratic upbringing to her heart, so for her it meant everything that she should stand with her entire family. Unfortunately, in her decision to stay with her family in England rather than join us in Canada, her grief struck her hard without our attention, and as a result she passed away earlier this year. In her last breath, my mother expressed to me her intent to be buried with her husband, but unfortunately, the French government could not allow a woman who did not fight in the war to be buried in a gravesite meant for veterans and the fallen casualties of war. For this reason, my wife and I endeavored to see to it that those two could be reunited on earth as they surely are in heaven.

"When my father died two years ago, I did not say a word in all those events that took place. On one hand, I was in shock at what had occurred like anyone: my father, a young and healthy man in his peak, sadly taken from this world through a tragic and avoidable accident. I had no expectation that he would leave us so soon, no less when I had not seen him in years at that time. However, I cannot say that it was the shock that kept me silent, but because it really was not the state of shock, but the lack of anything to say that kept me silent. I had nothing to say for the man who had raised me from my childhood, who had taken me to the unique sights of the world from the Middle to the Far East, and who in his heart wanted me to become a man in his vision. The only words I could speak were the obvious point of fact, 'my father is dead.'

"What I do know about my father, however, was that he truly would not have wanted to have been buried at the beaches of Normandy as he was. This decision-made without consultation from my mother, nor us, was made in part due to his status and services in the war, and also too because his accident had taken place not too far in Belgium. My mother urged me to do something, but like I said, I had nothing useful to say and did nothing. I spent some time in reflection over my father's death to process his untimely departure from us, and overcome all the words I wish I could have said to him before his passing. In honesty, I have still not yet overcome the depth that his untimely death has brought onto us... However, I know that we cannot stay stuck in the past, but we can correct the errors of the past, one of which was allowing the French and British government to bury my father in that lot in Normandy. I am very pleased to unite these two in a memorial to correct those errors of the past, but also too because what I do know about my father too is that he loved this land, this county of Nattau, especially in all its trees and hills, and mountaintops and plains. This land around us is a place of which he held very close to his heart, and his romantic ideals. I can be certain to believe that at the end of his life, they both would have wanted to have been buried here, in Allabrese Cemetery, together."

Everest folded the piece of paper before him, and then turned around where a velvet tarp was placed overtop the memorial.

"Without further ado, allow me to unveil the eternal memorial of Derby and Ophelia Cabernet," Everest said, beginning to clap.

The rest of those in attendance began to clap. A groundskeeper off to the side pulled the velvet tarp off and unveiled the joint tombstones of Derby Martel Cabernet and Ophelia Victoria Cabernet. These were large tombstones, with a firm base with a metal plaque in the middle that said, 'Together Again.' Beneath their full names, there were dates carved into the tombstone for each of them. For Derby, these dates were 10 August 1920 to 04 March 1969, and for Ophelia these dates were 14 May 1926 to 21 October 1970. Beneath those dates were two wide metal plaques for each of them, on the base of the memorial. On Derby's plaque, there was a quote that said, 'He heals the broken in heart and binds up their wounds' (Psalm 147:3), and on Ophelia's plaque, there was a quote that said, 'I shall dwell in the house of the Lord forever' (Psalm 23:6). The tombstones were directly in front of a cliff edge. Between the two tombstones was a circular pot where flowers could be placed. Vienna received flowers and proceeded to place the bouquet in the pot. The audience continued to clap, and there was a flash of a photographer as someone took a photo.

The couple stood before the memorial, the small carriage with their infant daughter at their side. Another flash from the photographer came, and then Everest took a seat with Allodia while Vienna went to the podium.

"Thank you, one and all, for your great hospitality," Vienna expressed in her Austrian accent. "I cannot be more thankful when in a time of need, the help of a human hand reaches over – when at a time of desolation and rejection, the good of humanity vindicates the worst of humanity. In my lifetime, I have found more hospitality in the company of strangers than I have in my own family, in Austria where I am from, although I can find it in my heart to pardon the hearts of those who rejected me in my home country. When I was young, my family threw me out from my home, and without anywhere to go, there was Derby Cabernet to welcome me in. He was not an easy man to understand, very intimidating at times, but through his hardness he was a caring man and with time he grew more kind to me. He cared for me as though I were his own daughter, and I felt so secure in his home that I felt confident I could truly become his daughter and marry Everest. I understood that both Derby and Everest shared each other's hearts, and that the Cabernet home was a welcoming home, a welcoming family, one that I could participate in. When Everest asked me to marry him, I felt no hesitation to officially become a part of the family and Cabernet name.

"When my husband asked me to help him with the relocation of Derby's memorial to this land, I was very pleased to say 'yes' and help him. Again, I found the generosity and goodness of people in our parish who helped pick out this plot and make arrangements for this tomb to be built just as it is now. Everest and I are ever grateful for the assistance of the parishioners with our quest, and I am certain that both Derby and Ophelia greatly respect the efforts we have made on their behalf.

I would now like to ask Fr. Wilfred to come to the podium, as he has a few words…"

The ceremony continued with a few more people after the young parish priest came forward to the podium to express words of admiration for both Derby and Ophelia Cabernet. Afterwards, the crowd left the cemetery and returned to St. Allan's Parish where a reception awaited them. Everest continued to sit in front of the memorial with Vienna and Allodia while the podium and velvet tarp were put away.

Vienna put a hand on Everest's shoulder as he leaned forward in silence. "Let's go now, my mountain. We have guests waiting for us at the parish."

"In a moment," Everest replied.

"Allodia is cold, you can return later," Vienna pleaded.

"I don't want to return later," Everest responded, a little annoyed, "just go on without me. I'll catch up later." He then took out the keys from his pocket and passed them to Vienna. "I'll walk home."

Vienna took the keys into her hand and then looked back at Everest. She looked at him with a bit of pity, placed a hand on his shoulder, and then kissed him on the head. She then took the keys into her coat pocket and strolled Allodia away as she left. Everest stayed put once the workers put the podium into a van and then drove off. The cemetery was now quiet.

Allabrese Cemetery was a large cemetery stuck between a canyon near the base of the rocky mountains. There were numerous lots around the memorial park, including a groundskeeper hut near the entrance. The front of the property was lined with a black iron fence, and the gate was arched with words 'Allabrese Cemetery' webbed in. There were a few deciduous trees around the property, whose leaves were a warm-palette of yellow-orange-red.

Everest finally stood up as he looked at the tombstone of his father and said, "Just because your dead, and that you died early, doesn't mean that I forgive you. You may have all sorts of people pardoning you, praising you as being some sort of hero from the war, but not me. I know exactly what kind of a man you were, and I…" he stuttered and tensed his hands, "… I won't let it down. You hurt me, your own son, and for what? What did I do to you?"

Everest knelt down as tears began to roll down his cheeks. He tilted his head down for a moment, raising it up later to read the epitaph on his father's grave. He then lowered his eyes down again.

"I hope you're happy. You got what you wanted; Charles is mine, and you've got a granddaughter now. I've submitted – I've submitted to what you wanted from me. Am I a man now to you yet, father? Are you pleased with me?" Everest paused and then said, "What's the point? You're dead now, gone and no more. When we last talked, you wanted to apologize to me, and I accept it now if you'll still let me accept your pardon. I want to forgive you, but I can't. I want to move on – I don't want to live burdened in guilt that I… I wasn't good enough for you." He then took a deep breath and began to stand up. "Just because I let you apologize doesn't mean that I have to kiss the ground you're buried in. I still don't like you. You were unkind and cruel to me, your own son – I won't be like that though. I won't be anything like you. I am my own man now. Your memory is confined to here, so I can move on and have peace." With those final words, Everest then left the cemetery.

Act 5, Scene 1

"Here I am," Roness expressed, meeting Everest in an outdoor parking lot in the midst of some woods. "I wasn't sure about today, but I've warmed up the idea – it takes me back to my days in the army when we would march for miles with full kit."

Everest retrieved his backpack from the back of the Spyros EX, which was seriously dirtied with streaks of mud at its sides and windows covered in dust. He then walked over towards the hiking trail entrance near where Roness was parked. Roness stood at the rear of his black Armstrong pickup truck. He wore a bluish-grey flannel and a vest overtop. He also wore greyish-beige cargo pants and hiking boots. Atop of his head was a beige leather cowboy hat. Everest on the other hand wore a greenish-grey flannel and grey cargo pants. He also wore hiking shoes, gloves, and had trekking poles. Roness took out his own trekking poles from the rear of his truck, as well as his backpack. He put his backpack around him, and carried both poles in one hand.

"What a lovely day for a hike," Roness said, walking forward. "Eh, Everest?"

"Indeed," Everest replied, shaking his hand, "I heard about this trail and thought it was a moderate one for the two of us. It's approximately three kilometers either way, a little steep at the start, but then smooths out towards the top."

"Excellent," Roness responded. "Let's get to it."

The pair proceeded forward, down a stoney path with trees and tall bushes on both sides. The path steered forward on the left, but a sign at a junction there pointed towards a slimmer path on the right. They proceeded through and continued along a stoney path that began to ascend slightly. They were surrounded by more bushes, some of which their branches poked into the trail itself. The path began to curve to the right and continued to ascend upwards. They came to a ditch in the path in which a spring of water poured through the cliffside. The ditch was not very steep but was U-shaped. They trekked down carefully to the base of the ditch and then climbed up to continue on their merry way.

"You do much of this on your own, in Allabrese?" Roness asked, lightly panting.

"Yes, as a matter of fact, I do," Everest answered. "There are not many trails as sophisticated as this one though, but even over the summer, my boy and I (my youngest), tried out a lot of the trails around here in New Harlech. What we didn't get to do was much camping though, and of course this trail. Behind our home in Allabrese, beyond the fields, there's a beautiful trail upwards the side of the Rocky Mountains. My... my father took me up that trail when I was a kid, on horseback though, and it came upwards to this beautiful, majestic view just before the steepest parts of the mountain. This view would look outwards to the entire valley of that county and could encapsulate so much in your field of view. I wish more people knew about that trail so they could share in that beauty. This trail is supposed to be something though, it goes up to a glacier lake and we should be able to see over the R'alagah area."

Everest paused for a moment as they continued up and began to go across a steep incline along the same stoney path.

"When I was younger, around my mid-twenties or so, I would spend a lot of time going out and around the property," Everest said. "I wouldn't necessarily just go up towards the mountains, but all around the property. The entire west side from the river is like an unexplored land, and it was all ours to explore and see fit as to what we could find. As a child, I enjoyed that plenty in the summers when I was home from boarding school."

"You went to boarding school, huh?"

"Yes, here in Harlech, down at the university. What about you?"

"I was in military high school before I went to West Point," Roness answered. "I graduated with honors and got to serve in the United States Army in both the Korean and Vietnam War."

"I had heard you fought in Vietnam," Everest replied. "How was that?"

"It was certainly something of a war," Roness remarked. "What I do regret is that we left, after all that bloodshed, and for what? I was disappointed when we left Korea only for the borders to remain just the same. I had heard that Douglas MacArthur - you know him? He wanted to nuke the Koreans the same way we did to the Japanese, but five-fold to show 'em not to mess with the United States, but he was removed from his post, and we left that war with our tails between our crotches. I thought for sure, not again, and there we were leaving Vietnam with just not our tails but our asses in our hand. I was offered a generous position in United States office after the war, but I declined – I instead accepted a position with Blackmore and that was that."

Everest did not immediately reply as they continued to ascend. He instead asked, "Pardon my ignorance, but I was young when those wars kicked off. For what reason did we go in to either of them?"

"To stop communism, of course," Roness answered. "North Korea (the communists) attacked South Korea, our democratic allies, and when we pushed them back, the damn Communist Chinese got involved too. The Soviets were helping them out with weapons and such, and it was nearly the start of another world war – and oh, I wish it was because we could have put the raps on communism back then in the fifties than to have held out to now. The same was essentially true for the Vietnamese."

"My father told me that both Korea and Vietnam had been formerly occupied as colonies," Everest said. "He said that the brutality of Japanese and French oppression had pushed the Koreans and Vietnamese to praise the communists. I'm not a communist. I think that a man should be able to own his property and give up his property without the government making the decision for him. I'm an advocate for the free market and such, but only as much as there is compassion and kindness towards others as long as others are not harmed in any way by the actions of another person. We should have that as much freedom; freedom from fear and oppression, so how can we place blame or believe that further brutality through war will solve the war ahead of us."

Roness began to laugh before he replied, "You were one of those pacifist protestors in the sixties, weren't you, Mr. Cabernet."

"I spent a lot of time in West Germany with my wife in the sixties, especially around the Berlin Wall," Everest answered. "We protested for that wall to come down, and we protested for there to be a common understanding between the humanity of the man in the West with the man in the East. I suppose, like you, I loathed the government because I did not understand for what so much bloodshed was being done for. So yes, in the sixties, I was one of the protestors who would shout out the slogan of 'Make Love, Not War,' because I knew it was within our human capacity; within our existence to love one another – to care for one another in peaceful co-existence, but for whatever reason the way of the world was not so. Even now, I don't understand why there is so much indifference towards one another in the world we share, especially in this part of the world here in Harlech. I can understand that not everyone is perfect, but is there even that much effort in a small act of kindness? If we all acted even a little bit more different towards each other, with kindness and compassion, it could revolutionize the world for the better."

"Ah, it has begun to make a lot more sense," Roness remarked as they continued to ascend the trail. "You were born at the end of the war, and through the sixties, you were a protest child. Now I understand what drives you; you're full of ideals from that era still. What you don't understand though is that the world doesn't work the way that you think it could. The free world is just like this great outdoors that we get to enjoy. At any point, we could be ambushed by a grizzly or a cougar, and who do you think would win in that situation? Whoever has got the better fight in him – not the most love and compassion."

"That's an unfair comparison," Everest complained.

"It's a fair one, because just like in the civilized world, there are savages, predators, looking to attack one another and you can't change that about them."

"I don't agree," Everest rejected. "I don't believe that man can ever be intrinsically evil. I've been to some parts of the third-world, the places where culture is different, and no matter how different the culture tends to be, there is an understanding of basic moral principles. Certainly there can be a savage desire in a person, but overcome through reason and willpower, it is what builds civilized worlds from the Wild West. The loss of it through lack of reason or willpower is what destroys civilization, especially when that rebellion against the basic moral principles creates something so revolutionary against the human spirit – something that it totally against the principle to love one another."

"Are you a Christian, Mr. Cabernet?"

Everest sighed and answered, "I go to church every Sunday with my wife, because she was born and raised Catholic, and she said that it was very important for her in the hardest parts of her life."

"I'm asking about you," he quickly replied.

"I was born but not entirely raised Catholic – my father seldom took me to church, although he put within me a basic understanding. My mother was Anglican, and like him, she did not care much about which faith I belonged to as long as I was baptized and christened. When I was a teenager though, around thirteen-years old, my parents got into a fight, a very serious one – from my sister who witnessed a lot of that tension and she said that they nearly got a divorce, but then nothing – there was no divorce and instead we came to learn that they had both become seriously religious. Through my adolescence, I was forced to go to church more, especially when Vienna joined the family. Yup, I guess Vienna and my dad shared that in common, which was part of the reason too why they got to get along so well. Her and my mother too. I didn't see what the big deal was though. I never really believed – even now, I just go along to appease my wife. I know the kids don't really believe either – all of them, even Charlemagne. What about you?"

"I'm a private fellow in that regard. My folks were Mennonites, but of course, being an army man, I couldn't hold to their pacifist traditions. I definitely believe that there is an almighty and powerful God above, but I also believe that religious faith is something that man should hold privately to themselves. Every man needs faith in a God above, whatever that religion is."

The pair came to a curve in the trail that took them in the opposite direction, although still climbing the base of the mountain. They continued upwards and passed a couple that were descending from above. They greeted them and then continued onwards. Towards the end of this stretch of the trail, the bushes grew shorter and there was an extensive presence of fireweed in the shrubs. Soon enough, the pair began to see the extensive view across the county they were in, stretching outwards to the ocean.

"Well, isn't that something," Roness said, looking out. "Yup, this land sure is blessed. I certainly can't wait to see the view up above."

They continued along the trail as it smoothed out although the ground was now gravel. The pathway ahead began to diminish and it consisted of little more than a simple slim dirt path. The dirt path went along the shrubs in an inconsistent manner, passing over patches of mud and a stream. The path proceeded to curve right as they continued upwards towards a grassy hill. They passed a small but long pond on their way up a hill and then over it to catch sight of a larger lake at the base of the mountain. The lake was calm and its water light blue. There were patches of snow about, and behind it was a tall peak with the rest of the mountain behind.

"You certainly know how to lead a man to water," Roness said, looking down towards the lake. "What a marvelous sight. Thank you, Everest."

"Yes, it is a sight for sore eyes," Everest remarked. "The trail continues upwards to the peak of the mountain, but we would need specialized equipment for the climb up."

"Not a problem at all," Roness remarked. "Let's rest here. It's been quite a journey."

From where the sun had been in the morning, it now loomed over them at noon. The pair rested for a moment as they looked outwards to the lake.

"Can I ask you a question," Everest requested.

"Certainly."

"At the casino, my older son, Charlemagne, made accusations towards you and the rest of the board of directors, specifically those who represent the investors. He made the accusation that all of you intended to squeeze Cabernet Industries to support the corporations of the investors. He provided one such example as the liquidation of R&D, in which the assets were overwhelmingly bought by companies that four of you came from."

"Yes, that is certainly a bold accusation from your son," Roness responded. "He's a character, isn't he. You should have seen how many times I had to politely ask him to leave my office since he returned to Harlech."

"I'm not hearing from you that those claims are not true."

"No, you aren't, Everest," Roness remarked. "You've received the information already, you know it's true, but what you need to understand is that from a certain point of view, the sale of such assets could fit into a conspiracy theory as your son suggests… Are you familiar with Occam's Razor?"

"No."

"Occam's Razor is a philosophical principle that points out that often times, the simplest explanation or theory is usually the correct one. Your son suggests that we sit on the board as representatives to the investors to see to it that Cabernet Industries can thrive, but that would imply that in the five years we have been in charge, Cabernet Industries has been in decline and will continue to be so with a projection towards bankruptcy. That projection is not the case; Cabernet Industries has never been better, and it is even in the investors interest that the company flourish. The sale of those assets to these companies comes because those companies are our partners in a certain sense. We would not want our rivals to buy out that material, so we pulled some strings to have a safe buyer take those items from us so that we could proceed with the liquidation and shutdown of R&D. Of course we will choose companies that we trust and have worked for over stranger ones."

"And what about the closure of Site C? How did that sale pass by me?"

"The decision to shutdown Site C was not communication to the board of directors, because the property belongs to the branch and subsidiary, and it is for them to decide whether it is in their interest to continue that operation. Unfortunately, it was not so…"

"I wish we were informed so that we could have vetoed the decision, given them support to keep the site afloat."

"If we were informed of every business activity across the multitude of subsidiaries and branches in our control, we would never get any sleep, Everest," Roness explained. "You have to trust the men in office to do their job and that they have the interest of the company in mind. You cannot expect to micromanage every facet of the company to fit your vision."

Everest sighed and replied, "It's tiresome. Really, it is. Whenever I come to believe that I am doing good work, something comes up to throw that belief out the window. I'm also exhausted with the immensity of this corporation, and the fact that we do not have good men we can trust in positions of power."

"Honestly, Everest, if you seriously intend to continue to be involved in your current role, you will not survive psychologically if you do not begin to just stop caring," Roness advised. "How else do you think that me, Lucius, or anyone else can function with such an immense workload on our plates without simply not caring about every little detail. We focus on the project at hand, and nothing more. Anything else is out of sight and out of mind."

"Seriously? That's how you cope with your position… with apathy?" Everest questioned. "I… I don't understand how that could seriously be wise advice."

"It is how any businessman can hope to succeed," Roness encouraged. "You need to have the right mindset for this line of work, and you're putting too much attention at caring for every worker, when, let me tell you, the workers don't care about you – with all the compassion you may have to offer to them, they will always vilify you as the evil employer, so stop trying to win their affection."

Everest looked down and towards the lake as he held two hands at either side of his face. He breathed in and out slightly rapidly with a minor pant as he closed his eyes, and then opened them, stood up, and pointed at Roness.

"You're heartless," Everest accused. "You're a heartless man if you believe that we truly cannot do something for the workers, or believe that because they see us as evil, any effort to see them as humans is in vain. How could you also hold such disregard, such indifference towards the people who keep the lights on for this company?"

"Hmph," Roness responded, "there's that spirit of the anti-war movement. I won't have you insult me, Mr. Cabernet. I'm sorry you don't like the way the company is run, but dammit, it's how it must be run in order to succeed, and I do intend to keep its success going even if you and your flowerchild endeavors to soften the company continue to come forward."

"I'm only trying to humanize this sociopathic corporation," Everest argued, "because admittedly when someone stops to give a crap, it cascades to result in the deaths of a few hundreds of innocent people. It's no wonder the collapse of the dam played no heed to you or the others – you're all amoral monsters with no conscience whatsoever. You – you're all…"

"Human," Roness answered, "just humans doing our jobs, in the same manner and likeness in which humans have built and shaped the Western world, the American way."

"Yeah," Everest agreed, "the same spirit that allowed the use of slave labor in the Americas, the development of nuclear weapons, and the massacre of innocents in both the Korean and Vietnam War. Boy, it must feel good to be an American… all that blood on your hands."

"I've heard enough from you," Roness remarked, shaking his head. "I won't stand for this nonsense – I'll be leaving on my own now. Good day, Mr. Cabernet."

"Yeah, well good riddance," Everest replied. "Go on, get out of here and I'll see you Monday, when you know for certain I'll be talking to the entire board about how I want everything run through me before it is approved!"

Roness left. Everest shook his head and stayed put above the lake for a while longer as he shook his head. After a moment alone, he sat down and brought his hands to the side of his head again. He growled and then went quiet. Everest stayed put for a few minutes to half an hour, at which point he decided to sit up straight and close his eyes. He began to breathe in through his nose and out through his mouth. He stayed quiet otherwise, listening to the howl of wind come from between two peaks nearby, and nothing else as there was an absence of wildlife around him. Everest continued to breathe in through his nose and out his mouth. He continued this for minutes on end, pausing ever so often, and then recontinuing. After an hour or so, he opened his eyes and looked before him. The sun was on its way down, and he remained put for another moment alone. After that moment, he stood up and turned around. Everest left.

Everest came down the mountain the same way he arrived, passing through the bushes and patches of mud to reach the gravel trail, and then passing the viewpoint with its steep cliff down too. Everest went down with careful steps to avoid slipping, staying to the left side of the trail. As Everest was about to come around to the curve, he stopped as he could hear a muffled noise. The noise repeated, and it sounded like cries and moans of a person. Everest came down a bit around the corner, but the noise became faint, so he attempted to locate the noise.

"Hello?!" Everest shouted. "Is anybody there?!"

"Oh, thank God," a faint voice could be heard. "Hello! I need help! I- I fell down the trail and I... I'm in so much pain and I can barely move!"

Everest identified where a small landslide in the path was visible, and then came around to some trees to look down. The steep drop was close to a few yards and at the ground level could be seen a person on their back.

"Holy..." Everest muttered. "Let me go and get some help!"

"No, don't leave me, please! I've been here for what's felt like hours already man. I can't stay here all alone, I- I need help now!"

"I… I don't know how to help you," Everest responded. "I'm not a paramedic. I'm not trained for these situations – you're going to have to-"

"No… please, I just… I need you to help get me out of here, please! Just throw a rope down and I'll grab on, or something… please…"

Everest paused for a moment and then asked, "What hurts right now?"

"My ankle," the hiker answered. "My right ankle, and my left wrist hurt. I… I can still move my left leg and right hand without any pain, but I'm scared I'll fall down further if I move, and I can't climb up."

"Okay…" Everest replied, taking off his backpack, "let me see." He took out a cord from his backpack, but it was not a very thick rope. He also had a few first aid supplies in a kit."

"Look, I'm trained in first aid," the hiker remarked. "Just come down here, or pull me up, and I'll guide you through the rest of it. I have some supplies in my backpack too."

Everest looked at what he had. He took the rope and then stood up. "Alright," he said, "I'm going to help you, don't worry. I'm not going anywhere." He began to tie the rope to a secure tree.

"Just toss the rope down… aargh!" the hiker complained. "Actually, wait… you're going to have to come down here. I'm going to need to splint this ankle before I move up."

"What?" Everest questioned, stuffing his pockets with bandage rolls.

"I'll tell you what to do, just come down here! Do you have any splints?"

"I don't even know what those are," Everest replied, placing a hunting knife on his belt.

"Just come down here then and use some branches. Just hurry…"

Everest tied the rope around his waist and then began to climb down the side of the cliff, grabbing at roots and tree trunks to make his way down the steep cliff. After a few minutes, he found himself next to the hiker. There was still a few yards down to the absolute bottom of the cliff.

"Thank God you're here, man," the hiker expressed. "You'll need to put at least two thick branches between my ankle and support it with some bandage. Any movement right now hurts a lot…"

"Okay," Everest responded, looking around, "let me see what I can find." He looked around and was able to find some moderately thick and straight branches around his vicinity.

"Good," the hiker said, "now put them in line with my boots and take some bandage rolls around it. Do you have any?"

"I do- I do," Everest replied, taking them out from his pocket. "I see what you want me to do too."

Everest placed the branches at the side of the ankle, restricting its movement. He then fastened the branches with the rolls of bandage, securing them tightly.

"Right, what about your wrist?" Everest asked.

"Don't worry about it," the hiker responded. "I can survive as is. Now just get me out of here somehow, please. Give me your rope, and then go back up and pull me out…"

"How much do you weigh?"

"Not that much, man," the hiker replied. "A hundred and something pounds."

Everest removed the rope from around his waist. He then removed the backpack from the hiker, cutting the straps. He tied the rope around the waist of the hiker, looping it around his hips.

"Alright, you wait here while I climb back up," Everest remarked. "I'll be just a minute."

Everest proceeded to climb up the hill. He treaded carefully up the steep hill, jumping to grab roots to pull himself upwards.

Once at the top, Everest removed the rope from where he tied it, and then began to tug on it.

"Okay, I'm going to pull you out now!" Everest called out. "Get ready!" He began to tug at the rope. "Feels like more than a hundred and a few pounds…" he muttered. He secured the rope around his gloved hands and began to pull, walking away from the hiker. He could hear the hiker yell out in mild pain as he did so, but he was also able to see from up top the hiker move. Everest planted his feet firmly on the trail, ensuring he did not slip and have a similar fate. He kept a close eye to navigate the hiker through the trees. "Easy does it…" he muttered too. "Almost there….!" Everest groaned as he continued to pull and pull.

The hiker began to laugh. "You- you're actually doing it! Oh man, you are awesome!"

Once Everest saw that the man was almost up, he shifted tactics and began to pull with his legs for the final stretch. The rope now moved quicker and in the last push, the man was raised from the side of the hill. Everest released his grip on the rope and quickly ran over, pulling the man by his clothes so he could lie flat on the path.

"Let me check your splint," Everest offered, securing it with more bandage. He then came around to the man's wrist to examine it and splint it too.

Once the bandages were secured, Everest began to help the man onto his feet. The hiker put his good arm around Everest's neck. He abandoned one of his trekking poles, but kept the other to stabilize each other as he began to make the long descent downwards together.

"I owe you my life, man," the hiker acknowledged. "You're the best, dude."

"Don't go thanking me yet," Everest responded. "We're still not back to the parking lot."

"I'm serious man," the hiker said. "Angels do exist- you seriously just saved my life. I could have died down there…"

"Yeah, well you didn't."

Everest and the man continued to descend downwards. At the U-shaped ditch and spring of water, Everest paused for a moment and then began to come around to the side to bypass it. They then went on the final stretch back to the parking lot where Everest helped him into the back of the Spyros EX.

"I'm going to take you to Ralagah Hospital back in town," Everest expressed. "I'm sorry about your backpack."

"Forget the backpack, man," the hiker replied. "I got my car keys and wallet. I'll be fine – but dude, thank you so much. You seriously saved my life – you are the best. I don't even know what your name is…"

"My name?" Everest questioned. "It's… Pepin."

"Well, Pepin, you are the best."

Act 5, Scene 2

Everest sat at his desk in his study, jotting down notes as he looked over some reports. There was a mighty downpour in the city, the skies were dark, and the patio was wet. He stayed put in the warmth of the study as he wrote down notes, then standing up to go to a folder box on a table to put these reports away and take out some others. He rummaged through the box, but could not find the reports he was looking for. Everest pulled out another box beneath that table and continued to search through, but among the boxes, the information he was searching for was nowhere to be found. Everest sat down at his desk and picked up the telephone.

"Kay, I can't seem to find those period reports anywhere in my office. Are you sure you left them here?" Everest questioned, waiting for a response. "No, I said put them in my office, my penthouse office. I don't even use that office downstairs..." He then paused again. "No, don't worry about it. I'll go downstairs and get them myself." He then put the phone down, stood up, and left the study.

Everest left the penthouse, got into an elevator, used his key card to go down a few floors, and then exited out onto the executive level. He turned right and then right again to go down the corridor towards his office. He looked up towards the corner of the corridor at the security camera, ignored it, and then walked through to come into the chairman office.

A flash of lightning could be seen through the curtains as he entered inside. The office was dark and cold. He walked across the large space to the other side where there were tables set up with various other boxes with files inside. He began to rummage through them to find the correct box, seeing a newer box to be set side atop of the desk. He opened the box and began to go through the files inside, quickly looking over the titles and then closing the box as he shook his head.

"There's quite a few missing," Everest expressed to himself. "I thought I said these needed to be submitted by the end of the week."

Everest left the room and came back into the corridor. He walked down, passed the boardroom, which was empty, and then came around to where Roness' office was. He observed another surveillance camera in the corner of the corridor, and ignored it as the sight of these were just about everywhere in Cabernet Tower. He walked into the executive office spaces and saw that it was mostly empty as the end of the day had passed. Kathleen Summers was sat alone at her desk, typing at her computer. She wore a long-sleeved brown plaid blazer jacket buttoned-up and a long skirt with it that went down to just below her knees. She also wore tan-brown high heels and tan stockings. Underneath her jacket she wore a white blouse. Her blonde hair was amess and tied in a bun. The clock ticked, and the keys on the keyboard clipped as she typed quickly. Everest came around to her desk and looked over.

"Mr. Cabernet," Ms. Summers remarked, "did you find the period reports on your desk?"

"I found some period reports," Everest answered, "where are the rest of them?"

Ms. Summers sighed and replied, "I could only submit to you what I had received. The rest are delayed and will be with you shortly."

"I'll have to have a word with Mr. Roness and Mr. Clifford – these reports were due one week ago, and the rest of the subsidiaries and branches need to understand that deadlines are set for a reason."

"Mr. Roness and Mr. Clifford are away," Ms. Summers answered. "They're on a business trip and will be back Tuesday."

"Dammit," Everest responded, "seriously? What for? I told Roness that I wanted to review the period reports by the end of the week, and he's now gone off for what?"

"I'm sorry, Mr. Cabernet," Ms. Summers replied, "I wish there was something I could do for you, but as you can see, I'm swamped and unlike everybody else, am still working so I can get out of here. I can hear that you are upset, but there's nothing I can do to change that – I can only send reminders to staff, not enforce them."

The printer behind Ms. Summers began to print some documents. She stood up, came around to the other side of her desk where there were tall stacks of paper. She began to open drawers in filing cabinets around her to file these papers.

"Where's everybody else?" Everest questioned, looking away from her and to the rest of the cubicles. He then looked at his watch. "Is it quitting time already?"

"Oh, it's Friday evening," Ms. Summers responded as she continued to work, "nobody stays behind on a Friday evening except little old me. Everyone else is straight out the door, if not in the staff room."

Everest did not respond. There were only a few desks, or cubicle spaces in the executive corporate office space. They each had a sizeable L-shaped desk with a computer.

"I can appreciate the efforts of your staff to cater to our administrative needs," Everest expressed, "but the consistent disappointment from branch and subsidiary leadership to deliver is unacceptable. I'm tired of people in this company not giving a crap about what needs to get done, because it really seems like nobody cares about anything around here."

"Complaining to me won't get them to do their work," Ms. Summers replied. "As you can see, I've got plenty to do and I'm not an executive, I'm an assistant and the least I manage is the team in this office."

Everest turned around and observed her continuing to sort files into filing cabinets. She sighed as she had to take out a thick bunch of papers from a drawer, place it atop of the cabinet, and begin to sort through them and place the papers into the correct divider.

"Speaking of not giving a crap," Ms. Summers complained, "I need to talk to my team about putting the correct files under the correct heading..." she growled. "There we go..."

"Why are you still here, Kay?" Everest questioned. "The day ended half an hour ago, you should be going home. As much as I would like to pay you for your time to stick around, you don't have to."

"Oh, I don't make overtime," Ms. Summers replied. "I make a salary under a management position, and the way it was explained to me was that I earn a fixed amount in a year, work a certain number of days, and it's on me to get my crap done within that day for the amount they paid me. Of course, what I didn't realize was that the volume of work could vary on a day to day, even week to week basis."

"That agreement hardly seems fair now, does it?" Everest questioned. "Call me old-fashioned, but I believe any worker should get paid a fair wage for a fair day of work. I see plenty of our people, directors and vice-presidents, leave early without a care in the world, and on time when there is still yet work to be done. I've spoken to a lot of our staff, and most of them stop thinking about the office after five o'clock."

"Some people around here just have easier jobs, I suppose," Ms. Summers surmised. "A part of me questions where else I'm supposed to go from here when the only position above me is John Bennett's job. I've surrendered though to the idea that I'm stuck here as coordinator for the rest of my lifetime. Just as I'm stuck here for the rest of my evening..."

"Let me help you," Everest offered."

"No, you seem like you need to go cool down and do your own work still," Ms. Summers responded. "I'll be fine, although less chit-chat would be helpful."

"I can help you and not talk at the same time. Please, let me help you."

"Honestly, Mr. Cabernet, it's okay," Ms. Summers remarked in a strict tone, reviewing some files. "We have a very certain system around here that I wouldn't have time to go through with you."

"How much do you have left?"

"All this," Ms. Summers said, turning around to stacks of papers behind her desk on a low counter. "Shouldn't take too long…"

"Let me help you," Everest again stated, "please. You shouldn't have to spend your evening in this office, no less unpaid – I'll sort your compensations with Mr. Bennett on Monday."

Ms. Summers did not immediately respond. She was reading some papers as she continued to sort documents. Everest waited for a response, but then none came so he sighed and then began to leave.

"Don't you have period reports to review?" Ms. Summers questioned, sighing as well. She looked at him. "Really, I insist that you just let me finish off here and you go what you need to do. I can handle it; not like I have a family to go home to at my apartment."

Everest turned around and replied, "I can hardly finish my work today, the least I can do is help you finish yours. I'm not going to leave here until you do."

Ms. Summers sighed again, turned to face Everest and placed a hand on her hip. "Alright then, Mr. Cabernet," she said. "If that's the case, then take a stack of papers. We organize according to quarter on some documents, period on others, and then week on the rest. It should be fairly obvious according to what you have where it should go because all the filing cabinets on this wall and the wall over are labelled. If you find anything you are unsure about, let me know. Sometimes information gets printed or winds up here from downstairs, so anything out of the ordinary may just need to be sent down."

"Got it," Everest replied. He proceeded to help Ms. Summers with organizing the files in the office. These files were general data reports, copies of reports from other subsidiaries that were faxed over for review and signature, or to be archived. Like Ms. Summers, Everest would sometimes pause to look over the files before he proceeded to file them away.

Between the pair of them, they were able to put all the stacks of paper away on Ms. Summers' desk and the counter behind into the respective filing cabinet in less than an hour. As Everest worked on the last few sheets, he looked at these items with careful eyes. Ms. Summers removed her blazer and placed it on her chair. Everest briefly glanced over to her and her slim figure.

"Well, that is the last of it," Ms. Summers remarked, looking over to Everest. "What have you got there?"

"Just some information on some project proposals," Everest expressed, "but I haven't seen these yet. I also have some raw data sets from today for Cabernet Extraction."

"Those project proposals should be in my inbox," Ms. Summers said, taking them. "I will need to make photocopies and pass them to Lucius for review."

"They seem important," Everest remarked. "Be sure Roness and I get a copy too."

"Will do," Summers responded, moving around to the copying machine. "Usually, anything from the branches or subsidiaries goes through Lucius before they move on to Roness and then you."

"I can only imagine the amount of content that does not get past him to Roness, or from Roness to me," Everest remarked, putting the last few files away. He then picked up the stack from the printer. "Oh wait, there's still some documents here."

Everest went through the papers that were printed out. These were minutes from meetings held throughout the day. He quickly went through each of them, reading the subject of the meeting held, from which department, and then placing them in the correct place. Ms. Summers finished photocopying the proposals and went to place them in the outbox for Everest, Roness, and Clifford. Ms. Summers then went around to join Everest as he continued to flip through minutes.

"I don't recall this meeting," Everest remarked, reading the subject headline. "This meeting had a few board members... What was it about? You took these minutes."

"You were in another meeting at the time," Ms. Summers clarified, standing behind Everest's right shoulder. "The meeting was not too long and to do with potential restructure of leadership and responsibilities. The board is interested in hiring a Chief Financial Officer to fulfill that role. You will want to put those minutes here..."

Ms. Summers walked over and opened the drawer. Everest came over and placed them inside. She then closed it and turned to face Everest. She stood a few inches from him and looked up at his face.

"Anything else?" Ms. Summers asked.

"Just these minutes from a meeting Mr. Holmes had at the end of the day," Everest replied. Ms. Summers continued to look at him. "What?" he asked. She took a side-step and went around to open the drawer. Everest stepped over and put them inside, and then she closed them.

"All done," Ms. Summers said, hand on her hip, other at the top of the cabinet, and herself looking at Everest still.

"So we are," Everest replied. "You should be going home now."

"I should," Ms. Summers agreed, "thanks for all your help just now…"

"No problem," Everest acknowledged. "I'm sorry if I seemed upset with you earlier. It wasn't for me to be upset with you because of other people's shortcomings."

"Oh, don't worry about it… Mr. Cabernet."

"Everest."

"Right, Everest," Ms. Summers said in a calm tone. "You know, I've noticed that you really stand out from the other executives around here. You have a warm heart… You want to do whatever you can for other people, whoever it may be…"

"I've always believed that we should do what we can to help those around us," Everest remarked. "I've held that belief since I was a teenager… A part of me believes that just because I was born into a palace, doesn't make me better than other people. In fact, I'm not any better than anyone, so why should I believe I deserve to be treated better? There are better people than me in this world who deserve better treatment then what they get, and then there are people in this world who get better treatment for what they deserve."

"What do you think I deserve?" Ms. Summers asked, bringing her hand from her hip to her blouse near the sternum.

"I think you deserve more than what you earn for this job as administrative coordinator, that's for sure," Everest remarked, looking at her hand. "You obviously care about your job, unlike other people. I think we should promote people like you to higher ranks than those who swung by on a basis of nepotism and cronyism."

"What do you think you deserve?" Ms. Summers questioned, taking her hand to Everest's hand.

"Nothing," Everest replied. "I'm not deserving of anything more than what I have, and even much of what I have is not deserving to me."

"What do you have that you feel like you deserve?"

234

"In honesty, Kay, none of it."

"Why?" she questioned, bringing Everest's hand to her chest.

"I... didn't do anything to earn it... even my wife and kids, I didn't do anything to deserve any of them. I've just... existed all my life. I've never done much in my life except that... to live with them. I try to love them, but sometimes it's hard because they don't want that particular love at that moment, especially the kids and others more than anything else, but since I was a youngster, I felt like I had so much love to give to this world... but people around me were not receptive to that love and rejected me. I wanted – desired, to love others, but they rejected me and it hurt, but rather than cower and love no more, I doubled-down on what it means to love – to sacrifice. If I had not met my wife, I would have been a miserable man. She kept the lights going on with me and received my love, but still there is so much more love yet outpouring from me, maybe that's why I'm here trying to find a place to put that care into."

Ms. Summers closed her eyes. Everest saw a tear fall from the corner of her right eye and down her cheek. She released the control she had on Everest's hand, and he slowly pulled it away.

"That's beautiful..." Ms. Summers acknowledged, "you really do have a loving heart... you're not lacking in what you deserve, you deserve better. I'm sorry, but I can't do this..."

"Do what?" Everest questioned. "What's wrong?"

Ms. Summers brought a hand to her face, picked up her blazer, and put her arm through one sleeve before changing hands to put the other hand through the other sleeve.

"What's going on? Why are you crying? Please don't cry," Everest pleaded. "I'm sorry for whatever I did to you."

"No, it's not you, Mr. Cabernet, it's me. I'm sorry..." Ms. Summers said, picking up her purse. Everest stood behind the desk, visibly puzzled and perplexed at her reaction. He stood there for a brief minute as though he attempted to process what transpired, but then he came around the desk and into the corridor. He looked down, but he could not hear Ms. Summers crying anymore. He walked down the corridor to come around the elevator lobby, but she was not around. He then went down to the chairman office, pushed through the doors, and then went across to the doors by the fireplace to look down the corridor through them, and then around to the doors behind the large desk to a small backroom where there was access to the stairwell. A lot of boxes were stored in this backroom. He returned to his office and then came around to his desk as he placed a hand on his forehead, still processing the moment.

A flash of lightning then filled the room, brightening it for a moment and allowing him to see through to the other side, specifically the portrait that hung above the fireplace. He squinted as it became dark again and began to walk over to the other side. As he was a couple feet from the portrait, another jolt of lightning lit the room and exposed the looming appearance of Derby Cabernet immortalized in the acrylic painting. The sight of Derby, dressed in his grey suit and with his eyes that carried the same hue as in life, caused Everest to grow pale. Derby held a displeasing look on his face as his eyes beamed down towards Everest. Everest clenched a hand into a fist and held it close to his breast. He held this fist tightly and pressed it firmly against his sternum. A tear came down his eyes, and he left the room.

Act 5, Scene 3

Everest and Vienna sat together in a pew towards the front of the cathedral, at the end of the seat with access to an aisle on the right. There were many people in attendance around them, especially towards the back. Vienna wore a green dress while Everest wore a brown suit. The people around them wore a variety of different clothing types, and among them too were some people that wore white robes with headdresses. They were elderly and middle-aged females, most of whom were Southeast Asian in appearance. There were seldom people in the cathedral who were also dressed in a similar appearance as them, although those that did wear formal clothes were older than them. As they sat together, the organ played from above the narthex and a female singer sang in English the responsorial psalm verse, 'Blessed the poor in spirit, for the Kingdom of Heaven is theirs!'

Pentateuch Cathedral had a modest-sized crowd in attendance in its many pews. Everest looked towards the sanctuary, past the altar, and towards the archbishop sat directly behind it in his cathedra. He wore a green chasuble, a mitre, and held in his hand a shepherd's crook. The archbishop was an older male with fair skin and white hair. He wore glasses too. On his right-hand side was an assistant pastor of Hispanic appearance, holding a book in his hands as he sang to the responsorial psalm verse. On his left was a deacon, wearing a green dalmatic. He was an older male with a greyish beard and fair skin. At their side, left and right, there were altar servers, older males in their twenties and thirties, one of whom was even in his forties most likely, dressed in black cassocks and with a white surplice overtop. Above the archbishop's cathedra was a circular stained-glass window, and above that window was a mural painted on the half-domed ceiling of the chancel that showed a depiction of God in three persons, the Virgin Mary, and onlookers on the left and right in the form of angels and saints. Beneath the mural and around the circular stained-glass window were arched windows that had visual depictions from key moments in the Gospel. Around the sanctuary where the ambulatory was, there were pillars with statues that looked towards the altar. The entire sanctuary was raised up on dark wooden floor that was polished and clean. This sanctuary was separated from the crossing between the transepts by altar rails built into the polished stone floor. Above the altar was a bronze crucifix that hung from the ceiling directly in front of the round stained-glass window. At the side of the sanctuary there were doors that went into the sacristy and chapel where the tabernacle was kept. On the left transept were confessionals as well as additional seats pivoted perpendicular to the rest. There was also a closed-off archway that led around to the sanctuary. On this side, at the corner of the sanctuary, there were stairs that led up to a pulpit. On the right transept there were cabinets that held relics to a local saint, lit candles for the people, and next to the sanctuary two shrines with kneelers. There were also pews perpendicular to the rest and oriented towards the altar too. These transepts each had large wooden doors that exited outside behind the pews. Everest fixed his eyes though on the crucifix, and the visual image of Christ nailed to the Cross with a look of suffering on his face.

At the end of the responsorial psalm, a layperson sat in the pews on the left transept stood up near the archway, walked forward and removed the velvet rope, and then came around to climb up to the pulpit.

"A second reading from the Second Letter to the Corinthians," the woman announced. She was an older woman and she wore a toffee brown blazer and skirt. She had short white hair and glasses. "Blessed be the God and Father of our Lord Jesus Christ, the Father of mercies and the God of all consolation who consoles us in all our affliction, so that we may be able to console those who are in any affliction with the consolation with which we ourselves are consoled by God." The women paused for a moment. "For just as the sufferings of Christ are abundant for us, so also our consolation is abundant through Christ. If we are being afflicted, it is for your consolation and salvation; if we are being consoled, it is for your consolation, which you experience when you patiently endure the same sufferings that we are also suffering. Our hope for you is unshaken; for we know that as you share in our sufferings, so also you share in our consolation... The word of the Lord."

"Thanks be to God," Vienna and others in the congregation replied.

A tune proceeded from the organ, and everybody in the congregation stood up, including Everest. A male singer in the choir began to sing, "Alleluia, Alleluia," followed by the rest of the people gathered who sang, "Alleluia, Alleluia." The male singer then sang, "I give you a new commandment: love one another just as I have loved you." The congregation and singer together then sang, "Alleluia, Alleluia" as the deacon came up to the pulpit.

"The Lord be with you," the deacon greeted as the singing stopped. People continued to stand.

"And also with you," the congregation replied.

"A reading from the Holy Gospel, according to Luke," the deacon announced.

"Glory to you Lord," the congregation replied. Vienna took her thumb and drew a cross on her forehead, lips, and chest as everyone else did. Everest did what he always did at this moment, and simply touch his forehead, lips and chest. The deacon then spoke, "A certain ruler asked Jesus, 'Good teacher, what must I do to inherit eternal life?' Jesus answered, 'Why do you call me good? No one is good – except God alone. You know the commandments: You shall not commit adultery, you shall not murder, you shall not steal, you shall not give false testimony, honor your mother and father.' 'All these I have kept since I was a boy,' the ruler said. When Jesus heard this, he said to him, 'You still lack one thing. Sell everything you have and give to the poor, and you will have treasure in heaven. Then come, follow me.' When the ruler heard this, he became very sad, because he was very wealthy. Jesus looked at him and said, 'How hard is it for the rich to enter the Kingdom of God! Indeed, it is easier for a camel to go through the eye of a needle than for someone who is rich to enter the Kingdom of God.' Those who heard this asked, 'Who then can be saved?' Jesus replied, 'What is impossible with man is possible with God.' Peter said to him, 'We have left all we had to follow you!' Jesus said to them, 'Truly I tell you, no one who has left home or wife or brothers or sisters or parents or children for the sake of the Kingdom of God will fail to receive many times as much in this age, and the age to come enteral life.'" The deacon then took the book he was reading from and had brought from the altar up in his hands, showing it to the people as he sang, "The Gospel of the Lord."

"Praise to you, Lord Jesus Christ," Vienna and the congregation replied. The crowd sat down as the deacon moved off the pulpit, met the archbishop at the altar, and they both bowed at the altar, in the direction of the people, and then traded places. The archbishop went up to the pulpit.

"My dear brothers and sisters in Jesus Christ," the archbishop greeted in a British accent, "the story of the Ruler, also known as the story of the Rich Man, is often a difficult reading, one wrapped in mystery. The reading can be summarized to a question, 'In order to be a disciple of Christ, do we have to abandon all that we own?' Whenever I come across this reading, and those alike it in the other Gospel books, what comes to the forefront of my mind is a rich man who embodied the message of this passage in his own life, St. Francis of Assisi. Now, St. Francis was a man born into wealth, and he was said to have also been an energetic young man who spent his father's wealth lavishly and could have whatever he wanted in life. However, some also believed that even before his radical conversion, he was a kind and warm-hearted man, at one point running after a beggar to give him what he had earned in the sale of some of his own wears in the market, to the ridicule of his rich friends. Although we can be sure that at some point St. Francis heard this Gospel reading as we have today, we were told that it was not this reading but being on the brink of death at a young age that radicalized him to the point that he sold his possessions. Perhaps St. Francis could understand today's psalm, Psalm 49, specifically the verse 'Do not be overawed when others grow rich, when the splendor of their houses increases; for they will take nothing with them when they die.' St. Francis would surely understand he would take nothing with him if he died as well, and knew that this desire was not what he wanted from his life.

"During his illness, St. Francis of Assisi had a vision of Jesus, and what did Jesus ask of him? He did not ask him the same question he asked the Ruler in today's reading, to abandon his wealth, or similar lines from today's psalm, but instead asked him to simply rebuild his Church – that was all. Rebuild my Church. In seeing Jesus before him, St. Francis of Assisi realized not only a mission, but a way in which he could not fear dying for nought. In the spiritual transformation to follow, St. Francis of Assisi would understand the deeper meaning of the Gospel message today, and that is not that riches are evil, but that those objects of which distract us, chain us, or are otherwise obstacles to our pursuit of love and goodness, are that which are evil. Jesus was not displeased with the rich, nor did he dislike the Ruler because he had riches, but he understood the heart of the Ruler, and although he kept the Ten Commandments, he had to take the next step and give up his riches so that he could fulfill the commandments on a greater level, the sum of which is to love God with our whole hearts, and in our love of God, to love our neighbors with our whole hearts and as we love ourselves – this purification of love was what the Ruler was afraid of, and which we hear in other gospel readings though not today's, prevents this Ruler from selling his belongings and following Jesus. St. Francis of Assist did not abandon his riches to prove a point, but to prove to God his willingness to love and follow Jesus without any obstacles or distractions. He was all-in, so to speak.

"The Ruler in today's Gospel had many riches and he was sad to abandon them. No doubt, living so many years in wealth and luxury, to abandon these objects would be a radical shift as it was for St. Francis of Assisi, which is why Jesus preaches on the difficulty of this step, and although we are all called to sanctification, Jesus understands all our hearts and the limits of our hearts to recognize that in some men and women, this call may be too much at initial glance. Not all will be able to answer the call, but to those that are able to answer and do, many riches await them in Heaven. For those who are not strong enough to make that leap of faith, it is still possible to do so with God, faith in God, and trusting in Jesus as we are able to do so as Christians, but also to receive the graces available to us as Catholics.

"Why is there is so much emphasis on love, especially of the poor? My brothers and sisters, we live in a fallen, unjust world and the poor are the most victim to that injustice. What Christ proposes in our joint mission with him in the world is to love one another, to expel evil through goodness, and keeping the commandments does its dues and is very good, but going above and beyond is what Chris emphasized in his ministry – he was all-in, whether it was to go the extra mile, or to abandon everything to serve his people, or to give up his own life on the Cross for each one of us, and suffer, because this world is one of suffering, because the desires of our hearts made for so much more do not align with the fallen world we live in. Jesus did no wrong in his life, and yet he suffered, and as we heard in the second reading, it is there that he meets us, in that suffering in a world that is imperfect, whether it be poverty, illness, or some other circumstance. For this reason, Jesus is the God of the poor, the afflicted, and the marginalized... and as disciples, asked more from us, giving us the grace to do more as his disciples. The commandments can be very well summarized as love God and neighbor, so when you fulfill the commandments, it is imperative that then you become beacons of love, loving God and neighbor as much as you can – that is the call of today's reading, and it one that can apply to any of us…" Everest went silent as the archbishop continued to preach. He held a frown on his face, crossed his arms, and simply looked blankly towards the altar.

At the end of Mass, Vienna and Everest left their pews and went up the aisle towards the back of the church and into the narrow narthex. They then exited out of the church and onto the patio, coming down the steps to the sidewalk to depart from the cathedral for the day. Vienna opened a small umbrella that Everest held, and they shared it. They crossed the street to come around to above-ground parking garage where the Spyros EX was parked.

"What should we do for the rest of the day?" Vienna questioned as they drove around to exit the parking garage. "What can be done when the rain comes down so often like this…"

"I have to work on a speech that I'm going to give at the next Cabernet Foundation event next weekend," Everest remarked with a sigh. "We're doing a fundraiser for local food banks."

Everest turned onto Bailey Drive and began to drive southbound to pass the cathedral and reach the large intersection that led to the highway or south part of the island. He stopped the car at the red light.

"If you will be in your study, then I will see if Allodia wants to go out," Vienna responded, lowly in spirit as she looked out the window. "We could go for a walk in the mall and have lunch together."

Everest did not respond. Instead, he eyed a beggar on the side of the street with a cardboard sign that read 'Need Money –

Stuck in Harlech.' He came out to the car stopped at the line at the intersection and then began to pass down the middle as he attempted to solicit drivers and their passengers. He rushed over to a car on the left as they rolled down their window.

"Oh, look, Everest," Vienna noted. "How can they just come onto the streets? It's so dangerous…"

"It is dangerous," Everest agreed, reaching into his jacket.

A whistle blew and a police officer came around on foot and yelled at the car and beggar. The beggar fled the scene, but the office called the driver to pull over up ahead. The lights then turned green, and the cars began to drive forward. Everest saw in his rear view mirror the beggar standing from afar while the car whose passenger gave money to this person was pulled over.

"Why did the policeman stop that man's car?" Vienna questioned. "Is he stupid?"

"No, actually come to think of it, I think there's a bylaw to do with giving money to panhandlers."

"What? Why?"

"I couldn't tell you. I heard about it though, supposedly it's a couple years old."

"Oh, that's awful…"

"Yup…" Everest replied, clearing his throat, "My fairest city? I had an idea."

"What idea, my beautiful mountain?"

"How about we go out to one of those Christian soup kitchens to just volunteer an hour or two together? I saw an ad in the lobby of the cathedral. I think it would be interesting to try it out. I wouldn't have time next week, but the week after would be a good time maybe?"

"What a wonderful idea, my dearest mountain," Vienna responded with a smile. "I love the way you think."

Act 5, Scene 4

"Welcome, Mr. Cabernet," Leanne greeted, shaking his hand. "We're still setting up for today's event, but hopefully the skies stay as they are, so we don't have any rain."

"Yes, the weather seems to be unpredictable lately," Everest replied, "but I suppose it's our fault for organizing a day of lawn bowling mid October. At least the tickets have been sold, and nobody should have not known what they were walking into."

"Let me show you around," Leanne encouraged.

Everest and Vienna both walked through the parking lot to two clear open rectangular patches of artificial turf where today's event at the Eastford Lawn Bowling Club was to take place. The club also had a small building attached at the side and to the sidewalk, and a patio plaza next to with a small clearing of grass. Around this clearing of grass, a sheltered stage was being set up with audio speakers. There were additional tents behind acting as a green room for performers and other crew members. The property was surrounded by a very low three-foot tall fence with gates at the sidewalk and parking lot entrances. The property in itself was situated in Upper Middlefield, surrounded by some suburban condos and near a local community centre. Directly behind them was the highway.

Everest wore a casual white-beige suit with a very light blue-white collared shirt and no tie. Vienna wore a white dress and carried around a clutch. She also wore a derby hat with a feather in it.

"Looks like we're making some progress here," Everest remarked, looking about. "The event doesn't begin until around ten o'clock, so we will still have some time."

"Just to go over the itinerary again, we have our opening at ten o'clock, followed by two hours of lawn bowling. At twelve o'clock, we have another speech, including one by yourself. The media will be here to report on the event. There will also be a banquet, and then two more hours of lawn bowling that results in a finale."

"Excellent, well thought through, Ms. McClaren," Everest remarked. "Who did we secure for the live performance."

"We were able to get a local band to play soft rock for the four-hours," Leanne answered. "They'll be playing while the guests bowl. Let me just take you to the back tents where you can familiarize yourself and also set up."

Leanne brought them around to the enclosed rear tent behind the stage where there were some seats and chairs, coolers with refreshments, and cases for AV equipment lying around. A table in the back also had food.

"This space is yours to share in," Leanne said. "Just through that exit over there you'll come up to the stage." She led them through the exit, up a set of stairs, and onto the stage. "Right here we have the podium and microphone. Ms. Walters has left her speech here, so if you have a speech, you can also leave it here."

"Ah, that would be convenient," Everest replied, taking out a piece of paper from his coat. "I wouldn't want to lose this – I'll just place it here. I spent a bit of time on the computer typing that out over the week and don't have a copy. Are you sure it'll be safe here?"

"Absolutely," Leanne assured him with a smile. "Now, we were able to sell all our tickets, so we expect a full house. We've also set up a section at the very back for media to set up their cameras and take pictures from. They will only be allowed in that zone. We have volunteers at the entrance gates to check tickets, and we also our caterers in the club house kitchen where they will be preparing lunch."

"Good," Everest replied, "if that's the case, then is there anything that either of us could assist in? Anything at all? Anything that needs to be supervised, or taken care of? Is there anything we've forgotten?"

"No, Mr. Cabernet, we're all set for today's event," Leanne answered. "Fingers-crossed, it looks like nothing could go wrong for us."

At a quarter to ten o'clock, the first guests began to arrive and filter into the plaza patio. Both Vienna and Everest stood at attention near the entrance, greeting people as they came inside and making conversation with them. Within a few more minutes, Allodia in a white sailor blouse, and white trousers and belt arrived with Salmar in a white polo, rain coat, and beige-white trousers.

"Hello!" Allodia greeted with a smile. "Glad we could make it!"

"There you two are," Everest said. "I was worried you wouldn't make it, or that something had happened with your cab."

"Yeah, about that..." Salmar responded.

Everest turned his gaze over to the entrance from the parking lot as Charlemagne walked in. He wore baggy white trousers, a plain turquoise shirt, and a white blazer overtop.

"Isn't this lovely," Charlemagne sarcastically remarked with a frown, looking about.

"Hello, Charles," Everest instead replied. "How nice of you to drive your brother and sister here, and save the cab money I gave them."

"Did you think I would allow them to slum it in a cab?" Charlemagne questioned. "Besides, I couldn't miss this event..."

"Right..." Everest responded, looking about, "well, as long as you are all here, why don't all five of us have a round together later? For old time's sake?"

"I don't recall ever a time in which all five of us had a round of anything together," Charlemagne responded. "I would rather not partake in such a common activity as bowling outdoors."

"Aw, come on, Charlie," Allodia complained. "Why not? It would make up for all those nights that we missed you on family board game night."

"Family what?" Charlemagne questioned.

"Shut up," Salmar said to Allodia.

Charlemagne simply looked estranged at their words.

"Come now, Charlemagne," Vienna encouraged, "do so for your *mutte*r, hm? A round of bowling could be fun, no?"

Charlemagne looked at his mother and the seriousness in his face broke down a bit. He sighed and looked to the side. "Oh, alright then…"

"Yay!" Allodia cheered.

"I will be right back," Charlemagne replied.

Charlemagne left, and Everest looked towards him for a split moment before he began to shake hands with the rest of the guests that began to arrive. The musicians on stage began to play some soft tunes to liven up the venue and at the background of all the participants and guests who were deep in conversation with each other. After a few minutes from when the last guests arrived and joined the others, the music began to soothe down and Leanne took the stage.

"Hello, everyone!" she enthused. "Welcome to only just our second fundraiser in the life of Cabernet Foundation. Today, we are here at the Eastford Lawn Bowling Club where we've partnered with the establishment for the cause of supporting our local food banks across Harlech. Everyday families who are not making enough income to survive rely on these food banks to provide them with the necessities they need to feed not just themselves, but often times entire families who depend upon them. We want to ensure that our local food banks have the funds needed to run successfully and also to provide the essential foods that every family needs. We appreciate all of you who have bought tickets for this event, a share of those proceeds of which go into the cost of this event and everything else towards supporting that cause. We would also like to thank all of you who have voluntarily chipped in and provided additional donations through Cabernet Foundation for these banks – your generosity will not go without praise, so thank you to all our generous donors. Now, without further ado, I would like to invite Yolanda Walters to the stage, Chief Executive Officer and President of Cabernet Foundation."

The crowd applauded and a woman walked up to the podium. She placed down a sheet of paper on the podium from her white blazer jacket and then looked at the crowd with a smile. She wore a white full-body dress underneath her blazer. She had medium-length auburn hair and black glasses. She was middle-aged and had fair skin. She also wore pearl earrings. A lot of people in the crowd wore white, beige and grey colors.

"Hello, everyone," Yolanda greeted, "thank you once again for coming to our event today. Just before we dive right into the fun of today's event, I wanted to talk a moment about poverty in our beloved city and what Cabernet Foundation hopes to do not just in Harlech, but across the world. The mission of Cabernet Foundation has been set to help the communities that Cabernet Industries does business with to ensure that our mutual experience with one another is always a positive one. We rely on the local communities not just to do business with them, but for them to also build up our branches and assist us in ways that we could not do otherwise. A lot of times, these communities in the poorer parts of the world are under-developed and/or are under regimes that are so corrupt that their local governments cannot provide for them the basic infrastructures they need. Cabernet Foundation aims to extend our charity outwards not just to our own people in Harlech who need a helping hand, but to extend that mission to all peoples. As part of my job with the foundation, I've been in charge in coordinating with branch leadership across the globe to see just how Cabernet Foundation can hope to make a difference in those different corners. I would just like to say, thank you for all your support towards Cabernet Foundation, because without it we would just be sitting ducks. Through your support, we will be able to make a wholesome impact on the world around us, and it is through that difference that we hope to ensure that the Cabernet Industries namesake is remembered upon with a smile. Before I pass the mic back to Ms. McClaren, I would just like to take the opportunity to thank our sponsors here at the Eastford Lawn Bowling Club, and also Mr. Archibald Simpson, City Councillor for Eastford, and his party, the Harlech Association of Liberals, who without this event would not be possible as well. Thank you."

The crowd applauded. Leanne returned to the podium while Ms. Walters walked off.

"Alright everyone, without further ado, let's get to some bowling!"

The crowds broke-off and each according to their ticket, went to their assigned lane. There were approximately ten players to each lane and twelve lanes in total. The musicians began to play music, and Everest and his family went to the last-most lane where they met with five more people. The Cabernet family quickly announced their intent to compete against the other five as a team, and then they proceeded to set up for the two-hour game.

"So... where's the pins?" Allodia questioned, looking at the small black bowling balls for them to use.

"There are no pins," Charlemagne explained. "Lawn bowls do not use pins. In lawn bowling, at least two players compete against one another each round as we attempt to roll the bowls down the grass and towards a mark called a jack. You see this white ball here," he said, showing it amongst the bowling balls to the other nine, "this little ball is the jack. It is rolled down at the start of the game, and the objective is rolling these balls, each of which are distinct in the color of their seal, towards the jack. After a round is complete, each ball is measured for proximity to the jack and scores tallied up from those measurements. The team with highest score wins the round. Since we have five players, which is an irregular size, I propose and believe we are expected to play four on, and one off, and then rotate one player off from each team per round as a moment to break. From what I can gather from the scoreboard here," he said, pointing to a chalkboard nearby for them to use, looks like we are expected to play ten rounds total."

"Have you played this before, Charles?" Everest questioned.

"No, father," Charlemagne responded with a sly smile, "I've just read about it beforehad."

Charlemagne volunteered to not play the first round and let the other four play instead. The game proceeded with Charlemagne setting up a mat nearby from which players would roll from, and then him also throwing the jack from the mat. Afterwards, one player from each team took turns rolling a bowl towards the jack, and each player went twice for eight throws in total. To keep all players engaged, those not throwing were responsible to go out and measure together, and then report back and collect the balls. After the initial round, Everest volunteered to sit out and take Charlemagne's place with the other player from the other team.

Everest cheered from the sidelines as his family gave their all. Vienna, Salmar, Allodia, and even Charlemagne became more engaged in cheering each other and giving words of encouragement as they competed against the stranger group, a group of strangers of whom were no strangers to the game and were natural-born players. At the end of the next round, Everest and the other player from the other team went out to measure the bowls and collect them before returning to write down each other's score. The game was close between the rounds. Next Vienna, then Salmar, and finally Allodia sat out the round. Everest continued to cheer as Charlemagne gave his second of two throws.

"Way to go, son!" Everest applauded with a smile. "Very nice!"

Charlemagne gave a timid and confident smile as the bowl nearly came near the jack. The next player from the opposing team came up to the mat and rolled the bowl forward. The bowl clashed with some others and caused some of the Cabernet family's to splinter off.

"Oof," Salmar remarked, "dirty play."

"Tisk, tisk," Charlemagne admitted. "Alright then, father, it's on you."

"The pressure is on," Everest remarked, stepping up to the mat with a bowl. He looked towards the jack and positioned his body towards it. The then bent his knees and threw the ball, landing it directly next to the jack. "How's about that!"

"Yes!" Charlemagne cheered, clapping.

"Well done, honey," Vienna agreed, lightly clapping.

"How about that, Team Cabernet?" Everest said, shaking hands with his family. "Alright then, Allodia, go on and count them."

The score was close with the Cabernet family in the lead. Allodia and the player from the opposing team went out to measure and collect the bowls, and when she came back, she wrote down a score for them and the opposing team wrote their score. They then added it up, and before it could be written down, Charlemagne clapped his hands.

"Nicely done!" Charlemagne cheered. "Are we not the greatest?!"

"Easy there, tiger," Everest laughed, putting a hand on his shoulder. "We were all great." He then turned to the opposing team to offer his hand and say, "Good game."

After a few more minutes as others finished their rounds for the morning, the music faded, and Leanne McLaren came around to the stage.

"Oh, I've got to go," Everest noted, "I have my speech – the press is here. Wish me luck." He then left and came around to the green tents where he stayed behind in anticipation of being called to the podium. Everest waited anxiously as he stood restlessly.

"And now, I would like to welcome Mr. Everest Cabernet, Chairman of Cabernet Industries to the stage for a few words..." The crowd applauded.

"Alright, Ev, here we go..." Everest muttered to himself. He then stepped up and onto the stage from behind, waving to the crowd and coming around to the podium. He moved his speech kept behind the sheets of paper to the front and then cleared his throat. "Thank you, Leanne, and thank all of you for coming out to our event today. I hope you've all been enjoying yourselves as I have been enjoying myself with my family here. A huge thanks and round of applause for our musicians, who have kept us also entertained, the event coordinators and volunteers, and also how about this weather? Beautiful and warm despite the time of the year..." he said, smiling as he looked towards the sunshine. "We've heard a lot from Ms. McClaren about today's project mission, and from Ms. Walters on what the Cabernet Foundation strives to do worldwide, but now I would like to take a moment to just share with you a personal story on why Cabernet Industries has become oriented towards these charitable objectives. I want to be absolutely transparent with all of you," he said, looking down at his speech, "the objectives here are nothing to do with publicity, or entertainment and enjoyment, although these are certainly beautiful results of our endeavors. The true objective here is to line my own pockets..." Everest paused for a moment as he finished reading that line and the crowd muttered amongst themselves. He then cleared his throat and looked to the crowd as he apologized, "Sorry, I made a mistake there. I meant to say, to give back to others..." Everest paused again as he continued to read what was written on the piece of paper. He went ahead, eyes shooting across the paper and reading perverse words rather than those of charity. "Hm... sorry," he said, looking up to the crowd. "I had a speech written, but it seems like something is wrong with it... uh..." Everest began to silently read his speech before looking to the crowd as they murmured to each other. "Alright, you know what – it's alright." Everest picked up the microphone from the podium and stepped out towards the center of the stage. "I don't need a piece of paper to talk... Ladies and gentlemen, the aim of Cabernet Foundation is to give back to those in need. I've never in my life have ever had to worry about money; it has just been there for me. Contrary to popular belief, but there are not millions of dollars in my bank account despite my 'net worth' being millions, because my net worth is based on what my assets, or shares, are worth, and those are worth what the company is worth – and the company is worth a lot in all it owns. Every year, Cabernet Industries earns profits, and for most of our history those profits went straight into the pocket of my family – admittedly, we shared it as I found out, through annual bonuses, which we still provide, but that was always a small percentage. We would then choose to either hold on to, or to spend those profits, and they would usually spend them to grow the company and invest in projects that would make Cabernet Industries continue to expand. Nowadays, that money doesn't go solely to me, it becomes dividends, divided earnings that go to each shareholder, and the other portion becomes retained earnings, capital for future projects. Why am I telling you all this? A lot of you own businesses, so you know what I'm saying. The reason I am telling you this story is because Cabernet Industries makes too much money that it knows what to do with, just like me. A man should only have as much money as he needs, and if a company is a person, then this company makes too much money that it knows what to do with too, so it is my commitment that this year's retained earnings be put forth in the investment of

Cabernet Foundations to extend its reach to all corners of this city and to all corners of the Earth. It is my commitment that my income that extends beyond what I need to sustain my family is given back too. I intend to lead by example. From this moment forward, no longer will profits sustain the investors, it will now sustain the poor, those in need of a dollar, and it will also fund projects that build a better world. From this moment forward, Cabernet Industries intends to give back to society, rather than to hold on to a wealth. We will invest back into the world. Thank you."

Everest returned the microphone to Leanne as the crowd gave a light applause. He came down the steps into the green room and slammed his fists into a foldable table in front of the musicians who looked at him. He then growled and exited the tent from the rear, eyeing Charlemagne as he stood nearby. He shot towards him.

"Charles," Everest grunted, "a word."

"How can I help you?"

Everest took him by his arm and pulled him around behind the tent. "You sneaky little runt... You did it, didn't you? You swapped my speech – I don't know how you knew what my speech was, but somehow you did it. You swapped it with one that had different words – did you really think I would be idiot enough to read that entire manipulated speech? I saw what you were trying to do – I mistakenly read some words, and then it's fine for a couple sentences, and then I say the bad part again... You tried to sabotage me because I took away your toy department!"

Charlemagne looked back at him with shock. He then cleared his throat and said, "I'm sorry, father, but I have the earnest clue of what you are talking about. I did not swap your speech as you suggest. I did not even know you were giving a speech today."

"Then how?"

"You've been manipulated again, father," Charlemagne warned. "If not me, then who else has been screaming for your blood but the cartel?"

"The board of directors has not..."

"Oh, listen to yourself, father," Charlemagne interjected. "You honestly know not what they do. They hate you; they loathe you – they've been conspiring against you, meeting in secret..." he said, causing Everest's eye to slightly twitch. "Oh... yes," Charlemagne affirmed. "You know it. I know it. What you've yet to do is act on it. They've been deceiving and manipulating you since you arrived here earlier in the year. All this pretty talk about realigning the goals of the company, but will you survive? You've become increasingly naughty with them having announced your plans to reduce dividends, cut executive salaries, and such. I would not be surprised if they are conjuring a way in which they may get rid of you to stop you from bankrupting the company."

"If I were to bankrupt the company, would that not benefit them? For them to buy it out with their masters?"

"Cabernet Industries is worth more to them alive and in their control. There is too much capital and assets to possibly divide, and it already runs everything so smoothly... What happened with R&D was a one time event, an opportunity to divide the spoils, but the entire company as a whole? It would be disastrous if it were all to collapse. The cartel need Cabernet Industries to survive, but they don't need its people to do well, or for money to be wasted in frivolous charity projects. Those are just distractions to keep you pacified. The cartel needs the company's broad control over the branches in the many parts of the world – that is something they cannot replace. They need Cabernet Industries so they can continue to exploit the world in our family's name."

Everest did not immediately respond. "Hmph," he finally replied, "even if what you are saying is true..."

"It is."

"How was my speech altered? I typed it on my computer in my study, which nobody except you and the rest of the family has access to. The speech was nearly identical to the one that I had written aside from the modifications. How do you suppose that was possible? If you ask me, it has your fingerprints all over it."

Charlemagne paused for a moment as he took his hands to his chin to think. He then snapped his fingers and replied, "The penthouse is only accessible to us, but the computer network is a part of the corporate network. They must have hacked into your computer to steal your speech and make the changes."

"Really? Hacked my computer?" Everest questioned, unconvinced. "And who is that's spent the last year in the United Kingdom doing computer research?"

"Oh, please," Charlemagne responded, "I'm no hacker."

"Even if that is how they modified my speech, how could anyone from the board of directors changed it – none of them are here."

"None of them are here, but I'm sure someone who is here could have changed it for them. I bet it was Ms. Yolanda Walters – she and Mr. Roness are good friends. If not, it could have been anyone within the foundation."

"That," Everest was about to respond, pausing for a moment, "makes a little sense actually…" He then went quiet as he let go of his son. Rather than continue to face his son, Everest stepped aside and left him. He was speechless for the rest of the day.

Act 6, Prologue

"Are any of you guys hungry?" Everest questioned.

"Yes!" young voices agreed.

Everest stood around a group of young adolescents varying between the ages of fifteen-year-old females and thirteen-year-old males. Amongst this group of youngsters was Allodia and Salmar, each those respective ages. There were close to seven adolescents in total, including Everest's own children. As Everest asked the question related to food, the youth began to shake the queue barrier in the corridor of the entertainment facility in expression of their anticipation and hunger. Everest and the kids were inside a long corridor, similar to the one in Polaris Arena, although this one appeared more rustic. The corridor consisted of smooth concrete floor and the walls were vertical dark wooden panels. There was a lot of horse imagery on one side of walls, and around some parts were large television sets that played videos on loop to do with equestrian races and show jumping. At the other side of walls there was the main entrance further ahead, a food vendor down the corridor, and also washrooms towards the other end. At the end of the corridor on the far side there was as fire exit, while on the other side near the food vendor there was a club member only entrance that went to the clubhouse and stables. The food vendor was a regional small business called Angel's Burgers, and rather than beer, they sold all sorts of family friendly foods: from ice cream and ice cream sundaes to chicken wings and chicken strips, pizza, burgers, and hotdogs, and French fries, poutine, pretzels and popcorn. They also had a variety of soda selections. Most importantly of all, the prices were cheap; a hot dog for a mere dollar and twenty-five cents for example. Everest stood back as he looked at the menu with the kids.

"Okay, everybody picks out one food item and a drink," Everest addressed to the youngsters. "Allodia, you and your friends go first."

Everest appeared much as he did in the present age, although a bit more youthful and his head fuller of hair and at a medium length. He wore a flannel shirt tucked into denim jeans. He also wore his leather coat. Allodia had wavy thick blonde hair and wore a denim coat. Salmar was slimmer than in the present age, shorter, and had nearly a bowl cut of light blonde hair. He wore a collared long-sleeve shirt with top buttons. He also wore denim jeans like his father.

Allodia and her three friends walked up to the counter to order food. Every one girl ordered one of the food items and a drink after much deliberation and harassment from the boys asking them to hurry up. Afterwards, Salmar and his two friends went up to the counter and they quickly ordered their food before Everest came up to make his choice.

"And for you sir?" the seventeen-year-old boy at the other side of the counter sheepishly asked.

"Hm," Everest thought aloud, "I'll just get a hotdog and cola, please."

The cashier punched that order into the cash register. He then said, "That'll come to twenty-five seventy, sir."

Everest raised his eyebrows as he took out his wallet. He took out a ten and twenty dollar bill. Salmar stood directly next to him as he paid. "Don't tell your mother I spent this much on you guys," Everest remarked. "She'll kill me otherwise." He passed the bills to the cashier who began to fetch the change.

"Four dollars and thirty cents is your change," the cashier remarked, passing two toonies and three dimes back to Everest. "Your order will be right up."

"Thank you," Everest responded, taking the coins into his hand. He then eyed a tip jar next to the cash register and dropped them inside.

"Thank you, sir!" the cashier thanked.

Everest and Salmar moved away from the counter and to the side to allow the next customer to approach. All eight of them began to wait for their food, which did not take too long to come around.

"I've got two chicken strips, one poutine, two popcorns, two hotdogs and one burger!" an attendant called out, placing two trays on the counter.

"Alright, that's us," Everest remarked, holding a beverage cup in his hands.

The kids moved forward to grab their food and then step out. Everest stepped forward in last place to pick up his hot dog. He then went over to the ketchup and mustard dispensers where like father like son, Salmar was putting both on his hotdog.

"Hey, we got the same thing," Everest noted, joining him.

Salmar went back to his friends, and now that everyone was nourished, they began to make their way up the stairs to the second floor. The second-floor corridor was plain in these days, consisting of a wide passageway with seats and windows that looked outwards to the street on one side, and doorways to the stands on the other side. Everybody came around to Gate C where they exited out to a stand of benches that looked outwards to a large equestrian racetrack. The benches went all the way down to the ground level where there was an approximately two-foot drop to the ground floor. They also went further up to the rooftop of the building where there was a judge's stand and exclusive boxes on the sides for very important persons. The benches looked towards the arena. The arena course was large and consisted of an oval-shaped track with a fence around both the inside and outside. In the middle of the course was a large, mowed field with obstacles placed around in a consistent pattern. Some haybales could be seen positioned along the backside of the track. Behind the haybales, there were rows of billboards that advertised local businesses in Allabrese. On the right, the start of the raceway began on a straight path appendaged to the oval circuit with starting gates. The clubhouse and stables could be seen extended outwards from the stands and main building, slightly bent inwards to the arena. Between the area of space from the stands, stables, and racecourse, there was a dirt paddock. This paddock was further divided by a fence between the space directly in front of the stands and the space directly in front of the clubhouse/stables. In the latter space, horses could be seen wearing jackets overtop their coats. These horses were on leads and had stable workers holding them in place as many of them were being brought out from the stables. Further to the right from the stands, another enclosure could be seen separate to the racecourse where more horses could be seen grazing in the grassy area. Finally, on the stretch of racecourse closest to the stands, around the middle was an archway that connected with both sides of the fence. Near this finish line within the inner field was a scoreboard with a ladder at the side and platform in front. The skies were mildly grey at this time, although the day had been dry, and the stands were sheltered. Across from the building, next to the scoreboard on the left, was a large stage from which a high school band was playing for the crowd as part of the pre-game show. Salmar went and sat next to his friends at the end of the bench, while Allodia and her friends went down a step.

Everest came around to the same bench as Salmar and his friends, but stayed a fair distance away as he saw his son chatting with his own friends. He gave a warm smile to them and then sat down. He began to eat his hotdog on his own as he listened to the band music playing from the ground below. A few workers could be seen setting up for the event, but there were no horse jockeys in sight. Everest looked down to his daughter as she and her friends chatted. He continued to give a warm smile. He also looked around him at the others in attendance in the stands. There was a modest crowd in the stands for today's events, mostly older folk and families. After a few minutes, the music from the high school band shifted tune and became more suspenseful. Everest straightened up as he realized the races were about to start.

"Ladies and gentlemen, boys and girls, welcome people of all ages. We are pleased to have you all come again to our grounds as we prepare for the thirty-ninth annual Nattau Derby and Spring Festival! Today, we have twelve contestants seeking to compete for one of twelve spots for the derby!"

The audience applauded.

"Without further introduction, allow me to introduce to you our contestants – it is always such a pleasure to welcome old faces and new horses. First, but far from the worst, we have Rye Toast and his rider, Dean Casset."

The audience applauded as a beige horse trotted forward. A jockey rode atop of the horse while a handler led the lead towards the gates. The jockey was a short male, less than average height by a few inches. He was also slim and wore tight white pants and a blazer. He wore a black helmet and tall black boots.

The master of the ceremony introduced the rest of the twelve contestants and their riders. The horses were named Gigi, Thumper, High Tail, Hammerhead, Gunner, Maple Leaf, Broomstick, Haha, Doppel, and Kebab.

"Last but not least!" the MC said. "Put your hands together for Milo Beckett and his horse Prudence!"

The audience clapped as a flamboyant jockey atop of a brown horse was led across from the stables. He waved at the crowd and blew kisses towards them. The audience cheered for him. He was brought to the end of a line-up of the jockeys beneath the stands.

"Twelve contestants, and only one spot in the tourney!" the MC declared. "We should all agree though that we should want the best and brightest of them all to represent Nattau County, so who is it going to be?! Let's find out!"

The riders split up from the pen and they were started to be led further towards the gates so that the race could start.

"That Beckett is a piece of work," Everest remarked as the MC continued to speak. "Last year he and his horse at the time got to represent the county at the derby and lost... badly."

The kids didn't reply as they looked at him. The horses were soon ready in their gates. Everest and the others could see and hear the horses kicking and neighing as they were confined into that small space. Some workers positioned themselves above to release the gates.

"Looks like we're just about set..." the MC remarked. "We're getting the thumbs up. Markers at the ready, and... they're off!"

A loud bell rang, and the gates were released open. The horses launched out from them like grapeshot cannonballs from a cannon.

"And they're off!" the MC declared. "Look at them go! We have Thumper taking the lead with Hammerhead and Kebab directly behind. Prudence and Haha not too far from them either!"

The horse ran down the initial stretch and reached around the corner. The kids were astonished at the speed of the horses as they zoomed forward. It wasn't long before they reached around the corner of the arena.

"Look at them go!" one of the kids cried out. Everest smiled at their own excitement.

"Hammerhead cuts-off Kebab. Thumper maintains the lead – oh wait! Hammerhead has now passed Kebab. Prudence is not too far behind, passing even Kebab, but Thumper continues to get the lead out!"

"Oh, I should have put a wager on this race," Everest remarked. "I forgot to pass by that man Barney at the bookmakers."

The horses began to come around the second corner. The MC announced, "Hammerhead is still in the lead. Thumper behind –

Prudence behind. Kebab has now lagged behind with Haha… Thumper is trying to make a push back into first, but he just can't do it… Here we go as they come across the next stretch. Hammerhead is still pushing on, and looks like Prudence is looking to pass Thumper too. Kebab and Haha are tied behind, and maybe we'll see Kebab fall back. We've got Gigi in the very back starting to just struggle to keep up with the others. Prudence is now right behind Thumper, and it looks like he may pass, but Thumper is denying the humiliation of going into third. Hammerhead standing strong as they reach the corner here. There they go, Prudence unable to push on past Thumper, and Thumper having the dilemma to catch up to the Hammerhead and not get beat by Prudence. Haha is now ahead of Kebab, and we have Gunner behind those two too. Who's it going to be?"

"Come on, Thumper," Everest remarked. "Let's go…" he muttered. "I'll tell you kids what, this really brings me back. I loved horse races, ever since my dad took me to one when I was a kid, I loved them. He loved them too. I suppose we had that in common…" He grew silent.

"Hammerhead is still in the lead! Prudence and Thumper tied for second place. Haha behind and Kebab has now been surpassed by Gunner. Those three are having their own tussle as this comes around the last corner! Hammerhead has got a bit of a distance, but Prudence is now catching up while Thumper struggles to hold on to second place – seems like he's falling back now – no, there goes Thumper with another push, but Prudence has got a bit more life within him too. Hammerhead is still in the first but those other two are now gaining on him. They're around the last bend and here's the final stretch. Hammerhead is going for it, but there's Prudence and Thumper. Thumper with a final push to pass Prudence. Gunner with a final push to meet Prudence too. Hammerhead is still going for it; Thumper is now right behind him – there they go! Thumper takes it! Hammerhead is in second place and Prudence falls back to fourth place. Gunner in third. Haha in fifth, and then we have Kebab, Broomstick, Doppel, Maple Leaf, High Tail, Rye Toast and Gigi."

The boys shot their hands up in the air in celebration, and the girls applauded, and the entire stand audience cheered the conclusion of the race.

"What a turn of events, folks," the MC declared. "A game like that really keeps you on the edge of your seat because you don't know who will come out on top…"

Everest simply stood at his bench, expressionless to the victory of his pitched horse. He briefly came to life as he realized the commotion and lightly applauded. The kids and crowd continued to cheer, but he looked towards them without a plain expression. He then took in a deep breath and let out a sigh.

"Congratulations to Thumper and his rider, Doug Kershaw, who have taken first place! An honorable congratulations to Hammerhead and his rider too, and also Gunner and his in their noteworthy push. Well everyone, that concluded the two-kilometer race, but don't go anywhere as we enter a brief intermission and carry on with the obedience and obstacle portion of today's day full of events."

Everest lowered his hands and continued to stare plainly forward. He took in another deep breath and then let it out. He then turned to a warm smile as he looked to his kids.

Act 6, Scene 1

Everest sat at the large desk in the chairman's office on the executive floor of Cabernet Industries. Light poured through the windows and past the curtains, creating beams of light that shined down on the floor. He held a pencil between his two hands, elbows planted on the desk cover, and he looked straightforward towards the portrait of his father. After a few more minutes as he was sat in the board room, some workers began to enter the room to set up chairs in front of the fireplace. They moved the couches and placed them on the sides of the room to create a larger space ahead of the desk and armchairs. They then began to place foldable chairs, a podium with a microphone, and some sound systems. A photographer also began to set up, placing photographer umbrellas around the corners. Finally, a worker entered the room with a ladder, placed it in front of the fireplace, and began to climb up to remove the portrait of Derby Cabernet. At that moment, Everest stood up and walked over as it was placed next to the fireplace and he looked at the image of his father.

The painting of Derby was not just life-like, but the frame was tall and the depiction almost the exact same height of Everest's father. The pair looked at each other, blue eyes piercing at another's blue eyes.

"Is everything okay, Mr. Cabernet?" a worker questioned.

"Yes, everything is fine," Everest replied, smirking. "Where will this portrait be taken?"

"Well, I don't have anywhere particular to move it, so it'll just go downstairs into the furniture depot. Is there somewhere in particular you wanted it to go?"

"No, nowhere," Everest answered, moving away. "Carry on."

The worker placed the painting on a cart and then hauled it away. As soon as the workers had moved the painting of Derby out of the office, another cart entered, veiled, and with a portrait underneath. The cart was brought around to the front of the mass of chairs where two workers then lifted it up to a stand. They maintained the veil. After the workers placed the painting on the stand, Everest came around and placed some papers on the podium to prepare.

After another hour, the room had a few people, including some from Cabernet Foundation who were seated at the front. Some chairs besides the stand with the painting were occupied, one of which had Lucius Clifford, Yolanda Walters, and another where Everest sat from.

"It's a pleasure to have you all here today," Yolanda greeted, taking the stage to speak first. "At the request of Mr. Cabernet, he wanted to keep this ceremony small and compact, despite our insistence that we take this moment to reflect and celebrate on twenty years in which he has been in his current position as chairman. I'm honored to have myself and few others from the foundation present on this occasion and have the opportunity to speak. However, as Mr. Cabernet has put it, and will likely go on to speak about, the Cabernet Foundation is his favorite part of the company, so it is not too surprising that many of us are from the foundation. I have not been with Cabernet Industries for too long, but since I started in my role, Mr. Cabernet has been as involved in the operations of the foundation as I have, and been there to guide us towards his vision for what the foundation aims to serve in local communities. We've sat together in many meetings, made many decisions together, and it has been a pleasure to be a part of what is a bright future for the company as it endeavors into a new century soon in an everchanging world. I won't speak for very long, so I just wanted to address that Mr. Cabernet has a particular skillset that has inspired all of us in the foundation. He is a born leader and a visionary. He is also very creative and a man with a mission, a mission of which the foundation is eager to fulfill. To honor this man who has given life to our charitable organization, despite his insistence that no such project be undertaken, the foundation at our own expense commissioned this painting for Everest."

Leanne McClaren stepped forward and drew the veil away. The painting was not a portrait, but a landscape painting of Mount Everest with its snow-capped mountains and many peaks. The audience laughed as they saw the portrait. Everest looked over and gave a sly smile as he saw the depiction.

"You may think that there was some sort of miscommunication between what we intended and what the artist thought we intended, but I assure you that this portrait was our true intent," Yolanda expressed. "To capture this brilliant image of the tallest mountain in the world was no easy feat. Our artist travelled to the Himalayas himself to get an idea of what needed to be painted, and before you ask, no he did not climb the mountain while there. He shared with us that the ascent can be very dangerous and not worth the risk, but he was able to see with his own eyes this scene that has now been captured on canvas. We thought that such a painting was appropriate for Mr. Cabernet given that he refused to allow a painter to capture his likeness in the flesh, and also because he shared with us a story about his father, Derby Cabernet, in his desire to be the first to climb the mountain and because of such desire, it became the reason behind his name. Nonetheless, we thank Mr. John Vivien for this masterpiece, and we present to you what has been the fruits of labor for several months now. I would now like to invite Mr. Cabernet to share a few words with us."

The audience clapped and Everest stood up went to the podium. Ms. Walters sat down, and he looked at the painting closely.

"Wow, what a sight," Everest expressed. "I had never imagined the mountain that I was named after was such a breathtaking view... Thank you, Yolanda, Lucius, and all the team members in the foundation and those of you gathered here. I did not want to make a big deal out of twenty years, no less since nineteen and a half of those years has been spent without the oversight I've provided nowadays with the board of directors. Such a painting is just so precious, I don't think I could accept this piece... I would have to insist it be auctioned for a project with the foundation, but that is a discussion we can have later. Right now, I would just like to be brief and touch on a couple points.

"You are right to say that the foundation is my most precious contribution to Cabernet Industries, and I do believe that we have made a step in the right direction in terms of the future of Cabernet Industries. From now on, the success of the company is intertwined with the charitable contributions that it can make, and no longer are our actions just a part of a growing worldwide capitalistic market order with communism in decline. However, even as the foundation moves forward in its actions, I still find something amiss within our internal organization. For this reason, I would like to announce at this gathering, a new vision that I have for Cabernet Industries.

"Cabernet Industries is a world-wide multimillion dollar organization that has reaches into all parts of the world. To think, all decision-making capacities are made within the boardroom on this floor, or from our individual offices, to dictate the path and destination of this company. The fates of so many lives are made in our uninformed and sometimes plain ignorant decision-making, and how could they be anymore informed when we are so invested in the larger picture. It is no reason we at times don't even care about what the smaller reactions or consequences are... Not anymore though. From this moment, I intend to transfer the decision-making authority for our international branches, into the hands of each respective branch through local executive councils co-chaired by a corporate executive leader from that branch and a member of the local government. These councils will have the complete oversight in their day-to-day operations, and work in tandem with our many subsidiaries to deliver services in a way that promotes the local communities and societies that we do business with. The introduction of these smaller councils at each branch, and the invitation of governments to invest in Cabernet Industries, will coincide with a reduction in the board of directors' oversight and occupation in large-scall big picture operations and pave the way forward for independence for our branches. The board of directors will be allowed to focus on home issues to do with the everyday corporate workforce rather than get involved in international affairs.

"To be honest, I've yet to propose this idea to the board of directors. I've yet to discuss it with anyone else. I've thought about it though and I feel as though I am ready for Cabernet Industries to take the right next step into the future. On Monday, I will hold a press conference where I will go into details about this transformative and exciting next step into the revision of Cabernet Industries. Since the corporation went public five years ago, it has been guided through a new leadership that has surely led the company through tough times and restored stability. However, now that those times have passed… it is time that we adapt before hard times come again. Thank you, Ms. Walters and Mr. Clifford, for organizing this event and presenting this paining for me and thank you all for attending this ceremony."

Everest removed his papers from the podium and then went to sit down next to Lucius. The audience clapped. Lucius leaned forward into Everest's ear and remarked, "We will need to talk about what you just said later."

After the ceremony, Lucius and Yolanda left the room with the other guests. The workers moved in again to remove the chairs and equipment. The painting that was given to Everest was moved next to the desk. He stayed there for a moment, expecting Roness to come or Clifford to return, but they did not arrive. After much anticipation, Everest picked up his suit jacket, put it on, and then went down the hall to knock on Roness' door.

"Who is it?" Roness questioned.

"It's me, Dwight," Everest responded. "Do you have a minute?"

Roness did not immediately respond. The door opened and Mr. Paterson looked back at him with straight eyes. Everest looked in and saw that Mr. Leroy, Mr. Clifford, and Mr. Wan-Cheung were inside already. Roness sat back in his chair and looked over to Everest.

"Mr. Cabernet," Roness greeted, "please, come in – we have all the minutes…"

Everest stepped inside the office which was dim. The curtains were closed although light poured in through the cracks. Paterson closed the door behind him and then came around to stand in the corner.

"Please, sit," Roness encouraged, gesturing for Everest to take Paterson's seat. "What can we do for you?"

The rest of the directors stared back at him with uneasy eyes. Paterson held his arms crossed. Roness looked at him with focused eyes. Everest sheepishly sat down and placed his hands in his lap.

"I take it that Mr. Clifford has already shared the contents of my speech," Everest said, "and perhaps that is what you are all gathered here to talk about…"

"No," Roness remarked, "I mean, we did hear about your speech, but right now, it's just old friends having a conversation, talking about work-related business."

"So, you have heard then," Everest pointed out.

"Yes, but please re-iterate for us if you could, just in case Lucius here misheard what he thought he heard you say… What are your plans for Cabernet Industries?"

"I plan to restructure it," Everest clarified. "I read it in a book… it's called rightsizing. Cabernet Industries has grown too large, and it is time since the restructuring that we did in 1985 to refocus our efforts to plan for the future. My proposal in plain language is two-fold. First, I intend to restructure the way in which our branches are led, eliminating the position of executive vice-president and instead creating a chief executive officer, president, and vice-president positions as part of the executive management team. Each branch will function like its own independent company, as they mostly do, and the executive power of each branch will be within their own councils of both management and investors, as we have here. There will be two chairs, a management chair and an investor chair, as we have here too, but these investors will be invited from the local government (and any local corporations able to invest). The co-chair on behalf of the investors will mainly be someone from the government investors. These councils or boards will be the primary decision-making authority for operations and administration within their region. They will work in tandem with our subsidiaries according to the best wishes of their board of directors. They will have the final say on projects in their region and oversee them.

"Meanwhile, for us here in the Pacific Branch, I intend a restructuring of the board of directors from a one-tier system to a two-tier system due to our size, forming a management board led by a chief executive officer, and a supervisory board led by a chairman. The management board will be responsible for the day-to-day operations of the Pacific Branch rather than that and the entire worldwide company. The supervisory board will compose of us investors and we will supervise the management board of the Pacific Branch. The rest of the company will continue to rely on the Pacific Branch for direction and advise but will be limited to advisement from now on as power will be provided to the branches to make their own decisions, as I said."

Everest nodded and did not immediately reply. The others were silent.

"Mr. Cabernet, that's quite the idea you have," Roness finally said. "Very thorough… there's but one problem that I have to…

advise on. Cabernet Industries has investors who have poured millions of dollar and placed people like me, Lucius, Brian, and such, in positions here on the current board and within the current management because they trust us to make decisions on behalf of the company and keep their investments safe and lucrative. They put their money forward to have the power to make decisions, not provide advice. What you are suggesting will guarantee their withdrawal from the company… We cannot support it."

"I don't need your support," Everest replied. "I am the majority shareholder, and it is up to me to decide on how the company is structured."

"You do understand that if we pull back our support from Cabernet Industries, all of us, the stock price will plunge – Cabernet Industries will not survive without our support."

"What I do understand is that if your investors leave, then so do you," Everest remarked. "I'm not particularly concerned about a lack of investors, and if the stock is cheap then that will make trade with government investors a lot better."

"You don't have the experience and knowledge to see that through yourself," Roness challenged. "We won't comply in this direction."

"Like I said, I don't need you," Everest remarked. "You are expendable, Mr. Roness."

"Expendable?" Roness questioned. "Oh really now? You are out of your depths, Mr. Cabernet. What you are proposing is unsustainable – it will result in the total collapse of this company. You will be penniless by the end of it all because all those stocks you have now and are worth something, won't be worth jack by the end of it. And do you know what will happen when the dust has settled? Blackmore, La Bastion, and every company that is better off will come in and pick the skin off the bones of whatever is even left, including this building so that it can be called Blackmore Tower instead to Cabernet Tower."

"I accept that sort of risk," Everest simply said. "You won't change my mind…"

"Then you better find someone willing to comply, because we won't."

"Then I'll sack you from your position, Mr. Roness, all of you who choose not to comply."

"For God's sake, Dwight, just do what we talked about," Leroy pressured. "Stop this madman."

Roness looked to Leroy and then back to Everest. "Alright then, it seems then you've left me with no choice, Mr. Cabernet. Bring in the TV," he said, opening a drawer and taking a video tape. "Let's watch a little movie."

Wan-Cheung pulled a television on a cart over and placed it next to Roness at the corner of his desk. He then plugged it in, took the video tape from Roness' hand, and put it in. He turned on the TV and pressed play. Everest sat back and watched as the video tape showed security camera footage, from within the corporate office area. He squinted for a moment and then saw himself come forward to Ms. Summers desk.

"What is this supposed to be?" Everest questioned.

"Shhh," Roness hushed, "let's fast forward…"

Everest continued to watch as the footage was sped up. The footage was from the day Everest offered to help Ms. Summers on a Friday evening with unfinished sorting. The footage came to the very end where Everest was positioned in front of Ms. Summers. The camera angle could see a brief glimpse of Ms. Summers behind him. Everest watched as the camera footage replayed the moment in which Ms. Summers took Everest's hand and brought it to her chest. From the angle that the camera recorded the footage, it appeared as though Everest had voluntarily raised his arm to touch her breast. The camera footage then showed Ms. Summers enter into a panic and leave.

"Isn't that nice?" Roness questioned, pausing the footage. "You naughty dog, Mr. Cabernet. Ms. Summers told me about what happened a few weeks ago. I had this footage pulled from security, and I was meaning to share it with you, but now seems like the right time. How could you?" Everest was silent. "If you want to carry forward with your proposals, Mr. Cabernet, you better find someone who will see them through, but here is my offer. I want you to sell your shares, every single one of them, and to take an early retirement. We will host a party, it will be nice, and I will destroy this tape when the time is right. I want you to leave Cabernet Industries in our good hands and abandon these destructive ideas, because otherwise I will ensure that this videotape is shared with your wife and the police so they can pursue charges for sexual assault, and she can file for divorce. How's that?"

"You... you want to blackmail me?" Everest questioned.

"Correct," Roness simply responded. "You've forced us to this point, Mr. Cabernet, but I believe I've offered a fair deal. We all know some investors who will be eager to invest back into the company at a reduced price, but it'll be a shaky transition, though sure enough it will be better than whatever you intend to do. Look at you, Mr. Cabernet, you're not a businessman. You – you're hardly a man at all, are you? Just a spoiled child, and what do you spoiled children do most? They whine, complain, and destroy that which they do not value, and that's what you are trying to do with Cabernet Industries. You are trying to destroy it just to spite us... this isn't about charity, it's about your ego."

"I..." Everest hesitated to respond, looking at the TV screen.

"Let's take a moment to think about our actions," Roness expressed, standing up. "It's a lot to think about, and it is Friday, so let's break here and wait until next Monday? How about that?"

The others stood up, and Everest slowly stood up as well. He made his way back towards the door, and Leroy opened it for him. He glared at him as he exited and then closed the door behind him. Everest quietly retreated to his office upstairs and hid himself for the rest of the evening.

Act 6, Scene 2

Everest woke up in his penthouse study, asleep on an armchair in the corner of the room with Baron licking his hand. He sat up and a book in his lap fell to the floor, spooking the dog as the hardcover hit the floorboards. He looked around and saw that it was just about dawn with a bit of light in the grey skies. He then leaned backwards into his chair and stayed put for several more minutes. Baron left, and within those few minutes, the door opened with Vienna dressed in a robe stepping inside with a cup of coffee. She placed the coffee on the small table next to the armchair and then put her hand on Everest's forehead, pulling the rest of his hair back to reveal the receding hairline. She leaned forward to kiss him and then took his hand.

"You slept here all night," Vienna expressed, "and left me all alone…"

"I'm sorry, my beautiful city," Everest responded, "but I must have dozed off. I have a lot going on at work right now."

"Do you still want to go out and volunteer this morning?" Vienna questioned.

"Hm? Oh, right," Everest replied, picking up his watch from the table and putting it on his left wrist. "I forgot we were going to volunteer at the soup kitchen this morning. Yeah, we can still do that – I really wanted to go down there."

"Have a drink in the meantime, and I will make you some breakfast," Vienna said. "Afterwards you can take a shower, and we'll be there just before ten o'clock to help. I spoke with the Sisters there, and they're eager for us to join them."

"Thank you, Vi," Everest responded. "You really are the best city, aren't you?"

Vienna gave a warm smile and then left. He stayed put as he tried to drink some coffee, and then he stood up and went to the dining room.

The couple left the penthouse at half-past nine and drove the Spyros EX into Keswick. They parked at the curb besides the same park in which Everest had parked besides when he was in Keswick earlier in the year. Both Everest and Vienna wore the simplest clothes they could find. For both of them that included denim jeans, and a long-sleeve plain black sweatshirt for Vienna, and a white t-shirt and leather jacket for Everest. The couple left their vehicle and went to the Christian soup kitchen, arms linked, and stepped inside to be greeted by other volunteers and religious sisters.

"Welcome!" a Filipino Sister exclaimed as she brought them around to the back of the kitchen. "We are so happy to have you join us…"

The sisters wore normal clothes for the most part, although some of them wore a white blouse with a cross necklace, while others wore black skirts. All of them wore a white headdress that covered their hair though. There were not many of them, only four in total while there were five volunteers with them. Everest observed a religious sister in the front, preparing the metal trays in the servery while the others were in the back. The building interior was not very large. The entrance led into a horizontal room with tiled floors and half a dozen wide tables with chairs. The chairs were stacked up on the tables. At the end of this room were several serveries with metal hoods and glass panels. An opening behind connected with the kitchen and allowed the rapid transport of food from one side to the other. On the other side, the kitchen was a similar-sized room with stoves, metal counters, and wide refrigerators. There was a smell of minestrone soup although the room was moderately quiet as people worked.

"Before you get started, you will need aprons," the Filipino Sister said, taking two aprons from a coat hook. "If you are going to be in the kitchen, you will need a hair net too. You will both need name tags with your names."

The religious sister provided these items for them to wear. Vienna wrote her name on a label and then placed it on her apron. She wrote "Vienna" with a smile next to it.

"I'm going to be lowkey," Everest expressed. "Not that I believe anyone would know who I am, but in case anyone does to avoid any publicity to my presence here."

"What business is it of anyone else that we are here on your day off?" Vienna questioned.

"Absolutely nobody's," Everest replied, "but they certainly will make it their business. I would prefer to avoid any praise that comes from my actions here the way they would for my actions in the foundation." He wrote his name as 'Pepin' and put it on his apron. "Right, so how can we help?" he asked.

"You are big and strong," the religious sister remarked. "You can help bring the groceries from the car, and you," she said, taking Vienna by the arm to guide her, "can help make sandwiches."

"Oh, yummy," Vienna encouraged, going over to a sandwich making station.

Everest went forward to a back exit where the door was open. A minivan was reverse-parked in the alleyway and the back door open. Another male volunteer, a young teenager, was assisting with the unloading of cardboard boxes with buns and vegetables. Everest followed suit and began to take out the boxes and followed the boy as he went back into the kitchen and then around a corner into a nook corridor where there were storage rooms with shelves on the left and a walk-in fridge to the right. He placed the boxes on a shelf and then went back to the van. Everest went back and forth with the boy, unloading items from this van and then another car that came with donation items.

By the time all these items were unloaded, the same Filipina religious sister directed Everest to bring some items out to replenish them as the Sisters and volunteers continued to cook and make sandwiches. Vienna had made dozens of sandwiches from the plain sandwich bread they had, placing a slice of cheese and sandwich meats between the slices, and then wrapping them up in plastic wrap. They were collected into a metal tray and then brought out to the servery for lunch time. Before the lunch hour, Everest was brought to the front servery where he was shown all the utensil and instructed on portions to give to people. He was then made to bring all the chairs down and then brought back around as people started to enter. By lunch time, a few more people entered and sat around. The smell from the patrons was foul, although the waft of soup nearly prevailed.

Each person who entered the kitchen was provided with a sandwich, a bowl of soup, and then some sort of dessert item, either a cookie or slice of a very thin cake. At the end of the servery there were insulated drink dispensers that provided either coffee or tea. If a person chose, they could have their food placed in disposable containers and placed in a brown paper bag for them to take with them. Each person varied in size and stature who walked in through the doors, but most of them were older males although a few females and even a young child could be found inside (albeit, the child was accompanied with an adult). For every ten person that was served, one gave thanks to the server while the others stayed quiet and simply sheepishly went to eat. Everest was not offended though if he wasn't thanked, but the words that came across to him from another person did leave himself quiet and stunned.

At the end of the lunch hour, by close to two o'clock, the majority of people had left and only a few stragglers entered in and received what was left. By three o'clock, the doors were closed, and the trays were empty so it was time to clean. Everest helped clean the front section while Vienna helped clean the back. He took a cloth and began to wipe the tables, letting crumbs and such fall to the floor. He wiped the tops of the seats too so he could raise the chairs up, turn them onto their seat and place them on the tables. Afterwards, Everest and another volunteer swept the floors. As he placed the contents of his dustpan into the trash bin, he looked across to the servery and on the walls where there was a Christian cross nailed in. He briefly looked at it and then lifted up the trash bag to bring it around back to the dumpster. At the end of the day, Everest and Vienna took off their aprons and prepared to leave, but not before being thanked by the Sisters.

"Well, that was nice," Everest expressed with a smile on his face, holding Vienna's arm in his arm as they left the building. "We don't have those opportunities in Allabrese, do we..."

"Everyday," Vienna corrected, "you just don't see it, my mountain. For me at least, it's every day I am in the kitchen making food for you and the children, or at the parish serving food too. You are right though, an extra remarkable opportunity to serve the community like today is lost in our little town..."

The couple came around to the Spyros EX where they stopped not too far and noticed some shards of glass on the sidewalk and gaping hole in the front passenger door.

"Oh Lord," Everest reacted, moving forward closely. "Who did such a thing?"

"Oh dear..." Vienna said, bringing a hand to her mouth. "Did they take anything?"

Everest removed some of the glass that stayed in place and looked inside. He looked around then brought his head out to look at Vienna.

"They stole some coins I had in the cupholder, but doesn't seem like anything else was taken. Unbelievable..." Everest remarked, looking about. "I'm going to have to call the police and get the car towed to a shop... Looks like there's a payphone not too far from here. I'll have to make change with a nearby store, but..." he stopped and turned to Vienna. "Why don't I get you a cab to take you home – I'll sort this all out."

"I can stay with you," Vienna proposed.

"No, it's fine, Vi. I... ugh, the stress from earlier is starting to come back to my mind as I look at this mess. Please, it would be best if I'm left alone to handle this stupidity..."

Everest didn't stay to argue with his wife. He left to go to a nearby store to make change, and then came around to payphone to call a taxi and then the police. A cab arrived before the police to take Vienna back to Cabernet Tower, while the police arrived ten minutes later to make note of the incident and then leave. Finally, a tow truck arrived to haul the vehicle off to a nearby shop in the industrial district not too far. Everest stayed in the shop for a bit as they helped him make the insurance claim on the phone, and then left on foot of his own accord.

From the body shop, Everest came out onto Manchester Street. By this time in the day, the sun was beginning to set, and it was twilight. He proceeded to walk on his own, going south to Federal Street, and then coming around westbound to reach Bailey Drive. From Bailey Drive, Everest walked south until he reached Campbell Street, but rather than cross the road to go home, he continued south until he came to Pentateuch Cathedral. The church bells could be heard ringing from afar. He stopped at the steps of the cathedral and looked up. The doors were open. Everest came up and entered through the doors, stepping through the narthex and entering into the church proper where he looked down and could see a few people inside.

The organ in the background played a gentle tune. Everest stepped forward a few steps and looked ahead towards the sanctuary. He took in a deep breath and then took a step back to leave, but before he could exit, he looked to his right where on the left-side of the church was none other than Conrad Adlington dressed in a suit. His eyes shot towards Everest, and they met each other's. They nodded to each other and then Everest left. He stepped through the narthex and came around to the front patio where he placed his hands on the prongs of the low iron gate above the stone bricks that bordered the patio. The organ continued to play, shifting towards a melancholic song that flowed out through the doors and onto the streets.

"Mr. Cabernet," Conrad greeted, putting his hat on.

Everest turned around and looked over to him.

"Fancy seeing you here," Conrad expressed. "Just out for a stroll, I take it."

"Yes," Everest replied, "I didn't realize you were in Harlech, or that you went to this church."

"The apartment I rent is not too far from here," Conrad remarked. "When I'm in Harlech, I come here for Mass. My wife and I used to always come to the evening services…"

"That would explain why we almost never see each other," Everest replied. "My wife and I go in the early morning."

Conrad nodded and then said, "So what brings you out and about at this time?"

"Where do I begin? Someone broke my car window, stole some money from me, and the police don't seem keen to do anything about it. I had to send the car to the shop to get its window fixed, and that left me on my own to walk home."

"You seem far from Cabernet Tower…"

"I'm walking around to clear my head," Everest replied. "Work has been… very tough actually. I never imaged how difficult it could be to do job of a chairman. I can't imagine how hard it must be for you to do your job…"

"I manage fine…"

"No less when we're dealing with borderline psychopaths in the board of directors…"

"Ah, yes," Conrad responded, "that does make it difficult at times," he said with a sigh. "I did not have the privilege to be a part of the executive council before that was dissolved, but as much as they became corrupt, they were at least not outsiders seeking to tear at the fabric of the company from the inside."

"What do you mean?" Everest questioned with a nervous chuckle. "You sound like my son and his wild conspiracy theories."

"Hm, conspiracy theories lack evidence, but these eyes, Mr. Cabernet, have seen what Mr. Roness and his clique have been up to for the past nearly five years. When you opened the company to investors, you invited opportunity to tear at one of the largest companies in the world from the inside to feed the growth of these other companies that hate us. Cabernet Industries has had its troubles, but it was projected to become one of the largest companies in the world until this scandal came with Medici Bank. Cabernet Industries could have stayed its course, but then these companies came in and worked to ensure that didn't happen. If the charges against the company were fought instead of settled, they could have been dropped because the men were guilty, not the company."

"How has Mr. Roness and the others acted against the company's interests?"

"Aside from what they've done since your return to Harlech, they've sold many assets and closed many subsidiaries and branches they viewed to have been a loss. These were not in a loss, but struggling because they were most impacted by the scandal. You may not have realized because you were not interested in the company's affairs, but they have surely pecked at what this company has to offer. Nearly all our business deals with other companies are with those invested into Cabernet Industries, and our ideas and successes are shared with them. Blackmore Industries, which was known to eventually surpass Cabernet Industries in growth, has done so tremendously, and even Ursicon will do so too."

"I see..." Everest replied, shaking his head, "I can't believe it... I mean, I can believe it, but it's just... so infuriating... There's no winning – either I let the board destroy the company, or I destroy the company."

"You destroy the company?"

Everest explained his plan to invite local government participation in foreign branches, and split the board of directors into a two-tier system. He also explained Roness' retaliation.

"Hm…" Conrad remarked, "very troubling, sir."

"I don't know what to do, Mr. Adlington," Everest expressed. "I'm at a loss. I feel the entire weight of this stupid company on my shoulders, and it's driving me insane. What if Roness shows the video tape? What if my wife thinks I cheated on her? He'll ruin our marriage – I'm so screwed…"

"Do you believe in God, Mr. Cabernet?"

"God?" Everest questioned. "What does that have to do with anything? I… I don't really believe in any of that. What reason is there to believe?"

"There are many arguments, but I will share a simple one. It is called Pascal's wager, and put simply, if God exists then there is more to lose in not believing and worshiping in God than there is if you do worship and believe. If God exists, and I believe and worship God, assuming these are all that are needed to go to Heaven, then it is better to do so for that gamble than it is to not believe and lose eternal life. If God does not exist despite our faith and worship, we lose nothing and become nothing. If God did exist and we did not believe or worship, then we lose a lot. Do you understand?"

"I can't believe that belief alone in a God is enough to save my soul."

"It isn't," Adlington remarked. "The Catholic Church holds that faith and charitable works together lead to salvation, but that too is a simplified framework as is what I'm trying to explain in Pascal's wager. The point is, we risk our souls in not believing and lose nothing if we were wrong, and I ask whether you believe to place your faith in something constant and have hope in a God who loves us."

Everest sighed as the conversation briefly grew silent.

"You are conflicted in the situation you are in right now," Adlington continued to say. "You are in distress. You are suffering. I understand your methods, even if I do not agree with them, but after much observations, I understand your aims. The sufferings that Cabernet Industries has caused make you suffer too, but you cannot root out suffering, Mr. Cabernet. You cannot pretend it does not exist either. God understands the sufferings of this world because he too suffered, but if you take decisions into your own hands, you will only worsen a situation. You must surrender yourself to the will of God, allow him to reshape your heart and guide you. Do you understand?"

Everest nodded. They then went silent for another moment.

"I need someone to manage Cabernet Industries," Everest pleaded. "I have nobody else to turn to because I don't trust anyone else, so I... I have to ask you because I've known you for a while and you seem to be last decent man at Cabernet Industries. If I go through with the dissolution of the board of directors, I need someone to do Roness and Lucius' job especially while they refuse to their job now. Can you help me out?"

Conrad took in a deep breath and replied, "I've been in service to Cabernet Industries for many years. I could not abandon this company now no less in a time of need. I am ready to assist you, Mr. Cabernet, do not worry."

"Thanks, Mr. Adlington," Everest said with a sigh of relief. "That's a lot off my chest."

"But to be honest with you, if you and your wife have such a bond as you express, I would go home to her now and tell her what is about to happen. Only then, with assurance that she will not leave you, will you be calm and collected to go forward with your plans..."

Everest nodded to him. Adlington took a sidestep and then turned to him.

"Goodnight, Mr. Cabernet. I will see you on Monday morning at the office."

"Goodnight, Mr. Adlington."

After Adlington left, Everest stayed put for another moment before he decided to walk back to Cabernet Tower. The front doors to the tower were closed by the time he arrived, so he went in through the parking lot and then up to the penthouse. He opened the door with his keys, and then stepped inside to the foyer where the lights were on. He came around to the stairwell on the right and then went upstairs. He opened the door to his bedroom and saw Vienna inside, in a change of clothes, but similar style. She immediately stood up and came forward to embrace Everest.

"Oh, there you are, my dear," Vienna said, holding him tightly. "You had me worried – what happened?"

Everest explained to her what happened after she left up to him leaving from the auto shop. He then took Vienna's hands and brought her around to sit at the foot of the bed.

"My dear city, I need to have a word with you about something serious," Everest said, looking at her. "My love, you know that I love you with my whole heart, right?"

"Of course, my dear mountain," Vienna replied. "What's wrong?" she asked, bringing a hand to his face. "You look upset, my mountain."

"I am upset," Everest responded, taking her hand and bringing it between them. "Ever since I came to this city, I hoped to make a difference. I didn't have a good impression of Mr. Roness and the other investors, and that's been reinforced because they're a bunch of evil men, but lately it's grown worse and worse... they're blackmailing me to prevent me from making a major decision that would reduce their power in the company and also relinquish control of our foreign assets. They... they have a video tape, and..."

"My dear mountain," Vienna remarked with a light smile, "say no more. Charlemagne has already told me all about this video... He said he found it in Mr. Roness' desk and watched it. He told me about what happened with you and that woman, but as our son does, he investigated before he came to me, believing something to be off with that man. He retrieved the video tapes from the other cameras from security and showed me what he found."

"You mean he's got the video tape?" Everest questioned. "And he's shown you?"

"Yes," Vienna replied, "you may not understand our son, but he means well in what he does. He was worried for you, for all of us..."

"Where is he now?"

"I don't know, but he has the video," Vienna said, "but he did mention that it is possible it is not the only one. He said that something like it could be duplicated and copies made."

"But you know the truth," Everest stated, "that I didn't cheat on you with that woman – that she took my hand, and I didn't realize how close it was to her breasts, I thought I was feeling her heart..."

"You don't need to worry about it, my dear," Vienna insisted, sharing a smile. "I believe you. I believe our son."

"Oh, that's such a relief," Everest expressed, letting out a large sigh. "You have no idea how stressful that's been on me – those fiends... they're awful, aren't they? They threatened to share that tape to the police, to accuse me of sexual harassment..."

"We have the other tape; it will not work."

"What if the girl testifies that I did touch her inappropriately?"

"It will not work."

"What if it goes to the press?"

"I am prepared for whatever storm it may brew," Vienna remarked, "and I will stay with you. I made my promise to you, Everest Cabernet. You are mine and we stay together, to the ends of the earth, my mountain." She embraced him.

"Oh Vienna, what did I do to deserve you in my life?" Everest replied, a tear falling from his eye. "You are the most precious soul I have ever met, and you are my wife…"

"You are the gentlest and kindest soul I have ever met, and you are my husband."

Everest laughed as they hugged. They then parted and continued to hold each other's hands. "I've had enough of this place. I've had enough of these people in office. Let's leave, Vi. Let's leave this modern hellhole and travel the world again, except this time, as we truly intended… Let's travel the world and lend a helping hand to all people that we come to meet. Let me take all that we have, sell it, and let us give to the poor what we can."

Vienna gave a wide smile as she heard these words. She replied, "If you want to travel the world, then abandon what you intend to do – abandon this fight with Mr. Roness and let us leave so we can live that life. Charlemagne is a grown man, Allodia is bright woman, and Salmar… he's grown used to the city and is itching to move out. As much as it hurts a mother to leave her children, I am yours, my mountain, and they no longer need their mother. Isn't that why we stopped travelling? For our children? We've given them more than eighteen-years of our lives, and they do not need us anymore. Let us live our life. Let go of your fight and we can leave tonight."

"Not yet," Everest said, "no. Not yet. Not until I've handled business here at Cabernet Industries will I turn my back and leave. I won't let us be seen as cowards to run away from a fight. I won't let us leave when there is still work to be done, especially for our children. If we will leave, it will be when the job is done."

Act 6, Scene 3

The next day, Everest silently dressed himself, left his room, and came downstairs to the penthouse study. He stayed put in that room through the early morning, bouncing a ball at his side as he stared across the room and towards the horizon view. At midmorning, Everest left the penthouse study and went downstairs to the corporate offices. He came around to the chairman office and walked around the perimeter, looking at the draft images of Cabernet Tower, Cabernet Manor, and Cabernet Court. He came around to the painting of Mount Everest and looked at it and its tall peaks. He then walked around to the fireplace and up to where the image of his father used to be mounted. Everest walked through the side door and came into the corridor that led to Lucius' office at the end, walking around and then down towards the one that went to Roness' office. He knocked on Roness' office and waited for a response, but none came. He knocked again and waited, and then he attempted to enter through, but the door was locked. He looked up to the surveillance camera above, and then turned around to walk down the corridor when he stopped to see Ms. Summers step out from the office spaces. She held papers in one arm and looked apologetically at Everest. Everest silently stood across from her as she closed the door behind her.

"Hello, Mr. Cabernet," Ms. Summers greeted.

"Hello, Ms. Summers."

"Are you looking for Mr. Roness?"

"Yes."

"He's in the boardroom," Ms. Summers remarked. "Since I have you, I also want to let you know that we've set up for the press event downstairs later this afternoon."

"Press event?"

"Your announcement for the company," Ms. Summers clarified. "Mr. Roness ensured me to have everything ready for you. He says you have a big announcement?"

"Yes," Everest replied. "I suppose I do." Ms. Summers nodded and then turned to leave, but Everest stepped forward and said, "Wait!"

"Yes?" Ms. Summers jumped and turned around.

"Kathleen, I am so sorry for what I did to you," Everest remarked, standing a meter apart. "That day when I helped you into the evening, I didn't mean to upset you if I did. I'm terribly sorry…"

"You don't need to apologize, Everest."

"I do," Everest insisted. "Mr. Roness told me that you were very upset about it all…"

"Wait what?" Ms. Summers questioned. "I haven't told anyone about what happened. How does Mr. Roness know?"

"You mean you never told him?"

"No, Mr. Cabernet, I didn't, and also too, I wasn't upset about anything you did to me. I was upset because… because he was pressuring me to make a move on you, and I didn't want to. I told him the following Monday that I didn't want to be a part of whatever was going on between you two. I backed out. I enjoyed my time with you, and as you told me about what you hoped to do for this company, for other people through this company, I began to realize what a warm-heart you have… and what an important, but also great part you have in this company as the man that you are – a great man. I didn't want to be a part of Roness' plan to ruin you. I'm the one that should be sorry…"

Everest didn't immediately respond as he stood where he was. He then replied, "I've been a fool, this entire time, Roness has played me as his friend when I've been getting in his way… He's been appeasing me for whatever intent that he has, and he was going to blackmail me with that footage and go to the police claiming that I had assaulted you."

"That's awful," Ms. Summers quietly said, looking about. "How though?"

"He has security footage," Everest replied, looking at the camera in the corner, "but my son caught on to him – he's a wylie boy. He found the video tape and he looked at the footage from the other cameras to verify it wasn't true. However, he believes that Mr. Roness may have another copy. If he releases that tape to the media, then it will create scandal and discredit me. It could ruin Cabernet Industries' reputation, and either I resign, or the company goes under and he and his friends can plunder the remains like the vultures they are. Dammit... I've lost this battle. Again, I am so sorry..."

"You don't need to be sorry," Ms. Summers clarified, stepping towards him. "All of this... this plan sounds like an awful situation, and I'm in the middle of it too."

"I don't know what to do," Everest confessed. "I'm a loss... My wife recommends that I submit to his will and let him have total control of Cabernet Industries. Roness wants me to sell my shares and relinquish control of Cabernet Industries. I don't want to sell my shares... it would mean that our family would have nothing left. We would be wealthy, but what good would all that wealth be when Cabernet Industries is worth so much more?"

"You cannot let him win," Ms. Summers encouraged. "He will tear this company apart, even if you let him have control. I... I know him, Everest. I've known him for years now, and he... he's a despot of a man who won't stop to have power over others. He believed he had power over me to get me to make you unfaithful. You need to stop that madman before it's too late."

"What can I do though?" Everest insisted.

Ms. Summers thought for a moment and then replied, "Mr. Roness is a gambling man. He won't back down from a chance to humiliate someone else and take from them. His favorite game is poker, so if you challenge him to a match, he'll surely accept."

"If I win, what makes you think he would honor the deal?"

"He wouldn't dishonor himself in front of others."

Everest nodded as he looked to the side. The two then walked together down to the boardroom and entered through.

"Ah, Mr. Cabernet, there you are," Roness expressed. "We were worried you would never show…" he said as Ms. Summers walked around to take her seat near him. "Please, sit down."

Everest did not respond and came around to sit down at his place in the room. The rest of the cartel was present, as well as Mr. Holmes, Mr. Adlington, Mr. Locke, and Mr. Bennett.

"I did not realize that we had a meeting," Everest remarked, looking across the table.

"Didn't you get the memo?" Roness questioned. "We all did because we heard you have some news to share with us before the press conference. Have you made up your mind?"

Everest looked over to Mr. Adlington, and then across to Mr. Roness.

"Why the deceitful game, Dwight?" Everest questioned. "I'm a man that believes we should be transparent with the entire board in what has been going on. After all, Mr. Clifford, Paterson, Leroy, and Wan-Cheung already know. I've also informed Mr. Adlington too, so let's be transparent."

Roness didn't respond.

"Last Friday, I informed Mr. Roness of my intent to announce later today the next path for Cabernet Industries. From this day, all branches of Cabernet Industries will become independent from the Pacific Branch and have their own executive council comprised of investors and management. These investors would be invited to join the executive council in agreement with local governments in order to ensure that decision-making served the local people. This autonomy would allow us to focus on the affairs of the Pacific Branch, while we also advise the other branches and subsidiaries in their direction. This board of directors would be separated into two-tiers, a board of investors and a board of executives, where the executives will manage the Pacific Branch, and the investors supervise and advise.

"In response to this proposal, Mr. Roness and other investor representatives here, announced their opposition to my plans. However, being a majority shareholder, I announced my intent to move forward without their support. They also announced their intent to not cooperate in the transition. Last of all…"

"Mr. Cabernet…" Roness grunted.

"… Mr. Roness and the other investors attempted to blackmail me into submission. They demanded that I sell my shares and retire, assuring me that the stock prices would bounce back when my part of the company is bought up by their friends. Isn't that right, Dwight?"

"You are a very difficult man, Mr. Cabernet," Roness barked. "Let me be absolutely clear to all of you, not a word of this business gets out from this room until we settle this dispute. These are outrageous allegations that I won't stand for…"

"I have a simple solution," Everest proposed, "something that will resolve all this business once and for all, and could win in your favor what you desire."

Roness raised an eyebrow.

"How about a game? A simple game of Texas Hold 'em between you and me until one of us busts. If you can defeat me, I will relinquish my stocks and give them up. I will even resign, but if I defeat you, then you must resign, Mr. Roness, and forfeit your blackmail attempts. How does that sound? Do you feel like you can win this fair and square?"

Roness did not immediately respond as he held a hand at his chin as though thinking. The others in the cartel looked at him. Mr. Adlington briefly looked to Everest and then to Roness.

"Very well, Mr. Cabernet, you've provided me with a persuasive bargain," Roness expressed, "but let me tell you, I don't lose. I've not busted in Texas Hold'em since the war, but I will take delight in your loss and assumption of your shares."

"What are we waiting for then?" Everest questioned. "Let's play."

"Gentlemen," Bennett interrupted, "this sounds ridiculous. On behalf of my own shareholders, I cannot endorse this frivolous play."

"Sit down, Bennett," Roness commanded. "For less than five percent, your handlers don't get a damn say in any of this. The future of the company is secure, and price of your investments assured... I cannot lose."

"How arrogant of you," Everest simply replied.

"Lucius, go and fetch a deck of cards from my desk," Roness remarked, putting a hand into his blazer jacket. "For a lack of chips, we will use cash. How much do you have, Everest? Does five hundred suffice a buy-in?"

"Good enough," Everest replied, taking out his wallet and placing down some cash.

Lucius returned with the deck of cards and took them out from their package.

"Lucius, be our dealer," Roness requested.

"Not so fast," Everest remarked. "We should have someone neutral do the honor."

"Very well then," Roness responded, taking the cards into his hand. He held onto them as he looked around the room. Everest looked around the room too. "You, Mr. Holmes, you will deal."

"With all due respect, Mr. Roness, but I do not know the rules of the game."

"I'm not asking you to know the rules of the game. We do. I'm just asking you to hand a card. We'll guide you."

Roness passed the cards to Mr. Holmes who sat between them on Everest's right. He began to shuffle the cards while the other board members watched.

"Kay, bring the cash together and go get us some change in tens and twenties from the safe," Roness requested as Holmes shuffled the cards. The money was brought to Ms. Summers, and she picked it up and went to the office spaces with it. She then returned and provided ten twenty-dollar bills, twenty ten-dollar bills, and twenty-five-dollar bills. "Alright, Mr. Cabernet, the small blind will be five dollars."

Since Everest was to the left of the dealer, he played five-dollars and Roness played ten for this round. Roness then guided Holmes in the division of cards, one each to a total of two. Everest received his cards: a six of hearts and a seven of hearts.

"I'll call," Everest announced, placing another five dollars forward.

"I'll check," Roness replied, looking over to Holmes. "Now place three cards between us."

Holmes placed three cards: an ace of hearts, a four of diamonds, and a two of hearts.

"I'll check."

"I'll raise," Roness remarked, placing another ten in.

"I'll call then," Everest said, placing ten in too.

"I'll check."

"Me too."

"Place another card," Roness instructed Holmes. "Mr. Cabernet, I think now would be a good time to establish when we raise the blinds. How about every five games?"

"Works with me."

Holmes placed a two of clubs.

"Check," Everest said.

"Check."

The last card placed was a five of diamonds. Everest grit his teeth. "Check," he said.

"Alright, show 'em," Roness requested.

Everest showed his cards. He then looked over to see what Roness had. He had a nine of clubs and ace of spades.

"Two pair," Lucius remarked. "Roness wins."

"I see what you were trying to do there, Mr. Cabernet," Roness mocked. "I think this'll be an easy game for me." He received the winnings and they proceeded to the second game.

This time Everest placed a large blind of ten dollars. Roness placed five dollars. They received their cards. Everest had a queen of diamonds and a nine of clubs.

"Call," Roness said, placing five more dollars.

"Check," Everest simply remarked.

Holmes placed the community cards: a king of diamonds, a seven of hearts, and a ten of diamonds.

"I'll check."

"Me too," Everest agreed.

Holmes placed the fourth card, an eight of clubs. They both checked. The fifth was a jack of clubs.

"I'll raise," Roness said, placing thirty dollars forward.

"I'll call."

"Show 'em."

Everest showed his cards, and he saw that Roness had a mere two pair to his straight. Roness growled.

"Alright, Mr. Cabernet. This one is yours…"

The two played the rest of the games in this set, resulting in $480 dollars in Everest's hands and $520 in Roness' hands by the end of it. At the sixth game, the blinds were raised to twenty dollars and they continued on. Holmes shuffled the cards.

"I never particularly liked playing with just two people," Roness remarked, "but with what's at stake, I will enjoy this victory."

Everest received his cards for the next round: a six of diamonds and a seven of hearts. They both checked at twenty and then the cards were put forward in the community: a seven of diamonds, an eight of diamonds, and a six of hearts.

"I'll call," Roness said.

"I'll check."

"I'll call your check."

They each placed in twenty more. The next card was a five of clubs.

"I'll call," Roness said again.

"I'll check.

They each placed in twenty more. The next card was a nine of diamonds.

"I'll raise," Roness finally said, putting in forty.

"I'll call."

They each placed forty more. The total pot was two-hundred dollars. They each revealed their cards.

"A straight," Everest chimed, looking over.

"A flush," Roness expressed, showing his ace of diamonds and four of diamonds. "Sorry, Mr. Cabernet." He took his cards into his lap and then threw them over to Holmes.

Roness received the pot, raising his earnings to $620 versus Everest's $380.

"Now this is starting to get interesting..." Roness said, returning his cards. "Let's keep going then."

At the end of the second set, Everest had $420 and Roness had $580. Holmes shuffled the cards and this time the big blind was at forty-dollars.

"Alright, Mr. Cabernet, ante up," Roness expressed, placing a large blind.

Everest put twenty in and then received his card. He had a five of clubs and a king of clubs. They both checked and at the reveal of the community cards, an eight of diamonds, queen of clubs, and six of clubs, Roness raised it to sixty each as Everest called. Holmes placed the fourth card, a two of clubs. Everest looked over and then at his clubs.

"I'll raise," Everest proposed, "let's keep it going."

"Fine," Roness replied, checking.

The final card was placed: a two of clubs.

"I'll check," Everest said.

"I'll raise," Roness propositioned, placing twenty.

Everest raised an eyebrow and raised even more. "Let's raise then."

"Right with you, Mr. Cabernet," he said, calling. "What do you have then?"

"A flush," Everest said, showing his cards. "You?"

"Three of a kind," Lucius remarked as he looked at Roness' cards: a queen of hearts and queen of diamonds.

"Damn," Roness expressed, "alright then, that one is yours, Mr. Cabernet, but don't get too comfortable with that win. I'm only getting warmed up."

Everest took in the winnings to raise himself up to $540 at Roness' now $460. They played the rest of the games carefully, placing himself at $460 as Roness recovered to $540.

"Ante up," Roness said at the start of the next set. The big blind was now $80.

The next game played. Everest placed a big blind and Roness a small one. Everest received a king of hearts and a jack of hearts. Roness called and Everest checked. The community cards were placed: a six of clubs, two of clubs, and a ten of hearts. They both checked. The fourth card, a six of hearts was placed. Everest looked at his cards and checked. They then went to the fifth card, a three of spades. They both checked again.

"Two pairs," Roness said, showing his four of hearts and two of diamonds. "You've got nothing there but a high card. Very weak, Mr. Cabernet."

Everest received his cards after he placed his small blind of $40. They were a three of clubs and five hearts. "I'll fold," he immediately said.

"There he goes again," Roness remarked. "Folding this early has its consequences, doesn't it? It's made me forty-dollars richer and you forty-dollars poorer, and closer to capitulation."

Roness received the winnings. Everest had $340 to $660. He folded the next game as he received a two of diamonds and four of clubs. The totals were now $260 to $740.

"I'm feeling very good," Roness bragged as he received his winnings. "How are you feeling, Mr. Cabernet?"

Everest did not respond. He placed his large blind and then received his next cards. He had a nine of hearts and king of diamonds. They called and checked, and the community cards were a queen of spades, ten of spades, and jack of hearts.

"Hm," Roness murmured. "I'll raise."

Everest glanced over to him and called. The next card placed was a jack of spades. He looked over at this card and then over to the queen of spade and ten of spades. He looked at his pair where he had a heart and a diamond.

"I'll raise again," Roness expressed. "I can afford it…"

"I'll call."

At the river, an eight of diamonds was placed.

"Well, that doesn't change much for me, but I'll still raise because I'm feeling good. Really good."

Roness put down another forty dollars. "How about you, Mr. Cabernet? Do you feel good?"

Everest looked at what money he had left. He then placed eighty dollars in.

"As a matter of fact, I do," Everest coldly replied.

"We'll see about that…" Roness grumbled, "putting in a hundred and forty dollars. Your move."

Everest saw how much Roness had put in, and then saw that what he had left was that exact amount. He looked over to Mr. Adlington who looked at him with concern. He then moved all his money in.

"Go ahead, try to have me beat here," Everest expressed, a drop of sweat at the side of his head. He looked over at Roness' cards as he placed them forward. He also placed his. Roness had a king of spades and jack of clubs. "Three pair? You only had a three pair?"

"A straight again," Roness observed aloud, looking at Everest's cards. "You really took a chance there, didn't you? You nearly lost it all on a whim?"

"What can I say, Mr. Roness? I'm a gambler," Everest remarked, taking in the winnings. "I knew the risks I was taking…" he said with a smile on his face. "Did you?" Roness frowned.

The pair went on to the next game and played through the rest of the set with caution. The totals were roughly even at $480 for Everest and $520 for Roness.

"Ante up," Roness expressed, placing his large blind of $160. Everest placed his small blind of $80 and they both received their cards. Everest looked at his: a two of clubs and eight of diamonds.

"I'll fold."

"You can't afford to do that all the time now," Roness expressed. "Look at me – I've never done that once and I seem to be on top here…"

"Your arrogance will be your fall, Dwight."

Everest placed a large blind this time and received his cards: a seven of clubs and an ace of clubs. They called and checked, and the community cards were a two of clubs, a four of hearts, and a queen of hearts. They both checked. The turn was a three of diamonds. Everest looked at his cards and then at the community cards. They both checked. The river was a queen of diamonds. Everest took in a deep breath as Roness checked. He looked at his cards and then the community cards. Everest put forward forty-dollars, causing Roness to raise his eyebrow at him.

"I'll call your bluff there," Roness expressed, looking straight at him as he put forty-dollars forward. "What do you have?"

Everest turned his cards, and then so did Roness. Roness had a four of clubs and six of clubs. He stood up to get a better look at Everest's cards and then sat down.

"You had a high ace and that's it? Do you think I'm stupid? I know when you're trying to bluff, and it won't work because I don't back down from a challenge…."

Each received their next cards. Everest placed his small blind and Roness his big blind. They received their cards. Everest had a queen of hearts and jack of diamonds. He called and was left with forty dollars. Roness checked. The community cards were a jack of clubs, two of clubs, and a nine of diamonds. They checked again, and the next card was a queen of clubs. Everest looked at what he had left and decided to put half of it in. Each placed twenty and waited for the river, a five of clubs.

"I'll check," Everest remarked.

"Hm," Roness expressed, looking at his cards and the community cards. "I will raise." He placed forty in. "Are you in or out?"

Everest looked at his twenty dollars left and then back at his cards. "I'm in, all in." He put his twenty in.

The cards were revealed. Roness had a queen of diamonds and ten of hearts.

"Two pairs," Everest remarked with a bit of relief to his one pair. Roness did not react. Everest received his winnings and now the game was at $420 to $580. They anted up, and Everest put his large blind. His cards were a six of diamonds and nine of clubs. They then called and checked. The community cards were a six of clubs, queen of clubs, and eight of diamonds. They checked. The turn was a two of diamonds. They checked. The river was a ten of clubs. "One pair, nines."

Roness revealed his cards, one pair of eights at an eight of spades and two of hearts. Everest received the winnings. Roness grew silent until he remarked, "What time is it? I could use a drink at this pace. Lucius, why don't you fetch something from my bar? Do you want a drink, Mr. Cabernet?"

"No, thank you."

Lucius left and went to fetch two drinks, but Everest refused to touch his as it was given to him anyways. They continued on for the rest of the set, going back and forth against each other to an equal total of $500 each.

"Ante up," Roness said in a strict tone, placing three-hundred and twenty in for his big blind. Everest only put in half of that for his small blind, and then he received his cards. He had a queen of hearts and a king of hearts. He called and Roness checked. The community cards were an ace of hearts, king of diamonds, and a queen of diamonds. They both checked. The next card was an ace of spades.

"I'll raise," Everest remarked, putting in forty.

Roness called and placed forty in too. The last card was placed, and it was an ace of clubs. Everest's eyes widened as he looked at the three aces and then the king and queen on the field, and the king and queen in his hand.

"I'll raise," Everest stated, putting in forty.

"I'll raise too," Roness remarked, putting in sixty.

Everest looked at Roness with a bit of surprise. Roness had a pleased look on his face.

"I'll raise you," Everest challenged, putting in forty more.

"You won't win this one over me, Mr. Cabernet," Roness confidently said with a smile. "You may as well back down." He raised another twenty.

"I don't think I will," Everest replied, going all in and causing a frightened look on Mr. Adlington's face. Even Mr. Bennett looked nervous as he watched on.

"Good," Roness remarked, hands and cards at his lap, "very good. All in."

Both Roness and Everest went all in, and with that move, they showed each other's cards.

"Full house," Everest remarked, placing his cards down.

Roness smiled and brought his cards forward onto the table. He had an ace of diamonds and a jack of diamonds.

"Four-of-a-kind," Lucius stated. "He's won."

Everest's expression dropped as he realized he had an ace of diamonds. "How? No – that can't be… I weighed the odds."

"Yes, but unfortunately, those odds were against you," Roness rebuked, laughing. He stood up and buttoned his suit jacket. "Good game, Mr. Cabernet. You had me at the edge of my seat there for a moment. Now you've not only lost five-hundred dollars, but your company as well – the members of this board are a witness to that defeat, so it's time to go and address the press. We won't want to keep them waiting."

Everest continued to sit. Roness looked at him without pity.

"You cheated," Everest accused. "You- you must have had that ace up your sleeve…"

"Don't be such a sore loser, Mr. Cabernet," Roness remarked, unbuttoning his jacket. "Look." He brushed his coat as he whipped it in the air and no cards fell out. "You see?"

Everest did not respond.

"We'll leave you wallow in your own self-pity for a while, but do not keep us waiting too long. We'll be downstairs waiting for you to make your announcement. It's been nice working with you, Mr. Cabernet. I'm sure you will enjoy your retirement. If you do not show in the next ten minutes, I will address the crowd on your behalf."

Roness and the cartel then left. Everest sat back.

Act 6, Scene 4

"You don't need to follow through with this childish game," Adlington assured Everest. Both he, Bennett, and Summers remained in the room with Everest. "You do not owe him your inheritance."

"I... I have to. He's blackmailing me."

"I won't support whatever he plans to accuse you on," Summers encouraged. "You can't let him take everything you've got."

"Mr. Cabernet, if you will... why not transfer your stocks to someone else?" Bennett proposed. "If your transfer control of the company, then it could put Mr. Roness in an awkward spot. You will have backed down from these changes you planned to make, and he will not dare to endanger the reputation of the company."

"Why not just back down entirely?" Everest questioned.

"Because it is clear that Mr. Roness intends to dispose of you by any means necessary," Adlington answered. "I would not advise transferring control to anyone, but to carry on and we can fight through any backlash. Mr. Roness should be removed from his position for his threat towards you and your family."

"I... I can't do it – I can't fight him. I'm... I'm not the right person for this job. I'm not a businessman. I... I'm not a leader either. No matter what I do, Mr. Roness wins somehow."

"Mr. Cabernet..." Adlington addressed, "for the sake of the company, please do not resign control to Mr. Roness. Think of your children, sir."

Everest paused for a moment and then stood up with a sigh.

"What are you going to do?" Adlington asked.

"I'm going to go downstairs and address the crowd before Roness does so for me. I can at least have the honor to say goodbye myself. It's over gentlemen."

Without another word, Everest left the board room and came out to the hallway. He went to the elevator and waited to be brought down. Adlington, Bennett, and Summers joined him. They went down the elevator together and came to the atrium. The atrium was set up with a podium to the right, curtains behind, and a few foldable chairs in front. The area was cordoned off from the public, although they were provided space on the sidelines and back. A separate cordoned area was provided for the media with their television cameras and equipment. Everest came forward to the area as he listened to Roness speak with the cartel at his side.

"I for one believe that we will have a very strong quarter," Roness expressed. "We've made a lot of new changes recently, and as an organization we have never been any better. The future of Cabernet Industries has always been on the upside luckily, and with what's been going on in Eastern Europe and the Soviet Union, we can be sure that whatever the future hold, the company will be right there. The new image of Cabernet Industries is compassionate, charitable, and open to the arms of the entire world rather than just another cog in the world economic machine. We will continue to play that part as we tackle issues such as global warming and overpopulation, rest assured." He looked to his side as he noticed Everest arrive. "I think that's enough from me though.... Ladies and gentlemen, thank you for gathering here this afternoon. As you were made aware, our honorable chairman, Mr. Everest Pepin Cabernet, has some words he would like to share with you. Please let us welcome our great leader." He then stepped aside and led the applause.

Everest came around to the podium. Adlington, Bennett, and Summers stayed on his left side while the cartel was on the right. Everest fixed the microphone and then looked towards the crowd. He could see Vienna in the front with Salmar and Allodia.

"Thank you, Mr. Roness, and thank you all for attending here today," Everest remarked. He then paused for a moment as he looked across the room with a pensive stare. He then cleared his throat and looked back towards the crowd. "I've been chairman of Cabernet Industries since I inherited ownership of the corporation from my father, Derby Cabernet, after his untimely death. I never anticipated having ownership of the company, nor did I anticipate my father to have died at such a young age. I did not know what to do with being the owner of such a large company, but luckily there were people in charge of the company at the time who assured me that I did not need to do a thing and that they would run the company for me. I was twenty-three years old at the time and I thought it was such a relief to know that all this – Cabernet Industries, would not need to be worried about. I could live my life, and the company would run without a hitch – after all, my father trusted these men. Of course, then we had the economic downturn in the early seventies and that hit Cabernet Corporation, as we were known in those times, badly. We survived, just barely, although in those times, some of the people in charge of our company made some bad decisions and the deals with the wrong people. After Medici Bank went under, it was discovered that some people in top-positions here participated in their money laundering scheme – a crime of which we were found guilty to have taken part in and those people are no longer with our company for good reason. For the first time in my life, I became involved in the affairs of the company, and at the advice from those around me, we went public. To this date, I do not know if that was a wise decision, or if Cabernet Industries as we renamed it, could have survived without going public. I do know that I sacrificed forty-percent ownership to off-set the costs that this Medici scandal had cost us, allowing us to resume business as usual. That forty-percent was sold to numerous investors who got to have a say in how the company was run, and through them we had Mr. Roness, Mr.

Clifford, Mr. Paterson, Mr. Leroy, Mr. Wan-Cheung, and Mr. Bennett join us as both investors and executive leaders. Their expertise in all things business has done a tremendous job for the company, but of course, nobody is perfect. I became focused on the company's affairs only recently after twenty years of not caring about the company other than to know it as a source of income for me and my family. My interest came from a selfish place; I was humiliated to not know what was going on in my own company, so I felt the need to learn, and what I did learn was that despite the excellent leadership of the current board of directors, we had room for improvement. For the past nearly six months, I've focused on improving the company by moving away from the cold and rigid management styles and organization, to a more humanistic touch; a compassionate and charitable one towards others. We are a company. We participate in the global economy, and as I've been told, our goal is to make money – that's not been my goal. We are not just a company, but we are an organization with people who work for us in all shapes and sizes, and whose activities influence the lives and wellbeing of not just our own employees, but those we interact and trade with. My proudest achievement since returning to Harlech has been the formation of the Cabernet Foundation for this reason – a successful vision of what I could hope for through the successes of Cabernet Industries. However, even that organization, as a charitable foundation, has its limits and I'm hopeful that in the future, as it continues to grow and fledge, it will become a very important component of the company. My time here overall has been an adventure… What is the next step for Cabernet Industries then? What does the future wait for us? I suppose I'm here to give you that answer…" Everest sighed. "I do not know what the future waits for Cabernet Industries, because I do not know the future. I do know that whatever this future brings, I will hope that it continues in the path and leadership that I've set out for, understanding that we are not just a corporate entity, but we are an organization of people and persons with emotions and experiences, who interact likewise with people and persons with emotions and experiences. I hope that Cabernet Industries will be a force of good for this world, always changing and improving the livelihoods of other people than to exploit and destroy. Whatever it takes, I hope Cabernet Industries will always do good. What then is the next step for Cabernet Industries?" he asked again with another sigh. "The future for Cabernet Industries will be one that does not have me as its chairman, I know that as much, because effective today, I will resign from the board of directors and that title. I have had a very interesting experience these past months having a chance to work and meet all sorts of people, but now this adventure for me comes to an end and begins for other people. If I had to say what moments I cherish the most, it would be those I spent getting to know individual people and understanding that our workers are not just workers, but they are people...

"Rather than elect a new chairman to take my place, I will let the investors decide who should be at the helm. Right now, I personally own sixty point six of those shares. Before the end of the day, I intend to..." Everest paused for a moment as he looked at Allodia's smile. He then looked at his boy, Salmar, and his smile upon his face, and then to his wife whose loving smile caused him to hesitate. "I intend to... transfer these shares, to all three of my children. The future of Cabernet Industries belongs to them, the children of tomorrow and the next millennium, and it will be for them to decide together who should be chairman and what the future of Cabernet Industries will be. Each of my three children will receive exactly a third of my ownership, and it will be for them to decide what they do and what decisions they make with that power. My advice to them, is to remember the words of your old man in this speech, and to be sure that Cabernet Industries also invests in the future generations, in the people that it serves, and ensure that the objective of Cabernet

Industries is always to serve other people rather than itself. In these past few months, it has been difficult to lead the company, but in the back of my mind, I've remembered the words of my father. Although he did not personally prepare me to lead this company, nor did he as I've mentioned take lead, he did share a particular bit of wisdom in leadership itself, and that is to lead is to serve – he found this wisdom in the company of men that he fought with in the war – men that he led through the war, through thick and thin. I want to share those words of wisdom as well to my children, that in their own leadership, they serve others too.

"Last but not least, I want to thank our staff at Cabernet Industries who deserve to be recognized for their efforts. Each and every one of them build up the fibres of this company, and this company is what it is because of you, so thank you for your service, and thank you for joining us today. If you'll excuse me, I will now be looking forward to my early retirement… Thank you."

Everest walked off from the podium. The media attempted to ask questions, but Everest ignored them. Roness and the cartel simply sat back, still in shock at the announcement. Mr. Adlington quickly came to the podium.

"Please, if you could please give a round of applause to our fearless leader, Mr. Cabernet, for all he has done for us. Through his family, this company exists, so let us honor him."

The audience and those around began to applaud Everest who turned around and looked over to them. Vienna came around with the kids to join him as the others celebrated him. Those who were seated rose to their feet to give a standing ovation. Everest saw Roness stand up, fix his coat, and then step around Adlington to come towards Everest. The crowd continued to celebrate Everest and his family.

"We should go now," Everest remarked, seeing Roness on approach. They turned around to call and elevator, and the doors opened. Everest rushed Vienna and his children in, but just as he was about to enter inside, Roness took him by the wrist.

"Where do you think you're going?" Roness snarled. "You made a promise – that was not the deal we made. I don't care what you just told the public, I want those shares."

"I'm sorry, Dwight," Everest responded as he stood in the elevator and shook off Roness' grip. "I am a man of my word though – I seem to remember that if you won, I would get rid of my shares... I never specified to whom I would give them to. I'm sorry if you thought that meant you."

"I have the tape," Roness threatened. "You've been a naughty man, Everest."

"Do you? I could have sworn my son swiped that copy in your desk," Everest replied. "Speaking of Charlemagne, if you thought I was a bad chairman, then wait until you have to deal with him. From my understanding, although each of my children get an equal share of what I own, he owns more than them which likely makes him my successor. Best of luck, Roness."

Roness stood back as Everest stepped back and the doors closed. He then took a sigh of relief and put his arm around Vienna.

"Well, kids, I think I've had enough of this city," Everest expressed. "Five or so months here, and I want to never come back."

"What are you going to do now?" Allodia questioned. "What does retirement look like for you?"

"Oh, I think your mother and I have the right idea..." Everest said, looking into Vienna's eyes, "but before we do that, I need to go back to Allabrese to pick up some things. I also need to sign off on the transfer of the shares and leave that with Mr. Adlington to handle."

"And then where?" Allodia asked.

"Wherever the winds take us," Everest remarked. "We are now free."

Act 6, Scene 5

Everest opened his eyes. He looked above him and could see light pour through the cracks of the ceiling above him. He lay on a mat, covered in blankets, and wore a simple white t-shirt. He looked up at the ceiling as his eyes analyzed it, seeing different types of branches tied together with straw that formed a thatched roof. The ceiling was tall and pointed. He also looked at the larger and thicker branches that acted as beams to support the ceiling roof. They came together to a central pillar in the shelter he was in, which itself was a single room. This was circular and there was space enough for a mat be placed on one side, a furnace at the other side, and a basin with water next to it. The mat he laid on was large enough for two persons and was placed directly on the sand-ridden floor. To the right of Everest was an archway in the walls of the room he was in, and across from them was another smaller archway window. The walls of the room consisted of smooth mud. The archway window was covered with more thatching, and the door of a straw bound together to form a flexible doorway that could be walked through. On the left from Everest were two backpacks placed aside. Next to him, on the mat and underneath the sheets, on her side, was Vienna. She wore a white t-shirt as well. Her hair was unbound and grown slightly longer since the beginning of their worldwide voyage. Likewise, Everest had grown a bit more hair, enough to cover his receding hairline. His skin was tanned too. Everest opened his mouth, took in a deep breath, and let it out as he stretched an arm around to embrace his wife.

Vienna moaned as she felt the embrace of her husband. She curled her head into his armpit and then placed her hand on his chest. She slowly opened her eyes as he felt him slowly breathe.

"Good morning, my mountain," Vienna greeted. "How did you sleep?"

"Horribly," Everest replied with a smile, "but it doesn't matter. Just laying here, looking up at this ceiling and listening to the movement and voices outside, tells me we are far from home and somewhere we have never thought to come to before. It's a strange thing, to take such excitement in being far from home and in a different place. Maybe that's why my father liked to travel abroad and go on his adventures..."

"We are not looking for treasure though," Vienna said. "We are here to see the many people of the world, to learn to say 'hello' in their language, and provide a helping hand to those around us as we journey."

"How long can we keep this up? How long before the money runs out and we really do have nothing left in our name?"

"We will always have something to our name, our children..."

"They don't even know where we are right now."

"Oh, nonsense," Vienna responded. "They know enough to know where we are going... I've been sure to write to them. Insofar as money is concerned, where we are going, we do not need that but the skills of our hands to help others."

"We've sold everything we own already," Everest said.

"Then we have done well to do so."

"What if we grow hungry?"

"Then our compassion for those who hunger should widen."

"What if we grow thirsty?"

"Then our appreciation for water will increase."

"What if we have nowhere to sleep? What if one of us gets sick?"

"We will have each other, and as I swore to you, my love, I will not part from you even when you are sick."

"What if one of these crazy governments throw us in jail?"

"Even prisoners are taken care of to some extent."

"And what if we have nothing left to wear?"

"There is always something to wear," Vienna assured him, "now come. Enough chit-chat, it is morning, and we must ensure that we help the villagers rather than laze here. We are not here on vacation. It is time for us to get to work…"

Vienna leaned forward and Everest looked over to her. He got out from their bed too and started to get ready for another day. They put their items into their backpacks, washed their teeth, and then stepped out into the midst of a village where many similar round huts were scattered around a clearing of sand in the midst of a savannah. Everest looked about as the heat of the sun pierced down upon him. They were not alone as many Sub-Saharan African locals with dark skin and shaven heads could be seen wearing rags, some of which were too large, too small, or barely put together to be worn. These people looked over at the couple with a smile as they greeted them, especially the children who began to gather around them. Everest gave a smile as he waved back to them, shaking their hands. Vienna leaned over and shook the hands of the children as they encircled them, making their way through the village as they came to their assistance in this village like the many they would come to visit throughout the third-world world in service to the poor.

Epilogue

Everest sat atop of a wooden plank beam as he hit a hammer into some nails to connect two sections of wall frames. He was young, seven years old, and wore denim jeans and a white t-shirt. Around his hips he wore a leather belt with a pouch that held many long nails. He sat amidst a skeletal framework of a house under construction, the initial floors of which were only just being laid down upon from the basement foundation. The building was large and had a U-shape to it. The building was also situated at the top of a hill near the cliffside that overlooked the Nattau River. A dirt path behind the clifftop passed the front of the building and went onwards to the south as it did to the north. From where Everest was sat, he could see a bridge northward that crossed over the river. Directly in front of the building was a pickup truck parked atop of a dirt path that stretched out from the main road in a stretched U-shape. Along this area, another road came out and went around to the north side of the building where there were tents pitched around a firepit. At a tree near those tents the leads of two horses were tied up. Numerous piles of lumber and wooden sheets were placed around the front of the under-construction structure. The front of the building was elevated up from the front dirt lot and so wooden sheets were placed down to create a ramp to allow egress up to the main entrance. The first room of the building was large and rectangular. It likewise went to a room to the north that was also large and rectangular, and then next to these rooms were two more rectangular rooms, although smaller. The rooms to the south were more complicated and had various rooms that led up to a large hall at the end. This large room, like the main entrance room, and the room besides had double sets of wall frames placed to indicate they would be two-story rooms. Everest sat in the midst of one of these second-floor frames, between the main entrance foyer and north wing.

Cabernet Manor was under construction, and Everest was busy at work connecting the second-floor frames with beams that stretched across the future living room and side bathroom. The second floor of the atrium was larger than the first floor because it outstretched on the sides into the south and north wings to create the viewing gallery around. Everest was not alone however as downstairs on the ground floor, busy at a table, Derby was sawing planks of wood into exact lengths. He wore a canvas collared shirt with the sleeves rolled up, top buttons exposed, and denim pants. He also wore a baseball cap to cover his forehead, the front of which showed the logo for the Harlech Hunters baseball team. Everest continued to hit his hammer into the nails, beating these long nails into the wood and through to the other frame to connect frame with frame more securely. When Everest finished this section, he came around to the next frame and started to do the same at that side. He made his way east, tightening the closeness of the frame and beam, and then came back east to look down at his father. Cabernet Manor was still in its early stages as the wooden sheets of the second floor were yet to be placed, and nor were any of the walls raised for the rest of that floor nor the roof except in the main atrium, although even the floor was yet to be placed for the viewing gallery.

Everest stood from the frames he had nailed in with a two-meter gap between him and the other beam, with small beams connected with the short side up to prepare for the wooden sheets. He looked down from where he was and took notice of the two-meter drop. He went around rather than return the way he came. He began to navigate himself around the front wall directly below the main entrance doorframes. He moved around to the west wing where he continued to work as Derby cut wood. When Derby was finished with the wood he had cut, he came around to place them in particular positions that needed exact shapes, especially future windows. When Everest finished nailing the frames into the beams, he looked up at the rooftop and decided he would do the same. He started to climb up, using the studs in between to prop himself. He then stretched himself took hold of the frame, using his strength to pull himself up, but as he brought himself up, he found himself awkwardly hugging the frame beam. Additionally, his hammer fell out of his belt and into the rear patio.

"Uh... dad?" Everest questioned.

"What?" Derby replied, looking over from the table. "Oh Christ... what the hell are you doing up there, Ev? Get down from there!"

"I- I can't get down..."

"What do you mean you can't get down? If you got up there, then that means there must be a way down!"

"I can't get down!" Everest insisted.

"I sweat to God, Everest..." Derby cursed, moving away from the table and going around to the stairs. "I'm coming..."

Derby stopped at the top of the stairs, as there was no floor, he stayed put and looked over at his son towards the left from him.

"Shimmy yourself forward and gently lower yourself," Derby encouraged. "You're going to need to shorten the fall somehow, you can't stay there all day. Come on..."

Everest continued to hold on and looked ahead. He began to pull himself closer towards the corner. He then looked down, looking on his left and straight down all the way to the ground floor and through the gaps in the planks of wood. The drop was at least four meters. On the other side, Everest looked and saw that it was a straight four-meter drop into the dirt below.

"You're going to have to shift your weight around," Derby instructed. "Keep your upper body tight to that frame and drop your feet. You're going to need to aim to land on the wooden plank below."

"Can't you grab me?" Everest questioned.

Derby sighed and began to move around to join him. He carefully navigated around the wooden frames and studs, while Everest began to do as his father said. He maintained his grip with his arms and pressed his chest closely into the frame. He then began to drop his feet so that they dangled, although for a seven-year-old boy less than five-feet tall, it was not much of a reduction in drop.

"Hold on," Derby remarked, nearly reaching him.

"I… I think I got it," Everest said, looking at where he wanted his feet to connect. He then dropped himself off.

"Everest!" Derby shouted.

Everest landed both feet onto the frame, but he lost balance and fell backwards immediately.

"Everest!" Derby shouted again.

Everest lay backwards on the dirt and rolled onto his side. Derby quickly came around to him. He knelt over at his side and looked at him as he lay his hands on his waist and head.

"Are you alright, my boy?" Derby questioned. "Are you hurt?"

"I… I'm okay... except my arm hurts. I think I landed right on top of it."

Derby finished quickly examining his son before he brought him onto his back.

"Let me see," Derby said, picking it up. He gently pressed in to see if it would cause a reaction in Everest. He seethed as his father pressed in, but did not wail out in pain. "How's your head?"

"It's okay… my neck hurts a little too."

"You're bleeding…" Derby noted, looking at Everest's hand. He wiped off some of the blood to see a thick cut on the top of his hand. "Come on, let's get you back to the camp and I'll wash all this blood. I'm going to need to stitch you up."

Derby picked up Everest and carried him in both arms down from the patio, which at this point was just another dirt lot that sloped down for them to come around to the camp on the other side. He brought him all the way around to the campfire and then helped him onto his feet so he could sit down at the bench. Derby picked up a first aid kit from nearby, some water from a bucket, and sat next to Everest to wash his wound and stitch his cut.

"Ow!" Everest exclaimed as the antiseptic ran over his cut.

"Keep your hand steady," Derby remarked, preparing to sow the cut together. "Here, bite into this…." He gave Everest a thick leather strap.

"Why do I need to… ow!" Everest complained. Derby sowed the wound quickly as Everest cried and bit down onto the leather strap. When he was finished, Everest looked at his right arm again and then his right leg.

"You look fine," Derby expressed, lowering Everest's right jean pant leg cuff. He let out a sight of relief. "Don't stretch your right hand too much or the stitches will tear, and we'll be back at it again, and I think neither of us want that. Let it heal… here." He rolled the wound with some bandage and then tied it together. "Best thing you can do is just heal…"

Everest looked back at his father as he worked on his hand. His starry eyes looked up at his father's focused eyes as he cared for him. When he was finished, Derby placed the bandage into the medikit and then kicked it aside.

"That'll do it," Derby expressed. "I need a drink after that…" He stood up and went around to a picnic basket where he fetched a bottle of rum. He then went back over to sit next to Everest. He gave another sigh of relief as he drank.

"I thought mom didn't want you to be drinking that…" Everest noted.

"Your mother doesn't decide what I put into my body," Derby responded, looking over to Everest. "What did you think you were doing up there?"

"I was finishing the job, just like you told me to," Everest said with a frown.

"I didn't tell you to go all the way up there," Derby complained. "Besides, the roof is secured already. It was just those loose bits I needed fastened. Did you get the ones all around the foyer floor?"

"Yes, sir."

"Good."

"I'm sorry I fell…"

Derby lowered the bottle from his mouth and looked over to his son. "Don't be sorry you fell, Ev. Besides, we all make mistakes…"

"Even you?"

Derby sighed and replied, "Especially me." He then quiet for a moment. He turned to his son and placed a hand on his lap to get his attention. "I want you to listen to me though son. We're allowed to make mistakes, so long as we learn from them. If we don't learn from our mistakes, then sometimes we make bigger mistakes, and you don't want to do that. The worst you can do is make a mistake that you could come to regret later in life. You understand?"

"Yes, sir…"

Derby sighed and looked ahead of him as he continued to talk to his son and say, "You've helped me a lot these past few weeks. You've done a good job too. You've really helped us build a shelter for us homeless folk although we've got lots left to do."

Everest didn't respond at this praise. His face attempted to maintain a neutral expression, although a smile could be seen raising through.

"You know, Everest, the best you can learn from me is to not make the same mistakes as your old man. I made that mistake with my dad, your grandfather… He told me I shouldn't have joined the army, and I did, so here's my advice – don't join the army, son."

"I thought you liked the army."

"I did," Derby said, "but only because of the people at the time. We were all a good company of people, but we... we shouldn't have joined the army to fight in the war, and those of us who survived, deserve better than what they've received from that war. Those who didn't make it, deserved so much more..."

Derby fell silent. He took one more swig from the bottle and then close the lid. He placed it at his side and then placed a hand on Everest's far shoulder.

"Come on, we've got work to do," Derby encouraged, taking off his hat to reveal his short blonde hair. "How about you supervise, while I work. Take it easy for the rest of the day – sun will start to set soon and then we can get to making dinner. Okay?"

"Yes, sir."

"Good boy," Derby recognized, placing his hat on his son's head, "let's go."

Everest looked up to his father with loving eyes, and without even saying the words, felt the love from him. Derby looked back at him and smiled. He placed his hand behind his back and walked with him back around to the main foyer where Everest sat down and watched his father work. He saw him saw the lumber and place them into the window sills, and then he watched him place sheets along the viewing gallery and cut particular shapes to fit all spaces. Derby looked back at his son with loving eyes, and although they didn't say it, his son loved him, and he loved his son.

"It is not just a matter of eliminating hunger, or even reducing poverty. The struggle against destitution, though urgent and necessary, is not enough. It is a question, rather, of building a world where every man... can live a fully human life, freed from servitude imposed on him by other men or by natural forces over which he has not sufficient control..."

– Pope Saint Paul VI